I0583522

FIRES OF ATONEMENT

THE BLOOD METAL WARS

FIRES OF ATONEMENT

THE BLOOD METAL WARS

Cameron Scott Kirk

Fires of Atonement © 2024 Cameron Scott Kirk

Cover art by Christian Bentulan © 2025

Edited by Amanda Rutter, Timothy Repasky

This book is a work of fiction. Names, characters, places, events, and dialogues are drawn from the author's imagination or are used fictitiously. Any resemblance to actual events, locales, or persons, living or dead, is coincidental.

Epic Publishing supports the right to free expression and the value of copyright. The purpose of copyright is to encourage writers and artists to produce creative works that enrich our culture. The scanning, uploading, and distribution of this book without permission is a theft of the author's intellectual property. If you would like permission to use material from this book (other than for review purposes), please contact us at publisher@epic-publishing.com.

Epic Publishing

www.epic-publishing.com

First Printing by Epic Publishing: 2025

Epic Publishing is an imprint of Mighty, LLC.

The Epic Publishing name and logo are trademarks of Mighty, LLC.

ISBN (trade paperback): 979-8-9987721-0-8

For Penny and Cody.

1

ON MOUNT ULFUR

A bloodied tongue lolled from a twisted mouth. The corpse of the goat lay deformed in rigor mortis upon the mountain path, its bulging eyes gazing sightlessly across the desert far below.

The high winds whipped at Brother Vernon's coarse brown habit as he sadly shook his head. He turned to the three young men following him and extended a skeletal hand towards the rock face towering above them. "You can see for yourself the result of a misstep, even for an animal born on this mountain. A tragedy and a lesson for us. We proceed with much caution." A light cascade of pebbles and rock dust whispered down the cliff wall as if to emphasize the wizened monk's warning.

Brother Vernon uttered a benediction for the soul of the dead animal and continued up the path. The three young men following him did not wear the vestments of monk, friar, or priest, or any man of a spiritual nature, but rather plain tunics and woollen trousers of brown or black. The three stepped warily around the stiff, cold corpse of the goat and hurried after the older man. The mountain path became steeper and morphed into a series of switchbacks before levelling out once more and disappearing into dense swathes of forest covering the mountainside.

"Ah, the woods are beautiful at this time of year," Brother Vernon said. "You're in for a treat, boys. May I never grow so old that I can never again walk these glorious mountain paths."

As the four men entered the forest, a mint-scented coolness washed over them. The sun no longer stabbed at their eyes or burned exposed skin. The track between the trees was carpeted with crisp brown-red needles and dried cones, providing a cushioned thoroughfare fit for the forest god Silvanus himself.

Brother Vernon inhaled the pungent air and smiled. Without slowing his pace, he said, "Deciduous or evergreen?" No reply attended his question. "Come, come, boys. Are the spruce and larch deciduous or evergreen trees?"

"The larch are deciduous, sir," came a voice behind the monk. "They are also coniferous, meaning that they shed needle and cone in autumn. The spruce and the juniper trees further up the mountain are evergreen and flower all year."

Brother Vernon stopped and turned around. His wispy eyebrows raised in surprise and appreciation. The three young men, in turn, came to a halt. "Yes, you are quite right." He nodded. "Who said that?"

A youth with large brown eyes beneath a tousled mop of black hair raised a solitary finger. "I did."

Brother Vernon squinted. The lad's features were pleasant enough, yet there was little to distinguish the face, or the youth himself, from a thousand others like him. Aesthetic, yet nondescript. Handsome enough, yet forgettable. "And your name?" Vernon asked.

The mountain breeze of mint and pine brushed through the young man's black hair. "My name is Julian, Julian of Dysael, sir."

"Have you been on this mountain before, Julian of Dysael?"

"No, sir. I only arrived in Re'Shan yesterday."

Vernon turned to the second of the three. The young Black fellow was completely bald, his skull an austere contrast to the lustrous growth sprouting untended from the head of the first youth. "And you? Your name?"

"I am Martin of Sil'Raka."

"Ah, a Freelander. You are familiar with Mount Ulfur, then?"

Martin nodded. "I've heard much of the famed mountain, though I myself have never set foot on its ... foot. The mountain's foot, I mean."

Vernon smiled. "Yes, yes, I understand what you mean." The old monk inspected the third of his charges. The tall young man with a long pale face fidgeted and glanced nervously from his companions to the old monk and back again.

Realizing that Vernon was waiting for him to say something, the young man spoke with a thick Germanic accent. "My name is Klaus of Habsburg, and this is also my first time on Ulfur, sir."

Brother Vernon rubbed at the spiked growth of his two-day-old beard. "Habsburg? My, my goodness. You have come far across the seas, young fellow." The aged monk measured all three. "You are to call me *Brother Vernon*, or simply *Brother*." The three young men nodded. Vernon turned to the first youth once more. Perhaps his features were not so nondescript after all. The eyes were unusual in that they were slightly larger than normal, almost cowlike, or similar to those of a deer, or even the dead goat on the path below. "How do you know so much about what grows up here, lad?"

Julian brushed an errant strand of black hair from his face. "I was an apprentice seedsman, Brother Vernon. I recognize these trees."

"A seedsman, eh? Mmm. Good. Good. You might just prove

useful. Well, why are you all just standing there? We have far to go. Come." The monk twirled, and with a spring in his heels, scampered off. The others had to rush to catch up, despite being several decades younger.

They climbed until juniper trees began to spread their roots among the spruce. Ignoring his earlier exhortation for speed, Brother Vernon stopped and picked some blue-black berries from a low-hanging juniper branch. "Taste these, boys." He held out the berries in the palm of his thin hand. Brother Vernon popped one in his mouth and grinned as he chewed. Julian, Martin, and Klaus each gingerly placed a berry on their tongues, rolled it around, and began to bite down. Each young face screwed up in distaste, but none stopped chewing.

Julian coughed as he swallowed. "Bitter."

Vernon winked. "Yes, a very astringent pine flavour, best used in cooking rather than enjoyed on their own. But I like them," he chuckled. "They're an acquired taste and I've had twenty years on this mountain to acquire it." The monk licked his lips. "They also make quite a good juniper gin. Do you boys drink?"

"Sometimes beer," offered Julian meekly. The others shook their heads.

"Never gin?" Another round of headshaking. Vernon shrugged. "Ah, well, there's plenty of time to convert you. Come, come."

After some time, the path left the mountain forests of spruce and juniper. It narrowed and veered towards the edge of a long, jagged cliff.

"We must cling to the very mountainside itself for the next length of our journey," Brother Vernon said above the cutting wind. "Do not approach the edge of the path. Remember the mountain goat." He turned to find the three youths ignoring his warning and gaping over the side of the cliff. From this height, the entirety of Re'Shan came into view below: the spires, domes, rectangular libraries, and open-air markets of the greatest city in the Freelands.

"It's a magnificent city, boys," Vernon said, following the gaze of the younger men. He nodded to himself. "Yes, a wonderful example of civilization. If you like gambling, whoring, and nameless other soulless and depraved activities, then Re'Shan is your town. But not for us, lads. Godliness is further up. Up there." Vernon pointed in a vague direction towards either the bright blue heavens or the ice-capped top of the mountain. "Come! Come, lads, we're only two thousand feet up. We have another thousand before we can rest. The sun is well past its zenith. Hurry, boys, hurry! If you wish to be Brothers of the Order of Ulfur, and it is a life with much to commend it, then you must follow!"

Brother Vernon's enthusiastic speech snapped the spell Re'Shan had woven over the three young men. They watched as the older monk girded his robes and strode further up the path. The three exchanged glances and hurried after Brother Vernon, making sure to stay far away from the sheer edge of the mountainside.

—————

For the most part, the mountain path was wide enough to fit three men abreast, or even a pack-laden mule. Julian's nerves began to settle. The journey up Mount Ulfur stressed one's lungs, no doubt, but there proved to be little danger of a fall, despite the bad omen of the dead goat further down. It was, however, becoming cold. The late afternoon wind cut at Julian's skin, freezing the tip of his nose and tossing his black hair wildly about his face. He hoped that Brother Vernon would soon lead them to shelter. He'd not thought to bring a jacket. In fact, Julian had nothing but the clothes he wore and a copper coin in his woollen trousers as an initiation fee into the Brotherhood of the Monks of Ulfur.

Julian was not the only one feeling the cold. He could hear Martin's teeth chattering as the young Black man walked behind him. Julian slowed down to allow him to catch up. "Are you alright, Martin?"

"It's cold up here."

"Yes. As cold as Hades."

"I thought"—Martin blew into his hands—"I thought Hades was hot."

Julian shrugged. "I think Hades is simply the worst of whatever you are feeling. An analogy for each situation that you find yourself in. For example, one might say that a disappointing potato tastes like Hades."

Martin slapped at his shoulders to warm them. "You will make a good monk, indeed."

"And why is that?"

"You have a knack for philosophy. I understand that the monks like to talk philosophy in the evenings. You should fit right in."

Julian raised a dark eyebrow. "I met you at the foot of this mountain. We have known each other less than a day. How is it that you know I have a knack for anything?"

"Ah, that is why *I* will make a good monk. I'm a good judge of character."

Julian smiled. "Why do you want to be a monk, anyway?"

"My father was a slave before Emperor Groubert came to power, before the Freelands were established. He once told me that if he had been born into a world where a man could choose his own way, as I was, then he would have been a monk." Martin smiled proudly as he related his story.

Julian frowned. "It seems your father would simply be exchanging one form of servitude for another. Monk is an odd choice of profession for a former slave, I might suggest."

Martin waggled a finger. "Ah, but a life given willingly to the service of others is not servitude."

"Excellent answer," Julian said, nodding. "I like that. How does it go? *A life given willingly—*" Julian stopped. "Where is Klaus?"

Julian and Martin looked back down the way they had come. There, sitting with his knees drawn up under his chin, his back to a solitary twisted juniper shrub, sat Klaus.

Julian hurried back down the path. "Klaus, what are you doing? The hour grows late. We must not be caught out here on the mountainside when night falls."

The German youth drew his knees tighter under his chin. "I can't go on. It's too high. I cannot bear to look down. I feel something dragging me towards the edge, willing me to leap over the side. I will sit here a while until it goes away. Just allow me a moment, please."

Brother Vernon had by now noticed his absent novitiates and came scurrying down. "Up, lads, we must be on our way. We're almost there."

"Come, Klaus." Martin held out his hand.

Klaus screwed his eyes shut and rocked back and forth. "I can't. I can't. It calls to me. It asks me to leap to my death."

Julian knelt by the agitated young man. "What calls to you? Klaus, what is it?"

"I will fall. I just know that I will fall. I cannot. Please leave me."

"You'll freeze to death out here," Martin said. "Come on."

Brother Vernon spoke calmly, as if to a child unsettled by a bad dream. "It is but vertigo, my son. You suffer vertigo, nothing more."

Julian nodded enthusiastically. "Did you hear that, Klaus? It is nothing but vertigo." Julian turned to Brother Vernon. "What is vertigo?"

The old monk took on a scholarly air, his hands clasped before him. "From the Latin *vertere*, a whirling in the head when in high places, a turning of the mind in the elevated realm. A common enough occurrence, in fact—many of the brothers above suffer the same affliction."

"You see, Klaus?" Martin said, kneeling and taking Klaus's shaking hand. "You are feeling something completely explainable, but which can be conquered with understanding. Think of the wondrous knowledge we may learn above. *Vertigo.* Even the word is beautiful. The Monks of Ulfur are wise indeed, and we shall soon be among them. Think on that."

Julian patted Klaus on his bony shoulder. "Martin is right. The things that terrify us, we will defeat them if we but carry on. We will be brothers, together. Come on, Klaus. Our education awaits us. We're so close now."

Klaus opened his eyes and looked from one to the other. "Vertigo? This ... condition can be overcome?"

"All things can be overcome," Brother Vernon said.

Klaus nodded and allowed Julian and Martin to pull him to his feet. He was a head taller than the others, gangly and thin, seemingly slight enough for the elevated breeze to send him sailing from the mountainside like a wayward kite. He took a deep breath and attempted a weak smile. They all continued further up the side of Mount Ulfur, the two shorter novitiates on either side of the taller one, supporting him when his step faltered.

It was not long before they came to a small plateau. Klaus

breathed easier as they moved away from the edge of the mountainside. Brother Vernon walked past a squat wooden hut and headed for a cave entrance farther on, a dark maw in the side of Mount Ulfur.

Walking into the cave entrance, Vernon held out an arm to prevent anyone passing him. "Mind your step in here, lads. Stay behind me. Wait for your eyes to adjust."

Without warning, a ghastly face loomed out of the darkness. Klaus screamed, causing Martin and Julian to jump. An enormous figure in a brown habit and black cowl moved out of the shadows.

Brother Vernon scowled in irritation as his charges trembled and clung to each other, and to him. "Settle down, boys. It is only Lay Brother Jacob."

The massive monk, as tall as Klaus and three times the girth, addressed Brother Vernon. His voice resonated around the cave entrance. "Is the cargo ready? It is not safe to delay."

Julian looked around. What cargo could he be referring to? They carried nothing with them that could possibly qualify as such. A moment later, he understood.

"Aye," Brother Vernon said, "they're ready."

"Ready for what?" Julian asked.

"To ride the elevator to the abbey," Vernon replied.

"What's an elevator?"

"There is no time to dally." Vernon waved a hand at the colossus in the brown habit. "Lay Brother Jacob, make the preparations."

Jacob placed two fingers in his mouth and let out a piercing whistle. The door to the squat wooden hut outside opened and four burly monks in matching brown robes and black cowls answered the call. As they approached, Lay Brother Jacob beckoned to Julian and the others. "Follow me."

Jacob lumbered further into the cave and the others had to

hurry to match his expansive strides. Julian stumbled over the hem of Brother Vernon's habit in the darkness. Rounding a curve in the cave passage, Julian was relieved to see an orange glow on the cave walls. They passed by three burning torches in sconces before arriving at a large wooden platform constructed of sturdy planks. Torches at either end of the platform illuminated twin winch handles. The monks from the hut outside had by now positioned themselves at the winches, two at each long handle. The four men stood waiting, bald heads shining in the flames of the torches.

Lay Brother Jacob indicated for Brother Vernon and the novitiates to step forwards. Approaching the edge of the platform, Julian noted an open wooden carriage waiting for them, strengthened with a cross seam of metal. The elevator carriage was spacious but had no guardrail.

"This is the elevator," Brother Vernon said. The device seemed to be floating on the very darkness itself. Two thick ropes disappeared upwards into the pitch black. "The next one thousand feet of our journey shall be in the bosom of the mountain herself. Mother Ulfur welcomes you all home, boys."

The platform under Julian's feet had been constructed over a chasm. If it were to collapse, they would all plummet into the blackness below. Klaus had realized the same thing, for his eyes stared wildly, his mouth opening and closing wordlessly.

"Brother Vernon," Julian whispered. "I think this is not good for Klaus's vertigo."

Lay Brother Jacob overheard and laughed heartily. "Ha ha! Vertigo? You want to be a monk on this mountain, you'd better leave your vertigo down in Re'Shan!"

Brother Vernon made a clucking sound of disapproval. "Have a care, Jacob. Not everyone is as comfortable up here as you are. Come on, lads." Vernon stepped forwards onto the carriage. He turned and waved the three young men after him.

Julian put his hand on Klaus's shoulder. "Klaus. We can do this."

"This *elevator* will take us up there?" Klaus whispered in horror, pointing up into the darkness. Vernon nodded and gestured for them to join him. Klaus stammered, "Wh ... what if ... what if it falls?"

"Have a little faith," Brother Vernon said. "Lay Brother Jacob and his men haven't lost a soul yet. Isn't that right?"

The huge man nodded. "Not a soul. Safe as suckling at your mother's teat."

Vernon frowned. "The boys have no need of your colourful expressions, Lay Brother."

The lay brother bowed his head. "Sorry, Brother Vernon."

Julian and Martin each took an arm and guided Klaus towards the carriage. The tall young man resisted. "I can't ... I'll go back down the mountain."

Jacob shook his head. "Too late for that, boy. Get on."

Klaus tried to back away. "I'll sleep here. I'll sleep in the hut outside and make my own way down tomorrow."

"You can do this, Klaus," Martin said.

"There is no time to waste," Jacob growled. "You'll only have an hour of daylight remaining when you get to the upper station, and you'll need that to make the abbey safely. Go now or *all* of you must bed down here tonight."

"No, no." Brother Vernon waggled a finger. "Abbot Howard is expecting us today and we must not keep him waiting. Not in his condition."

"Then I have no choice." Lay Brother Jacob stepped forwards and grabbed Klaus in a headlock. The gangly youth struggled ineffectually.

"What are you doing?" Julian shouted. "Leave him alone."

Martin and Julian tried to pry the big man from Klaus's neck but could not match Jacob's power.

Brother Vernon sighed. "Is this really necessary?"

Jacob released his hold on Klaus and the German slumped. The big lay brother gently placed him on the carriage, which creaked under the weight of both bodies.

"He sleeps, nothing more." Jacob stepped off the elevator carriage. "He'll probably wake on the way up and then you'll have to deal with him, but that won't be my problem anymore, will it?"

Vernon waved his hand. "Come, boys." Julian and Martin stepped lightly onto the creaking carriage.

"Stay away from the edge and sit down," Lay Brother Jacob warned. Julian and Martin did as they were told.

Brother Vernon sat and cradled Klaus's head in his lap. He looked up and said, "How long do you think, Lay Brother?"

Jacob ran an eye over Julian and the others. "Not a heavy-weight among you. We'll have you up there in forty-five minutes."

Vernon placed two fingers to his lips and kissed them. "Farewell."

The master of the elevator returned the gesture and approached a bronze bell sitting at the edge of the torchlight. It looked heavy, but the big lay brother picked it up with ease and slammed the clapper against the sound bow once. The ring died away, and he followed with four more quick rings in succession. The monks gripped the winch handles and began to vigorously wind them. A grinding sound echoed through the dark chasm as the carriage began a juddering ascent. Within moments, Lay Brother Jacob and his men disappeared below, the glow of the torchlights fading soon after.

Julian was glad that Klaus was unconscious. He would not be coping well with this situation. Julian, too, was afraid. The carriage tilted sickeningly at one end before settling level once more. A sense of isolation and weightlessness overtook him as all light disappeared. He became aware of the sound of his own breathing and tried to ignore the steady squeaking of the wooden carriage as it oscillated like a slow-moving pendulum, tried to block out the image in his mind of four tiny figures swinging precariously back and forth over an endless black abyss.

2

A BLACK WING

The cold metal cross seam of the wooden carriage sent a chill through his legs and body, and Julian hugged himself. The four men continued to ascend in echoing space, though Julian could not tell how far or how fast the carriage rose. All sense of direction and time disappeared in the blackness.

Klaus groaned and stirred, his foot brushing against Julian's leg.

"Be still, lad," Brother Vernon whispered.

Julian's heart began to beat faster. If Klaus were to panic and lash out, he could send them all sprawling to their deaths.

"Where are we?" Klaus muttered. "I cannot see."

Julian blindly reached out and patted the tall man's leg. "Klaus, listen to me. We're on the elevator. Don't move."

"No, no, let me off." The carriage began to swing as Klaus attempted to get to his feet.

"Klaus, no," Julian said. "Stay where you are. Stay down."

"I can feel something," Klaus whispered.

"What is it?" Julian asked, feeling his own panic begin to rise.

"I feel something crawling on my arm."

"It's only an insect," Brother Vernon said. "Calm yourself."

"I hate the insects. I ... they frighten me."

Martin's disembodied voice came through the darkness. It was not sympathetic. "If you move, Klaus, I swear, I'll knock you out myself. Do you hear me? Stay still."

Martin's warning seemed to have an effect. Klaus whimpered but he no longer attempted to stand. "Take my hand," Julian said. A moment of fumbling in the dark, and then two hands clasped. The carriage moved steadily on up. Soon, a patch of blackness above them lightened somewhat. Julian let out a breath. "We're almost there, Klaus. Do you see? We're alright."

"I don't feel good about this," Klaus whispered. "There's evil on this mountain."

No one chose to respond to Klaus's augury of doom. The young man was, after all, severely affected by his fear of heights. He wasn't himself. All things considered, he was doing well to sit tight. The patch of lighter gloom further up brightened: burning torches, a welcome sight. Julian wanted off the elevator almost as much as Klaus did. Soon, they could make out faces peering down at them. A bell rang from above, one long clanging sound followed by four shorter ones: an echo of the bells that accompanied their setting off from the lower station.

The carriage stopped short of the upper platform, and Julian's heart jumped in his chest. Then, it began to ascend again. Julian noted four more monks straining at the winches. The final stretch of their journey had been taken over by the upper station crew.

"Stop," called a voice, and the carriage shuddered to a standstill, perfectly level with the upper platform.

Julian, Martin, and Klaus stumbled off the carriage, arms

outstretched and feeling off-balance. They followed a short passage to the outside world while Vernon stayed behind to talk to one of the upper elevator crew.

The three novitiates emerged into a cool early evening. Though the sun was setting behind the mountain, the sky seemed as bright as that of a midsummer's day. Julian passed several monks who cast sideways glances at him. He approached the edge of a rise and gasped. Above him a cloudless azure sky stretched away forever. Hawks circled below, and far below the hawks lay the city of Re'Shan, a sparkling jewel in the Great Southern Sands. The city was situated in the shade of Mount Ulfur, the mountain's shadow precipitating true night, but the city twinkled with the light of ten thousand gas lamps.

Martin joined Julian at the edge of the mountain and the young men exchanged breathless smiles at the wonder of the view. Klaus hung back from the edge of the path and, hands on knees, vomited. Brother Vernon arrived, patted Klaus on the back, and hurried on up a gravel path edged with wind-tossed purple bellflowers and fragrant gardenia shrubs of white.

Julian breathed hard; the air at almost four thousand feet seemed unwilling to inflate his lungs, yet his body thrilled at the magnificence of his surroundings. He could well understand why the Brotherhood of Ulfur had chosen to establish itself on the mountain. Closer to God, indeed.

Small stones crunched under their shoes as they journeyed ever upwards. The sky darkened perceptibly with each step. They rounded a curve in the mountainside and came to a set of stone steps laid into the path. Climbing them, the party came to an open flat space and Julian laid eyes for the first time on the monastery of the Ulfur Monks.

Nestled at the foot of a cliff face veined with trickling streams of ice-cold mountain water, the central edifice rose high in the air, as if to offer a challenge to the cliff and the very mountain itself. At first glance, it reminded Julian less of the religious buildings he had seen in the past and more like the paintings of the ancient Greek temples with their white columns of marble. It was breathtaking. Several smaller wooden or stone buildings of a less sophisticated nature formed a cloister, but his eyes were transfixed by the central building and its columns of grandeur.

Brother Vernon huffed and puffed as he reached the top of the steps. He beamed a proud smile and waved his hand in an expansive gesture. "Welcome, lads. Welcome ... to your ... new home." When Vernon had gathered his breath, he turned and pointed at the steps that they had just ascended. "Three hundred and thirty-three steps. Three times three, and your vows shall number three."

Martin turned to the old monk. "May we know these vows, Brother Vernon?"

"Obedience, stability, and conversion of life."

"What is this, *conversion of life*?" Klaus asked.

"Death to the self brings life to God," Vernon said.

Klaus looked horrified. "Death?"

"Material death, boy. Do not be alarmed. You must forego the earthly pleasures of man and commit yourself to God." Vernon stared hard at the three young men. "Good lord, do you boys know nothing of the lives to which you now devote yourselves?"

"We will learn, Brother Vernon," Julian said. "We are ready."

Vernon nodded. "Very well. Come, come. Night falls and the abbot awaits. Almost everyone is inside for the evening."

No gate or walls surrounded the central building, the cloister, or the other freestanding structures making up the grange. Julian wanted to enter the impressive central edifice and explore inside, but Brother Vernon led them towards a small hut nearby. He knocked at the door and entered, followed by the three curious novitiates. Brother Vernon stopped and raised a wispy eyebrow at the sight of the man in a pure black robe sitting at a plain wooden desk. "Prior Blackwing, forgive my surprise. I was expecting the abbot." Collecting himself, Vernon lowered his head and touched two fingers to his lips in the monastic *kiss of life*.

Prior Blackwing stood and returned the greeting. He was a tall man, not as tall as Klaus, but tall, nonetheless. His cheeks and nose appeared flushed with blood. Julian had known a drunk or two in his life and wondered at the florid appearance of the superior.

"Abbot Howard is unwell," Prior Blackwing said. "He has retired early, but he will welcome our new lay brothers at sunrise tomorrow before prime." The superior's eyes roamed over the young novitiates. He did not seem pleased at the quality of recruits. "They need habits and tonsures. Their faces must be shaved clean so that no consecrated wine shall become attached to the moustache. This will be done before they are shown to the dormitory. Is that understood?" Brother Vernon nodded. Prior Blackwing folded his arms and went on, "Three? This is it? That's all?"

Vernon nodded again. "There were two others, but they turned back very early on. Still, these three young lads are made of sturdy stuff." Here, he turned and patted each man on the shoulder. "They will do the Brotherhood proud, of that I am sure."

The red-faced superior did not seem to concur. He cast a doubtful glance over the three. Putting his hands behind his back, Blackwing stepped out from behind the desk. "The office of monk is both a vocation and a respected career path. A chance for advancement. I do not understand the reticence of the folk below. They are happy enough to send their sons to their deaths in distant lands, foot soldiers in wars that have little to do with them. They let wastrel teens and even children run the streets of Re'Shan, begging and stealing, and the Senate do nothing to stop it. Why they do not send them to us, I will never understand." Prior Blackwing let out a long sigh and shook his head again. "But we must make do with what we get. Sign here." The superior pointed to a large book on the desk. "You can write your names, can't you, or does the ignorance of the folk below outdo even my expectations?"

Brother Vernon placed a hand on each shoulder and guided the three young novitiates forwards, and one by one each picked up a quill and signed his name in the large book.

"And place your coins in that bowl," Blackwing added. The three young men dropped their copper coins in the indicated collection bowl on the desk and moved back a respectful distance. The tall cleric in black seemed lost in thought for a moment. He chewed at his lip and put his fingers to his red cheeks in an absentminded gesture. Then, Blackwing ran a final disapproving scowl over Julian, Martin, and Klaus before dismissing them with a wave of his hand.

Brother Vernon gently ushered the three outside and the door closed behind them. "You must forgive Prior Blackwing's excessively sober greeting," Vernon said. "He is greatly worried by Abbot Howard's illness. The burden of responsibility for the entire community rests on his shoulders until such time as the abbot is fully recovered."

Julian, though entranced by the impressive edifice in the centre of the plateau and the mountain environment in general, did not miss the note of pessimism in Vernon's voice. Abbot Howard was an ill man by all accounts.

Brother Vernon led them across the stone courtyard of the cloister and towards the central edifice. "This way, lads. This way to the Grand Chapel." As darkness descended, Julian's skin prickled in anticipation. "We call it the Grand Chapel,"

Vernon continued, "yet the prayer chapel itself constitutes only the first floor. The sleeping cells for the ordained monks are on the second floor and on the third is our magnificent library, curated by Brother Cohen. Scholars come from all manner of places to read our books. I believe it is world-renowned, if you will forgive the overt pride of such a statement."

"What's on the fourth floor, Brother Vernon?"

Vernon gave Julian an odd look. "Eh? The fourth floor?"

"Yes, I can see from the height of the façade above the third floor that there must be a fourth level, though I can make out no windows."

Vernon rubbed his hands and frowned but did not answer the question. "Um ... please follow. No time to dally."

They passed under a columned portico and entered a large wood-tiled antechamber lit with candles. The aged monk put a finger to his lips in a gesture of silence and then indicated for the three novitiates to follow him. They approached two large sliding doors, each on ball bearing rollers and possessing panels of frosted glass. The doors were now closed.

"In there," Vernon whispered.

Julian peered through a frosted glass at a prayer chapel burning brightly with what seemed like a thousand candles. A hundred figures knelt, perhaps more: monks lit by flame. Each figure faced away from Julian, motionless, head bowed under habit and cowl. The figures seemed to move and sway, warped by the frosted glass.

Brother Vernon smiled and whispered, "We must not disturb vespers. Come along."

Following the portico, the four came to a side exit leading to a space of alpine grass lit by a brazier half the height of a man. By its light, Julian realized that the cliff face behind the Grand Chapel comprised not one but two sheer vertical walls, and between their joining was a pool of dark water stretching away and narrowing until it disappeared under the granite cliffs.

"You shall bathe here," the old monk said. "Pile your clothes up by the banks of the water and climb in. You will find soap in a bucket. Lay Brother Rollant will come shortly to begin your initiation into the Order." Vernon took a step backwards. "I will say goodbye at this juncture. I commend you, lads. I commend you all on the choices you have made. Welcome to the Brother-hood of Ulfur." Brother Vernon bowed, placed two fingers to his lips, and walked away into the gathering gloom.

The light of the brazier cast dappled flame across the pool. Julian glanced at Martin and Klaus and then shrugged, pulling his tunic over his head. Martin laughed and followed. Klaus looked about nervously and began to undress slowly.

Julian and Martin jumped into the water with a splash; Klaus folded his clothes neatly and then eased himself into the pool. Each gasped with the shock of the cool clear mountain water.

"It's freezing," Martin said.

Julian laughed again. He jumped out of the water quickly and picked up two cakes of hard orange soap, which he threw to the others before entering the water once more. "It's cold, no doubt, but beautiful. Look." Julian pointed to the sky. Stars dimpled the heavens, brilliant points of distant light.

Martin gazed upwards in wonder. "We're closer to heaven than we've ever been. Enlightenment is within our reach." Julian ducked his head underwater and came up with a sharp exhalation of breath. He shook the water from his mop of black hair and grinned. He reached out and took both companions' hands and together they formed a circle.

"Enlightenment, my arse," a voice in the darkness said. "You're a long way from that."

The three bathers froze as a thin form came out of the

gloom. "I am Lay Brother Rollant, and I am here to instruct you in our ways." The newcomer bent and laid three brown robes on the grassy bank, and on each he placed a white undershirt. Finally, he rested a lacquered wooden crucifix on each pile of clothing. The gaunt, sallow-faced monk stood straight and placed his hands on his hips.

"Rule number one," Rollant said. "No putting your cocks in each other's mouths."

3

THE RULE OF ROLLANT

"Celibacy means just that," Lay Brother Rollant said as he cut chunks of hair from Julian's scalp with a sharp knife. Julian knelt naked by the brazier, his skin barely dry. Klaus had already been clipped and shaved, his new tonsure glinting in the light of the brazier. Martin, naturally, required no haircut. Both Martin and Klaus now wore the brown robes of the monastic order, though Klaus's ankles were exposed above his sandals as apparently no one could find a habit long enough to accommodate his length. Klaus and Martin examined the wooden crucifixes now about their necks.

Lay Brother Rollant's narrow eyes puckered around a sharp nose. "Remember, no intercourse of a sexual nature. No touching and certainly no penetration."

Klaus frowned as he watched the thin lay brother spread an oily cream atop Julian's head. Letting his cross fall to his chest, the young German said, "But there are no women on the mountain to touch or penetrate. Surely this forewarning is unnecessary?"

Lay Brother Rollant froze, the shaving blade poised above

Julian's scalp. The blade began to shake and then Rollant exploded in scornful laughter. "German idiot," he said. Julian closed his eyes and hoped his head would remain unscathed. Martin looked sideways at Klaus, who shrugged, a mystified expression on his long face.

When Rollant's laughter faded, he wiped at his eyes and began to scrape at Julian's head with the shaving blade. "More fools I must deal with. Listen to me. You won't be monks for at least two years. You are lay brothers. Do you understand that? *Lay brothers.* The library, the meditation, the *lectio divina* will be as attainable to you as the sky is to a fish. Only when you have shown your true worth, only when you have proven yourselves useful and sown your seeds of diligence, only then will you be ordained as choir monks and find yourselves in the bosom of enlightenment." The thin lay brother squinted at Julian's head, checking his handiwork. "You've got grey in your roots. How old did you say you were? No, don't answer that. I don't care." Rollant continued to shave the tonsure, and Julian shivered in the night air despite his nearness to the brazier, his discomfort heightened by the growing chill at the top of his skull.

"I've done my time," Rollant continued, "and I will be a cleric. Oh yes, very soon now I shall be ordained. Part of my final obligations are to make sure that you three cretins learn our ways. I am also to assign duties that you must carry out. Listen well to this warning. If you don't pull your weight, if you *in any way* prevent me from getting my holy orders, it will not be a pleasant life for you here. Do you understand me?"

Julian did not nod his head for fear that Lay Brother Rollant would nick the skin of his raw scalp.

———

The monastic habit worn by the skeletal Rollant was identical to that worn by big Jacob and his men in the lower elevator station. It was the garb of the lay brothers as opposed to the choir monks like Brother Vernon. The difference was simply in the colour of the cowl: black for the lay brothers but a uniform brown for the ordained monks. Thus, Julian, Martin, and Klaus wore brown habits with black cowls.

Over the next few weeks, a routine developed. Julian and the others slept with two dozen other lay brothers in a dormitory between the abbot's office and the cliffs which formed a rear wall to the grange. Due to the proximity of the lay brothers' sleeping quarters to the cliffs, Julian was often lulled to sleep by the calming sound of water trickling down the rock face. The falling water soothed the turbulent thoughts that plagued him, and he was grateful for it.

The lay brothers attended their own less frequent versions of the liturgy hours within their own dormitory, not in the Grand Chapel with the holy monks. Outside of his duty to pray three times a day, Julian spent much of his time in the vegetable gardens on the slopes around the grange, a task deemed the best use of the skills acquired as a seedsman in his secular life. Julian longed to see the inside of the Grand Chapel and read in the library, but these he could not do. In fact, Julian had found no excuse to set foot within the central edifice of the Brotherhood of Ulfur since he had arrived two weeks before. But of the layout of the Grand Chapel itself, he remembered what Vernon had told him: the prayer chapel was on the first floor, the ordained monks slept in individual cells honeycombed throughout the entirety of the second floor, and the library could be found on the third floor. Lay brothers, of course, remained forbidden from accessing the accrued wisdom held within the library.

No one knew, or at least no one spoke of, what might be found on the fourth floor. Whatever the upper level contained was forbidden from both lay brother and choir monk alike. As he crossed the courtyard, Julian glanced at the columned Grand Chapel and decided that he would one day find out the secrets of the uppermost level, but for now he was famished and hurried past the bread ovens, the storehouse, and the choir monk dining hall to find his seat with Martin and Klaus in the lay brothers' refectory.

Mealtimes on the mountain were silent affairs as a matter of code. Many of the lay brothers had developed a sophisticated form of sign language to overcome this, but Julian had yet to learn its more subtle complexities and was therefore unable to ask Klaus what ailed him when his tall friend slumped down beside him for the midday meal. Klaus looked miserable, more so than usual.

Julian gently elbowed his sullen friend and pointed at the bowls of steaming onion and leek soup on the table. He beamed and proudly thumbed at his own chest, indicating that he had been involved in the harvesting of the vegetables involved in this day's meal. Klaus attempted a smile as his fingers danced, spelling out the letters for 'well done.' Julian raised an eyebrow in surprise. Klaus was picking up the symbols at an impressive rate, much faster than he. The gangly youth's dejected expression, however, resumed a moment later. Julian looked enquiringly across the table at Martin, but his friend simply shrugged as if to suggest that Klaus was being oversensitive and Julian shouldn't fret.

The other lay brothers at the dining table were too busy slurping at their soup or tearing at their chunks of bread to notice, so Julian leaned in and whispered, "What's the matter?" Klaus frowned and shook his head, but Julian ignored him. "They can't hear us. Tell me."

Klaus made several movements with his fingers, but Julian shrugged in confusion. Sighing, the tall German youth lowered his head and whispered, "Meet me at the goat sheds."

Julian nodded. "Yes, as soon as I can. Do you like it, by the way? The soup?" Klaus formed the letters for 'well done' once again. Julian smiled, turned to Martin, and with a wink whispered, "I miss steak."

Every lay brother along the table stopped eating and stared at Julian, open mouthed. Several wooden spoons clattered to the table. Julian's face turned red as he busied himself with finishing his onion and leek soup.

When the choir monks were attending midafternoon prayers, and when he was sure Rollant would be busy in the bread ovens, Julian strolled away from the vegetable gardens to a grass track leading southwest out of the compound. This path wound its way down and around the side of the mountain to the remaining buildings that made up the Brotherhood's grange: the goat sheds and Brother Vernon's gin mill. He followed the path, its grass unstirred by even the slightest breeze, and soon tasted the bitter tang of juniper berries on the still air, and the even more pungent whiff of goat shit.

Brother Vernon stood at the door of his gin mill, smiling and waving at Julian as he passed by. The old monk held out a tin cup and raised both wispy eyebrows in invitation. Julian smiled back, shook his head, and pointed at the sky as if to suggest the hour was too early.

Julian found Klaus in the goat sheds further on, standing and staring absentmindedly into space. A dozen goats chewed grass about him.

"What's wrong?" Julian asked.

Klaus blinked and turned at Julian's voice. "I've been tending the goats since we arrived. I like it. I'm learning to make goat's cheese. It's a fascinating process and I think I may even be good at it."

"So, what's the problem? I cannot linger, Klaus. I am expected back in the vegetable gardens."

Klaus kicked at a tuft of grass. "Lay Brother Rollant has decided to change my duties. Tomorrow, I begin in the storehouse. I must keep account of all goods coming up or going down the mountain. I, myself, am required to go down to Re'Shan for purchases each week."

"Well, I see nothing ... oh, your vertigo."

"Yes, the vertigo. I ... I cannot stand the thought of traversing the path again. I'm alright up here, you see, up here on the plateau. The goat sheds stand back from the mountain's edge. Sometimes I forget that I am even on a mountain. But the path ... and the elevator. Oh, Julian, I cannot bear the thought of the *elevator*." Klaus's hands started shaking. "I cannot do it." Suddenly, Klaus burst into tears.

Julian tried to console his friend. "Just explain to Rollant. I'm sure he'll understand and let you stay with the goats."

"He will not listen." Snot bubbled from Klaus's nose and the tall lay brother turned away, wiping at his face with the sleeve of his habit.

Julian laid a hand on Klaus's shoulder. "Let me talk to him. Surely, he will see reason." Klaus turned and without a word grasped Julian in an enveloping embrace, squeezing the air from Julian's lungs. Klaus was more powerful than he looked.

———

Rollant spat onto the stone floor and did not turn from where he stood at the bread oven, his face sheened with sweat from the heat emanating off the bricks. "Lay Brother Klaus is going down the mountain and that's final."

"But Klaus has vertigo," Julian said. "It makes him quite unwell. I have seen how it unmans him. Surely there is someone else."

The bony supervisor rounded on Julian. "Look, Kristoff and Lawrence fell into a gully last night, broken ankles both. They were barely able to help each other limp back into the compound. Cursed fools. I don't know what they were doing up there in the dark, but I have my suspicions." Rollant threw a long-handled spatula into the corner, put his hands on his hips, and glared at Julian. "At any rate, I need two men to go down the mountain for supplies, at least until those idiots recover. That mewling German bastard is one of them."

"But it makes no sense to choose Klaus because—"

Rollant held up a hand to cut off any argument. "I despise the man. Klaus is afraid of heights, he's afraid of insects. He's terrified of *everything*. This is not the life for him unless he can overcome these fears. If he can't complete his duties, he's out. As for myself, I soon leave the ranks of the illiterate and ascend to a higher status. When I am ordained, I won't have to deal with you or him anymore but for now I am senior lay brother, and you must obey my commands. Do you understand? I have the authority to have you thrown out of this place on your arse."

Julian placed his hands together and bowed his head. "Yes, Lay Brother Rollant. I understand. I wish for nothing more than to see you became a choir monk. I'm just not sure that Klaus is the right man for this task, and surely you would prefer your last few weeks among the lay brothers to go as smoothly as possible. But I have spoken all that I will on the matter."

"You have and you are dismissed," Rollant said shortly.

Julian made the kiss of life and backed away. As he turned to go, Rollant called after him: "Lay Brother Julian, wait." Julian waited. Rollant sighed and then reached inside a sackcloth at the entrance to the bread ovens and pulled out a rolled-up parchment. He held it up. "Alright. Tomorrow morning, immediately after lauds you and Lay Brother Martin will descend to Re'Shan. You will take some of Brother Vernon's gin to the address at the top of this parchment."

"Me? But—"

Rollant cut Julian off with a sneer. "You've convinced me that Klaus is not a suitable candidate. *You*, however, will suffice. Now, pay attention." Rollant unrolled the parchment. "You shall receive five coppers for Vernon's gin. With that money you must purchase items one through eight on this list. Do you understand?" Julian nodded and reached for the parchment, but Rollant held it away. "A moment. It's written in Latin. Listen carefully and I'll tell you what each item stands for in the common tongue."

Julian listened as the thin lay brother slowly pointed to and translated each word on the list. Rollant was wasting his time: Julian could both read and write in Latin but simply nodded along to each of the items explained to him.

"Items one through eight." Julian took the parchment. "I understand, Lay Brother Rollant."

Rollant scowled and scratched his temple. "You'll need a pack mule. See Lay Brother Jacob at the lower station. You will also pick up the gin there." Julian nodded again. "You are not to touch the gin. It must arrive intact. Two small barrels evenly weighted on the mule's flanks."

Julian spread his hands. "I would not dream of interfering with Brother Vernon's prized gin."

"Yes, yes. Don't lose the money or any of the items you purchase with it. If there's any money left over, it must be returned to me. And remember, this does not absolve you or Lay Brother Martin of your duties in the gardens. You shall spend two days in total each week attending to supplies and the other days you will continue to work the gardens. Understood?"

"Yes." As he backed away, Julian bumped into something. Turning, he was startled to find the tall Prior Blackwing staring down at him. The man's expression seemed eternally frozen between contempt and irritation.

After what seemed an uncomfortable length of time, the superior's narrow eyes flicked to Rollant. "How goes the bread, Lay Brother Rollant?"

"Fine, just fine, Prior Blackwing." Rollant smiled ingratiatingly. "Lay Brother Julian here will bring us more wheat and millet the day after tomorrow."

Blackwing looked down his nose at Julian, a nose which seemed more inflamed than usual. "I suffer from rosacea," the superior said suddenly, flicking a small white spot from the shoulder of his black robe. Julian stared in confusion as the tall monk went on, "rosacea is a rash about the face, you see. A flushing of the blood beneath the skin. I do not drink on most occasions and am certainly no drunkard. People spout the most ungracious nonsense, the petty-minded down in the city. Those in Hell. The unholy and weak of mind like to gossip. But we are above all that here." Julian could not quite understand what the superior was getting at. He could only nod again under the man's intense stare. "Are you committed to the Brotherhood of Ulfur?"

"Yes, Father. I am committed."

Blackwing flicked his fingers at Julian. "Go about your duties."

Offering the monastic kiss of life, Julian walked quickly from the bread ovens, his mind uneasy at the odd conversation with the senior monk, and indeed the man's very presence. Truth be told, Julian *had* seen the prior's ruddy appearance as evidence of heavy drinking. Had Blackwing read his mind? Julian shivered and turned his thoughts to the city of Re'Shan below and his new duties that would take him there. He did not want to go. He hoped for nothing more than to remain cloistered high on the mountain, where his past could remain buried deep. Too many eyes in the city, too many that might recognize him.

But to the city he must go, with care. With great care.

4

TWIN GREEN

The sun had already disappeared behind the snowcapped head of Mount Ulfur when Julian and Martin reached the city gates. The heat of the day still radiated from the grit-covered paving stones underfoot. Armed soldiers wearing light surcoats of black and green gave the two lay brothers and their pack mule only a cursory examination as they passed under the massive open portcullis and entered Re'Shan, the city at the edge of the Great Southern Sands.

Martin excitedly pointed out some of the more impressive buildings along the main avenue. "There," he said. "Mosque and church, side by side, do you see? Temples and civic buildings of a democratic nature. I have heard so much about this city. They say Re'Shan is truly a place of peace and enlightenment where all people can worship and live together."

Julian tried to take in the sights of the city while keeping his cowl firmly over his head. "It is truly magnificent, though Brother Vernon certainly does not approve. He thinks it a den of temptation. I suppose he's right, but it's such a *vibrant* den of temptation."

The two men led the pack mule along the avenue until they

33

came to an intersection with a fountain spouting bright, clean water from the mouth of a large brass fish. Several women in light flowing robes of pink and pale purple scooped at the water with clay jugs and carried them away on their heads. Next to the fountain was a signpost giving directions to different sections of the city and the two men approached it.

As they were discussing which road to take, their pack mule defecated with a loud whinny. Immediately, a small barefoot child in a dirty tunic approached them from the lengthening shadows of a nearby apartment and used his hands to scoop the mule dung into a small jute sack. The boy's hair was a matted brown, almost the colour of the dung now covering his hands.

Upon completing his task, the boy held out a filthy palm towards the two lay brothers. "City ordinance as relating to public health and safety, oh, and beautification. That will be one copper, sirs." The child had bright emerald eyes and could be no more than nine years of age.

Julian shook his head. "We don't have any coppers. And that seems a rather excessive amount of money for collecting mule shit."

The emerald-eyed boy replied with an earnest air, "We must keep Re'Shan clean and beautiful for both visitors and locals alike. You can ask anybody, sirs. City ordinance, regulations, and things of that ilk. As a city officer, it is my responsibility to keep these streets right and proper and I take my duties serious."

Julian found himself vacillating between amusement and annoyance. "We don't have any money, *officer*, not until we sell the gin."

The boy looked from one lay brother to the other and then to the gin barrels on the mule. A slight frown relaxed into a smile. "Gin? Oh, in that case, you'll be wanting the Vestibule."

"The Vestibule?" Julian glanced at Martin. "It's a church?"

"Pubs, sir," the boy replied. "Eateries and whatnot. Down that way." He pointed with a shit-stained finger towards a long street running between tall wooden apartments.

Julian glanced in the direction indicated. "I see. Well, we're looking for a man called"—Julian fumbled for the paper with the name on it—"*Theodore Axel*, of the ... of the ..."

"*The Whore's Chastity*," finished the boy.

Julian paused in surprise, his face reddening. "Yes, *The Whore's Chastity*. A fine establishment by all accounts."

The boy smirked at Julian's discomfort. "Are you two monks down from the mountain? I can tell from your kit, sirs."

"Yes, we have recently joined the Brotherhood of Ulfur."

The boy nodded. "Well, sirs, come along and bring the gin. I shall take you to the *Chastity* before the sun sets."

Still carrying his bag of shit, the emerald-eyed boy with the matted brown hair padded off down the street. Exchanging surprised glances, Julian and Martin dutifully followed.

———

"Get off with you, lad. Stop molesting honest folk."

The boy backed away, bowed to the lay brothers, and twined his two little fingers together in an obscene gesture known only too well by its rotund recipient. Theodore Axel took a lumbering step towards the street urchin and made to kick the child's skinny arse, but the emerald-eyed boy evaded the fat man's foot and disappeared into the pooling shadows of the street.

"Little bastards," Theodore Axel commented. "Cut your throat as soon as look at you." The proprietor of *The Whore's Chastity* rested his hands on the apron covering his swollen belly and turned his attention to Julian and Martin. "Hope you didn't let that one sell your own shit to you for a copper."

Julian smiled. "He tried."

"Pen them up, I say, like the animals they are. The Senate is too lenient. Nothing good will come of letting them roam the streets like feral dogs. Democracy, my arse. We were better off *before* the republic." Axel raised an eyebrow and looked at Martin. "Even the slaves. Anyway, where are the other two monks what usually come, Lawrence and whatshisname?"

"Kristoff," Julian offered. "The victims of an unfortunate accident. Lay Brother Martin and I will be providing you with the gin while they recover their health."

"Alright, bring it in and through to the kitchen. This way." The two apprentice monks unhitched a gin barrel from either side of the mule and heaved them up several steps. Theodore Axel turned at the entrance to his pub, scratched at his mutton-chop whiskers, and pointed to the floor. "Roll them from here, brothers. Save yourselves a hernia. That's right, roll them through here."

The two men rolled the gin barrels inside *The Whore's Chastity* and across a sticky rosewood floor. The few patrons eating or drinking at the tables around the large dark room paid no heed to the two men in habits.

"Alright, just stand them in the corner by the kitchen door," Axel said. "Your beds are upstairs, second door on the left. Here" —Axel reached past Martin and handed a handful of copper coins to Julian—"keep those well-guarded. You can stable your mule two doors down at the blacksmith. Food is on the house, as per our agreement with your Abbot Howard, served in your rooms in half an hour." Theodore Axel wiped his hands on his apron and walked away.

"Thank you," Julian called after him before slipping the coins into a small pouch stitched inside his habit.

Martin laughed bitterly. "What was all that talk about slaves? Did you notice how he gave you the money even though I was standing right beside him? Wouldn't trust it with a Black man, obviously."

"Don't let it bother you, Martin. We're holy now. We turn the other cheek and all that."

Martin smouldered for a little longer but eventually shrugged. "You're right. Look, I have a plan. We buy supplies at daybreak, yes? But tonight, after supper, we're free. I want to explore the city."

Julian frowned. "I don't think that's wise."

"Come on. Where's your sense of adventure?"

"We're monks, Martin. We have no sense of adventure."

Martin scoffed. "Lay brothers, we're not choir monks, not yet. You must be as curious as I am to see the greatest city in the Freelands."

Julian would have preferred to stay inside, unseen. Martin's childlike enthusiasm, however, was touching. It would be dark and the chances that anyone would recognize him were remote. Still, he would wear his cowl and keep his head down, just in case. Against his better judgement, Julian nodded. "Alright."

———

As the sun set, the creeping shadows had a moment of unmitigated power before the turbaned lamp lighters made their rounds, dethroning the early darkness. The foot traffic on the streets of Re'Shan intensified. Martin's excitement at exploring the famed city gave vigour to his steps, and he had to slow down on several occasions to let Julian catch up.

"We can't go far," Julian warned. "It's very easy to get lost in a city this size."

"Look over there." Martin pointed to a low orange clay

building. "We have places like this in Sil'Raka. It is a public bathhouse. You see, the evening is when a desert city truly comes alive. Is it not the same where you come from in the north? Dysael, isn't it?"

Julian nodded. "Perhaps, but Dysael can be a dangerous place after sunset, so I rarely ventured out in the evenings." Several men wearing togas wandered from the low-roofed building. "Who are those people, the patrons coming out of the bathhouse?"

"They are civil servants, *senators*, more specifically." Martin chuckled. "Some say the Blacks of Re'Shan and Sil'Raka were freed from slavery as they oiled the backs of the white senators discussing its abolition."

"Perhaps, if we have time," Julian said, "we can go inside."

Martin frowned. "Monks don't bathe in public bathhouses with senators, Julian, or anyone for that matter. What would Abbot Howard think?"

"I don't know what he'd think. I haven't seen him yet. Have you?"

Martin shrugged. "He is ill."

"No sign of the man in over two weeks. Is he even alive?"

Martin leaned his head towards Julian and whispered conspiratorially, though no one on the street gave the two apprentice monks even a passing interest. "The brothers say that Prior Blackwing is preparing to step into the senior position on a permanent basis. It would seem Abbot Howard is at death's door."

"He's a prickly one, isn't he?" Julian said.

"Prior Blackwing? Yes, quite dislikeable. I had always imagined abbots as fat jolly fellows, but the superior looks more like red-faced Death without the scythe."

Julian put on a mock scowl. "We mustn't talk ill of the next abbot, Martin." He pointed towards a square four-story pink building with blue trim. Several young women sat reclining outside next to a blazing brazier, smiling at passersby. "Even I know what that place is."

Martin took Julian by the elbow and led him away. "I don't think we'll have reason to step foot inside there."

Julian nudged Martin. "Well, you never know." Both men laughed.

A group of children ran across their path and disappeared into the shadows between the pools of lamplight. Just then, a woman sidled over to Julian and laid a hand on his shoulder. "Half price for men of the cloth." She winked, and her rouge-tinged cheeks dimpled.

Martin spoke before Julian could reply. "We have taken a vow of celibacy."

The whore's painted eyebrows rose. "I won't tell God if you don't. Besides, even Jesus needed a jolly good pull on his pudding now and then. Am I right?" She gave another lascivious wink, but the two men demurred and moved on. On a quieter section of the avenue, a small girl came hurtling towards them. She slipped and crashed to the ground in front of Julian.

"Please, your Lordship," she said. "Don't let them hurt me." The girl clung to the hem of Julian's habit.

Julian helped the girl to her feet and blinked in surprise. She had freckles on her cheeks, but it was the eyes that made him catch his breath: the same startling emerald eyes as the previous street urchin, the collector of mule shit and their former guide to *The Whore's Chastity*. "Hurt you? Who would seek to hurt you, child?"

The girl's bright green eyes were round with fear as she pointed at a group of bigger children coming closer, a group comprised of four boys. A burly lad led them, ginger hair hanging over his eyes, giving him the appearance of a sheepdog.

"Hand her over, mister," the big boy growled. The slight girl huddled closer to Julian.

"What's going on here?" Martin said.

The hefty ginger-haired boy cracked his knuckles in a threatening gesture. "None of your concern, sir. She's simply out after her bedtime."

"Don't listen to them," the girl said. "They mean to do me an awful harm."

The big lad pointed at the girl. "This is my wee sister. And me mum is waiting at home for her, sick with worry, Mum is. Come along, Yerty." The large boy held out his hand.

The girl looked up at Julian with pleading eyes. "Me name's not Yerty. They're liars."

"Be gone," Martin said to the boys. "God does not condone bullying."

The group of boys looked from one man to the other and then backed away. They turned and ran off the way they had come.

"Perhaps you should accompany us, child," Julian said.

The girl brushed her long black hair and surprisingly clean white tunic. "No. No. I'll be alright. I'm alright now. You are me heroes, both of you, sirs. May the Lord be with you always."

Martin knelt to look the girl in her bright green eyes. "Do you have somewhere to go? Somewhere safe?"

"Aye, aye. I'll be fine. Thank you." The girl curtsied and ran off in the other direction.

Julian looked to the stars in the sky. "A good deed done, but now I think we should get back to our lodgings. It is late and we must be up at first light."

"But there is much more to see," Martin said, disappointment in his voice.

"I'm quite overwhelmed already," Julian said. "Oh no."

"What is it?"

Julian was patting at the inner pocket of his habit. "The money. It's gone."

"Oh, shit," Martin gasped. "We'll be expelled for this. The prostitute?"

Julian shook his head. He swung around but the child had melted into the night.

———

Three children stood together on a rooftop overlooking the sparkling evening view of Re'Shan. The girl with the eyes of cold green light pushed the five coins around her palm with a finger.

"Five coppers." She looked up into the small boy's equally luminescent green orbs. "Only five coppers."

The boy, the shit collector who had shown Julian and Martin to *The Whore's Chastity*, shrugged. "They're monks, hardly rich folk, but five coppers is five coppers. Don't be sniffing at it."

The girl screwed up her freckled face and put a thin forearm to her nose. "I'm sniffing at *you*, Dylan. You stink. Why don't you bloody wash yourself before you show up here?"

Dylan looked offended. "I can't smell nothing."

"You reek of camel shit. I'm ashamed to call you my brother."

"I ain't gathered no camel shit today. Mule shit. A lot of it."

The girl scowled. "Camel, mule. What do I know the smell of one animal's turds from another?" The girl turned to the other boy, the big ginger-haired lad who had played the role of bully on the street. "And, Olaf, you stupid bastard. Don't use my real name!"

The big boy grimaced. "I'm sorry, Yerty. I forgot. It's just that Yerty and Gertrude sound similar."

A look of disgust passed across Yerty's freckled face. "They don't sound *nothing* alike. Now *Olaf* and *oaf*, they sound the same, don't they? *Olaf the oaf.* You use my real name again and I'll cut you, stupid big lump."

The ginger-haired sheepdog protested. "But *Yerty* and *Gerty* do sound the same. They sound alike."

"It's *Gertrude!*" the girl exploded. "You're to call me *Gertrude* when we scam!"

Dylan held up his hands. "Calm down, Yerty."

Yerty turned on her twin brother. "This is a very precise operation. Each part must work in perfect timing with the other. Remember, *I'm* the one taking all the risks. *I'm* the one getting in close and doing all the pilfering. I don't know why I even bother sharing."

"Hang on," Dylan said. "I found the mark, and without Olaf, the scam wouldn't work."

Yerty sighed angrily. "Alright, alright. Like I said, we work together. Just like Miss Cass showed us. We mustn't let her down. She's put a lot of faith in us. I ain't letting Miss Cass down, are you?" Dylan and Olaf shook their heads. "Good. We do it like we practiced, and for Christ's sake get the names right."

"Uh, we have a problem," Olaf said.

Yerty scowled again. "What problem?"

Olaf pointed behind Yerty, and she turned and gawked in amazement. The monk was standing there at the end of the roof: the doe-eyed one with the pleasant face. He'd climbed the drainpipe, just like she had. How a full-grown man had done that without tearing the pipe off the wall, she did not know.

"Run," Yerty said. She didn't wait for Dylan or Olaf. *She* was carrying the money, and the monk was after *her*.

She hurtled through an open window at the far end of the gabled roof and into a vacant top-floor bedroom. She bolted for the open door and ran down the stairs, taking them three at a time. She heard Olaf huffing and puffing behind her, and then a clattering. The idiot had fallen on his face. Hopefully, his fat arse would block the narrow winding staircase long enough for her to escape. She burst out of the stairs and onto the second floor. She didn't continue down the stairs but rather headed for another window at the far end of the dusty hallway. Glancing behind she caught a flapping of brown robes. He was right on her. Yerty leaped from the open window and grasped the rope spanning the street, a rope upon which a banner proclaimed the coming visit of Archbishop Fancypants and repent now all ye sinners. The archbishop be damned. All she knew was that the rope carrying the banner was a lifeline, a thread to safety, a finely weighted strand that would take her but exclude any pursuit. Neither Olaf nor even Dylan could swing across the rope without causing it to break free of its anchors. But she'd done it before, trusted the rope to carry her insubstantial frame. Planned on it, in fact.

With a firm purchase on the cable, she swung hand over hand like a tropical monkey, over the street and across the distance between apartments. She didn't stop to look behind her. The monk wouldn't be foolish enough to follow and over-load the rope, sending them both crashing to the paving stones below.

She reached the other side and dropped down onto a canvas awning. The monk was not behind her, nor was he peering from the open window across the street. Yerty skirted around the awning, bouncing with the motion of the canvas but was confident that it, like the cable above, would support her weight.

She gripped the edges of the awning and flipped over, hanging suspended for a moment before dropping to the side alley below and startling a hungry dog digging at something, sending it yelping into the shadows.

Yerty followed the dog down the alley and came to a tall, slatted fence. The dog had squeezed under a nearby building and the girl considered following the animal. Going through the crawl spaces was always a filthy undertaking and only attempted when there was no other avenue. The monk had given up his pursuit, so Yerty decided to climb the fence. Her clothes would remain clean, well, cleaner at any rate, and she wouldn't need to beg any more soap from the washerwomen.

She took off her canvas shoes and threw them over the fence, backed up, and sprinted. She made it halfway up before her momentum stalled. Inserting her hands between the slats, she held on, reached up, and climbed to the top. Dropping to the other side, the copper coins fell from her tunic pocket to the street. She picked them up, blew them clean of dust and sand, and ran again.

Several minutes later, a breathless Yerty was climbing a set of twisting stairs. At the top was a small wooden door. She pushed it open and entered a dark gabled attic. An armchair, half its stuffing oozing from a tear in the seat, squatted in the centre of the room and a desk with a broken leg slumped in the corner. Yerty threw herself into the chair which served as her bed and tried to catch her breath. She removed the coins from her pocket and cast them into the shadows.

"More trouble than they're worth," she muttered.

The room was lit by moon and stars through a smudged skylight above. Yerty pushed herself from the chair with some effort and fumbled through the desk drawers for a candle. She found one and stood on the armchair, reached up, and clambered through the skylight onto the roof above. Yerty took a moment to admire the view she never tired of: the desert city by moonlight. Re'Shan stretched on forever with its spires and minarets, curved domes and long rectangular gabled roofs. The city threatened to engulf even the Great Southern Sands in its majesty and expanse.

Yerty turned away from the vista of twinkling stars above and glowing gas lamps below and clambered softly across the angled roof. Careful, a fall from this height would mean instant death. She came to another skylight and rapped at it three times. The skylight opened and Yerty whispered, "Light." She passed her candle within and a moment later it was returned to her, its wick aflame.

Yerty clambered back to her loft and entered once more, gingerly for fear of dropping the candle and setting the attic, and indeed the entire building, ablaze.

She placed the candle firmly in one arm of a three-armed candle tree on the dilapidated desk. She opened another drawer and took out a small wooden horse in midflight, its mane flowing in an invisible wind. She brushed a finger across the wooden animal's flanks and sighed.

Yerty turned around and the monk stood there, looming over her silently like a flickering ghost.

5
THE MISTRESS AND THE MONK

Yerty bit back a scream. The monk stood between her and the door, like some hooded boatman standing on the shores of the Styx. She had no chance of getting past him or making the skylight. She backed away into a corner, clutching the wooden horse to her chest and feeling it vibrate with the beating of her frantic heart.

The monk removed his cowl and glanced around the loft. "I'll take my five coppers."

Yerty nodded to the moth-eaten carpet where the copper coins glinted like dull bronze in the candlelight, but the monk did not fall for the distraction. He stood motionless. "Collect them and hand them to me. I mean you no harm. I simply want the coins."

Yerty tried to control her breathing. She found herself in a position she had always tried to avoid: trapped like a kitten in a stormwater drain. Her brain railed at having no escape route, fear threatening to drive her wild. She considered attacking the man, clawing at him with her fingernails. Or yelling for help, that's what she would do. It was *all* she could do.

As if sensing her unease, he put a finger to his lips and said softly, "I simply want the money and then I shall leave you in peace."

Yerty peered at him in the wavering light of the candle. The doe-eyed naïvety in his eyes was no longer there. A hard edge had replaced that softer element, an authority that had nothing to do with his role as God's representative. "You won't seek retribution?" Yerty asked.

He smiled. "I'm a monk. We deal in forgiveness. I am Brother Julian, *Lay* Brother Julian as it is, for I shall not be ordained for some time."

"I don't know nothing about *ordained*," Yerty said suspiciously, her bright green eyes narrowing.

His smile did not dim. "It means that I will not be a *real* monk until I have served the Lord in a manual capacity." Yerty merely nodded and let the man ramble on. The monk, or lay monk, or whatever he was, put his hands on his hips. "What's your name?" he asked.

"Gertrude."

"And the horse?"

"What?"

"The fine horse that you hold. Does he have a name?"

Yerty glanced down at the wooden horse. "*She* doesn't have a name. It's not a real horse." She was lying; the horse had a name, but she wasn't telling him that. If he knew, he'd have an advantage over her. Things like names were never offered up to a stranger. Not for free.

He smiled that pleasant smile again, but Yerty wasn't falling for it. "Of course," the man said. "She is simply a toy. Gertrude, the coins, please."

A woman's voice said, "Leave the child alone. Raise your hands."

A cold blade at his neck prevented Julian from turning around and the smile on his face melted like overheated candle wax. He held his hands up.

The woman addressed Yerty. "Child, be a dear and extinguish the candle." Still clutching the small wooden horse tightly to her chest, Yerty walked warily past Julian and extinguished the flame with a quick breath. The room fell into darkness once more, lit only by the moon and stars through the skylight. "This girl is under my protection," the woman said. "Leave."

Julian swallowed. "She has taken money from me, from the Brotherhood of Ulfur. I must have it back."

The woman wore a long, flowing abaya of midnight blue that brushed the mouldy carpet and hid the curves of her body, though the monk could know nothing of her clothes or figure as he dared not turn around with the knife still pressed against his throat. She glanced from Julian to Yerty with eyes bright brown even in the shadows. "Monks? I told you to leave the brothers alone."

Yerty shrugged. "You said it was not *advisable* to work with them, but you never said we couldn't. Anyway, he's not a real monk."

"I must apologize for my little friend," the woman said to Julian. "She is young and has erred, grasped the wrong end of the stick, so to speak."

Julian nodded, slowly, very slowly. "Of course. A straightforward misunderstanding. I will take the coins and go."

The woman sighed. "If it were only that easy, Lay Brother Julian. You know who I am."

Julian gently scoffed. "Despite the fact you overheard *my* name, I do not know *yours*. I have not seen your face, nor do I know anything about you. Besides, I have no intention of informing anyone of anything. What you do here is none of my business. We all must make a living, yes? Only God shall judge. I will avert my eyes and leave—with the money, of course."

Yerty pointed an accusing finger at Julian. "He climbed a drainpipe, straight up three floors. He followed me here though I swear I covered me tracks like you taught me, miss. This has never happened before. It's supernatural."

The woman's brown eyes sparkled with curiosity, or perhaps amusement. The darkness made it hard to tell. "This child is among the most talented of the street artists and yet you managed to hunt her down. Impressive, lay brother."

"Artists?" Julian said. "Thieves, more accurately."

The woman gave a subtle shrug. "Depends on one's perspective."

Yerty waggled a finger. "He's no monk, miss. No monk could follow me like he did. He's a liar."

"Our little friend is suspicious, Lay Brother Julian, and I must admit, so am I. If you're not a monk, just what are you?"

"I suppose that depends on one's perspective."

The woman smiled in the dark. "Have you been to the top floor?"

Julian frowned. "What?"

"The uppermost floor of the Grand Chapel, the fourth floor. Have you been in there?"

"Why would I want to go up there?"

The woman tut-tutted. "Come now, don't be evasive. Have you been on the fourth floor?"

"I am a monk in training. Novitiates do not have access to the top floor, nor any part of the edifice for that matter. I am not familiar with the upper floor nor its contents."

The woman's voice became a whisper. "There's treasure up there, or so it is rumoured."

Julian said nothing for a moment. Then, he spoke quietly. "I have heard no rumours of ... *treasure*. Can I put my hands down?"

"No. Take it from me, the rumours are persistent. It's quite some situation, isn't it? The monks accrue wealth on high, while down here the children are forced to collect shit from the gutters to sell to the tanners just to survive. No one cares. The Senate doesn't care and the Brotherhood of Ulfur doesn't care. Archbishop Courtenay is coming to save souls, but it's a pretence because the church is so wrapped up in its own politics that nothing ever changes. No one can save the children from their despair, no one."

Julian smirked. "Except you?"

A weighted silence followed Julian's comment. Then, the woman said, "Careful, monk. Mocking a woman with a knife to your throat is never a good idea."

Julian swallowed. "I mock no one."

"I am sensitive to tone."

"I'll mind my tone. I apologize if I have given offence."

"Hold on to that apology. I'm going to let you sit down in that comfortable chair. Wait, do not move until I tell you."

The woman kept the knife at Julian's neck and patted at his habit; she stopped abruptly when she came to his waist. "You have a concealed weapon." Placing her hand on Julian's shoulder, she leaned in and quietly hissed in his ear, "Take it out slowly and drop it. If you move in any way that discomforts me, I'll cut the artery in your neck. This would upset the child, so for her sake, if not yours, move slowly."

Julian reached under his habit. A moment later he removed a dagger and dropped it on the floor.

"Kick it away," the woman said.

Julian did so and Yerty leaped across the floor to gather it. "It's bone-handled, miss. Very fine make." The girl threw the knife in the air, and it spun three times before she deftly caught it.

The woman cocked her head and whistled softly. "Well, well, Julian. A man who clambers up drainpipes, pursues a target through the maze of city streets and rooftops, and carries an exotic weapon. I think the child is right. You're not a monk."

"There are myriad kinds of monk," Julian said.

The woman nodded. "True. Some take vows of poverty and humility while others hoard wealth to glorify God. Which kind are you folk up on the mountain?"

"The former, or so I am led to believe."

"I think you'll find the only place you've been led, Julian, is down the garden path." With one hand, the woman took a grey scarf from her head, revealing dark brown hair that swept from one temple to the other in a wave. The hair at the sides and back of her head was short. "You may sit now." She glanced at Yerty and said, "Child, tie this for me."

As Julian sat in the gutted armchair, Yerty approached the woman and tied the scarf over her mouth and nose as a makeshift mask. The woman put her own knife away in a concealed sheath somewhere within a discreet slit in her abaya and took Julian's dagger from Yerty.

"You may call me Cassie," she said.

"Is that your real name?"

"For you it is."

Julian muttered, "May I go now?"

"Look at him, child," Cassie said behind the mask. "Such a sweet, docile face, such a polite manner. His piss wouldn't melt the mountain snows. But we know different, don't we?"

Yerty squinted through the gloom at Julian's face, luminous and smooth in the moonlight. "Aye, miss. We know different."

Cassie examined Julian's dagger carefully, tracing a finger over the white bone handle and the cameo of a gold star on one side and a blue star on the other. "This is an interesting piece. Unless I am mistaken, these stars are a symbol of our sister province to the north. It's an old symbol and not often used, but I recognize this as King Lyle's ideogram, or more precisely that of the royal line of Otago. What would you be doing with this if you were not at one time in the service of the Northern king?" Julian licked at dry lips but said nothing. Cassie stared at him for some time. "A man becomes a monk for one of two reasons. Either he's running away from something and hopes to find salvation, or he's running away from something and hopes to find a place to hide."

Julian cleared his throat. "That's a rather narrow spiritual view."

"Is it? If you're seeking to disappear, I'd recommend not carrying around souvenirs of your past life. This," she said, hefting the weight of the dagger, "could get you exposed by less scrupulous people than me."

"I appreciate your advice and your scruples."

Cassie winked at Yerty. "Our monk friend has a past he'd prefer to remain buried. We'll help him with that. We'll keep his secrets as we keep our own."

"You are very kind, Miss Cass. What can he do for us in return?"

"I like the way you think, child. A favour for a favour." Cassie pointed skyward with the dagger, its blade glinting in the starlight. "I believe the monks have quite an amassment of secular wealth. But no one can get up there to steal it. The giant guards the passage."

Julian drew his brows together. "The giant?"

"The big monk and his crew."

"You must mean Lay Brother Jacob."

Cassie held Julian's dagger by the blade and tapped the handle into her palm. "Is he as big as they say?"

"He's a large man, no doubt."

"He is the keeper of the elevator, correct?"

"He operates it, yes."

"He was a warrior of some repute in his secular life. Did you know that? A ferocious killer before he found God, apparently."

Julian turned the edges of his mouth down. "No. No one on the mountain speaks of their former lives. Not to me, at any rate."

Cassie flipped the dagger in the air and caught it expertly by the handle. "You're not the only one with secrets. No one accesses that elevator without Jacob's say-so. The secret paths, the alternative routes up and down the mountain, and once again rumour says that these paths do exist, are known only by the senior monks, and that secret is jealously guarded."

"I am aware of no other paths," Julian said.

"You wouldn't be. But to the point. You have been to the main edifice on Mount Ulfur."

Julian shifted uncomfortably in the chair. "You do not seem to be listening, madam. I am a novitiate monk, a mere *lay brother*, for the time being. I live in the monastery and walk past the Grand Chapel every day, but I know nothing of its secrets as I am not granted permission to enter."

"To clarify. You're telling me you've never been inside the main edifice itself, the prayer chapel and library and so on?"

"That's what I'm telling you. Well, one time ... just to the prayer chapel, and only from the outside. I did not enter."

"But you could get in if you so desired?"

Julian breathed in sharply. "I don't know what you're suggesting. Rather, I do, but absolutely not. It's forbidden."

Cassie ignored him. "Anything you find up there, I have a buyer for. We'll split the profits evenly. You could never distribute these goods alone. I can help." She gestured to Yerty. "With my share, the children could have decent clothes and food, education, a chance to better their lives. And you could end up wealthy, and your past would remain undisclosed."

"Are you threatening me?"

Cassie shrugged. "I merely negotiate the terms of a business partnership."

"I just want my coins and to leave. That is all."

Cassie pointed at Julian with the sharp end of his own knife. "I thought monks helped those in need. Isn't that the whole purpose of your order? *Any* monastic order?"

"I'm very new to the life of a monk," Julian said. "I have yet to learn the ways of the Brotherhood of Ulfur."

Cassie stared and then gave a quiet sigh. "Give him the coins."

Yerty gathered the copper coins from the musty carpet and handed them to Julian. He examined them. "Five. There should be five. She only gave me four."

Cassie shrugged. "A transactional fee. Listen to what I am about to say."

Julian slipped the four coins into his habit. "I am not a thief, despite what you are insinuating. I maintain that I am a monk in training, nothing more."

Cassie put a finger to her concealed lips. "Just listen. There is something on that mountain, something that could free the children from a life of slavery."

Julian frowned. "There are no slaves in the Freelands."

"Don't be stupid. The street urchins have no choice in how their lives play out. A child born into poverty will always feel its yoke. If you were born into such a life, *you* would do anything to free yourself from it. Wouldn't you? You would lie, cheat, steal. You'd even take on an identity that is not yours." She handed the dagger back to Julian, hilt first. "Hypocrisy is everywhere."

Julian took the dagger and stared at Cassie. Finally, he

stood, secreted the blade away, and said, "I'll be going now. Good evening."

Cassie stepped aside to let him pass. "Get rid of that dagger, Julian. It was foolish of you to keep it."

Julian put two fingers to his lips, bowed, and silently left the room.

When he had gone, a wide-eyed Yerty turned to Cassie. "He makes me skin crawl."

"*My* skin crawl," Cassie corrected. "You do not play the role of gutter snipe when we are alone, nor use its language. Proper diction, child, proper diction is power. You'll never extract yourself from the shit and filth of your current life without it."

Yerty's tone changed. She spoke with an exaggerated enunciation, as Cassie had shown her, and as the mistress herself used when speaking. "I'm sorry, Miss Cass. I forgot for but a moment. However, he's an odd one and I am not sure that you should trust him."

"I trust no one, my dear, except you. But there's something about him, something I think I recognize. I sense goodness in him." Cassie removed her mask, revealing a cleft palate that twisted her lip under her nose.

"You are romanticizing again, Miss Cass," Yerty said. "You're always finding the good in people, even bad ones. I sometimes think you're too beautiful for this world."

Cassie touched her twisted lip. "Sadly, the world does not share your view."

"Fuck the defect," Yerty said. "Fuck the world."

Cassie gasped and looked sternly at Yerty for a moment before laughing and sweeping the girl up in a hug. She looked deeply into the child's green eyes. "On the chance that Julian alerts the authorities, tell everyone to find alternative sleeping quarters. This building is now *defunctus*, to use the Latin term. The artists are to move to the north quarter a cycle earlier than planned. Get everybody out. Tonight." Yerty nodded, clutched her wooden horse in one hand, and headed for the skylight. Cassie stopped her. "Two hands for climbing, child, two hands. You must stay safe."

Yerty carefully placed the horse upon the armchair. A moment later she was back out on the rooftops of Re'Shan, but this time she did not stop to admire the view.

6

A SPITEFUL VENDETTA

The breeze was chill on the mountainside, but both men's blood warmed with the exertion of the climb. Martin patted the mule on its heavily laden flank as they turned away from the cliff edge and followed the path into the pine-scented forest of larch and spruce.

"We have adequate amounts of millet and barley," Martin said. "We have enough rye, lentils, and peas. We're a little short on the required amount of wheat. The bread will have a slightly fibrous texture, but I think we have done well with only four coins instead of the allotted five." Julian did not reply, and Martin went on, "Still, I imagine that Rollant will be furious. However, when he hears of your miraculous recovery of the coins from the thief, he will not fail to appreciate—"

Julian interjected. "I do not think we should mention the girl. It would be better to say we performed naïvely in our nego-tiations with the vendors, that we were simply unaware of prices and will do better next time."

Martin nodded and spoke no more of the loss or the recovery of the coins, for which Julian was grateful. *Cassie.* In his brief encounter with the woman, Julian had ascertained that she acted as handler for the street urchins, a mentor of some description, or perhaps even a guardian angel. She had spoken of lifting the children out of their lives of poverty. She had also spoken of the means of doing so: the hidden treasure in the Grand Chapel of the Monks of Ulfur. Julian looked up the mountain towards the edifice in question. *Treasure? What do monks want with earthly treasures?* He doubted the veracity of Cassie's story, doubted that such hidden wealth existed. Still, Julian burned with curiosity. If it was somehow true, then he would like to look upon whatever it was that constituted this *treasure,* if even for a moment.

By late afternoon, they had arrived at the lower elevator station and Lay Brother Jacob greeted them with a bare grunt and nod. The mule was unloaded, and Martin and Julian stepped onto the elevator. The wheat, barley, and rye remained with the massive lay brother as he explained that the combined weight of the produce and both Julian and Martin would potentially overload the elevator, and Jacob would not be responsible for the death of a brother. Safety came first and the goods would come later in the hands of the upper station crew. The two lay brothers were to go on to the storehouse above to make preparations for its arrival.

Jacob, himself, operated one winch, his immense power counterbalanced by two lay brothers at the twin winch on the other side of the platform. The lower station crew began to grind away, and Julian and Martin ascended into the darkness. Julian watched Lay Brother Jacob disappear below and was reminded of what Cassie had said about him.

A ferocious killer before he found God.

Julian had no doubt the big man could throw his weight around, but something about him, despite his stern and intimidating exterior, spoke of gentleness. Perhaps it was merely wishful thinking, for Julian had no desire to see any of the brothers in a bad light. They were his new family, after all.

Julian waited until the darkness had swallowed them and reached beneath his habit. He removed his ornate dagger as discreetly as possible and let it slip into the abyss. He'd steal another when he could, one that wouldn't give him away.

Klaus hugged Julian and Martin as they entered the community upon the plateau. The hug probably came from a deep wellspring of relief that Julian and Martin had absolved Klaus of the responsibility of climbing the mountain paths and, more specifically, riding the elevator through the eerie, hollow places within Mount Ulfur. Julian smiled and patted the tall German's hard, angular back.

The sun was setting, and shadows began to pool around the compound, melding the wooden huts and buildings together, yet the stone columns and façade of the Grand Chapel itself shone in pristine glory, a light against the encroaching darkness.

Julian, having only just recovered his breath from Klaus's crushing embrace, let his eyes settle on the top floor of the Grand Chapel.

"Come on, Julian," Martin said. "We must get to the storehouse before the goods arrive."

"Coming," Julian said, absentmindedly. He stared at the Grand Chapel for a moment longer.

———

Lay Brother Rollant did indeed fly into a rage at the lack of wheat brought back from the markets of Re'Shan. He swore all manner of vile punishments upon Julian and Martin, carried out none, and continued to send them down the mountain on a weekly basis, warning them to do better or suffer the Fires of

Hades upon their return. And upon each return, Rollant would complain and bluster, but not before Klaus had gathered his friends up in a fierce embrace, never failing to drive the wind from either Martin's or Julian's lungs.

After some time, Klaus began to smell of the goats he worked with every day. It was a comforting smell, a warm welcome home, and the odour of goat's cheese also signified that the tall German was happy in the sheds, far from the mountain path and the elevator he so loathed.

Julian's thoughts were never too far from the city at the edge of the Great Southern Sands. On his weekly trips to Re'Shan, Julian became aware that the street children were watching him. It was a feeling at first, a tingling at the nape of his neck, but as time passed, he became convinced that the urchins shadowed him, watching him go about his business in the markets, yet none approached him directly. They were waiting for an answer, and this answer they would relay to the woman known as Cassie.

Once, he saw the small girl with the emerald eyes, Gertrude, standing in the shadows of a tall apartment, staring at him with those orbs of cold light. Julian shook his head and the little thief scurried off.

Not today. I will not explore the secrets of the monastery today. But soon. Very soon.

———

The day that Elsie headbutted Rollant in the balls was the day that the gaunt lay brother took a true dislike to Klaus.

Julian was roused from his daydreams in the gardens by the sounds of shouting and distressed voices. The tall figure of Klaus seemed to be at the centre of the disturbance. Martin, too, straightened and rubbed at his lower back, his eyes fixed on the milling figures in the stone courtyard leading to the Grand Chapel.

"Is that Klaus in the middle of all that?" Martin asked, squinting in the early afternoon sun.

Julian nodded and gently placed the bag of cabbage seeds upon the furrowed earth at his feet. Cabbages had been Julian's suggestion, one which the brothers had agreed was worth a try, providing the winter frosts stayed away. When he and Martin were not on their weekly journeys to Re'Shan, they maintained their activities in the gardens and hoped that the cabbage seeds would take.

But the cabbages were forgotten as Julian stepped gingerly over the laid seeds and made for the grass path to the cloister. "Klaus is in trouble." Martin followed at his heels and the two lay brothers arrived at the courtyard to find Rollant in a fetal position on the flagstones, clutching at his groin, surrounded by several monks and Klaus, who had hold of a goat by the scruff of its neck. The recalcitrant animal twisted and turned furiously in the young German's grasp.

"I'm sorry, Lay Brother Rollant," Klaus said.

"You'll pay for this," Rollant grunted breathlessly.

"Elsie got away from me. She is a playful creature. It's not her fault."

Rollant's teeth were clenched in pain. "Elsie? What kind of fool names his goats? Oh, that hurts. I swear you engineered this."

Several monks and lay brothers stood nearby, some of whom had hands over their mouths to hide their smiles. Martin snorted with laughter. Rollant shot him a venomous glare.

Julian offered a hand to help Rollant to his feet, but the small lay brother swatted the hand away.

"I'll cut that goat's throat," Rollant said, his eyes watering.

Klaus gasped in distress. "No, no, please, I swear she won't get out again."

A dark voice commanded the situation. "Get up, Lay Brother Rollant. You're embarrassing yourself." Startled clerics and lay brothers made way for Prior Blackwing. The superior had appeared from nowhere and without a sound.

Rollant removed his hands from his crotch and scrambled to his feet. He continued to breathe in short gasps but stood straight with a visible effort. "Klaus set his goat on me, Father," Rollant complained.

Klaus looked as if he was about to burst into tears. "That is not true. The goat escaped her pen, and before I could—"

"He unleashed the creature on me in a vicious and unprovoked attack. I was innocently going about my business and the next thing this feral animal goes for my privates. Unprovoked, I say. Klaus knew exactly what he was doing."

Prior Blackwing's ruddy face showed no emotion, and Julian waited for the man's inevitably harsh response. To his surprise, Blackwing actually smiled.

"Are you suggesting, Lay Brother Rollant," the tall superior said, "that Klaus has control over his goat's actions? That he manipulated the animal in a spiteful vendetta against you, *you* in particular?"

Rollant's heavy scowl lessened somewhat. "Well ... yes."

"You give great credit to this animal's ability to discern one man from another. You do realize how preposterous an orchestrated attack by a goat sounds, do you not?"

"Uh ... well, I, uh ..." Rollant's face turned white.

Blackwing turned to Klaus. "Are you alright, young man?"

Klaus looked surprised. "Yes, Father. I'm ... I apologize for Elsie. She's a well-behaved animal on most occasions. She's just ... just a ..."

"A spirited creature?"

"Yes. Spirited, but not malicious."

Blackwing nodded sagely. "Then she belongs on Mount Ulfur with us, for if there is one thing that you can say about the members of the Order of Ulfur, it is that we are spirited. Is that not so?" Blackwing looked around at the gathered monks and lay brothers, and each nodded in turn. Rollant himself was forced to join the general bobbing of heads or risk looking even more like a fool.

Blackwing clapped his hands. "Good. There shall be no retribution for today's events. Am I understood?" The superior stared straight at Rollant, and the gaunt lay brother once again nodded though Julian could tell the man was quietly fuming. This wouldn't be good for Klaus in the long run, despite Blackwing's stern warning.

Elsie did not possess a malicious nature, but if anyone was capable of a spiteful vendetta, it was the skeletal Lay Brother Rollant.

7
EARTHLY TREASURES

Julian carried no candle as he silently crept under the portico. He wore no sandals. He could not afford to alert either eye or ear of a choir monk not yet deep in slumber.

The hours between compline and night watch, those precious few hours of stillness in which an ordained monk might indulge in the joy of unadulterated sleep, offered the best chance of getting in and out undiscovered. The only light on the plateau came from a waxing crescent moon edging its way over the cliff top far above, but within the Grand Chapel itself, even this light would not penetrate. The cold wood tiles chilled his feet as he padded silently past the prayer chapel. Julian breathed deeply. This was a risky enterprise. Were he to be caught, Julian's vocation as a brother in the Order of Ulfur would come to a premature end. He had told neither Martin nor Klaus of his plan. If he was caught, their ignorance would save them from a similar punishment.

At the darkened stairwell, Julian paused until his eyes adjusted to the lack of light. He cocked his head and listened; no sound, nothing but a cool draught wafting downwards over his cheek and his scalp. Even after two months with a tonsure, the bald patch prickled with sensitivity, as if freshly shaved.

He moved on up the stairwell, hands outstretched. He blindly felt his way to the second floor and the ordained monks' cells. Here, he must be very careful. It would only take one monk with a full bladder on his way from cell to privy to expose Julian and sound the alarm. Julian's luck held. The cells remained darkened and quiet, the sounds of holy snores echoing from open doorways lining the hallway. He crept higher, heading for the third floor.

Moonlight issued softly through clear panes of glass on the third floor and Julian heard the familiar tinkling of the glacial waters rushing down the cliff face at the back of the Grand Chapel. He glanced through a window, careful to stay low, and could make out the silhouettes of the abbot's office, the storehouse, the bread ovens now cool and dark, and the lay brothers' dormitory and refectory. Off to the side, just barely visible at an acute angle, he glimpsed the cliff walls.

There were no stairs leading further up to the fourth level. Julian found himself at the beginning of a long corridor possessing only one door. Approaching it, he discovered that the door comprised two parts, set on rollers like those of the prayer chapel below. But unlike the door below, this contained no frosted glass through which the interior might be viewed; rather, the sliding doors were made of a solid wood. Behind these doors was the library. All he had to do was reach out and slide one of the doors open just enough to allow ingress. But he wasn't here to indulge in the lore of forbidden books. That could wait for another time—if he escaped from this night's adventures undiscovered.

No, Julian's game was above, and he would not take unnecessary risks.

At the opposite end of the corridor, he found another stairwell leading up but not down. Julian took a long breath and ascended the steps. As he approached the fourth floor, the urge to flee overtook him. This was a mistake. To risk everything because of a rumour of hidden treasure, because a woman down in the city had threatened to expose him? Cassie wouldn't wish to draw attention to herself and her little thieves. Her threats were empty. But then again, she might do it out of spite. He couldn't be sure. In his own heart, too, Julian wanted to know. He had to know. Silently cursing Cassie and his own willful curiosity, his heart pounding in his chest, Julian moved higher.

On the fourth floor he crouched low and peered into a windowless hallway that ran away from him. This corridor did not follow the same orientation as those below: it seemed to run at right angles to the façade of the Grand Chapel. This made sense, for in his wanderings around the compound below he had noted the presence of windows in the far side of the Grand Chapel, up high and facing the cliffs. Those windows gave indication that there were several rooms here, yet in the hallway Julian could find no hint of a doorway.

The further Julian moved forwards, the darker it became, but finally his hand touched a cold doorknob. Julian turned the knob, but the door was locked. Odd, because no other door in the Grand Chapel required a key, not even the library. Blind and fumbling in the darkness, Julian felt for the lock plate and found it. A simple dead bolt design, full turn. Any key of even approximate fit would retract the locking bolt behind the plate. However, despite the lack of sophistication inherent in the locking system, Julian did not possess a key of any kind, approximate or not.

The night's escapade had come to an abrupt halt. Julian turned away and began to creep back to the stairwell. He had almost made the stairs when he heard a soft click. He held his breath and turned. A shaft of dim moonlight painted the floor of the hallway, a long sliver signifying that the door now stood slightly ajar, as if blown open by a gentle breeze.

Yet locked from within a moment before.

A chance gifted by God? Or a trap laid by the Devil? Julian crouched motionless for many heartbeats. Then, slowly, he returned down the hallway towards the door. Still crouching, his knees beginning to burn, he peered within; the crescent moon floated soundlessly in the window, its light sheening a floor that seemed made of polished red marble. Several plinths of black stone stood in a semicircle around the room, but their pedestals held nothing, nothing of holy or secular value. The room was empty except for two chairs pulled up to a small wooden table, upon which sat a stone game board divided centrally into two colours, black and red. Several game pieces of black and white stood silently on the board. It did not look like any game Julian had ever seen, for the pieces were not balanced: the black pieces were more numerous than the white, but the white avatars were larger than the black. The game had seemingly been paused midcampaign as both pieces occupied all parts of the board. But this was of little interest to Julian.

There. In the shadows of the corner of the room, something he had missed on first inspection: a chest, not of wood but some kind of rock crystal. Julian approached the chest and, once again, a surge of disappointment greeted him. He knelt at the translucent container but could see that it held nothing. What was this place of empty promises? It was almost as if the room was in a state of readiness to display something later: a gallery frozen in eternal preparation awaiting its latest exhibit.

A dry voice whispered, "The young seek the wrong things and in the wrong places."

Julian whirled and fell backwards onto the gauzy chest. An old man in a white sleeping gown leaned heavily on a walking frame in the centre of the room. A door behind the old man, a door previously unnoticed by Julian, stood open, and through it Julian glimpsed the end of a bed. The old man, his wispy hair matted to one side of his head, placed two fingers to his lips and breathed the kiss of life.

Julian, his back still against the translucent chest, could only stare open mouthed at the wizened stranger.

"I am Abbot Howard," the old man said. His white gown showed patches of ruby red, reflections from the marble floor.

Julian had been about to close his mouth, but this revelation kept it wide open. "I thought you were dead," he whispered.

The abbot raised an eyebrow. "I feel very much like it, young man." He cocked his head. "Has your training been so lax that you do not know the greeting of the Brotherhood of Ulfur?"

Julian crawled forwards onto his knees, brought two fingers to his mouth, and bowed his head. "Father Abbot, I apologize for the unseemly position in which you find me."

"And what position is that?" The old man smirked. Julian looked about the room and swallowed. Father Howard briefly waggled a finger and went on, "You're looking for the wrong thing. You're looking in the wrong place. What is your name?"

"I am Lay Brother Julian."

"Stand up, novitiate." Julian stood and brushed at his habit nervously. "What do you seek? Earthly wealth? Possessions of a monetary nature? Such is worth nothing to your immortal soul."

Julian met the abbot's eyes. "I seek atonement."

Abbot Howard stared silently at Julian for a moment. He nodded to himself. "Ah well, that, young man, *that* is worth something."

A scuffling noise and Prior Blackwing glided silently into the room from the darkened corridor outside, a scowl across his already stern features. Julian's knees weakened. It was over. He was to be expunged from the Brotherhood. Or worse.

"What are you doing here, lay brother?" Blackwing asked, his face as red as the floor. He held a vial of dark liquid in his long fingers. "You have disturbed Father Abbot, and he needs his medicines and a great deal of sleep. You are forbidden here."

Julian glanced from one man to the other and realized that any fanciful tale he attempted to weave would be fruitless.

Abbot Howard spoke. "I asked Lay Brother Julian to come." Julian contained his surprise and kept his eyes down.

Blackwing continued to frown. "How could that be? You have not been outside ..." He waved a long slender hand around the red marbled room. "You have not been outside your quarters for weeks."

"True, true." The abbot nodded. "But from my window, I saw this young fellow and waved to attract his attention, and through the use of symbols I made my intentions quite clear. *Come for a chat*, I indicated."

"At this hour? This is rather inappropriate, Father Abbot."

The old man bristled. "I am not dead yet, Prior Blackwing, and as the abbot I maintain the authority to see *whom* I will *when* I will." He paused and the fire seemed to ebb from his eyes. Abbot Howard resumed the form of a tired old man slumped on his walking frame. "But you're quite right, Superior. One loses all sense of time when one is bedridden. I had no idea it was so late." He sighed heavily. "Forgive me, both of you, for the nuisance I have caused. I pray to God for the strength to descend from these high places and walk among you once again. For now, I shall retire."

Julian played along. "I will come whenever you desire my company, Father Abbot."

Abbot Howard smiled. "Good, good. I hope we shall meet again but for now return to your bed." Julian almost ran for the door. "And remember what we spoke of," Abbot Howard said, causing Julian to turn back. "We leave behind the pleasures and temptations of our old life, and we find true solace and peace on this mountain. This life is a gift worth more than all earthly treasures. And *atonement*, young man, is priceless."

Julian nodded. He felt the cold hard eyes of Prior Blackwing at the nape of his neck as he left.

————

The next day, Julian could not take his mind off the meeting with Abbot Howard. The old man had saved Julian from expulsion from the Order of Ulfur. The abbot had even lied to protect him from the austere Blackwing. He had known Julian's motivation for ascending to the top floor of the Grand Chapel. He must have, yet did not condemn him.

Over the following days, Julian would frequently glance towards the fourth floor, not in awe at what treasures might be hidden above, but in the hope of seeing the kindly old monk. Julian would welcome the opportunity of an uninterrupted private audience with the abbot, for he had many questions, and he owed him a debt of gratitude. The chance meeting with the abbot had made up his mind. He'd been uncertain but now his resolve was firm. He would become a monk in his heart and soul. No more treasure, no more deceit, no more skulking in the dark doing the bidding of a criminal.

To hell with Cassie. Let her come for him if she would.

8

THE SEED

Yerty stamped her foot. "It's not fair, miss! It's just not fair!"

Cassie ignored the petulant child and examined the small circular bamboo frame in her hands. White linen stretched within the frame like the skin of a drum. Embroidered on the linen was a red needlework horse with a bright yellow mane; its hind legs, however, were absent.

"You've had a week to complete this." Cassie turned the object over. The embroidery reflected the light of an oil lamp hanging on the wall. "Mistress Zane is unhappy at your tardiness and so am I."

Cassie tossed the object towards the girl and Yerty fumbled it to the floor. Picking it up, she glanced at Dylan on her right and then at Olaf on her left. The stocky ginger-haired boy had a smirk on his square face. Without warning, Yerty struck Olaf across the face with the embroidery.

"Ow! Hey!" Olaf shoved Yerty. The girl returned a kick to the boy's shins, causing him to cry out once more.

"Enough, enough," Cassie said. "Yerty, control your temper."

A pained expression came over the girl's freckled face. "But, Miss Cass, it's not fair. Why must I embroider? Dylan doesn't have to do it, nor does Olaf. Why me?"

Cassie folded her arms and sat back in the wicker chair. "Because you will one day be a woman." Yerty stared, uncomprehending. "Let me explain. At some point in your future, you'll find a husband and ..." Cassie trailed off.

"And what, miss?"

"Well, men expect certain things of their wives."

"Like embroidery?"

Cassie nodded. "Like embroidery."

"But why, miss? It don't make no sense to me."

"Check your diction, child."

Yerty rolled her eyes. "It *doesn't* make any sense to me, Miss Cass."

"Quite honestly, Yerty, I fail to understand it myself, but that's how it is."

"What else do men expect of their wives?"

Cassie cleared her throat. "Uh ... other domestic tasks. At any rate, you'll finish the embroidery or face the wrath of Mistress Zane and me. Do you understand?"

"She's an old troll, miss."

"Silence. She was my teacher and though she may be irritable, I promise you that she is a woman of excellent character and I'll not have you speak ill of her."

"Sorry, miss. But I don't want to get married." Yerty stood straight and put her hands behind her back. She spoke with a scholarly air. "*Ipso facto*, to use the correct Latin, I do not need to learn embroidery. I have noticed that you do not embroider and would like to be afforded the same privilege."

Cassie wanted to laugh out loud but did not do so. Yerty was charming in her earnestness, but also a sensitive child and not one to lightly take mockery, perceived or otherwise. Cassie replied in a measured tone, "I *can* embroider, quite well, though have not done so for some time." Yerty lost a little of her authority, shifting her weight and blinking. "You're young," Cassie said. "Now is not the time for you to be making decisions on what skills you will or will not require in your future, or whether you will marry."

"But *you're* not married."

"I'm a thirty-year-old spinster because no man will have me."

Yerty frowned and stared at the floor. "That's not true, miss."

"It is true, child. I am ugly."

Yerty's voice quivered when she spoke, her eyes flicking to Cassie's cleft lip and away again. "Don't say that, miss. You're beautiful and many a man would be lucky to have you."

Cassie smiled. "That may be true, but I wouldn't have any man that would have me."

Yerty's frown deepened. She began to worry at the frame of the embroidery. "I don't understand."

"I'm picky. I won't marry any man unless he is of adequate quality, and those type of men could have any woman they want."

"That seems a little self-defeating, miss, if I may be bold enough to say."

Cassie raised an eyebrow. "Perhaps it is *self-defeating*. But that is none of your concern." Cassie pointed to the embroidery. "Finish that."

"Yes, miss."

Cassie turned to Dylan. "How go your Latin lessons?"

Dylan's green eyes widened in anxiety. His voice tremored when he spoke. "*Ego sum puer.*"

Cassie nodded. "Yes, you are." She turned to the large ginger-haired child. "*Quid est nomen tuum?*"

"*Mihi nomen est* Olaf," Olaf said.

Cassie turned to Yerty and waited expectantly.

Yerty let out a heavy sigh and rolled her eyes again. "Alright. Um ... Dylan *est canis* turd." Dylan frowned in confusion. Yerty went on, "Olaf *stultus est*."

Cassie pressed her lips together to suppress a laugh. "Well, you're using the language creatively. I suppose you get credit for that."

Yerty spoke up. "Latin, math, *and* embroidery, miss? Why must I learn more just because I am a girl?"

"It's because you are a girl that you must work harder."

"But that's not fair."

"Stop using that phrase!" Cassie's outburst froze Yerty in surprise. Cassie took a deep breath and made an effort to calm herself. She continued more evenly, "I'll have no more talk of fair or unfair. You are female. A woman in waiting. Forget about fairness because your gender is the burden you carry. Accept that now and you'll be better off." Yerty looked as if she would protest once more but Cassie held up her hand. "Stop, listen to me. All of you. The Republic of the Freelands does not currently prosecute children for crimes of a petty nature. That will change when you are grown. As adults, stealing will no longer be a viable career option for any of you. If you attempt to do so, you risk prison or worse. But, and here is the wonderful thing, your current education is bought and paid for by the proceeds of your artistry, your thieving. You are, in effect, raising yourselves out of the gutter by your own efforts and for that you should all be proud of the ends, if not the means, by which you better yourselves."

The two boys stood a little taller, their chests rounder, yet Yerty continued to slouch and sulk. She had tears in her eyes. "I don't want to go away, miss."

Cassie wanted to sweep all three up in her arms. She didn't

move. How does one apply the salve of logic to the hurt feelings of a child? They all stared at her, trembling, even the normally stoic sheepdog Olaf. None of them wanted to leave the comfort and security of the only home they'd ever known. How could she blame them? But leave they must.

"When adulthood comes," Cassie said, making sure to keep her voice steady, for she, too, wanted to cry, "there will be many in Re'Shan who remember what you once were and will judge you accordingly. But one day, somewhere far away where you are unknown, you will have the education and the skills to set up a new life for yourselves, to be reborn. And you'll have money. This new life is what you are preparing for. That is the agreement and the price you all promised to pay. Now, no more arguments, and no crying." Yerty bit her bottom lip and screwed her brows together in a brave attempt to hold back the tears. Cassie went on, "I'll have no more complaining about your classes or Mistress Zane. You'll do what she tells you and be grateful. Am I understood?" The three children nodded. Cassie ignored the lump in her throat. "I thank you for coming. The day is breaking, and opportunities do not wait. Get out and bring in more coin. Get to the gates and search out new marks." The stifling heat of the morning sun began to penetrate the blinds and Cassie pulled at the collar of her midnight-blue abaya. "It is going to be hot. Fill your bellies with water, like the camels do."

Dylan wiped at his face. "I should say so, Miss Cass. Very hot. Two suns today."

Cassie blinked. "Say again?"

Dylan shifted from foot to foot. "There are two suns in the sky. The big one and the little one."

"I think that you have not been paying attention to your Celestial Studies, Dylan. Nor the sky for most of your life. We have but one sun. Just one."

"No, miss," Yerty said. "Dylan is right. The big one has had a baby."

Cassie frowned and looked from Dylan to Yerty. The brother and sister wore serious expressions, their matching green eyes wide. Olaf nodded in support of his colleagues.

Cassie got to her feet and crossed the room, causing Yerty's long black hair to wave in the current of her passing. Opening the door, Cassie entered a long attic, stepped over the still sleeping forms of several children in rucksacks, and reached up to a rectangular frame set in the angled roof. She removed a hook from a ring and pushed the trapdoor open. Cassie hitched her abaya above her knees and, with catlike grace, leaped upwards and out onto the tin roof.

The sun had not yet fully lifted above the desert horizon, but there in the lightening blue sky, seemingly motionless, hung a small replica of Solis. Cassie looked from the glowing orb to Mount Ulfur and back again. She did this twice more and gasped. This second sun was not, in fact, motionless; this she could now tell by measuring its distance to the great mountain. The miniature sun ate leagues in mere moments and possessed a tail. She jumped back inside and began shouting for the sleepers to awake and they did so instantly, for the sleep of a child-thief is always light.

"Yerty!" Cassie shouted. The small child came running. "We are going to get everyone below ground, to the Rabbit Hole. You take the lead, and I will make sure none lag behind."

"Yes, miss."

"Go, child."

With Yerty leading the way, Cassie pushed and prodded the children out of the room and down the stairs, counting numbers. Eight children in total. Eight developing souls in her charge. They must hurry and get underground to a safe house, for Cassie understood what it was that hurtled through the sky.

Julian knelt in the gardens and pointed towards the glowing orb in the sky. "Martin, do you see that?"

Martin nodded. "Yes, what is it?"

"I don't know. Perhaps a messenger from God?"

"Are you jesting?"

"Yes. You're sweating."

Martin wiped at his bald head. "It's a warm morning."

Julian stood and stretched his back. "But the sun has barely risen. It's usually cool at this time of day, especially up here."

The other lay brothers were now putting down trowel and digging fork and looking to the sky. "You're right," Martin said. "What's happening?"

"I think we should inform the superior."

Martin pointed across the compound to the entrance of the Grand Chapel where Prior Blackwing was surrounded by several monks, all of whom were staring at the sky. "I think he is aware, Julian."

"It's getting closer," Julian said.

"To us?"

"As far as I can tell."

"Oh, is that good?"

Julian shielded his eyes against the light emanating from the orb. "I don't think so. It's getting brighter."

"What should we do?"

"Um ... where's Klaus?"

"At the goat sheds as is his custom. Why?"

"I think we should get Klaus and get inside."

Martin shook his head. "We cannot leave the gardens until noon."

"Just ... shit. Come on!" Julian broke into a sprint, heading for the goat sheds.

One man who had not noticed the danger was Lay Brother Rollant. When Julian sped towards him, Rollant stepped in front of Julian and shouted, "Hey, get back to the gardens." Julian pushed him aside and Rollant fell. The lay brother got to his feet, fuming and dusting himself off. "How dare you touch me in such a way!" When he finally spied the fireball in the sky, Rollant gawked along with everyone else, his anger instantly forgotten.

Julian and Martin had barely reached the path leading down to the goat sheds when they saw Klaus and several other lay brothers running up the path towards them. Klaus was hitching his habit with one hand and pointing to the sky with the other, shouting, "Have you seen—"

The tall German had not finished his sentence when a thunderous clap rang out, causing each man to stop and put his hands to his ears. Julian winced and looked around. The cracking sound had seemed to come from a place just above and to the left of his head, but there was nothing there.

Julian's ears were ringing. "We have to get inside."

"Get inside where?" Klaus returned breathlessly as he joined them.

Julian gestured up the path. "The prayer chapel."

Just then, a deep roaring sound like an enormous wave crashing on rocks caused Julian to look up. His jaw dropped as a flaming ball passed overhead, a shimmering vapor trail of white heat in its wake. Somewhere higher up the mountain, a sheet of rock slowly blossomed outwards, and a shuddering came violently underfoot.

"Get to the prayer chapel!" Julian shouted. "Get inside!" Then, the world turned upside down. A wave of invisible energy knocked each man to the ground.

A sound like rushing water grew as they scrambled to their feet and ran towards the Grand Chapel. The sound expanded in volume to become a hissing roar, not of water, but of rock and stone clattering down the mountainside.

Debris began to carve divots out of the mountain grass.

To Julian's left, Lay Brother Curtis dropped, his skull smashed by a rock half the size of the man's own head. Martin stopped and attempted to haul the lay brother to his feet.

Julian pulled Martin away. "He's dead. Save yourself."

But Martin did not listen. With an impressive display of strength, the bald lay brother lifted Curtis onto his shoulders and ran.

Every other monk in the compound, ordained or otherwise, had already entered the prayer room of the Grand Chapel. Julian and Klaus hurtled under the portico and into the chapel, joining the more than one hundred ordained monks and Prior Blackwing himself. Martin was the last man inside. Several monks helped bring Lay Brother Curtis gently to the floor, but it was apparent to everyone that the man was dead. Many men retched at the sight of the shattered skull.

Julian had little time to admire the monastic beauty of the Grand Chapel with its polished mosaic floor of white birds in flight across a bright blue sky and the ornately decorated columns of grey marble marking out the central nave. Frightened brothers clung to one another as a harsh sound like rain on a tin roof roared around them. Then came louder crashes and judders. It seemed as if the entire mountain was coming down on the Grand Chapel. If the cliff wall behind the main edifice were to give, it would spell the end for all of them.

Julian thought of Cassie. Odd, that he should think of her at this moment.

———

The first of the children clambered down the ladder leading to the Rabbit Hole. Cassie shouted for them to hurry. She turned just in time to witness the impact of the meteor on Mount Ulfur and admired the ferocious beauty of it. She could see the plume of smoke and rock spout from the side of the mountain, the arc of detritus reminding her of a cut artery spraying blood. A moment later her hair was blown backwards. She almost lost her footing and then felt a small hand grasp hers. She turned to see Dylan standing there, breathing hard, a worried frown on his grubby face.

"Come on, Miss Cass."

Cassie followed Dylan down the ladder. She stopped to slide a wooden panel over the entrance. No sooner had a candle been lit in the abandoned cellar than a rattling came from above.

———

The cliffs behind the Grand Chapel held strong and the rocks stopped falling.

"Alright," Prior Blackwing commanded. "Ordained monks may remain. The lay brothers must leave the chapel."

"It is not yet safe," Julian said.

Prior Blackwing drew his brows together. "I am in charge, and I say it's safe for you to leave the chapel. Lay brothers cannot stay here."

"This is not the time to invoke monastic rank, Holy Father."

The tall, ruddy-faced monk shot back, "There is never a time not—" A juddering came under the floor and Blackwing stopped midsentence. The shaking faded and the superior went on, "There is never a time *not* to obey monastic rank. The danger is over. Take this man with you." Blackwing pointed at the corpse of Lay Brother Curtis.

Martin protested, "He is dead. Surely, he belongs here, now more than ever."

Blackwing turned his bitter red face to Martin. "Do not question my orders. The man has not received his last rites or his sackcloth. He is not yet holy."

Martin did not relent. "We are all holy in death."

"Get out!"

Julian pulled at Martin's shoulder. His friend was outraged, but this confrontation could have only one outcome. Julian whispered in Martin's ear, "Come on. Your father is proud of you, don't let this bastard end your dreams of being a monk."

Martin and Julian lifted the corpse of Lay Brother Curtis and took him outside. Rollant cast dark sideways glances at the two of them, as if the whole incident were their fault. Julian was relieved to see only a plume of smoke and light ash in the sky. They would not breathe clean air for a while, but nothing threatened life or limb for the time being. Mount Ulfur had staggered at the impact of the meteor but absorbed it and stood strong.

The body of the dead lay brother was carried to the mountain grass near the bathing pool and laid down with the tenderness and respect of brotherly love. Julian and Martin had known Lay Brother Curtis well, for the Brotherhood of Ulfur was a tight-knit community. Each man came to touch Curtis on his chest and wish him well in his journey to heaven. Scattered about the ground were sizzling and smoking rocks of various sizes, like small chunks of the mountain's very flesh.

The ground tremored and then the Grand Chapel, with its huddled congregation of choir monks, sank into the ground right up to the second floor. Amid the gasps of shock from the lay brothers, Julian crept closer and peered over the lip of a freshly opened pit that now acted like a moat surrounding the ground chapel.

"Don't get too close, Julian!" Klaus shouted. "It's not safe." A small section of the edge of the pit collapsed as Julian took a step back. The Grand Chapel shuddered again and sank a few more feet.

The ordained monks within the building had wasted no time in ascending the inner stairwell and now gathered at the shattered second-floor windows of the sleeping cells. The monks clambered onto the sills, cutting hands and feet on glass shards, yet the distance from the sinking Grand Chapel to stable ground was too far to jump.

"For Christ's sake," shouted one of the monks inside. "Get us a plank!"

Men scrambled here and there, and Julian caught the acrid scent of burning. Two lay brothers brought a plank of wood, standing it erect and letting it fall. The ordained on the other side caught the plank and rested it against the sill, creating a makeshift bridge, and one by one, Prior Blackwing first, of course, each man wobbled and lurched his way to safety.

Men hugged each other in relief, lay brother and choir monk alike forgetting rank for a moment, yet one man remained in the sinking edifice: Abbot Howard. Julian looked to Prior Blackwing, but the superior showed no indication that he even recalled Abbot Howard's existence. The fourth-floor windows were on the other side of the structure, so Julian ran around the pit and scanned the top floor. There! Standing at his bedroom window, the abbot was leaning on his walking frame. He raised a hand towards Julian in supplication and mouthed two words. *Help me.* Smoke issued in swirling tendrils from somewhere on the roof of the Grand Chapel.

"Prior Blackwing!" Julian called, running back around to the half-buried façade of the Grand Chapel. "Prior Blackwing, Abbot Howard is still inside, and I think there is a fire."

The superior froze, seemingly unsure of what to do. He

shook his head and sighed. With a clicking of his fingers, two choir monks came to his side. Julian recognized the two men: Brothers Arnold and Harkness. The two clerics, arms outstretched to maintain their balance, followed the prior as he crossed back over the makeshift bridge into the Grand Chapel.

A moment later, Julian stepped onto the plank.

"What are you doing?" Martin put his hand on Julian's arm. "You can't go in there."

"It's dangerous," Klaus said as he stood next to Julian, a look of horror on his long face. He peered into the pit and shivered. "Don't cross over, Jules."

"I must help the abbot," Julian said.

Martin frowned. "If you're going, I'm coming with you."

"No. This is for me to do. Wait here."

Rollant came scuttling towards them, a deep-set scowl on his gaunt face. He grabbed Martin and pulled him away as Julian clambered across the plank, following Prior Blackwing and Brothers Arnold and Harkness into the doomed Grand Chapel.

9
OPALS IN THE ABYSS

"I'm scared, Miss Cass," Dylan said.

Cassie put her arm around the boy. "We're safe here. You have no need to fear."

As if to make a lie of her reassurances, the ground trembled. Eight frightened children clung to each other around a single candle. Empty barrels rested on dusty shelves in the corners. One fell to the floor and broke, causing many children to cry out in terror. Cassie shushed them and they all listened, the only sounds their own ragged breathing.

"I think it's over, miss," Olaf said.

"Stay here, all of you," Cassie said.

Yerty reached out to clasp Cassie. "Where are you going?"

"Just stay together. I'll be right back."

Cassie climbed up the ladder and slowly pushed aside the wooden panel. The alley was unpopulated, so Cassie eased herself to her feet. Wisps of smoke rose here and there around Re'Shan, but the city remained relatively unscathed. Darker plumes of smoke rose from the mountain and a thin grey cloud of ash hung above it. She thought of Julian and the brotherhood of monks. They had been closer to the point of impact. Much closer. She hoped Julian was alright. The man was intriguing, and their business partnership had got off to a bright start. Julian didn't know that yet, of course, about their partnership. The poor fellow seemed under the impression that this was a one-off. Julian seemed to even dislike her, but that didn't matter. They had a relationship of circumstance now, and it would be a shame for that to come to a premature end before Cassie managed to squeeze whatever she could from it.

————

Julian put one foot in front of the other on the flexing plank serving as a makeshift bridge to the Grand Chapel. He didn't look down into the dark chasm surrounding it. When he considered all his comings and goings on the elevator up and down the mountain, Julian had spent altogether too much time suspended above the abyss within Mount Ulfur. Shrugging aside the thought, he arrived at the broken window and, avoiding shards of glass, leaped into the second-floor hallway. No sign of Prior Blackwing and the other two monks. They must be ascending the stairwell to the top floor in search of the aged abbot. Julian moved up to the third floor. The library door stood open, and within Julian caught sight of toppled bookshelves and scattered books, spines open and pages exposed. But he had no time to read. No, he must follow Blackwing up to Abbot Howard's bedroom before the Grand Chapel collapsed once and for all.

Arriving at the top floor, Julian recognized the long hallway. At the end of it, on the left, he would find a brass doorknob that opened the door to the room of red marble, and off that, the abbot's room. As he passed down the corridor, a noise alerted him to another room on the right side, one that he had not seen on his previous visit. Figures within whispered, hard to make out against the dark marble of the room. It could only be Prior Blackwing and Brothers Arnold and Harkness. Julian poked his head inside and gasped. This room had a floor of polished black marble with lighter veins of white and the prior and his accomplices were standing over several large wooden chests, stuffing objects into their pockets: jewels, gems, opals of the most exquisite luster even in the half light. Some objects were so large that the superior and the monks could not store them on their persons: pure gold candelabra, ruby-encrusted goblets. These larger items they placed in sacks.

The treasure of the Monks of Ulfur. It was real, after all. Julian had missed it, missed this room on his first foray into the Grand Chapel. He shook his head in wonder. There was enough here to fill the coffers of all the Northern Kingdoms combined. *Lying bastards. Forego all earthly concerns, my arse.*

Blackwing whirled about and scowled. "What are you doing here, boy?"

"I thought we came for the abbot," Julian said.

Blackwing lost a little of his bluster. "Yes, of course, be a good lad and get him."

A weak cry from somewhere nearby. Julian scurried from the room of black marble and entered the room of red. He could smell something burning and above him wisps of smoke twisted and curled along the cornices like thin grey snakes. Julian grasped at the handle to the abbot's bedroom, but it did not open. Locked. Why would it be locked? Or had the collapse of the Grand Chapel jammed the door against its frame? It did not matter; Julian had to get in quickly before the smoke overwhelmed him or the entire edifice toppled into the endless chasm within Mount Ulfur.

"Stand back," Julian said, hoping that the abbot could hear him. He kicked at the door several times until it eventually exploded inwards. He found the abbot on the floor, his walking frame on its side, buckled and useless. Julian hauled the old man to his feet.

"Can you move?"

The abbot coughed and nodded. "With you at my side, lad, yes. I feel your strength."

"Come on." Julian and the old man hobbled into the corridor. Suddenly they were thrown against the wall, the old man crashing into him and both tumbling to the floor. The edifice had shifted its orientation. Julian's backside momentarily left the floor as the building tipped again. Someone gave a shriek. Precious baubles came scattering out of the room of black marble, followed by Brother Harkness. The man flipped upside down in an obscene show of crazed gravity. The entire building was tilting and falling.

Julian was going to die trying to save the old abbot, who was nothing but a hypocritical charlatan. They all were. They had talked about foregoing mortal pleasures, turning their back on greed and embracing poverty, yet here they were clasping and grabbing gems, jewels, and gold. The tenets and principles of the Order of Ulfur were lies. The abbot had seemed genuine, yet corruption ruled. *Hypocrisy is everywhere*, isn't that what Cassie had said? Julian should save himself and let the old man fall into the abyss.

Another shriek, another sickening lurch downwards, plaster and dust falling onto their heads. The building swayed as if poised on a fulcrum, the entire edifice now a child's seesaw. To make matters worse, a growing heat caressed Julian's cheeks: the Grand Chapel was on fire. Then, the movement stopped, the building having retained an even keel. Several gems and opals skittered at Julian's feet, and in the gloom, Julian grasped a handful and shoved them into his habit pocket. If it was good enough for the ordained monks, then he'd take his share.

Hauling the old abbot to his feet once more, Julian headed

for the stairs. Prior Blackwing and the other two monks overtook him, their hands clasping sacks of priceless objects, but they stopped at the stairwell.

Prior Blackwing turned with a look of horror on his face. "We have sunk below the level of the plateau. The stairs down lead to our deaths. We must go up." Blackwing was right. Their only hope of escape was making the roof of the Grand Chapel, and quickly. But as far as Julian could ascertain, there was no internal access to the roof, which might very well be on fire even if they could get to it. "This way," Blackwing said. Their pockets stuffed to the brim with glinting jewels, Blackwing and the two choir monks lurched unsteadily back down the hallway.

Julian followed more slowly, still supporting Abbot Howard. Blackwing stopped at a section of the wall and searched frantically for something that Julian could not see.

Blackwing turned to the wizened abbot. "The old door. Where is it?"

Abbot Howard croaked, "There, just where you are, surely. The third wood panel from my room. Count them."

"One, two, three," Blackwing said. "Yes, this must be it. Pray that the passage beyond remains free. Get to it, brothers."

Arnold and Harkness kicked at the wall, but for the most part their attempts were ineffectual, barely creating a crack in the wood panel. Something collapsed above and to the right and a surging wave of black smoke burst through the ceiling and rolled towards them. In seconds they would be drowned in choking ash.

"Hurry, brothers," Blackwing urged frantically. "The Grand Chapel rests on the precipice."

Julian watched the two monks flailing away. There was no time for this. "You say there's a door here?"

Blackwing nodded. "Sealed many years ago, but it exists."

"Support the abbot."

"What?"

"Do as I say. Take the abbot."

Blackwing leaned his tall frame down to prop up the abbot and Julian pushed Brothers Arnold and Harkness aside. He planted the same powerful kicks against the panel that he had used to open Howard's door and within moments the wood panel disintegrated, revealing a dark but clear space beyond.

"Well done, lay brother," Blackwing said. "You kick like a pregnant camel."

Prior Blackwing practically threw the abbot into Julian's arms as he scuttled through the opening. Julian and Howard brought up the rear and in total blindness ascended several steps, each man's breath rasping in the enclosed silence, but the smoke did not pursue them up the hidden stairwell and the air, for now, remained clear. In the blackness came another sound, an ominous rumbling under their feet. If the edifice were to fall again, it would perhaps be for the final time.

"Bring forth the lay brother," Blackwing whispered, as if afraid his voice might send the building over the edge and into the depths of Mount Ulfur. "We have need of his power once more. Here, my young friend. Force this hatch open if you can."

Julian placed the old abbot gently upon the stairs and felt his way forwards.

"A square hatch," Blackwing said. "Can you see it? If you can open it, we're free."

Julian bent his head and braced his shoulders against the hatch. He heaved, but it would not give. From the folds of his habit, he removed a hunting knife that he had stolen in the city and slid the blade into the merest sliver of a crack.

Blackwing squinted into the gloom. "Is that a dagger?"

"For peeling vegetables, Your Reverence."

"Of course, just get us out of here, lad."

Julian pulled down on the handle of the knife and something popped. The trapdoor opened partially, and Julian forced his shoulder upwards. The panel gave with a loud snap and sunlight filtered weakly down through the smoke and ash in the sky.

Martin, Klaus, and the others were peering down a dozen yards above them. Two ropes appeared and landed with a thud on the roof at one end; the other end of the Grand Chapel was ablaze, the intense heat burning exposed skin even at this distance. They had mere moments to get out before the flames spread to engulf them all.

Julian wrapped a rope around Abbot Howard's waist, and Arnold and Harkness fastened Blackwing to another. As the two senior members of the Brotherhood of Ulfur were being hauled upwards, the Grand Chapel tilted in a slow, sickening arc and slid into the abyss.

Amid the horror of weightlessness, Julian heard the screams of Arnold and Harkness as they fell flailing into the flames. Julian curled into a tight ball and a brief intense heat passed over him. Then, the brooding darkness within Mount Ulfur reached out and claimed him.

Claimed him with a cold, black finality.

10

A TASTE OF GIN

Cassie picked up the watermelon and slapped it gently. A firm, hollow sound revealed the ripeness of the fruit, and she nodded in satisfaction. She approached the fruit vendor fanning himself under the shade of a brightly striped canopy and paid for the watermelon. There were no customers ahead of her, the midday heat having cleared the market square an hour before. Cassie didn't mind the heat. She did, however, loathe waiting in line, but at this time of the day many merchants and housewives were inside napping.

A small child walked down the almost empty street towards her, the girl's clean white tunic shimmering in the heat haze: Yerty. Cassie flicked her eyes around the square and prayed the child would not be so foolish as to attempt to communicate with her in broad daylight, no matter how few people strolled the market. Cassie needn't have worried. Yerty simply met Cassie's eyes from afar, crouched, and swiftly scratched a series of figures in the dirt. She regained her feet and disappeared in a matter of seconds.

Cassie casually strolled over to where Yerty had scribbled the message and glanced at it. It read, *Medicus rediit.*

The physician has returned.

Cassie smiled. Yerty's Latin was impeccable. Cassie rubbed her sandalled foot across the dirt, forever obscuring the letters.

———

Stoppered bottles of green and blue liquid in the window. Myriad herbs hanging from the ceiling and laid out in small bundles on the counter: rosemary, sage, marjoram, thyme, mint, lavender, and tarragon. A thousand different aromas mingled into one heady, suffocating miasma, the potent broth enhanced by the humid midday air. Objects of unimaginable organic origin floated in murky, viscous liquids within glass jars. This was the physician's premises, the apothecary.

Cassie cleared her throat and the young man at the counter looked up from where he was counting out small white pellets and placing them in paper packets. The man's coat was bright white, his moustache pure black by contrast.

"I would like to see the physician," Cassie said.

The moustachioed youth dabbed glue on a flap and sealed one of the paper packets. "Master Corbin is extremely busy." He placed the packet on one end of the counter with several others.

"You're new here. He'll see me."

The young pharmacist continued to seal another paper packet. "He has just returned from an extremely tiring venture, madam."

"I know. Up the mountain and back again."

The young man raised an eyebrow in surprise. "Yes, well, it's not just that. Master Corbin spent a week up there in conditions of minimal comfort. He is extremely weary."

"I understand," Cassie said. "The monks are famed for their ascetic lifestyle. I will not keep the physician long from his rest."

"I'm afraid that I cannot—"

"It's alright, Stephen. She can come in."

In the doorway to the back office stood a portly gentleman of middle years wearing an identical white coat to that worn by the younger employee behind the counter, albeit a tighter fit around the belly. He was cleaning a pair of large round spectacles. Cassie followed Physician Corbin, who looked more tired than Cassie had ever seen him, into the back office. He closed the door, pulled a wooden chair from the wall, and offered it to her. He took his own seat behind a desk layered with randomly assorted parchments, which he scooped into some semblance of order. Corbin bent down behind his desk and produced a human skull, which, to Cassie's distaste, he used as a paperweight for the sheets of paper.

The medic sat back and clasped his fingers together. "I hope none of the children were hurt by the—"

"Meteor," Cassie provided. "From the Latin *meteorum*."

Corbin lifted his spectacles and poked a finger at the bags under his eyes. "Yes, the *meteor*."

"The children are well. It's those on the mountain I wish to ask about. I am given to understand that you've been up there?"

Master Corbin frowned. "How would you know such a thing? My journey was undertaken in quite some secrecy, or so I thought. Do you have a network of spies keeping an eye out?"

Cassie smiled and felt the pull of her cleft palate the same way she always did when mirth played at her mouth. "Something like that. What can you tell me of Lay Brother Julian?"

The physician leaned back in his chair and appeared startled. "How do you know about him?"

"Is he dead?"

"No." Relief coursed through Cassie. This puzzled her. Why was she so happy that the doe-eyed monk still lived? The medic rubbed at the growth on his double chin. "How could you possibly know that Julian is one of my patients?"

Cassie folded her arms and looked around Corbin's cramped office with its small sleeping cot under the one dirty window. "The monk has been a regular visitor to the streets of Re'Shan of late, acquiring produce for his brethren on the mountain. I bumped into him once and we got to talking. But since the meteor struck, well, it's been a month now and no sign of him in the markets. Naturally, I feared the worst and since you've been up there, I thought perhaps you would know something of him."

"I see. Well, I can tell you that three men died on the mountain that day, but the young fellow in question was not among them. He suffered a blow to his head, however." The physician grabbed the skull from the desk and pointed somewhere behind where one of the ears would reside had the skull flesh. "Here. It took two days, apparently, to raise him from a ledge on which he had fortunately landed. Very lucky not to fall into the chasm. He lapsed into a *coma*, which comes from the Latin word of the same name. Have you heard the term?"

"I understand the notion of a coma, Master Corbin, and the etymology of the word. Thank you. What ledge and chasm do you speak of?"

"The whole bloody Grand Chapel caught fire and fell into a pit in the mountain. Would you believe it?"

"What are you saying? It *fell*? It's gone?"

"Yes. The entire thing just disappeared in a hole in the ground, it seems."

Cassie held back a stream of curses. All that loot, the treasure, gone? She cleared her throat. "And Julian fell with it?"

The physician nodded. "Yes. As I said, a ledge broke his fall, but he was severely injured. I was able to stimulate the brain stem with a combination of ammonia and alcohol, restoring some movement to his extremities."

"He's awake?"

"Yes. But he is groggy, as you can imagine. Doesn't quite know where he is. The monks fed him while he was in the coma, liquids of course, bathed him, exercised his limbs. I think he's going to be alright." Corbin sighed and shook his head. "They should have called for me earlier, but you know how stubborn the monks can be. Julian will pull through. I'd stake my reputation on it." The medic scratched at his double chin and peered at Cassie over his circular glasses. "Your friend is something of a hero on the mountain."

Cassie leaned forwards. "He is? How is that?"

"He saved the abbot's life. Abbot Howard. It seems Julian dived into the destroyed chapel and dragged Howard bodily from the ruins before ... well, before Julian himself fell, though I fear that his efforts may have been wasted. The old man has cancer and will pass before the summer does."

Cassie nodded to herself. Julian was a man of surprising talents. She would give him that. Very much the dark horse. "You said that Julian went *inside* the main chapel?"

"Yes. That's what I said. That's what I was told at any rate."

A thought struck Cassie. "Did they pay you?"

Corbin frowned. "For my services, you mean?"

"Yes. You were gone a week according to the young man outside. You must have lost much custom in that time."

"I had Stephen to run things, but yes, the brothers did pay me."

"The monks paid you?"

"Yes. Why is that so surprising?"

Cassie decided to press her luck. "The austerity of the monks. I mean, they don't have a lot. How could they afford to pay you?"

Cassie could tell she had probed a little too far. Master Corbin began to look at her with a suspicious air. "It is no crime to wish to help one's fellow man, Cassie. That is why I became a medical practitioner in the first place. But yes, they offered me ..." The physician seemed to lose his train of thought. A moment later he resumed more brightly. "Yes, they gave me this." Master Corbin opened a drawer of his desk and pulled out a small stone on a leather chain. Cassie peered at it. It was a necklace of some kind, a beetle of rather rudimentary design, but recognizable as such. It wasn't stone; rather, it was metal, metal which glowed and changed colours. One moment blue like the sky, the next a pulsing purple, then a vibrant yellow to match that of the goldenrod.

Cassie could barely drag her eyes from the object. "What is it?"

The medic blinked and put the enticing object back in the drawer. "A recently discovered metal from the ... what did you call it?"

"Meteor."

"Yes, from that, or so the monks say."

"Is it worth anything?" Cassie asked.

"I am not sure of its worth. The monks are using it to make items of jewellery. I admire them, don't you? This *sky-metal* almost flattens their community, kills three of their number, but they survive and now use the same material to prosper. It's a tale of fortitude and spirit. And this material may appreciate in value, who would know? I can arrange to have some jewellery sent down for you, if you so desire."

Cassie shook her head. "I prefer my beauty to remain unadorned."

The medic cleared his throat, the irony of Cassie's comment not lost on him. Looking everywhere except at Cassie's cleft palate, Corbin said, "How did you meet the young fellow Julian again?"

"In the market one morning." Cassie stood and gave a bow. "I must be going. Thank you for your time, Master Corbin."

Cassie stepped out of the apothecary into the blinding, dusty streets. She looked to the skies and shielded her eyes. The snowcapped mountain loomed against a background of cloudless blue. Julian was alive.

And he'd been inside.

———

"God is good. Yes, he is." Brother Vernon grinned from wrinkled ear to wrinkled ear.

Julian was sitting up in bed, his back resting against the cool stone wall of the small infirmary, a cup of Brother Vernon's gin in his hand.

Martin and Klaus sat on the other side of the bed to Brother Vernon. The tall German was sobbing. Martin smiled and patted Klaus on the knee. "Every time, Klaus? You cry every time we come here. Julian is fine. Look at him. He is recovered. You do not need to cry anymore."

"These are tears of joy." Klaus sniffed. "Tears of joy." He dabbed at his cheeks with a cloth.

"Come, come." Brother Vernon smiled as he passed cups of gin to Martin and Klaus over the bed. "We will toast the health of young Lay Brother Julian. God is good, yes."

Julian grimaced as he drank the gin, which was a little bitter, but truth be told he didn't care. He was just happy to be alive, happy to have the option to be drunk.

Klaus coughed and spat gin down the front of his habit. Vernon gave a puzzled glance into his own cup. "It's a little immature but not that bad, surely."

"I'm sorry," Klaus said. "This is my first time with alcohol."

"Well, I suggest there is no better reason for a first drink than a friend returned from the abyss!" Vernon grinned and took another mouthful.

"We should leave Julian to rest," Martin said. "He needs time to convalesce."

Julian demurred. "No, no. You stay here. All of you. Brother Vernon is right. This is a celebration. Cheers." Julian raised his cup and drank deeply, finishing the gin. "May I have more?"

Vernon beamed. "May you have more? Yes, yes. God is good and so is my gin."

"God is good." Julian nodded as he held out his cup. He felt his shoulders ache with the effort, but he held the cup steady.

"You've had your walk?" Brother Vernon asked as he finished pouring.

"Yes, I've been out and about," Julian said. "I think I can return to the storehouse today, or even the gardens."

Vernon shook his head. "Oh, no. Oh my, no. The impetuousness of youth, God forgive you. It's bed rest and light exercise for the next week. Prior Blackwing would not like to see all of his good work undone by a premature return to the gardens."

Julian frowned. "Prior Blackwing?"

Brother Vernon nodded. "He is the community physick, among his other duties. It is only his skill that kept you alive. Yet even his abilities were not enough to awaken you, so we sent for assistance down below. Between Prior Blackwing and Physician Corbin, and God, of course, you received the utmost care."

Julian touched the stitches behind his ear. "Blackwing cared for me?"

"That he did," Vernon said, sipping at his gin.

Julian could not reconcile what he knew of the cold superior with this tale of the man who had apparently saved his life. Blackwing had seemed much more interested in the valuables in the Grand Chapel than in saving the abbot, and Julian couldn't imagine that his own life was worth a whit to the man.

"For a month? You say I was asleep for a month?"

Martin nodded and Klaus covered his mouth with the cloth, tears building in his eyes once more. "We thought you would never come back to us," Klaus said, his voice trembling.

Julian looked down at his body beneath the undershirt. He *had* lost a lot of weight. But a month? He rubbed his hands over the spiky growth of his disappearing tonsure.

"What do they say about keeping a good man down?" Vernon said. "Simply cannot do it." He raised another toast.

Down. A long way down. The bulk of the treasure was down there, too, still in the Grand Chapel. Julian dismissed the idea of trying to retrieve it, even were it possible. He'd risked enough. Risked enough for treasure, risked enough for Cassie. A thought struck him like a shock of cold water. *His habit*, the gems and opals, perhaps even diamonds he'd grasped. It had been dark in the collapsed chapel, and he couldn't be sure, but whatever he'd managed to pick up was in his habit.

"Where is my habit?" Julian asked, trying to stay calm.

Vernon swallowed some gin. "Bloodied and torn. You'll get a new one."

"What has become of the old one?"

The old monk shrugged. "I don't know."

Damn it. He couldn't push the question without raising suspicion. He had to get his strength back and soon. He had to get out of the infirmary and find his habit before it was too late. It had been a *month*. Still, the monks never wasted anything. His habit had to be somewhere.

"God is good indeed." Vernon pulled a crucifix from around his neck and kissed it. The object glowed.

Julian stared. "What's that?"

Brother Vernon patted the object now resting on his chest. "My crucifix. What else?"

Gone was the simple enamelled wooden cross. This object pulsed with an internal light, a metal of some kind that Julian had never seen before. It changed colours as he gazed at it. One moment it was crimson, the next pure aqua, and then summer-dusk orange.

Vernon smiled and nodded. "A gift from God." His smile faded and he sighed. "That sounds fatuous, even to my own ears. We paid a heavy price for this." He held up the crucifix. "Poor Brothers Arnold and Harkness. We could not find them. And Lay Brother Curtis, his skull so terribly crushed. A tragedy." Vernon shook his head sadly. "Three lives taken, but we do not question Him in His eternal wisdom."

Julian was puzzled. "I don't understand."

Klaus spoke up and gestured at Brother Vernon's crucifix. "This is what fell from the sky, Jules. It was hot to the touch at first, even molten. But when it cooled, well, it is what you see. It's beautiful, is it not?"

Julian murmured, "Yes. Beautiful. Such beautiful colours."

"There are traces of it higher up the mountain," Brother Vernon added. "It's malleable, quite soft until it takes shape. You'll each get your own cross like this when you become ordained."

"That is so long away, Brother Vernon," Klaus complained.

"Ah, patience. Time is so often miscalculated by the young. Patience."

"But on the bright side"—Klaus beamed—"I find the metal beautiful to work with."

Julian turned his aching head to the tall youth. "What?"

Vernon explained. "Young Lay Brother Klaus is now working the metal into items of jewellery with Lawrence and Kristoff. Something of a talent for design, has our young German friend."

"Won't you miss your goats, Klaus?" Julian asked.

Klaus laughed. "I am told I smell of goat, so they stay with me no matter where I go. And I shall visit Elsie when I have time."

Julian wasn't sure if the tall German was actually joking, so said nothing. He stared once more at the object hanging from Brother Vernon's neck. The crucifix pulsed a deep shade of red like the colour of freshly spilt blood.

"And of course," Vernon said, "you wouldn't be here without Lay Brother Martin. He went down to find you when all others had given up hope. He was the one who pulled you from the darkness."

Julian turned to Martin. "Is that true?"

Martin shrugged. "You risked your life to save the abbot and you would have done it for Klaus or me or any of us."

"I can't ... I can't thank you enough."

Klaus burst into tears and hugged Martin. Julian sat forwards and attempted to embrace him, too, but winced in pain. Martin and Klaus leaned in and the three clasped each other.

Brother Vernon sat back grinning. He sipped at his gin and said, "Now this, this is brotherly love. *This* is why we become monks. A beautiful moment, one I will treasure, but we must allow young Julian to recuperate. Time to go."

They stood to leave and Julian said, "Martin, could you please stay a moment?" Martin sat once more as Vernon and Klaus left the room, the one still drinking and the other still crying. "Thank you, again. For saving my life."

"You are welcome."

Julian made sure no one was listening at the door. "Did Prior Blackwing carry anything that day? When he and Abbot Howard came up on the rope?"

Martin shook his head soberly. "No. What would he be carrying?"

"I saw ... I saw precious stones and other things in the Grand Chapel. He emerged empty handed?"

Martin fell silent for a moment. He reached into his habit pocket and removed something. He opened his palm and held it out to Julian. In Martin's palm rested a purple opal of extraordinary sheen. "Blackwing carried nothing, but you had this in your pocket the day I found you."

Julian's face reddened. "I didn't steal it. Well, I did, but I thought I was going to die."

"I'm not judging you. Take it." Julian hesitated and then took the opal. He grasped it tightly, feeling its cool smoothness in his hand. Martin said, "Does this mean you're leaving? Do you need money for a life somewhere else?"

Julian sighed. "I considered it, if I'm being honest. But no, you and Klaus are family. I'm not leaving, but I think I owe you an explanation."

Martin stood and smiled. "You don't owe me anything. I'm just glad you're staying. I have to get back. I'll visit again after vespers."

When Julian was alone, he held up the opal and admired it. He didn't have a lot of use for it, not now that he had decided to stay. His second chance at life had made him see what was truly important. No, he had no use for the stone.

But he knew someone who did.

11

ASCENSION

The day's produce came into the city before the sun rose. Wines and coconut oils, dates, watermelons, carrots, lettuce, peaches, pears, and nectarines. Nuts, beans, alfalfa, slices of meat packed in salt, and even cow's milk at prices the average housewife could not afford but would try to haggle over anyway. Re'Shan's proximity to the Great Southern Sands mattered not at all to the types of delicacies one could purchase. With an ingenuity to make the ancient Greeks proud, the farmers of Re'Shan had found a way to irrigate their crops and grow whatever it was that you desired to eat, drink, or smear over your body or between your toes.

The market at the city gate hummed in the early dawn with an energy and excitement that would not return until the dusk, when those with bellies filled with desert fruits and the choicest cuts of meat would walk the streets seeking to fill their bellies further with ale, wine, and perfumed liquors.

Julian had missed this: the bartering and joking with the sellers and farmers in the morning markets. It felt like an age since he had walked the shops and stalls. There was something familiar and comforting about the sights and sounds of earnest business. Many of the vendors asked about Julian's absence and the terrible events on the mountainside. They gasped in horror at the story of his near death and then congratulated him on regaining his health, shaking his hand and even going so far as to offer discounted prices on the already discounted goods. Special prices for an old friend, they would wink.

Julian was tying a bag of wheat to the side of the mule after one such successful trade when a woman standing nearby said, "I'm glad you are well, Lay Brother Julian. Thinner, but well, by the looks of you."

Her face was hidden behind a hijab, but Julian instantly recognized the honeyed voice and bright brown eyes. *Cassie.*

Martin was talking to a fruit salesman a few yards away, out of earshot. Julian continued to tie the wheat sack to the mule. Cassie stepped closer, her long white dress flowing around her as if billowing in a breeze, though none caressed the market.

"You went inside the main chapel," Cassie said.

Julian glanced at her sharply as he finished tying on the sack. "How would you know that?"

She shrugged. "Word travels up and down the mountain. What did you find?"

"Nothing."

"You're lying."

Julian pulled hard on the saddlebag strap and turned to face Cassie. "It's gone. It's all gone. Leave me alone."

"What's gone, Julian? What are you talking about?"

"You know what I'm talking about. The Grand Chapel and everything in it."

"But you saw it, didn't you? Before it fell. You saw something."

"Lay Brother Martin and I will soon be leaving. We have a long climb ahead of us."

Cassie's voice held a smile in it, and something else, a touch of desperation. "I won't pry into who and what you really are. I don't care, Julian. Just tell me what you saw inside the Grand Chapel."

Julian took a deep breath. He looked to Mount Ulfur and admired the icy peaks in the haze of distance. Perhaps it was time to right some wrongs. He reached within his habit pocket and pulled out something small. He held it out. Their fingers touched as the thing dropped from his hand to hers.

Cassie's eyes grew wide as she stared at the lustrous purple opal. She glanced around the market and quickly closed her hand. "Do you have more?"

"No, and that nearly cost me my life."

She nodded. "You shall get a share of the sale."

"Keep it. A gift to you and the children."

Cassie frowned. "But I promised to—"

"Just keep away from me. Consider that"—he gestured at her hand—"a fee for doing so. You're wrong about me, Cassie. I *am* a monk. That's what I want to be. No matter what I was. Do you understand? I don't want to see you again."

"But we could do many good things together. Our partnership—"

"We have no partnership, of any kind."

Cassie bowed her head. "As you wish."

When Martin joined Julian, the bald lay brother found his friend standing alone and staring vacantly into the market crowds.

———

The chapel brimmed with clerics, and every pair of monastic eyes rested upon Lay Brother Rollant as he knelt before Prior Blackwing. Today, Gabriel Rollant would join the ordained monks; today he would receive his holy orders. No longer *lay brother*, but fully fledged *brother*. Rollant tried to contain his grin. He couldn't wait to see Julian's smug face the first time he was forced to call him *Brother Rollant*.

Hah! *Brother Rollant*. He liked the sound of that. No more sweating his arse off in the bread ovens or trying to direct the labours of the other lay brothers. Never again forced to mediate with idiots. Today he would get everything he had ever wanted. Today he would rise above the muck and ascend to a higher plane. Yes, that fool Julian and the others would no longer talk of him in scornful terms behind his back. He knew what they said about him in private. They had never respected him. But they would respect him now.

Song filled the chapel, one hundred ordained monks singing in pure harmony to welcome him into their ranks. Even Abbot Howard had made an appearance, leaning heavily on a walking stick but smiling and singing along with everyone else. The old man was, however, still too ill to carry out the rituals, so that duty had been taken up by Prior Blackwing.

Rollant had only one regret. He wished, oh, how fervently he wished, that he could be ordained in the original prayer chapel in all its glory, but that had sunk into the abyss the day the sky-metal had fallen upon them. The monks had worked hard to build a makeshift chapel and dormitory, toiling without rest until both structures were complete. But this chapel was a pale shadow of the former one, makeshift in every sense of the word. To make matters worse, the new chapel had been built near the goat sheds and the incessant bleating and pungent odour of those filthy animals invaded his peace of mind. Though Klaus no longer tended the goats, Rollant could not help but think of the German and the time his favourite goat had nearly crushed his testicles. The fool had even named the animal. Rollant took a deep breath and dismissed thoughts of the former chapel, the goats, and the idiot German. He would let nothing diminish the joy of his ascension to a higher plane.

This was *his* time and he'd be damned if he'd let anything spoil it.

Prior Blackwing removed Rollant's wooden cross and replaced it with a shining crucifix of metal: the sky-metal. It bled colour, glowing at first purple, then shimmering and filling from top to bottom with a deep red, and then a wave of aqua swept away the magenta. The thing was extraordinary. Brother Rollant closed his eyes amid a wash of ecstasy, his tears dripping to the floor of the chapel. *Brother Rollant.* Oh, how sweet the sound.

"Do you refrain from false speech?" Prior Blackwing asked.

"Yes," Rollant replied through his tears.

"Do you refrain from stealing?"

"Yes."

"Do you refrain from sexual misconduct?"

Rollant's balls tightened. He choked on his answer, cleared his throat, and said, "Yes." Sweat broke out on his brow. Merciful Christ, he was getting an erection at a most inopportune moment.

"Do you refrain from killing?"

Rollant almost did not hear the question, so forcefully did his blood flow through him. "Yes," he said. For a moment his heart leaped. What was the question again? Should he have answered yes or no? He stole a glance around the chapel with its plain, unadorned window looking out onto the goat sheds. No one seemed to notice anything out of place in his response. He must have answered correctly.

Rollant's thoughts ran away with him. *Unadorned windows. Goat shed.* It wasn't fair. He should have been ordained in the original chapel. The others had been ordained there and yet all Rollant had for his special day was this ramshackle hut. Even the name was pathetic: the *Second Chapel*, they called it. He was to be ordained in the *Second* Chapel.

Then the initiation ritual was over, and the choir monks began to disperse. Rollant had to resist the urge to run from the Second Chapel and find Julian so that he could parade his newfound power. Klaus would have to pay proper deference, too. Rollant's skin crawled. He couldn't stand the way the German moaned about his vertigo and shrieked at the merest sight of an insect, or the way he minced about like a princess.

Blackwing patted Rollant on the shoulder as he stood. The ruddy-faced prior smiled. "Brother, there is some time before terce, and the new library is currently open." The prior's knowing smile suggested that Rollant would wish for nothing more than to enter the library for the first time as an ordained monk.

Rollant nodded. Yes, the library. He should go to the library. The current library was a pale version of the old one, which had fallen with the Grand Chapel. The new library was a scant collection of books haphazardly gathered from the city below. But that did not matter. He was *permitted* to enter the library, as limited as it was, and that was the important thing to remember. Yes, he would go to the library. He could rub the lay brothers' faces in his holiness a little later. For now, he should read.

But before that, he had to find a quiet corner, perhaps in the library, to masturbate.

———

"I don't think I ever thanked you for saving my life."

Julian turned in surprise to see Abbot Howard standing at the entrance to the storehouse. The old man was wearing a flowing habit of white. "Father Abbot. It is not wise for you to walk outside. The air is chilled. You need bed rest."

"I'm feeling much better," Abbot Howard replied. "Perhaps I experience the last rays of the sun before it sets forever. I do not know, but whether I live or die is not of any importance, for today I feel fine and I shall walk our community. Besides, I've had enough bed rest of late and I wish to talk with you."

"Yes, Father Howard. At least come in out of the wind."

Without the aid of his walking frame or even a cane, Howard walked into the storehouse. The abbot must have noted Julian's surprise. "As I mentioned, I am feeling better. I only hope it lasts. How I've missed everything, I've missed the people, people like you, trustworthy and loyal. Where is the other young man that I always see you with? The Black brother?"

"Lay Brother Martin is in the gardens, where I shall shortly join him." Julian gestured around the room with its sacks of various grains, crates of vegetables, and bread. "There's not much to do in the storehouse today. Everything is in order. I was just making space for the eggs."

"Ah, yes. The hens are in lay, or so I hear." The abbot paused for a long moment and then met Julian's eyes. "You risked your life to save me. I only hope you do not regret it."

"Of course not, Father Abbot. Why would I?"

"I think you may have witnessed some things that ... confused you. I wish to explain."

Julian waved the older man away. "You have no need to explain anything to me."

"But I must, you see. Even an abbot must clear his conscience on occasion."

Julian nodded. "Alright."

Howard glanced around the storeroom. "As a young man, I started out here, not this storehouse in particular, you understand, but one just like it in another abbey. I was entrusted with the management of foodstuffs, a weighty position, for without food, we shall wither away in hunger and die." The abbot said nothing further, and Julian wondered if he was meant to fill the silence with an observation of his own. Father Howard came out of some distant memory and went on, "As the body desires, nay, requires sustenance, so, too, does the spirit. What you saw, the jewels, are not intended as a hoard of material wealth, but of a *spiritual* one. All things are created by God. It is within these physical objects that we perceive God and serve Him. These perfect things, the precious stones, are a medium, if you will, by which God talks to us and we Him."

"I see," Julian said, though he was not entirely sure he did.

Father Howard sighed. "Prior Blackwing was right to attempt to save the jewels. In the great scheme of things, I am not important. You must not judge him for what he did that day."

Julian put his hands together and bowed his head. "I judge no one, Father. I have given myself to the Brotherhood of Ulfur and simply seek to know its ways. If this is one of its precepts, then so be it."

The abbot looked embarrassed. "I am aware that it may have looked ... other than it was."

"These precious things are gifts from God. I understand."

"Yes. A gift from God. Like this." The abbot pulled out his crucifix. It sparkled and changed colour exactly like the one Brother Vernon had. "This was sent to us by God, do you see? It shines in a way that is crystalline, beyond crystalline. Surely this is the Holy Father trying to speak to us. Of all the places it could have landed, why here in the very midst of the humble Monks of Ulfur?" He sighed, sadly. "A price was extracted, but look at the beauty of it. Life is passing, transient, but this ..." Father Howard stared at the crucifix. "This is forever." The abbot turned to go but stopped and looked back. "I hope that you will not speak of what you saw in the Grand Chapel."

Julian had already confided in Martin, so he lied. "To no one, Father."

The old abbot smiled. "Good lad. Trustworthy and loyal." He lifted the cross from his chest and kissed it as a youthful sparkle glinted in his eyes. The abbot no longer seemed old, but rather a fatherly man of middle years, the wrinkles about his eyes no longer deep set, merely gossamer strands of silk speaking of experience. The abbot seemed almost ... *robust*.

With a spritely step, Father Howard left the storehouse and entered the biting winds. Julian closed his eyes.

He could still see the afterimage of the sky-metal crucifix.

12

THE CORVID

Klaus turned and beamed, his smile like a shard of setting summer sun. "It's just up here. We're close now."

Julian's back ached and he rubbed at it. He peered back the way they had come. From this vantage point he could see the small wooden and stone buildings serving as the community for the Ulfur Monks and the gaping pit near the cliffs where the Grand Chapel once stood. Water from the cliff face now splashed into the chasm, the rushing gurgle faintly audible even from this distance. Further below, in the distance across the desert, the horizon was a lighter shade of blue, deepening to an indigo towards the zenith. A few twinkling stars lit the blackness far above them. Perhaps a half hour of late summer light remained. Despite the season it was frigid at this altitude.

"Are you alright?" Martin asked.

Julian nodded and the two men followed Klaus along a high narrow ridge, each pulling his habit tighter around his throat against the cold. Oddly, in light of the tall German's vertigo, he skipped along the ridge with a carefree manner. Julian was about to remark on it when they arrived at a wind-warped juniper tree leaning at an acute angle, its trunk blackened, branches snapped. Beyond the tree was a small gully.

Klaus whispered almost reverentially, "Part of it landed here. Look." He pointed at a pool of water that had accrued in the gully below. "A small impact crater, one of many on the mountainside."

Julian and Martin crept close to the edge of the gully and looked down. Below them, the pool seemed luminescent, small grains of glittering colour glowing on its bed. Klaus came to this place every day with Lawrence and Kristoff to find the sky-metal and shape it into new crucifixes, but it was not just ecclesiastical items they fashioned from the metal; items of secular jewellery were also proving popular in the city below: bracelets, necklaces, earrings, and other accessories. The monks had started to turn a small profit from the sale of these items, coin that was needed to restore the Brotherhood of Ulfur and rebuild their lives after the recent disaster. Once again, Julian was reminded that even holy monks needed money for basic earthly needs.

"It is a beautiful metal to work with," Klaus said. "We are finding good amounts, almost everywhere we look. We'll soon need more brothers to work alongside us in order to keep up with demand. Perhaps you two can help."

"No, thanks," Martin said warily, looking down over the lip of the gully. "I'm happy in the storehouse and the gardens."

Laughter came from behind them in the deepening shadows of night. Two smiling lay brothers had followed them up the darkening path: Lawrence and Kristoff. It had been several months since the two men had broken their ankles in a nighttime escapade and though those joints had fully healed, the two men had not learned any lessons about climbing the steep places in the darkness. The newcomers greeted them and began to strip off their habits and underclothes.

"You can't seriously be going in there?" Martin asked, pointing to the luminous water below.

A smile spread across Lawrence's face. "Why not? It's warm."

Kristoff repeatedly raised and lowered one dark, bushy eyebrow to comic effect. He slapped Lawrence on his bare arse, and the naked lay brothers edged out onto the trunk of a dead tree overhanging the pool and jumped. The distance between tree bole and the water was not inconsiderable. For this reason, Julian gasped when Klaus began to slip his habit over his head.

Klaus winked. "I'm going in, too. Join us."

"What about your vertigo?" Martin said.

"I have no vertigo."

Martin glanced at Julian with a puzzled frown. "But you do have vertigo, Klaus. You've always had vertigo."

Klaus scoffed and waved Martin away. "I mean to say that my affliction has lessened of late. Coming up here every day to look for the metal helps me get over my fear of heights. It is ... what is the word ... *therapeutic*. As is the water. It invigorates body and mind." Klaus stepped onto the tree trunk. "Are you coming in? It's beautiful. Come, Martin. Come, Jules, it may help you recuperate your strength. You are still weak. Come on."

Julian shook his head. "It's late, Klaus. If we don't get back now, we'll be stumbling around in the dark."

"Nonsense," Klaus said. "The stars offer plenty of light."

Above Julian, the Southern Cross was barely visible. "No, there's not plenty of light. This is dangerous, and besides, Martin and I have a long climb down the mountain tomorrow for supplies. We can't be up here all night, cavorting."

Klaus snorted. "Cavorting? Hah, you sound like Rollant or Prior Blackwing." Klaus edged along the fallen tree. "Where's your sense of fun?"

Before Julian could reply, Klaus spread his arms wide and

allowed himself to slowly fall backwards. A splash followed by more laughter. Julian walked to the edge of the gully and shouted down to Klaus, "We're going back."

"You go." Klaus laughed and flicked water at Lawrence and Kristoff. "I'll come down with the others later." Julian shrugged and he and Martin began their descent to the compound below.

"At least he is over his fear of the high places," Martin said, bemused. "That has to be a good thing."

Julian nodded. *A good thing.* He supposed. When they returned to the compound, they found Rollant, or *Brother* Rollant as it was now, waiting for them in the dormitory.

"Where is Klaus?" Brother Rollant asked.

Martin cleared his throat. "I believe he is working the metal in the ... site above, brother."

Rollant gave an exasperated sigh. "I admire the man's work ethic, but it's late and evening prayers are due. Still, I am no longer concerned with the affairs of the lay brothers. I will attend compline with the choir monks in the chapel."

Rollant flicked a condescending smile at them and swept out of the dormitory. The arrogant bastard had taken every opportunity of late to remind Julian that he was now an ordained monk, but Julian had prepared himself for it, steeled himself against the man's smirking pride. Rollant mattered little to him anyway. Julian had dealt with worse, far worse.

———

Yerty and Dylan rifled through the unconscious man's pockets.

Miss Cass had warned Yerty several times never to steal from a drunk. There was no great difficulty, or art for that matter, in going through a man's pockets as he lay in a state of comatose nirvana in the streets. Drunks were easy marks. But there were three very good reasons for leaving them be. Foremost was that drunks had often exhausted every coin in their pursuit of oblivion. That was, after all, why they were drunk. The risk for return was too low. Or too high. Yerty could never quite get her head around which it was. Secondly, any drunk that awakened midrobbery was likely to lash out in violence. Try to nick his, or sometimes her, purse during the day, and the worst you'd get was a swift kick up the arse and camel curses. But get caught with your hand in a drunk's pocket down a dark alley at night and you could get a knife between your ribs, or your nose bitten off before the drunk realized you were only a poor wee urchin. Apologies wouldn't count for much then, not when you didn't have a nose, or your heart was good and punctured.

The third, and most important, reason street children should avoid drunks was that they attracted a more dangerous type of street criminal: the big thieves, the adults who stole to survive. They were not common because thievery on the part of a grown man or woman could mean a death sentence if caught. As a child you didn't want to come across a big thief when they crawled under the city walls at night, coming in from their holes in the desert, more animal than human. Woe betide any child who got in their way, for they would kill to get first rights to whatever the drunks carried. The big thieves didn't like the light—if you kept to the light, they wouldn't bother you. They weren't as dangerous as Miss Cass made out. They were just the bottom of the barrel, the least fortunate among the street people. There was nothing to fear from them. Not really.

"We shouldn't be doing this," Dylan whispered.

"Just get on with it," Yerty said.

"Miss Cass told us not to touch the likes of these."

"He's not drunk."

"He smells drunk."

"He's just sleeping. Shut up, Dylan. You'll wake him."

The man whose pockets Yerty and Dylan were currently patting down had a black eye and a bloodied nose. He was lying in the shadows at the mouth of an alley that opened onto a reasonably busy thoroughfare. It had been an opportunity Yerty had spied from a nearby rooftop and one too good to pass up.

"This is wrong," Dylan whined.

An unconscious man, a man knocked clean out in a barroom brawl such as this man evidently was, did not constitute a drunk, of this Yerty was sure. He *might* have been drunk before he found himself on the end of another man's brutality and been cast outside to sleep off the booze and the bruise, but that was splitting hairs.

"Got one." Yerty pulled a coin from the man's bloodstained vest pocket. "Lord, it's silver."

Dylan gasped and reached out for the coin. "Let me see."

Yerty swatted Dylan's hand away and hissed, "Grubby paws to yourself. Check his arse pocket and his boots." A big, bearded bloke shouted from a pub across the street. One of the man's companions, perhaps. "Run," Yerty said calmly.

Dylan and Yerty ran side by side to their prearranged escape route. The bearded lout chasing them down the dark alley didn't have a chance. In times like this, you must know who your friends are. Yerty's frail frame was her best friend. The darkness that covered the city was also a close companion. And the high places, yes, the places only the agile could reach. No big boozed-up lump straight out of a pub could steal through the shadows and clamber upwards like Yerty and Dylan could.

Looking down from the rooftop, they saw the fat bastard clenching his fists and shaking them in frustration. Yerty could tell that he didn't even know where they were; the idiot was waving his meaty fists in completely the wrong direction. The darkness blinded them, always did coming from a well-lit pub.

The beefy man turned in circles and scratched his thick skull before lumbering off and disappearing in the shadows.

Yerty held the silver coin to her nose and sniffed it. Miss Cass would be pleased, as long as Yerty didn't tell her where she'd got it. She smiled but that smile faded when a scratching noise alerted her to the presence of something on the rooftop.

"Whassat?" she whispered.

"What? Didn't hear nothing," Dylan nervously replied.

"Ssshh, listen." No further sound came.

"Maybe a hawk nesting in the guttering," Dylan suggested in a low voice.

The skin at Yerty's scalp began to prickle. "Maybe. I don't know. Something's up here." All was quiet. Then, the sound came again: the weight of a body on the shingles, a clipping sound, feet scratching at tiles.

Dylan must have heard it because he whispered, "Is he up here?"

"The fat one down below? No chance."

"But then who?"

Yerty held her hand out to Dylan. "Come on." She turned and scuttled away from the sound, her twin brother holding tight to her hand. The two children came to a section of the roof that had been removed and was now covered by a tarp and four heavy bricks. Pulling the tarp up at one end, Yerty allowed Dylan to crawl under and down into the attic below. Yerty glanced around and then followed.

The attic was warm. Below them, the sounds of a large family eating dinner drifted upwards: the clicking of plates and other utensils, the murmuring of conversation. The Johansen family, new immigrants to Re'Shan from the far north, ate, talked, laughed. The elder members of the family discussed something in low voices, something about a new business venture, while the children made mock of each other with high-pitched laughter. A woman's voice warned the children to behave themselves. That would be Margarite Johansen, mother, wife, and business partner. Yerty liked Margarite. She had spirit, just like Miss Cass. Yerty wondered if Margarite had a knack for embroidery, too. The Johansen children, Paulie, Roald, and Franny, were often ill-mannered, even insolent, but they made Yerty laugh. The Johansens were rowdy but happy. Perhaps it would not be such a bad thing to marry one day if it could be like the family below. Maybe embroidery wasn't so bad after all.

There was no time to stay and listen, not today. The family was at dinner and that meant the twins could drop down into the empty drawing room and get to the stairs, their usual way to the street. Yerty and Dylan clambered stealthily along the roof beams until they came to a hatch. Dylan went first and landed softly below. As Yerty slipped down through the hatch, she caught sight of something bursting soundlessly into the attic from the opening they had just come through. It was cloaked in a black feathered robe, giving it the appearance of a crow, but it was no crow. Yerty caught a glimpse of shining, malignant eyes within the darkness and her heart skipped a beat. She let herself down into the drawing room and hurried for the passageway leading to the front door, dragging Dylan with her.

Dylan must have sensed his sister's agitation, for when they had made the stairwell and were clattering downwards, he whispered, "What's wrong?"

"Big thief," Yerty replied, but immediately doubted her own words. The big ones did not usually take to the rooftops. Still, what else could it have been? They came to a window over-looking a dark alleyway and Yerty indicated for Dylan to leap down to the small side street below. The moment Dylan made the jump, Yerty regretted her decision. Better to stick to the main streets, stick to the light, even if they were hunted by the fat man or the drunk wanting his silver coin back.

She leaned her head out and reached down. "Come back up, Dylan. We'll take the front entrance."

"But someone'll see us," Dylan whispered.

Before Yerty could utter another word, something dropped on Dylan from above, swallowing him in darkness. Yerty screamed. For a split second, fear set her legs in stone, and then she leaped on the thing that had enveloped her brother.

———

"Shush," Margarite said.

The warning was unnecessary. The children were all staring at each other in fright, the scream having come from nearby, the scream of a child. Faf Johansen stood and looked to his wife. Margarite nodded and, as Faf was making for the front door, gave him a long, serrated kitchen knife.

Another scream sounded as Faf descended the stairs and came to the apartment entrance. It was coming from the side alley. He rounded the corner and saw a shadow of what looked like an enormous, feathered corvid. He shouted and the thing moved swiftly away, leaving a small figure prone in the dirt and sand of the alley.

Faf rushed forwards to find a bleeding child, a girl. She lay still and Faf knelt beside her. The crow-like creature was gone. Suddenly, the girl kicked out, catching Faf in the chest. He restrained her as she screamed again, blood on her face and in her eyes, blinding her.

"Be still, girl," Faf said. "I will not harm you."

The girl blinked and wiped frantically at her face and eyes.

Opening them, she stared wildly around. "Dylan. Where is Dylan?"

Faf shook his head. "I found only you."

The girl screamed again.

13
DIAMONDS AND LEATHER

Cassie rapped three times on the door. When it opened, she brushed past Stephen, the moustachioed pharmacist, and made a beeline for the back office. Physician Corbin sat next to a cot where Yerty was sleeping.

"How is she?" Cassie asked. "Any change?"

"The child is suffering from hysteria, and as a result her mind has frozen. I've given her a mixture of valerian and lavender, but her sleep is fitful at best."

"I'm sorry for bringing her here, but I didn't know what else to do."

Corbin waved Cassie away. "We do what we can."

"I'm going out to look for her brother."

"I would not advise that, Cassie."

"Dylan has no one else. I'm meant to ... protect him. He's my responsibility."

Corbin scratched at his double chin. "I feel that the streets are not safe, for either the children or you."

"I'll not go unarmed."

"Armed or not, it would be foolish to go out alone, especially to the dark places."

"I am familiar with the dark places," Cassie murmured.

"So was she and her brother, apparently." The physician nodded towards Yerty. "It did not help them. I urge you to reconsider."

Cassie shook her head. "I must try. I can't just abandon the boy when he needs me."

"Very well. If you are set on this, my lad Stephen shall accompany you."

For a moment, Cassie considered rejecting the offer, but she was tired and scared and the company would make the search faster and safer. "Alright. Thank you, Master Corbin."

———

Cassie and Stephen found no sign of Dylan, not in the streets and alleyways, nor in any of the safe houses in which he might hide. It was a long and exhausting night. She was grateful for the company of the moustachioed pharmacist, though they spoke very little.

When she returned to her bedsit in the late morning, she lay down and stared at the ceiling. Horror settled in Cassie's stomach. Yerty had been frantic when she'd come the night before, her face scratched and bruised, her normally clean white tunic covered in blood and filth. Cassie had attempted to calm her, to make some sense of the story that Yerty, through her sobs and shrieks, had tried to relate.

Cassie wanted to throw up. She had feared this. These children lived in great peril: every night, they stole and ran the rooftops. It was only a matter of time before one of them got hurt. But not this. A fall, perhaps, a beating from an irate mark, but not this.

Not this.

A large, bearded man patted Cassie down and did not spare her modesty as his hands lingered over her buttocks and inner thighs.

Satisfied that she carried no weapon, the bearded man slyly winked and stood back, allowing her to approach a circular table around which several men drank wine and smoked scented hashish. The open window allowed a quiet night breeze to play among the smoke. At Cassie's approach, several men stared at her, none of their glances friendly.

The man shuffling the deck of cards said, "Deal you in?" He was in his forties, beginning to soften around the middle, and had a scar running down his forehead from hairline to the bridge of his nose. If you didn't know better, you would think it was merely a deep-set worry line. Cassie knew better.

She shook her head. "I don't gamble, Carl."

Carl Braithwaite snorted forcefully. "Yeah, no. You only gamble with your life. What the fuck are you doing here, Cassie?"

"You going to leave a lady standing? Manners, Carl."

Carl waved his hand at the bouncer. "Chair for the *lady*." The big man obliged and took the opportunity to leer in Cassie's face as he placed the chair at the table.

Cassie squeezed in between two men she recognized: one was the owner of a local tannery, the other a fabric merchant. Both men wore halos of pungent vanilla hashish. The fabric merchant stood and left the table, muttering the word *"bitch"* under his breath.

Carl smiled and dealt the cards. "Making friends again, Cassie? I appreciate you using the door, by the way. You nearly gave me a heart attack the last time you appeared at my window."

"You know what it's like, Carl. Old habits. I want you to organize the militia."

Carl stopped dealing and looked around the table at the other men. "Are we under attack?"

"Dylan is gone. He was abducted last night."

"*Dylan.* One of the twins, yes?"

"Yes. We must do something. He's been missing a day, and I don't know who else to approach for help. He is an innocent child."

Carl sat back and sneered. "I don't wish to argue over your choice of words, Cassie, but there's not an honest businessman in Re'Shan that hasn't suffered at the hands of your charges. Thieves are not *innocent*." Several men around the table nodded in accord.

Cassie bristled. "I don't wish to argue over *your* choice of words, Carl, but there's not an *honest* businessman at this table. Are you insinuating that Dylan deserves to be abducted and murdered?"

Carl spread his hands in a defensive gesture and raised his eyebrows. "No one has said anything of murder. Calm down before I have you thrown out of here. I can't call the men to arms for one missing child, a thief no less."

Cassie reached out and rolled something across the table. The object attracted every pair of eyes in the room as it came to a halt under Carl's hand. He picked it up between thumb and index finger and examined it. Pursing his lips, he reached within a tunic pocket and brought out a small magnifier with which he inspected the opal more closely, turning it against the lamplight.

Carl nodded appreciatively. "Mosaic pattern, a very rare purple. Extraordinary. Now this, *this* is why we put up with you and your scallywags. For this very reason."

"Make your best offer."

"This is worth twelve gold pieces in the right market. Calculating my cut, I'll give you six and you won't get a better offer anywhere else."

"Keep it. Call out the militia."

The jeweller sighed. "I can't do that. Archbishop Courtenay has taken up residence for God knows how long. He's here to oversee the construction of a grand new cathedral, drumming up new recruits for God. Imagine his surprise when he sees a military force turning the city upside down. Questions will be asked, questions that will lead back to me, and you. No, out of the question. However"—he held up the opal—"this will buy you half a dozen men for a week. They shall discreetly scour the streets for your missing urchin, but *not* under the colours of the militia. That's the best I can do."

Cassie nodded. "Agreed. Get them out there now."

"Do you have more of these?" Carl asked.

Cassie shook her head impatiently. "No. The men, Carl. Have the men begin the search immediately."

Carl ignored her and gazed at the opal. "A shame. This is truly beautiful. I would not be so idiotic as to ask where you … found it, but I'm tempted." Carl looked at Cassie, who shook her head. "Ah, well."

"Why do you not simply ask the City Guard to help you?"

Cassie turned to the man who had spoken. The tannery owner had a look of contempt on his stubbled face. A hashish cigarette hung from his mouth under a large flat nose. The man went on, "Or maybe you've fallen out of favour with the law and would be arrested on sight, hardly surprising since you and your filthy little rats shit on said law every single day."

Cassie snarled, "Do not speak of my children."

But Ivan the Tanner would not be silenced. He chewed on the cigarette and between clenched teeth said, "Perhaps if

Mother didn't teach her children to steal, the boy wouldn't have met his fate."

Carl's forehead scar deepened as he frowned. "Ivan, leave it."

Ivan blew hashish smoke into Cassie's face and sneered. He stared at her cleft lip. "I say we kill her and throw her in the sewers with the other ugly filth and scum, where she belongs."

Cassie's hand moved and an instant later a blade pressed against Ivan's windpipe. "Say that again." Ivan's cigarette fell from his mouth as he held his breath.

Carl scowled and looked at his bouncer accusingly. The big man's mouth was hanging open. "Cassie," Carl said evenly. "This is not how we conduct business. I'll get the men out on the streets at once. Take the knife away from Ivan's throat."

Cassie didn't move and continued to stare unblinkingly into the tanner's bloodshot eyes. The man made an attempt to draw his head away from the blade, but she kept it gently caressing the skin of his throat.

"Cassie," the jeweller said. "You'll need to tell me what we're dealing with. Who took Dylan?"

"A raven."

"What?"

"Yerty said it was a raven. Or a crow. A big black bird."

"I know what a raven is, but ... do we even get ravens near the desert? Please, the knife."

Cassie whispered to Ivan, "You wouldn't be so nonchalant if your own child was taken." She removed the blade from the tanner's throat. Ivan rubbed gingerly at his Adam's apple. Cassie stood and approached the window, keeping the blade poised and the bouncer in her line of sight as she did so. "A man in a black feathered robe. Yerty insisted that he looked like a raven, that he scratched her and made sounds like a bird."

Carl blinked. "Alright. I'll tell the men to get on the streets and keep an eye out for this ... raven."

"Promise me. Promise me that the search will be carried out with intent."

Carl touched the gouge on his forehead. "From one scarred soul to another, I give you my word." Cassie perched on the sill of the open window and Carl said, "Cassie, unless you come up with more of these"—he held up the opal again—"don't come back here anytime soon."

Cassie pointed her blade towards Ivan the Tanner and then silently drew it across her own throat.

Then she dropped out of sight.

14
DESCENT INTO MADNESS

Julian and Martin arrived at the lower station elevator late in the afternoon on an overcast day, their mule heavily laden with supplies from the city below. The grey, muddy skies gave vent to a gentle rain, barely noticeable under one's habit.

Lay Brother Jacob was waiting for them at the entrance of the cave, a concerned look on his face. "Have you seen Larson?" the big man asked. "He disappeared from the station last night. No one has laid eyes on him since vespers. We think perhaps he has travelled down the mountainside. About this tall." Jacob put his hand out at the level of his nose, marking out the vanished lay brother as a large fellow in his own right. "A mole upon his nose."

Julian and Martin exchanged glances. "No, we haven't seen him," Martin replied.

"It doesn't make any sense." Jacob shook his head in confusion. "He's a steady man. I wouldn't have picked him for just up and leaving."

"Can you still operate the elevator without him?" Martin asked.

"Yes, yes, of course. We have enough hands. I'm just concerned for him, that's all."

"What do you think could have happened to him?" Julian said.

"I don't know. But ..." The big man trailed off.

"What?" Julian prompted.

Lay Brother Jacob looked to the cave mouth and the cliffs looming over it. "I'm a bad sleeper. When I cannot rest, I lie awake thinking of past follies, as a man does. I know every sound up here on the mountain, each bird call, the sounds of the mule as she eats and sleeps and even breathes, the way the wind plays in the juniper trees. It's all second nature to me now after all these years. But ... I swear I've been hearing strange things, calls of animals I do not recognize. Even the wind has changed the way she plays across the cliff walls." Julian and Martin stared silently. "I realize that doesn't make sense. Anyway, you'd best be getting up before dark. Larson will return. I have faith."

———

Klaus did not greet Julian and Martin upon their return to the community high on Mount Ulfur. It was an odd experience not to receive the German's hugs and beaming smile as they walked into the compound. Klaus would always run down from the workshop where he and Lawrence and Kristoff shaped the sky-metal, somehow always knowing when Julian and Martin would arrive. But not this time.

Martin must also have felt his absence. "Where is Klaus?" He rubbed at his bald pate. "You know, he still smells of the goats." Martin laughed and added more seriously, "And something else. A new scent."

Julian thought of the missing Lay Brother Larson, and a

dread began to settle on his heart. Could there be two missing men on the mountain?

The sound of snorting and clattering drew Julian's attention to the far end of the grange. A pig was running towards them, pursued by two lay brothers. One of the men managed to tackle it to the ground and the other bound the feet of the animal with twine so that it could no longer flee. Julian glanced in bewilderment at Martin, who returned the look. The only animals on the mountainside were goats and hens.

The two lay brothers began to haul the squealing pig away, and one of them winked at Julian as he passed. "Abbot Howard has decided that we should supplement our diet," he said, breathing heavily with exertion but grinning, nonetheless.

The following day, quite contrary to the regular custom, the lay brothers were invited to dine with the one hundred or so ordained monks in their refectory for the evening meal, though not at the same tables. Fraternal spirit did not extend quite so far.

Klaus was there. He winked at Julian from where he sat on the other side of the dining table with Kristoff and Lawrence. The tall German had yet to explain his absence the evening before. In fact, Klaus had not returned to the lay brother dormitory before Julian had fallen into an exhausted, restless sleep. Julian supposed that Klaus had been overwhelmed by whatever tasks he had found himself occupied with and had simply been unable to get away. Besides, Klaus was not obligated in any way to be there when they arrived. Still, Julian could not help but feel a change in his friend.

Before he could think on it further, and before the food arrived, Abbot Howard cleared his throat in preparation for a speech, another exception to the normal routines of the holy brotherhood. Silence, it seemed, was no longer golden at mealtimes.

"Holy brothers and lay brothers, I welcome you," the white-robed abbot said. "Today we start a new chapter in the Order of Ulfur."

Julian was struck by how healthy Father Howard appeared. He walked without the aid of a frame or cane. His wispy grey hair had recovered some tone of youth, the grey about his tonsure now interspersed with strands of almost golden blond. Julian scanned the room and found Prior Blackwing, draped in black in contrast to the abbot's white. He, too, was a new man. The superior's face had lost its angry red rash, and he seemed less stern and threatening because of it. His complexion was almost flawless, the constantly frowning disciplinarian now revealed as a handsome man in his early forties. The abbot and prior had overcome their afflictions. Klaus had even conquered his vertigo. It should have been a joyous thing, all this newfound physical and mental health, but something nagged at Julian.

The abbot continued to smile. "God gives sustenance. Prior Blackwing and I have conferred on the matter and have decided that meat shall once again be part of our dietary fare. There is no shame in partaking of the flesh if it is with His blessing." With a wave of his hand, the abbot signalled for the platters of food to be brought forth and along with the standard leek and onion soup, goat's cheese, and bread came boards of sliced meat, the pig from the previous day most likely. "Sup in the bounties provided by our Lord," the abbot said. And then the meal began in earnest.

To Julian's horror, the pork was undercooked, bloody, and too pink. No one seemed to notice, except Martin who screwed his nose up at the meat and didn't take any, settling for the soup, bread, and goat's cheese.

Klaus bit into the pork and his grin now displayed teeth laced with blood as he nudged Lawrence with his elbow. All around the room, lay brother and choir monk alike bit into practically raw flesh.

The skin at Julian's neck began to crawl.

—————

It wasn't just the abbot and prior who had recovered their health. Julian, also, had healed well from the injuries he sustained in the collapse of the Grand Chapel some three months before. The scar on his head was no longer noticeable at his tonsure and he no longer suffered aches or dizzy spells. His frame had filled out once more. In fact, he was heartier than ever, at least physically. But his spirit was troubled. Events on the mountainside had become increasingly strange of late, culminating in the bizarre nightly rituals of monks tearing at bloodied meat.

He climbed the path above the community, up to where the fireball had fallen, up to the scars and gullies on the mountainside where Klaus, Lawrence, and Kristoff sought its remains and fashioned the metal into trinkets that Julian and Martin now took on their weekly trips to Re'Shan below. The metal was proving popular with the jewellers in the city at the edge of the Great Southern Sands, and Julian and Martin now found themselves returning with a surplus of both produce and coin.

Klaus and his two new best friends, Lawrence and Kristoff, had disappeared after the evening meal. They could always be found together these days, and if the three of them weren't in the grange or cloister, they could be only one place: swimming in the water laced with particles of the sky-metal.

Sure enough, the sounds of splashing and laughing came to Julian as he neared the elevated gully by the blasted juniper tree. Without really knowing why, Julian crouched and approached the lip of the water-filled gully as soundlessly as possible. The Southern Cross burned brightly in the darkening sky, its brilliance outshone by the glowing particles of metal in the water below, giving a luminous blue sheen to the clear water. Klaus and Lawrence floated in the pool, naked and face to face, exchanging a passionate kiss.

"Hello, Jules." Julian whirled around and Kristoff, also naked, walked out of the darkness. "What are you doing here?"

"I ... I wanted to talk to Klaus."

Klaus and Lawrence stared up at Julian, still embracing and with smiles spreading wide on their wet faces.

"Take your clothes off, Jules," Kristoff said, eyes bright beneath thick black eyebrows. "Join us."

"No, I can't. I can't swim."

Kristoff laughed and ran his gaze up and down Julian. The young lay brother licked at his lips and grinned. Suddenly he lunged and pushed Julian backwards over the edge. Arms flailing in the air, Julian entered the warm waters with a loud splash. Julian had barely broken the surface of the water before Lawrence started tugging at his habit, trying to lift it over his head. Julian shoved him away. Klaus pushed Julian's head back under the water. Julian came up again, gasping for air. He broke free of Klaus and Lawrence and made for the edge of the pool. A loud splash came from behind him: Kristoff had plunged into the water a few feet away and began to stroke powerfully through the water towards him. Before Julian could reach solid ground, Kristoff had him by his habit and was pulling him back into the deeper water.

Julian struck out on instinct, catching Kristoff across the nose. The lay brother cried out in pain and momentarily loosened his grip on Julian's habit. Julian broke away and thrust his way through the blue water to drag himself soaking wet onto the edge of the pool. He stood, slipped on the damp earth, and got to his feet again. He turned and the three men were wading through the water towards him. Kristoff's nose was bloodied, his thick dark eyebrows drawn together in a frown.

"Come on, Julian," Lawrence said. "We won't tell anyone. We know you want this. You're beautiful. Let me show you how beautiful you are. Just let me ..."

"Stop." Julian held out his dripping hands. "I don't care what you're doing up here, but I ... I don't want any part of it."

"You don't like boys?" Lawrence asked.

"I'm a monk. Doesn't matter what I like."

Kristoff scoffed and spoke through a blocked nose. "Lay brothers, not monks, not yet. Come on. Live a little. Let me suck your codger. You'll enjoy it."

Julian could not believe what he was hearing. "What the fuck is going on with you three?"

"Language, Julian." Kristoff snorted blood from his nose and cleaned his hands in the pool. "You're a holy man, after all."

Julian looked to his old friend. "Klaus, what the hell?"

Klaus just shrugged. "It's alright. We're friends. Join us."

"I don't want this."

"You have no choice," Lawrence said, moving forwards out of the water.

Julian kicked the man's testicles. Lawrence grabbed his crotch and dropped to his knees. Julian drove his knee into Lawrence's anguished features and the lay brother collapsed back into the pool.

Klaus called out, "Stop, stop!" The tall German pulled Lawrence's head above water before the man drowned. "There's no need for violence. Nobody's making you do anything you don't want to." He patted the sputtering Lawrence on the shoulder. "Lawrence didn't mean what he said. We *are* friends. Jules, I think you've misunderstood some friendly banter. That's all."

"Friendly banter, my arse." Julian pointed to Lawrence. "If he touches me again, I'll cut his throat."

"There is no need to threaten anyone, Jules," Klaus said.

"Where did you learn to do that?" Kristoff asked.

"What?" Julian said. "Kick a man in the balls? Hardly requires fancy training."

"No. The knee, the whole thing. You can fight, Jules. I can tell."

"Then you won't fuck with me."

"Not me." Kristoff held his hands up in a gesture of nonconfrontation.

Klaus frowned. "Julian, I'm concerned for you. You're not behaving ... like yourself. What's happened to you?"

"Me? There's nothing wrong with me. *You*, Klaus. You've changed."

Klaus shook his head, drips of water flicking through the cool air. "No, it's me. I'm still Klaus. Still the same old bumbling Klaus."

"What happened to your vertigo?" Julian said accusingly.

Klaus shrugged. "I'm cured. That's all. I've become accustomed to the high places. Why do you focus on my vertigo, or lack of it? What does that signify?"

"You don't greet us upon our return anymore," Julian said.

Klaus gave a small laugh as if Julian were being overly dramatic. "I've been busy with the metalwork."

"And the fornication."

"Jules, you're being too sensitive. Please, let's not mention this to anybody. Agreed?"

Julian pointed a finger. "Don't ever touch me again. Any of you."

Klaus sighed. "I'm sorry you have reacted this way, but your message is understood." As an afterthought, he said, "Don't tell Martin about this."

Lawrence had by now got to his feet, his nose bloodied worse than Kristoff's. At the mention of Martin's name, Lawrence giggled. Klaus turned to the man and slapped him on the back of his head.

Julian stared from one man to the other, a dark thought worming around in the pit of his stomach. "You're not to touch Martin," he said.

Klaus nodded. "Of course."

"I'm serious about that. Leave Martin alone."

Klaus nodded again. Julian warily walked the path back up to the lip of the gully. He left the three men laughing in the pool and splashing each other as if nothing had happened.

———

The elevator gently oscillated in the darkness. Normally, the carriage would not move in such a fashion, and Julian's stomach began to protest the motion. Martin and he were descending on a fine morning before the sun's first rays. The descent was carried out in total darkness, as was every descent or ascent on the elevator.

"I feel sick," Martin whispered.

"Me, too. Just breathe." Then, shouting came from above, angry voices echoing down to them in the hollow places.

"Is the upper crew drunk?" Martin asked.

"I don't know. I wish I was." Julian remembered the unpleasant encounter with Klaus, Lawrence, and Kristoff in the pool the night before. He considered telling Martin but decided against it. Perhaps it had only been friendly banter. Perhaps he *had* overreacted.

"Something is wrong," Martin said.

"Don't worry. How many times have we been on this thing? Dozens. Jacob won't let anything go bad."

The next voice they heard belonged to the big man himself. He was shouting something from the lower station, but the cavernous spaces within Mount Ulfur distorted his voice so badly that neither Julian nor Martin could understand what he was saying. But they understood the tone. The big man was not happy, nor particularly calm.

Torchlight from below gave a murky pallor to the darkness. They were approaching the lower station. As the torchlights became more distinct, Julian heard something. He lifted his head. A man came hurtling out of the darkness. The falling monk hit the elevator with such force that the carriage tilted violently; shards of wood and bone spat through the air. Julian fell off the elevator into space. He recalled the moment that the Grand Chapel had collapsed under him. The weightlessness of the abyss, the slow turning. It was happening again.

Lay Brother Jacob caught him as if he were a baby thrown into the air by his father. It was a very fortunate thing that Julian had been thrown from the near side of the elevator, Lay Brother Jacob said afterwards. Anywhere else and he would have plummeted to his death. Martin was shaken but unharmed. The elevator was, mostly, intact.

Later, Julian would hear that it had been suicide. Brother Hoffner had been acting strangely for several days, they said. He had entered the upper station ranting and raving about God and the Devil, forced his way past the winch crew, and threw himself into the abyss. It was odd for a monk to commit suicide, true. Not unheard of, but odd. An isolated event. There was nothing for Julian and Martin to fear about taking the elevator again. It would be patched up by their return.

And so they continued down the mountain path as the sun began to shine. Neither man spoke of the horror they had just witnessed, neither man willing to relive the moment of sheer terror in which he thought his life had come to an end.

Julian thought of the missing Lay Brother Larson from the lower elevator crew. He thought of Klaus and the sudden disappearance of his vertigo. He thought of Lawrence and Kristoff and the way they had begun to leer at him. He thought of the transformation of Abbot Howard, his newfound health and vigour, and the clear and clean complexion of Prior Blackwing. He thought of the sickening way many of the brothers tore at the pig and lamb meat, grinning bloody grins. And now the suicide of Brother Hoffner. Something Klaus had said on their first day came back to him.

There is evil on this mountain.

Julian shivered. He was now inclined to take note of the warning.

15
THE CONFESSION

"I wish to speak to your mistress."

The ragged child looked up from where he sat cross-legged in the dirt street, his eyes milky white orbs. "My only mistress is poverty, sir," the child said. "A coin for a poor blind boy? Please, sir."

Julian bent down and placed a copper coin in the child's begging bowl, making a total of two. He whispered, "Have Cassie meet me at the Cenotaph of the Lost Soul in the east quarter before dusk. It is an apt place for our appointment."

The child said nothing, and Julian walked away. When he had gone, the child took the copper coin and touched it to his cheek, feeling the coolness of it against the warmth of the late afternoon sun on his face. "Thy will be done, brother."

———

The Cenotaph of the Lost Soul was a sandstone obelisk standing twice Julian's height. It cast a long shadow over the street where several children played jump rope. Julian took a swig from a leather pouch and closed his eyes against the last shards of a setting sun over Mount Ulfur.

Cassie sat down beside him. "Can a lady get a drink?" Julian passed the pouch to Cassie without a word. She was not wearing a hijab or abaya; rather, she wore a simple white tunic and dark brown trousers. Her face was exposed. Julian was at once taken by the beauty of her bright brown eyes and dusky complexion and set back by the disturbing sight of her curling lip. She had been born with a cleft palate, yet somehow it did not detract from the regal quality she possessed.

Cassie must have noted Julian's confusion, for she smiled in an odd fashion, perhaps pleased with his discomfort. She took a drink and grimaced. "Christ. Straight gin? Brother Vernon's"—she coughed—"finest. Or maybe not." She took another pull, handed the flask back to Julian, and fanned at her mouth. "I thought you didn't want to see me again."

"I didn't. I still don't."

"Oh." Cassie shrugged and gestured to the gin. "Aren't you supposed to be selling that to the pubs around town?"

Julian shook his head. "We took a little extra."

Cassie ran her fingers through her long fringe, brushing it back out of her eyes. "I have heard you and Lay Brother Martin are bringing something more than just gin down from the mountain."

A slow nod from the monk. "Trinkets made from the sky-metal."

Cassie frowned. "*Sky-metal?* That's the second time I've heard that expression. Is that what you people up there are calling it?"

Julian stared at the cenotaph. The sun had now begun to set, and the children packed up their rope and ran off down the street, laughing. He took another drink. "What else would we call it? It fell from the sky."

"Fair enough. Why am I here? Why are you so glum?"

"I have need of confession."

Cassie laughed. "A monk seeks *me* out for a confession? Surely, there are many upon the mountain far more qualified."

A group of six men came walking down the street towards them. Four of the men were military, wearing the blue and gold leather armour of Otago, the neighbouring province to the north. The other two figures wore long white robes. Upon spotting the group, who had now stopped at the Cenotaph of the Lost Soul, Julian placed his hands together and bowed his head as if in prayer. After exchanging a few words among themselves, the men moved on.

Cassie had noticed Julian's attempt to hide his face. She said, "Soldiers from the north accompanying two very high-ranking clerics. A diplomatic legate from Otago here to join Archbishop Courtenay. Now, why would a monk hide his face from King Lyle's men, particularly a monk who carries a weapon bearing the same king's insignia?"

"I don't carry it anymore."

"Wise. What are you hiding, lay brother?"

"You'd like more secrets to threaten me with?"

"You called me here for a confession, so confess."

Julian glanced after the receding dignitaries and their entourage. "Can we talk somewhere a little more private?"

Cassie nodded. "I have the perfect place."

———

Cassie and Julian sat on an angled rooftop facing out over the streets of Re'Shan. A cool wind swept away the heat of the day as the stars came out above and the oil lamps sprang to life one by one below.

"It's a beautiful view," Julian said. "But I'm afraid of sliding off. Why here?"

"I spent much of my youth walking the rooftops, thieving as you've probably guessed. I'm still most comfortable up here." Cassie studied the man's face in profile. He was handsome enough and he had pretty eyes, but she couldn't read anything in them. Julian was a man who remained guarded, at least from her. But perhaps that was about to change. "Isn't your friend going to note your absence?"

"Martin won't say anything. I trust him."

"Then why not confess to him?"

Julian closed his eyes and tilted back his head; his black hair, though cut short around his tonsure, gently waved in the night breeze. "Sometimes it's easier to speak to a stranger, do you not find?"

"Are we strangers?" Cassie asked.

Julian opened his eyes and looked at her quizzically. "Are we not?"

"Dylan is gone," Cassie said, surprising herself with the suddenness of the statement.

"Who is Dylan?"

"Yerty's brother."

"Who is Yerty?"

"You would know her as Gertrude."

"Oh. The green-eyed child. Her brother? What do you mean, he is *gone*?"

"Abducted."

Julian frowned. "By whom? Who would take a child?"

Cassie's tears overwhelmed her. She could not respond for a moment. She shook her head, trying to force the tears back down. "I ... I don't know."

"I'm sorry, Cassie."

"It's my fault."

Julian looked away. "You're not responsible for every street child in Re'Shan."

"But I ... I taught him how to steal, how to scam."

"I know that full well, having been on the sharp end of it, but this is the harsh reality of life on the streets. They'd be stealing anyway. Without you, I daresay many more—"

"No. Don't say it. I put him in harm's way. It's my fault." Julian reached out and patted Cassie on her knee. He seemed about to say something more but apparently thought better of it. Cassie brushed away tears and steeled herself. "If Dylan lies dead somewhere, then it's on me. It's on me."

Julian ran his eyes out over the city, his face limned in the dying rays of the sun. "Life is not so black and white," he said. "There are complexities to the decisions we make."

"It's on me." Cassie took a deep breath. "I was one of them, once. I was ten when I was adopted, taken off the streets. God, I feel drunk."

"Maybe you should stop drinking."

Cassie reached out and took the pouch of gin. She swallowed deeply and wiped her mouth, handing the flask back. "Thanks for the advice, monk. They adopted me because of this." She pointed at her mouth. "There were two of us, but they took me because of this."

Julian shook his head in confusion. "I don't understand."

"It came down to Gertrude and me, the real Gertrude, not Yerty. I'm sorry. I'm not explaining myself well."

"It's alright," Julian said softly.

The man's doe eyes shone in the moonlight and the stars began to spin. "When I was a child, my best friend was a girl of the same age, Gertrude. She was beautiful, a truly angelic child. We ran the streets together. I believe, though my adopted parents never admitted as much, that I was taken in because I was imperfect, unlike Gertrude. I was a message, you see? My adopted parents were senators trying to demonstrate the generosity of the state. I was a totem, nothing more, a totem of the scarred street child and what could be achieved with a stable family. My *rescue* was meant to erase the stigma of adoption, to encourage more families of the elite to do the same."

Julian shifted uneasily. "You sound resentful. You cannot, surely, be angry that your adopted parents took you off the streets?"

"No, I don't resent them, not for that. As an adult, I returned to the streets to help children like me, to give them some kind of life, and that's when my parents turned their backs on me. I haven't spoken to them in many years, and they refuse to see me."

"That's tragic."

"Fuck off. I'm alright. What happened to Gertrude was tragic."

"What happened to her?"

"She was molested and abused by her handlers, sold to men, sick men. She killed herself when she was twelve years old."

"Oh, Christ. I'm sorry."

Cassie raised her head to the stars. "I did not find out any of this until more than a year after the fact. What twelve-year-old suffers so badly that she chooses to take her own life?"

"I'm sorry."

"It could have been me. But fortunately, I am ugly. A pity project for my adopted parents. That was all that saved me from Gertrude's fate. I have sworn to protect the children from a similar fate."

"You're too young to be this bitter. And you're not ugly."

Cassie laughed scornfully. "What would a monk know of beauty? Aren't you supposed to forego all of that when you take up the ... whatever it is that you take up, your vows and so on?"

Cassie shook her head. "Why am I even telling you this? We're here for *your* confession. It's your turn, Julian. Who are you?"

Julian leaned over and kissed Cassie on her mouth. He smelled of soil, but it was not unpleasant. He leaned back and Cassie stared at him. She said, "Why did you do that?"

He kissed her again and she felt the softness of his mouth, and for the first time in an age was unaware of the constant tug of her cleft lip. Damn, he was a good kisser, for a monk. Were monks even allowed to do this? Shut up, Cassie, and kiss him back.

Julian leaned forwards and the weight of his body pressed her against the tiled rooftop. She felt his fingers at her hips, working their way upwards and pushing her shirt up over her breasts. His hands began to pull at her trousers, but he couldn't get them past her hips. Cassie reached for her belt, but suddenly Julian pushed himself away.

"I'm sorry," he said. "I'm sorry. This was not what …"

"No, it's fine." Cassie sat up and readjusted her tunic. "It's fine."

"I don't know what's gotten into me. Into *all of us*. I want to be a monk, I do."

Cassie tucked her tunic back into her trousers. "Well, I'm hardly stopping you. You asked to see me, remember?"

"I did, but … this was not what I had in mind."

"I wasn't holding a knife to your throat."

"Not this time."

"Excuse me?"

"Sorry. I must go. This is wrong."

"You didn't come for a confession. You wanted an easy lay. Bastard."

Julian shook his head. "No, no. That wasn't my purpose here. Something's wrong."

Cassie frowned. "With me?"

"With everything up there. There is evil on the mountain. Evil in us."

"You're not making any sense, Julian. What's wrong?"

"I have to go."

Julian scrambled into an open window and disappeared. He stepped out into the street a few moments later. Cassie watched him move down the empty street. She was disquieted by the way his habit flowed and flapped about his body as he moved quickly from lamplight to shadow and back again.

From this distance, he looked like a raven taking flight.

16

JEWELS IN THE MORGUE

Ashley knelt among a bed of spruce needles that had fallen the previous autumn. She gathered them into a pile and arranged them over her legs and torso. She completed her makeshift hiding place by dragging small branches with attached needles and cones across her face. It was an uncomfortable position, the branches scratching at her nose and cheeks, but at least now she was out of the high mountain winds, still bitter even in late summer, and more importantly her pursuer would never find her under the browning foliage. The needles still retained a sharp citrus smell, despite the fact they were dead almost a year. Ashley tried to breathe slowly and listen for the telltale cracking and popping of crisp needles underfoot, the approach of her pursuer.

After a few minutes, and unable to restrain her curiosity, Ashley lifted her head and peeked out between the branches covering her face. The sun had passed beyond the head of Mount Ulfur, and the boles of the nearby spruce and larch began to take on an indeterminate quality, each tree a menacing but motionless intruder.

Ashley's heart thumped in her chest so loud that she

thought her pursuer must be able to hear it. Her heart stopped completely when she saw a shadow flit from behind a larch tree and run off up the slope. She waited until it had gone and then sat up, puzzled. Brushing twigs from her tunic and hair, Ashley got to her feet. She kept brushing. It would not do to upset Mother by bringing half the forest into the house.

She moved in the opposite direction to where she had seen the dark figure and came to a small path through the woods. Ashley began to run when suddenly a small boy leaped out from behind a tree.

"Found you!" the boy shouted.

Ashley jumped in fright. "What? How did you get here? I just saw you over there." She pointed towards the gently rising slope.

Nathan shook his head and put his hands on his hips. "I've been here the whole time. Anyway, I found you. I win."

Ashley protested, "Hang on, I didn't … that's not fair. Let me hide again."

"Father says it's time to go. He's cut all the wood he can today. The cart's loaded and ready. Come on."

"But I saw you over there." Ashley gestured once more towards the larch tree.

"Wasn't me."

Ashley folded her arms petulantly. "Then who was it? There's no one else up here at this time of day." Nathan shrugged but Ashley went on, "Right over there behind those trees." Ashley began to walk back to where she had seen the figure.

"Hey, you're going the wrong way. Father's waiting for us. Listen."

Ashley did indeed hear her father calling their names, and she hesitated. "Just a quick look," she said.

Her brother followed and the two children ran to the larch

tree among the spruce. Ashley recognized signs of activity, the way that the needles and cones had been scattered. She was old enough now to pick up the indications. One day, she would be as good as Father at reading the mountain woods.

Nathan saw it before she did. "Over there," he said.

At first Ashley thought it was a mountain fox lying on its side. As she approached, she realized it was a sleeping child curled up on a carpet of needles. "Hello?" The figure did not move. "Hello?"

Nathan began to tug at her arm. "I'm scared. Let's go."

"Don't be scared. It's just a boy. Look, it's a boy. Hello, boy, what are you doing here?" Ashley reached out to touch the shoulder of the child. He looked like Nathan in many ways, all dark hair and pale face, at least from this angle. Ashley shook the child by his shoulder. "Hello? Wake up. You can't sleep here. It's cold in the evening, and there are foxes, sometimes they bite."

Nathan began to whine. "No, no, don't. We must get Father."

"Why? He's just—"

Ashley rolled the boy onto his back. She screamed. Nathan screamed. It took less than half a minute for their father, axe in hand, to come sprinting along the path to where the children stumbled towards him. Ashley pointed to the corpse of the young boy on the bed of spruce and larch needles.

Ashley could not get the image of the boy's face out of her mind, not then, not that night, nor ever. She would see it from time to time for the rest of her life. On the day she married, on the day she had her first child; it would come to her at the oddest moments, in the midst of the greatest happiness. The boy's face would be there without warning. The soul screaming silently out through the wide dead eyes. The mouth stretched open yet flaccid. An empty shell of eternal agony and ruptured innocence.

———

Edgar Thyme felt underappreciated. People didn't seem to understand the sacrifices a coroner had to make. He couldn't, for example, close his eyes and fall asleep without the possibility of a knock on his door startling him awake. Most people took their sleep for granted. When *they* closed their eyes, they had the soft warm assuredness that they wouldn't wake until the predetermined time. Edgar Thyme had none of that assuredness. The only sure thing he knew was death.

And death kept irregular hours.

"Strangulation, you say?" The young clerk from births, deaths, and marriages held the parchment at such an angle that it would best pick up the light from the torches, but the only thing the torchlight picked up was his long hair flailing about as the wind whistled through the dark trees.

Edgar Thyme shook his head. "No. I said asphyxiation. Quite clearly a different thing. There are no marks around the boy's throat, pay attention. No ligature marks anywhere on the body, in fact."

"How do you spell *asphyxiation*?"

"I don't know. You're the clerk." Edgar Thyme looked around at the ominous shadows among the trees, and shivered, not just from the cold. "How far up this bloody mountain are we?"

The clerk looked around and stuck his tongue out as if he could ascertain altitude by tasting the wind. "A thousand feet, coroner."

"A thousand bloody feet at God knows what time of the morning."

"It's three o'clock in the morning, or thereabouts."

"Jesus Christ, it's freezing up here. Why couldn't the boy have been murdered in the city?" The clerk paused in his writing and glanced sharply at Edgar Thyme, who cleared his throat sheepishly. "Uh, that's not what I meant. It's just that I'm not as young as I used to be, and I've climbed half the night. Of course, we don't want murder at all. Not at all. Murder is bad." The clerk nodded and resumed taking down his notes. "Alright," the coroner said, "get the body on the cart. Let's get him down to the mortuary." Two men standing by rolled the child's body onto a sackcloth.

———

Carl Braithwaite rubbed a forefinger down the vertical scar on his forehead. The groove had been carved into his face long ago by a man who died shortly after making it. Carl did not remember much of the man who cut him. The only thing Carl remembered was that the man was big, moved fast, and was intent on killing him in a dark alley. Carl was only seventeen at the time, out with a friend and both drunk and overconfident, thinking company meant safety. It was a harsh lesson in human nature that he almost did not survive. His best friend certainly hadn't. But survive Carl had, and now his instincts were sharpened like the polished and glinting diamonds he dealt with almost every day. No one would get the jump on Carl Braithwaite the Jeweller ever again.

The body under the grubby sheet set Carl's nerves on edge. He was reminded that it could have been him all those years ago: dead meat on a coroner's table. The body was that of a child, by the size of it, just lying there on the cooling board under the harsh light of an oil lamp hanging too low from the ceiling. He'd seen plenty of dead men in his life, but a dead child was something altogether different. Carl shuddered. He did not want to be here.

"A boy, approximately nine years of age," Edgar Thyme said. "A woodcutter's children stumbled upon the corpse at sundown yesterday."

Other than a first quick glance, Carl steadfastly refused to gaze upon the body under the sheet. "Why am I here, Edgar? I have no children to identify."

"I know that, Carl."

The jeweller's curiosity got the better of him. "What happened to the boy?"

"Murder happened to him. That's what. The child was starved of air, perhaps his lungs compressed by a heavier weight from above."

"He was smothered?"

"Yes, by a much larger and more powerful person. No one has come to claim the boy. Perhaps you could take a quick look?"

"No, no, I told you. I am no father. I don't know any children." *Not strictly true, Carl.* "No. No. I can't help you." Carl could think of nothing worse than gazing upon the face of a dead child. At that moment a crying woman and a man holding her by the arm, his face as ashen as hers, came to the door and stood staring with wide eyes.

"Just a moment." The coroner gestured for the terrified couple to come forwards and, as they took halting steps to the table, Edgar drew back the sheet.

Carl averted his eyes. The woman screamed and the tears came streaming from her, but not tears of sadness; rather tears of joy, or at least hope.

The child did not belong to her.

The couple left the room with more gusto than they had entered, and Edgar closed the door behind them. "Good fortune for one bodes ill for another." He turned back to the jeweller. "I asked you here for a reason quite unrelated to the death of the child."

"Could we discuss business elsewhere, for God's sake?"

The coroner shifted his weight, slightly embarrassed. "Perhaps not entirely unrelated. I found this inserted in the boy's nostril. It was placed there forcibly, so much so that it was lodged in the boy's sinus."

The coroner handed over a small object and placed it in Carl's palm. It was an opal. Carl got out his magnifier and examined it. The opal was a beautiful piece, a rare colour and pattern: an entrancing purple mosaic, exactly like the one Cassie had given him as payment to search for her boy, Dylan.

Carl's blood came to a sluggish halt in his veins.

Edgar Thyme smiled and winked. "I was hoping that you and I could come to an arrangement regarding this item. You can broker a deal with your buyers and—"

"Remove the sheet from the child's face."

The coroner stopped, puzzled. "What?"

"Remove it."

"But I thought you said—"

"Remove it. I need to see him."

Edgar Thyme stuck out his bottom lip. "Very well."

"Has the boy been ... interfered with?"

"If you're referring to a sexual motive for the attack, I see no evidence of such." Carl did not move. The coroner looked at him expectantly from the side of the corpse. "Well? Are you coming over to see the child, or aren't you?"

Carl swallowed and reluctantly joined the coroner. Edgar Thyme pulled the sheet back from the child's face. Carl shook his head and whispered, "Fuck. This is trouble."

———

Cassie stared at the opal sitting in a porcelain dish on the card table.

"Why are you showing me this?" she said. "Are you giving it back to me? Have you found Dylan? Please, tell me you've found him."

Carl frowned, increasing the depth of the scar on his forehead. "I'm not giving it back to you. This"—he gestured to the object in the dish—"is a different opal."

"But it's identical to the one I gave you."

"You're right. It is, or very close. This one was found on the corpse of a child on the mountainside last night."

Cassie gasped. "Oh, God. Dylan? Was it Dylan?" Cassie pushed herself off the chair and sank to her knees. "Oh no, no, no. Please, no."

Cassie put her head in her hands, and Carl let her moan for a time before he said, "It's not Dylan."

Cassie looked up, her eyes wet with tears. She began breathing again, short sharp puffs. "You bastard. You let me think it was Dylan. You bastard."

"Get off your knees and back into your chair, Cassie. It wasn't Dylan, but you may well wish it was."

Cassie screwed her face into a snarl, her cleft lip only adding to the savagery of her expression. "What are you saying?"

Carl traced the groove in his forehead with his index finger. "The boy is Jake Levin, Ivan Levin's son. Ivan the Tanner."

Cassie slumped into her chair. "What? That's ... but that ..."

"That's a relief? Is that what you're attempting to say?"

Cassie shook her head. "No, no, of course not."

"Ivan is at the morgue now. He's upset. Murderous, even. Did you kill Jake Levin?"

Cassie gasped and her snarl returned. "I would never hurt a child!"

The jeweller nodded. "I don't believe you would, but you realize that Ivan will blame you."

"What?" Cassie lost some of her anger. "Why would he blame me?"

"Think back to the last time you saw Ivan. As I recall, you threatened the tanner with a knife, in this very room."

"What does that have to do with anything? I threaten lots of people with a knife."

"Grief," Carl said. "Grief has everything to do with it. Grief over the loss of a child. Let me explain. Firstly, you come pleading to me on behalf of a disappeared child, Dylan, and then you threaten to cut Ivan's throat due to his lack of sympathy. Finally, Ivan's own child is found dead with an opal in his nose, an opal of the exact same kind that you gave me in plain sight of every man in that room, including Ivan. It looks like payback to me. What was it you said to Ivan?" Carl scratched at his scar. "I recall now. *You wouldn't be so nonchalant if it was your child.* I heard it. We all heard it."

"Shit. But ... no, no. Wait. Wait a minute."

"What is going on, Cassie?"

Cassie shook her head. "I don't understand."

"I haven't shown Ivan this yet." Carl picked up the opal and closed his fingers around it. "Despite your obstinacy and the fact that you train children to steal from me and the other guild members, I like you. I do. God forgive me. But if I reveal this opal to Ivan, you're a dead woman, daughter of a senator or no. Do you understand me?"

"I can't think clearly."

"You'd better. I want answers."

"You think I don't? I'm as confused by all this as you are."

Carl pointed at Cassie. "Ignorance, true or feigned, is no longer good enough. I'm going to speak frankly, and you'll hold your tongue while I do so. Your ragamuffin child Dylan is most likely dead. That's a shame. But the true tragedy is the death of a hardworking tanner's son." Cassie made to object, but Carl cut her off. "Silence. I haven't finished. Death befalls those of … less robust economic means, on a common basis. However, a guild member's child abducted and murdered is a different thing. It's a different thing. *This* death matters. *This* does not happen to upstanding members of our community." Cassie opened her mouth to protest again. "Shut up, Cassie!" Carl stood and approached the window. He put his hands behind his back and said, "If the same man took Dylan and Jake, then he does not discriminate in his choice of victim, and that is a concern. You're going to tell me where you got the previous opal. You will tell me, or I will hand this one"—he held up his fist—"to Ivan. The guilds look after their own. Ivan has many friends. You will be punished, and the children you currently manage will find themselves without a mistress. Then, who is to say what will happen to them, that this monster out there will not take them all one by one?"

Cassie swallowed hard. "Are you threatening the children? You bastard."

"I'll ask you once more. Where did you get the opal?"

Cassie muttered under her breath, "But it couldn't be."

"What? It couldn't be what? Speak up. Think of the children."

Cassie pointed slowly towards Mount Ulfur. "I got it from a monk, one of the Ulfur Monks. A lay brother, in fact."

Carl peered out of the window. He said nothing for a few moments before nodding vigorously to himself. "You wanted the militia to take action. Well, I think it's time we dusted off our swords and headed up that mountain. You're coming with us. We're going to find that monk, or lay brother. Do you have a name?"

"You prick. You wouldn't help me when it was Dylan, but

for one of the city elites, one of your wealthy friends, you'll engage all your resources."

Carl turned from the window and held the opal up. "The name?"

Cassie hesitated. Finally, she said, "Julian. Lay Brother Julian."

The jeweller cocked his head in surprise. "I know the man. I have bought certain items from him, items made of an unusual metal."

"The sky-metal," Cassie said.

"I believe that's what they're calling it, yes."

"You don't need to go up the mountain. Lay Brother Julian will be down in a few days, on his weekly errands."

"We can't wait a few days. I thought you wanted your boy back as soon as possible."

"I thought you said he was dead."

"Most likely, but his body isn't anywhere in Re'Shan, of that my men have made sure. If he's anywhere, Dylan is up that mountain. Alive or dead."

"How can you be so sure he's up there?"

"Ivan's son was found on the mountain, a place he never frequented. He was taken from the streets of Re'Shan, just as Dylan was. My instincts tell me that we will find our answers on the mountain."

Cassie got to her feet. "My instincts agree with yours."

"Well, at least we can find common ground on that. Do you have any loyalty to this Julian fellow?"

Cassie blinked far more than she needed to. She shook her head. "No."

"Good. Because this could get very political. If we're wrong ... well, it won't do to falsely accuse a monastery of monks. But I see no other way. It is time for martial law, regardless of whose toes we step upon."

Cassie made for the door. "When?"

"At daybreak. You will find us along the avenue of silver birch trees outside the main city gate at dawn."

"I'll be there."

"You'd better be." Carl scowled. "Something unpleasant is lurking up that mountain, and we're going to discover what it is."

17
QUITTING TIME

"Aren't you tired of onion and leek soup?"

Martin looked up from his steaming bowl and arched an eyebrow at Julian. "No. I like it." Despite the chill of the evening outside, Martin's bald pate was coated with a sheen of sweat, partly due to the excessively hot soup and partly because of the body heat generated by two dozen hungry men huddled together at the dining table in the lay brothers' refectory. "It's nourishing and doesn't taste so bad."

Julian sighed and with no appetite dipped his bread into his broth. "I wish that just once we'd get a different soup."

Martin blew on his spoon. "The cook is set in his ways. Besides, he has little to work with. We grow onions, leeks, and very few other vegetables up here. It's a shame that the cabbages didn't take. Perhaps it's just too cold." Martin indicated a plate with cuts of pork. "Have some meat."

Julian grimaced. "It's always raw. Have you noticed?"

Martin nodded. "I've noticed. I don't touch the stuff myself. It's odd that the abbot decided to introduce meat into our diet."

Sensing an opportunity to broach a delicate subject, Julian

leaned forwards. "Since you've mentioned it, there are a lot of odd things happening of late."

"What do you mean?"

"Well, for one, we're allowed to talk at mealtimes. What happened to our vows of silence?"

Martin shrugged. "We're trying to be a little more progressive, as far as I can tell."

"Progressive? Eating bloodied animal flesh is not progressive. It's barbaric. They could at least cook it. And it's only the ordained monks that eat it, have you noticed?"

Martin stared. "Is it?"

"Yes. Few lay brothers touch it. And surely, you've noticed the other strange goings on."

"What strange goings on?"

Julian spread his hands as if to suggest the answer were obvious. "Consider the disappearance of Lay Brother Larson from the lower elevator station. Where did the man go? Jacob is certain he didn't leave of his own volition."

"The mountain is a dangerous place," Martin said. "He could have fallen in the darkness, his body lost or lodged in a crevice somewhere."

"And what about the abbot? Have you noticed he's getting *younger*? There's something unsettling about that, and Prior Blackwing no longer has a rash about his face."

Martin looked confused. The wind howled at the windows of the refectory and the bald lay brother spoke above the noise. "As far as the abbot's health is concerned, should we not be joyous at his miraculous recovery?"

"Miraculous alright. It's bizarre. And we haven't even spoken of Brother Hoffner's suicide. No one has. It's like the man never jumped from the upper station, as if he never existed. Martin, I think we should leave."

Martin almost choked on his soup. He sat back and frowned. "Leave?"

Julian put his finger to his lips and leaned in. Quietly, he said, "Yes, I think we need to get the hell out of here. This is not how I imagined the life of a monk. It's not ... it's not right."

"I can't leave." Martin shook his head slowly. "My father would be broken-hearted. I haven't spoken to him for some time, but I know he was extremely proud of me for choosing this path. I can't just walk away when things get a little tough."

"Listen, I'm not saying we abandon the monastic life. We just take it up somewhere else."

"Where? Where is somewhere else?"

"Anywhere but here," Julian whispered urgently.

"Are things so bad?"

Julian sighed. "Klaus ... Klaus has changed."

Martin looked around the lay brothers' refectory. Klaus, Lawrence, and Kristoff were, as usual, absent. "People change, Julian. I also feel he is no longer the man we knew. He has new friends, that's all. It's natural to feel a little upset, hurt even."

"I'm not hurt. I'm greatly disturbed by his behaviour. He, Lawrence, and Kristoff ... they ..."

"They what?" Martin prompted.

Julian considered telling his friend of the incident in the pool, of the unwanted sexual advances of the three men, but decided against it for fear of truly upsetting Martin. Besides, he understood that the tale would be difficult to digest, much like the onion and leek soup. "He's changed," Julian said finally, "and not in a good way. I think we should leave."

"You're being oversensitive, Julian. I know things have been a little strange, but after the destruction of the Grand Chapel, we lost so much. I think it'll take time for the ship to find an even keel, to use a maritime expression."

Julian was not convinced. Still, if Martin was intent on staying, he would stay. He could not abandon his closest friend and the man who had saved his life.

The heat of the room began to make Julian drowsy. Perhaps Martin was right, perhaps he was simply overreacting. Perhaps all he needed was a good night's sleep and everything would look better in the morning. Julian stood and the room whirled around him. He staggered and reached out, steadying himself on the table. Martin frowned and got to his feet but immediately fell backwards to the floor.

The last thing Julian remembered was blurred figures rushing into the refectory, tackling him and the other lay brothers to the ground.

———

Julian dreamt of fire. He stood before a burning mound of small wooden figures, children's toys with painted faces and hair. The paint curled and crackled as the flames licked at the tiny wooden bodies. The screams of women and children came from somewhere behind him, and Julian turned.

Abbot Howard stood there. He was young, Julian's age. He had a cleft palate and bright brown eyes. The abbot smiled and said, "Atonement, young man, redemption, now *that* is worth something."

Julian gasped and opened his eyes. He sat up in the darkness, disoriented. His stomach rose to his throat. Lying back down, he turned on his side and vomited.

"Gently, young fellow," came a voice in the darkness. "You mustn't rush the process."

Julian recognized the voice. Wiping bile from his chin, Julian struggled to sit once more. He could see nothing, or was there a hint of colour somewhere in the thick blackness? He tried to speak but his voice issued in a dusty croak. "Brother Vernon?"

"Yes. It is I," the old monk said. "Rest, Julian. You must rest and then your eyes will open, and you will see the true glory of God. Your sleep was troubled, your dreams pungent."

Pungent? What was the old man talking about? Julian took several deep breaths and tried to quell the next wave of nausea.

"You are the first of the lay brothers to awaken," Brother Vernon said. "You are a remarkably strong young man. Prior Blackwing assured us that you would all sleep for twice the length of time, and yet here you are. I should not be surprised. After all, you showed remarkable resilience to survive the chapel's initial collapse. You have an immense will to live."

It was difficult to make sense of Vernon's utterings, or to understand where he was and what was happening. "Have I suffered another injury? Am I in the infirmary once more?"

"No, no," Vernon replied. "No injury. The soup contained a sedative, a sleeping powder."

Julian paused, unable to comprehend the answer just given to him. "A sedative? Why? Where am I?"

"Slow down, lad. All in good time."

"I cannot see anything."

A candle appeared in Vernon's wizened hands, the wick glowing brighter. The old man was sitting outside a small stone cell, and Julian realized that he had been asleep inside the cell.

"Is that better?" Vernon asked.

The coolness of metal chilled Julian's chest. He withdrew an object from under his habit: a sky-metal crucifix pulsing different colours. Without knowing why, Julian removed the crucifix and sent it clattering to the cold stone floor several yards away.

"Don't do that, lad," Brother Vernon said. "You mustn't do that. The metal is healing you, don't you see?"

"No, I do not see. Where are we?"

"Stay calm. In time you will adjust to the dark places. In time it shall become a part of you. This is a process you all must undergo."

"All of us? Martin, where is Martin? Where are the others?"

Vernon gestured down the hallway. "Still sleeping. All of the lay brothers are sleeping."

"I don't understand. Why are we here?"

"I would like to talk about your dreams."

Julian frowned. "What of them?"

"I saw what seemed to be children's toys burning on a funeral pyre. I heard the screams of women and children."

Julian gasped. "How could you know this? Did I speak of it as I slept?"

Vernon leaned in and winked. "I *saw* it. It is my gift, you see, to know the dreams and thoughts of others. Your past is troubled."

Julian's head throbbed. He rubbed at the temple where the scar remained from his fall several months before. "Brother Vernon, I cannot understand anything of what is happening."

"Patience." Brother Vernon collected the crucifix from the cell floor and handed it to Julian. "Put this on and breathe." Julian shook his head and Vernon sighed. "I admire your will, but not your willfulness. We all must wear the holy cross. Put it on."

Julian shook his head again. Something in the old monk's insistence that he wear the sky-metal crucifix made him uneasy. No, not uneasy. True dread began to tickle at his heart. "Am I a prisoner?" he asked.

"Only in so far as we are all prisoners of God."

"What does that mean?"

"Put the crucifix around your neck, young man."

"Enough. I want to speak to Martin." Julian stood and the

cell around him swung back and forwards. He reached out to lean against the cold cell wall until the dizziness passed.

"Steady. Martin is sleeping." Brother Vernon waggled a finger. "To wake him prematurely would be harmful. You don't want to do that. Do not interfere with the process."

"What process?"

Vernon did not answer but simply glanced at the sky-metal crucifix hanging from his wrinkled fist. Julian stepped outside the cell. Brother Vernon placed a hand on Julian's wrist. The old man's grip was surprisingly powerful.

Vernon leaned in close, his eyes twinkling in the candle-light. "It is not permitted. You must understand that I cannot allow you to disturb them before they emerge, enlightened, from their cocoons."

Something in the term *cocoon* horrified Julian. He made to break Vernon's grip, but the old man resisted and held on. Pain shot up his arm. On instinct Julian headbutted Vernon, sending him sprawling backwards against the wall, blood spurting from his nose. Vernon slumped to the floor. Julian grasped the candle from the old monk's shaking hands and stepped back.

"I'm sorry," Julian said. "I did not mean to hurt you."

Vernon simply shook his head and when he spoke, his voice trembled. "It is I who am sorry, my boy. I ... do not know if we have ascended or fallen. I have doubts. Oh, I have doubts. Yes, I think it best that you run now. I'm sorry for everything. Do not think ill of us, for we are all God's children."

Julian moved away, but Vernon called him back. "Wait, Julian. Wait. Here, take this." From within his robes, the old monk produced a dagger. "I think you'll need it. Be careful, lad. Oh, I think we have erred. Forgive us. God forgive us."

Julian took the dagger and left the old monk muttering to himself. He followed the dank stone passageway until it branched in two. When he heard whispering voices up ahead, he killed the flame of the candle and flattened himself against the wall in a darkened recess. Two monks scurried right by him, their heads bowed and whispering to each other. Instinct told Julian that these men were not to be trusted, that he should avoid them. After they had passed, he took a deep breath and tiptoed on. More passageways branched off: he was in some kind of underground catacombs. There was a faint light coming from one tunnel, and for want of a better option, Julian crept towards it.

18

LIGHTER THAN AIR

"My father doesn't care about me at all."

"Why do you say this, child?" the man asked.

Carmelita tried to open her eyes, but his voice was deep and soothing, lulling her to sleep. "Because," she said drowsily, "he is always working. We never play together. Mother says he is an important man in the Senate. He does not miss me, nor does he care what happens to me." Her bed was hot, almost suffocating. She wanted to open the window and breathe the fresh air, but her legs were too heavy to carry her from the bed to the window.

"The work of the Senate is important," the man said. "The affairs of state require great dedication. The life of a civil servant is onerous, indeed."

His voice was droning and musical at the same time, sending her in and out of consciousness. "What does *onerous* mean?"

"Difficult and very demanding of one's time."

"Oh. You have a pretty voice."

"Thank you, child. Are you sleepy? Would you like to feel the breeze on your face and taste the clouds?"

"That sounds lovely. But how does one *taste the clouds*?"

"Let me show you. I'll take you higher than you have ever been, to the very top of the mountain."

"Am I dreaming? I feel I'm awake, but I cannot open my eyes."

"If it makes you feel better, then this is a dream. Come, the mountaintop awaits."

"How can I go so high? I'm heavy. I feel so heavy."

The man smiled; Carmelita heard it in his voice, the way it lifted and stretched with mirth. "Innocence, your innocence is lighter than air. Did you know that?"

"I didn't know that."

"Yes. Your innocence will lift you up and you will fly."

"But what about you? Will you come with me?"

"Oh, yes, child. I shall attend you. Do not fear what comes next. You will not fall."

Carmelita was lifted into the air by strong arms, and she caught the scent of cloying grease like that of the seabirds she had seen and touched in the market. Then, she heard the window open. "I want to see," she said sleepily. "I want to open my eyes."

"Not yet, little sister. Not yet. But soon." The cool air caressed her legs. "You are wrong about your father," the man said. "He cares. And when you are gone, he will miss you very, very much. This I promise."

"Will I be gone long, sir?"

The man did not reply. He merely stepped out into space.

19

A KILLER OF SOME REPUTE

Ivan the Tanner wanted to stab Cassie through the heart.

Cassie couldn't blame the man. The purple opal retrieved from the nasal passage of his son's corpse was, by anyone's standards, damning evidence. Carl had felt obliged to show Ivan the offending item. Ivan had jumped to a few nasty conclusions and punched Cassie in the face before Carl had managed to drag him away and force him to listen. Cassie hadn't struck back at Ivan. She'd give him this one. The death of a child does things to people.

The truth was that the tanner wanted Cassie dead even before his son had turned up cold and lifeless in the forests on Mount Ulfur. Carl, somehow, managed to make the distraught tanner understand that it was Julian they wanted, the apprentice monk who had given Cassie the identical opal, the one who regularly travelled the mountain paths near which his boy's corpse had been found. It all pointed to the lay brother up on the mountain.

Now that his rage had found a new outlet, Ivan would not listen to Cassie when she said that they were just going up to the community to talk to the man. She had been wrongly implicated by the evidence, and it was possible, then, that the young lay brother had been similarly misrepresented. Ivan was not receptive to Cassie's argument, ignored her with a cold brutality, his rage seething beneath the surface of his skin. He and Carl and a dozen men of the militia, members of various merchant guilds, had met at the foot of Mount Ulfur the next morning in a hastily arranged search party, ostensibly to look for Dylan, but more accurately a mob set on revenge for the death of Ivan's son.

Dawn spread across the desert horizon in pinks and oranges. As the group of men prepared to make the trek up Mount Ulfur, John Cartwright, a pudgy man and baker by trade, spoke in whispers of another disappearance, once again of a child, but this time the daughter of a senator, taken from her bed in the night. The Senate would assemble in an emergency meeting, and Archbishop Courtenay would be in attendance.

On the outer edge of the group, Cassie listened to the fat baker. This could not be mere coincidence. No child was safe, not the street urchins nor the sons of merchants or daughters of the elite and powerful. The gathered men exchanged nervous glances, grumbled, checked their swords and pikes, and set out for the community on the mountain. Cassie knew that none of them gave a shit about finding Dylan or the senator's daughter: this was a revenge mission, a badly organized one. Cassie still wasn't sure Julian had anything to do with the disappearances of the children or the death of Ivan's son. Still, she would go along in the slim hope that Dylan was still alive somewhere up there on Mount Ulfur.

The group climbed throughout the morning, making good speed before the true heat of the day started to burn their exposed skin. In the early afternoon, Cassie stopped to admire the view of the city from the heights of the mountain. The militia men did not wait for her and soon disappeared around a bend in the path above. She hurried to catch up. The mountain winds probed at the tender bruise under her left eye, the mark of Ivan's temporary madness.

In the forests of spruce and larch, Ivan stopped near the place his child had been found—as it had been described to him by the coroner—and clenched his fists into tight balls. He began to sob. Each man maintained a respectful silence and only began to move on when Ivan did. Cassie kept her distance from the tanner.

It was now late afternoon and the sun disappeared behind scudding grey clouds, easing the humidity not at all. Carl walked back to Cassie from the main group of men, his face sheened in sweat.

"By my estimates," he puffed, "we'll be arriving at the elevator in an hour. We must get past Jacob."

"And how do you propose to do that?" Cassie said. "You're not going to take the big man and his crew with a bunch of disorganized bakers and cobblers. And besides, who's going to operate the elevator?"

"He will have no choice but to allow us to pass. We are the official militia and martial law now applies."

Cassie grimaced. "There's nothing official about this. Only the Senate has the power to instate martial law."

"Fuck the Senate. When have they ever helped us?"

"*Us?* You include me in your ragtag bunch of merry men?"

"Come on, Cassie. You weren't always a daughter of the state. You were born on the city streets and to the streets you have returned. You threw all that luxury away by coming back to the gutters where you started. Back to us."

"I'm not one of you. Never have you offered a hand to help the children. You're as useless as the Senate."

"That's harsh, Cassie. Very harsh."

"Why are you up here with Ivan and his blustering goons? This has nothing to do with you."

Carl wiped at the sweat on his scarred forehead. "I disagree. Ivan's son was taken. Mine could be next."

"You don't have children."

The jeweller shrugged. "Somebody has to do something. Anyway, it was you who called for the militia in the first place. Or have you forgotten that?"

"I know you, Carl. You smell profit. What are you going to do? Slay the entire brotherhood under the guise of righteous retribution and confiscate their wealth? You don't have the authority to take the law into your own hands."

"Hah! You talk about the law? How ironic. You don't care a fly's arse for regulations."

"Maybe not but you're no swordsman, nor a diplomat. Things could get ugly up there."

The jeweller smirked. "Perhaps, but what have I to fear from a bunch of monks? Anyway, I'm not planning on killing anyone. As you say, we're there to talk."

Cassie touched the bruise under her eye. "Ivan is not in the mood for talking. He's eager for blood. You should have left him in Re'Shan."

Carl smiled, not pleasantly. "The only thing you ever had going for you was a pair of pretty brown eyes. With that black eye, you have no saving grace."

"Shut up, Carl. Keep your sword sheathed while we talk to Julian. We're just making enquiries."

Carl clenched his jaws together. "Why are you so concerned for this monk? Did he not abduct your precious little Dylan?"

"We don't know that."

"We don't know he didn't. Something is going on up there."

"No violence."

Dappled shadows from the trees passed over them as they

walked. "Alright, alright." Carl fanned at his face. "I'm not going to bite the hand that feeds anyway."

Cassie looked at the jeweller sideways. "What do you mean?"

"The metal. The monks have, of late, been bringing me the sky-metal. It's proving quite popular with my customers. While I'm up here I hope to look at the mother lode."

"I *knew* you had money on your mind."

"Who doesn't? That doesn't make me a killer. Besides, I've donated money to the monks myself over the years. I don't want trouble with them."

"Hoping to buy that ticket to heaven, are we, Carl? A consecrated plot bought and paid for somewhere up on the mountain?"

Carl laughed and shrugged. "Insurance, that's all. *Soul* insurance. Relax, I'm not up here to hurt anyone. I'm not a killer."

"We're all killers. It's just circumstance that opens the door."

Killers. Was there a killer on the mountain? Was Carl a killer? Was Ivan? Was Cassie, herself? And what about Jacob? She had heard the stories about the big man who kept the elevator, heard what he used to be. She wondered if the stories were true. Was Jacob an ex-mercenary who had found God and changed his ways? Perhaps he and Julian were cut from similar cloth.

They walked higher up the mountain path, through the larch and spruce and then further, past the juniper trees until they approached a large shack outside a cave mouth. This had to be the lower station for the elevator. The perfume of pine hung in the air. There appeared to be no one in the shack, the windows shuttered against both a dying sun and birthing wind. As the men prepared torches with which to enter the dark cave mouth, a voice deep and resonant echoed from within.

"Turn around and go back. You are not welcome on the mountain."

Ivan stepped forwards and spoke, spitting bitter venom at the dark gaping maw in the mountain. "My son was murdered by one who lives among you. The murderer's name is Lay Brother Julian. I will take this man back to Re'Shan where he will face justice, or I will slay him where he stands."

A tense silence ensued. Then a shadow took shape among the darkness of the cave mouth. Lay Brother Jacob lumbered out into the pine-scented air. To Ivan's credit, he did not take a backwards step though the man before him seemed made of the granite cliffs, a massive stone golem.

Jacob stared down at Ivan. Then he cast his eyes over the other men, and finally his gaze came to rest on Cassie. "You are mistaken." He whistled and four more men came out of the depths of the cave to stand behind him.

Ivan reached within his pocket and brought forth the purple opal. "I am not mistaken." His voice shook with fury and agony. "This was found on ... on my son's body. The origin of this stone is the Brotherhood of Ulfur. This is fact. This is *evidence*. I will travel to the monks above. Do not stand in my way, or I will cut you down."

Ivan drew his sword and Cassie cursed under her breath. Like dominoes falling in succession, swords hissed from scabbards and pikes were brought to bear. Jacob and his men made no move. Cassie noted Carl's hand shaking around the hilt of his weapon. His bravado was simply a disguise. Carl sensed the danger here just as much as she did.

Ivan's chin jutted into the breeze. "We have cause for a legitimate search."

The elevator keeper remained impassive. Then, Jacob said,

"Very well. An interview with the man in question. This I will allow. But I must accompany you, and I want one vote as an estimator among a total of five."

"No." Ivan shook his head vehemently. "No, you will not select the jury."

Jacob spoke low, "You may not harm a monk, or anyone in the Freelands, without trial by jury. I will listen to the evidence in full. I will cast one vote. The other four votes belong to your party. This is clearly weighted in your favour. Do you accept?"

Ivan looked around at his men and then back at the giant. "Three votes will win the day?"

"Aye, three. But one of the other votes must be hers." Jacob nodded at Cassie. Cassie's eyes grew wide as a dozen armed men and five burly monks all stared at her.

"No," Ivan said. "Not her, anyone but her. *She* doesn't get a vote."

Jacob folded his arms. "Then you do not ascend. I remind you that you select the other three estimators, and you may include yourself."

Ivan gritted his teeth before cursing loudly. He walked away and kicked at the ground. When his tantrum was over, he agreed to the conditions. Ivan put his sword away and moved forwards, but Jacob held out an enormous hand.

"Wait. Only the five estimators may take the elevator, for it will not hold any more. Everyone else stays down here." Ivan looked as if he were about to draw his sword again. Finally, he nodded. "No weapons," Jacob added.

Ivan fumed. "Absolutely not. We have the right to protect ourselves."

This time it was Jacob who hesitated and finally conceded. Ivan chose Carl and John Cartwright the Baker to join him. Cassie and Jacob completed the five-person jury. They entered the cave and followed the tunnel to the elevator. When all were aboard, Jacob nodded, and the winch crew began to grind away. The elevator groaned under their combined weight as it ascended into the darkness above.

Cassie sat down, her life in the hands of the winch team below. Within an arm's length sat Ivan the Tanner, a man who would gladly push her off the carriage and to her death if he could only see what he was doing. She didn't trust Carl and knew nothing about John the Baker. The other man on the carriage was a behemoth who had most likely taken a life or three in his time. Cassie struggled to control the panic rising in her breast. She was among a dangerous crew in a dangerous place.

But Cassie couldn't shake the feeling that something up above was going to prove much more dangerous.

20

THE CHECKUP

For two days Re'Shan had resounded to the sounds of music and laughter. On every street corner, jugglers performed, troubadours played, and jesters pranced. Acrobats tumbled and dancers twirled. Hawkers wandered the streets selling sweetmeats and dried fruits. The archbishop had decided that a festival should play out for the entire month, in his honour, of course. He would even appear in a parade, in the flesh, for the populace to gaze upon in wonder and the people had duly come in their droves.

People lined the streets waving flags, entire families waiting in the heat of the midday sun. Thousands of people all standing around just sweating and grinning, waiting for a glimpse of Courtenay, the archbishop of all the Freelands and far beyond.

Fools, every one of them, Yerty thought from where she lay in the shade of a pigeon coop three floors above the street. The archbishop was no better or worse than anyone else. He was just a man. Why all the fuss? Besides, if you wanted a glimpse of God's representative, then the rooftops provided a better view than the dusty, crowded streets, especially if you were a child of under four and a half feet like Yerty.

178

Several fathers lifted their young children up to their shoulders, allowing them to witness the twelve papal cavalrymen on proud horses with beads of grey and black tied through their manicured manes. The animals trotted in perfect unison, two abreast and six deep, three black on one side, three white on the other. Yerty had no father to lift her onto his shoulders to appreciate such a display. She dismissed the self-pity inherent in the thought and crept closer to the edge of the roof, making sure to stay low. Daylight was not the time to be seen up here, yet all eyes were on the soldiers on horseback below, so the risk was worth taking. The horses were beautiful and immaculately trained. The archbishop be damned: the horses, at least, were an impressive sight. Tears came to her eyes. She longed to stroke her own wooden horse. She longed to see Dylan again.

Yerty shook her head to clear away the tears and waited for the main act. There he was, riding into view at the end of the avenue, the man of the hour: Archbishop Courtenay. This was his parade: a celebration of his presence and the new cathedral that was being built in the city. He sat tall on the back of his horse, dressed in a purple robe and wearing a funny, pointed hat of white. Yerty had never seen an archbishop before and didn't know much about the church or God, but she knew horses and this man rode a beautiful black Friesian.

The crowd below fell into a hushed silence as Courtenay came down the avenue. When he smiled and waved, every voice rose in a roaring cheer. He seemed genuinely pleased, the smile broad across his face, though from this distance it was hard to make out his features.

Yerty had seen enough. Not for her the worshipping of false vessels. He was just a man, just a man like any other. He had a good eye for horses, though. She'd give him that.

Yerty crept down the stairwell and made the dusty streets. She walked unnoticed through the crowd and headed for

Master Corbin's medical practice. Miss Cass had insisted that she visit the physician to make sure she was healing. Yerty had complained that she was fine and didn't need a medic, but Miss Cass worried about everything. Since the night her brother had been taken by the raven-man, Yerty understood why. She, too, carried fear now, a constant weight in her chest and head. On her arms she carried red scratch marks from the same event.

She padded down the hot streets to the apothecary, but it was shuttered. Yerty frowned. Perhaps Master Corbin had closed for the day to attend the parade. That made some sense, but surely the assistant, Stephen, would be tending to business. Or perhaps Yerty did not quite understand the import of today's celebrations and the clinic was truly closed for business. She peered through the window and caught movement, though it was difficult to tell what was shuffling about inside because the dim interior contrasted sharply with the blinding sunlight outside. She knocked again, and when no answer came, she shrugged and turned to go.

Just then, the door opened, and Corbin blinked in the sunlight. "What is it, child?"

"Master Corbin. Cassie sent me."

"Yerty?" The man seemed almost half-blind, or perhaps hungover: he had that bleary squinting look about him that Yerty recognized in the morning-after drunks. "Yerty, is that you?"

"Yes, Master Corbin."

"Come in, come in, child."

When Yerty's eyes began to adjust to the gloom inside, she noted that the apothecary was a jumbled mess. Several medicines covered the counter and the floor, and many glass jars lay on their sides.

"Come to the back office," Corbin said, yawning.

The physician guided Yerty to the cot, and he pulled up a

low stool. He tilted Yerty's head back and examined her face by the light of the rear window. He checked her arm. "Your scratches are healing. I see no indication of festering."

Yerty nodded. "I told Miss Cass that I was right as rain, sir, but you know her. She insisted I come by for a checkup."

The medic smiled. "Yes, yes, I know Cassie. A very cautious woman, which is a surprise really, considering all the risks she takes with her own life and yours."

A faint odour of stale sweat and a tinge of something metallic caused Yerty to wrinkle her nose. "What do you mean? Miss Cass doesn't risk our lives."

The physician rubbed at his jowls, a week's unshaved growth peppering his jaw. "Come now, Yerty, the lives you lead are not without hazards. You prowl the streets at night, stealing. That is not a life without risk."

"We'd be doing it without her, anyway, sir. She teaches us the safe ways. Or *safer* ways, at least."

"Yes, yes. I understand the theory. Where is Cassie anyway?"

"She's gone up the mountain, Master Corbin, sir."

Corbin looked thoughtful. "Up the mountain? Why?" He moved to his desk, opened a drawer, and took out a small amulet. He returned to the stool and sat heavily. He rubbed at the amulet, almost thoughtlessly. It was a scarab beetle, made of a metal that seemed to glisten with different colours, or all colours at once.

"I cannot say, sir."

Master Corbin frowned. "Why the need for secrecy, child? I've been up there myself, you know."

"I heard about that, sir. You went up there when the meteor fell."

Corbin raised two eyebrows. "You know that word? *Meteor?*

Yes, I was up there. That's where I got this." He held out the scarab beetle. "It's an extraordinary thing, isn't it?"

Yerty gazed at it. "Extraordinary, Master Corbin."

"Made from pieces of the meteor."

"Is that right, sir?"

"Yes. I understand that the Monks of Ulfur are now producing items from the metal and bringing them to Re'Shan."

Yerty nodded. "The monks and the jewellers are making a steady profit, or so I hear."

"Yes. That's right. Is there anything you don't know, Yerty?" The girl shrugged. "Come now. Why is Cassie going up there? Is she planning to pilfer this material and sell it herself?"

"No, sir. Miss Cass doesn't steal, not personally."

"Tell me, Yerty. What is she doing up there?" Yerty did not answer. The medic's forehead began to glisten with sweat. "Why won't you tell me? I am a physician, and people in my profession often serve as ... a shoulder to lean on, an attentive ear to those in need. I cannot profess to having saved *your* life because I believe you would have pulled through without me. But the young man up there," he said, pointing to Ulfur. "I can categorically state that I saved his life."

"Lay Brother Julian."

"Yes. Well, well. You know about that, too?"

"Yes, sir."

"Does Cassie going up there have something to do with him?"

"I couldn't say, sir."

The medic rubbed harder at his scarab beetle. Then, he placed it under his nose and sniffed at it. Finally, he put it in the pocket of his white coat. Yerty noticed the man's clothes about his pocket were stained with a dark material. Master Corbin normally kept himself relatively clean, if not a little shabby, but the medic had truly let himself go; he was as ramshackle as his premises.

"If you have finished your examination," Yerty said, "I'll be going." Corbin did not answer. He stared blankly at the wall behind Yerty, so she got up and left the room. She found the front door locked.

She called out, "Master Corbin, the front door is locked." No reply. The skin at the nape of Yerty's neck began to crawl, a feeling not dissimilar to that she had experienced the night of her brother's abduction. Yerty quietly walked behind the counter and approached another door, thinking that it might provide another way out. The door was heavy, but it wasn't locked. Yerty pushed against it and entered a storeroom of pharmaceutical concoctions. The smell of all the herbs and plant extracts was overwhelming, stinging her nostrils. But beneath all of this, she smelled something else, something familiar. Above her, a small skylight gave ingress to sunlight, but the window was so small and so high that it provided only a modicum of light in the lower extremities of the narrow room. She could probably scramble up the shelves and make the skylight, but if it was also locked then she would have to climb back down again, and she might end up breaking many medicines in the attempt. She decided to rouse Corbin from his stupor and insist he open the front door. She turned around and found the door to the storeroom had swung back behind her.

The naked body of the young pharmacist, Stephen, hung impaled on the door, dried blood from his nose coating his chin and chest, his body punctured by sharp objects including knives, needles, and thin rods of metal. Corbin's ashen face appeared at the crack in the door. He smiled and said, "I ran a little experiment and—" Yerty kicked the door closed in his face and jumped frantically at the shelves.

The skylight above seemed a hundred miles away.

21

BITTER MEDICINE

Corbin burst through the door and grasped for Yerty. His fingers closed around her ankles as she scrambled up the shelves in the narrow medical depository, but she wriggled through the physician's grip and jumped to a higher shelf. Corbin began to climb after her, but he was too heavy, and the shelf collapsed. He screamed as a glass vial containing a pale yellow liquid shattered in his face, the potent herbs getting into his eyes. Yerty hauled herself onto the highest shelf and reached for the skylight embedded in the truss roof. The enraged physician began to climb the shelves on the other wall, perhaps to leap at her across the gap when he had deemed himself close enough. To Yerty's horror, the first shelf on the opposite wall held the man's considerable weight.

Yerty stood on her tiptoes. The skylight had been permanently set in a partly open position, perhaps to ventilate the storeroom. She managed to disengage the end of the locking bar but didn't have the reach to open the window fully.

Corbin was now climbing the second shelf, but it collapsed under him, and he fell back to the storeroom floor, shrieking in rage and covered in pungent herbal concoctions. Yerty was thankful the shelves had been individually attached to the storeroom wall. Had they been part of a single unit, the man below could easily have sent the whole thing toppling and her with it. Corbin continued to howl his frustration, a feral, inhuman scream. His eyes were red, and not just from the medicines that had scoured them. He had gone mad. Corbin scanned the room and pulled out a stepladder from a darkened corner.

Yerty had to get out and quickly. She felt light-headed, the acrid fumes from the medicines now threatening to overwhelm her. Had she not been near the skylight, she would already have suffocated.

Then Corbin began to laugh. This, more than his murderous rage, chilled Yerty.

When he stopped laughing, Corbin cast aside the stepladder. He inhaled deeply and the air within the medical depository cleared instantly. Yerty gaped at the man below, his chest and cheeks puffed out. He looked up at her, red eyes crinkled in a smile. Slowly, he exhaled, sending wispy tendrils of chemical vapor directly at Yerty. She had no time to process what she was witnessing. All she knew was that the man, if he could still be called a man, was trying to kill her, or send her falling unconscious into his clutches.

The frightened girl leaped for the skylight and gripped onto the sill. She hung suspended for a few seconds, holding her breath as the foul miasma engulfed her. Pulling herself upwards, Yerty used her head to force the skylight window back. She heaved herself out onto the roof and slid down the steeply angled tiles, gasping for breath.

She braced her feet against the guttering. She estimated that she was over the front door. It would not do to fall and snap an ankle at the very doorstep of the crazed physician. How had the medic been able to inhale an entire room of air? Was he the one that had taken Dylan? No, that other creature was different in aspect and scent.

No time for wasted thought. She had to focus on escape. The pharmacy was a free-standing structure; there was no way of using her favoured rooftop routes. Yerty had to get to the street, had to get to the safety of the crowd and disappear. Checking that the mad medic was not waiting below, Yerty clung to the edge of the roof and then dropped quietly to the empty street.

There were no safe houses nearby, so she decided to run back to the parade. Surely, there would still be people out enjoying the day's festivities on the avenue. Perhaps Market Square, that would be populated. Somewhere, anywhere with people. She sprinted as fast as her legs could carry her. She glanced behind and saw Corbin loping down the street after her, his bloodstained white coat flat against his bloated belly. Yerty didn't scream. That would do no good. She pumped her legs faster and hoped the man's supernatural abilities did not extend to foot speed.

Nearing the main avenue where the parade had recently passed, Yerty spotted a good-sized crowd still lining the street watching something. She didn't know what they were observing and didn't care.

"Help me!" Yerty screamed.

Not one head turned in her direction. She was still too far away. The creature must be right on her now, but she dared not break her stride to look back. Only a few more yards.

"Help me!"

This time, several people turned: a mother holding her baby, a child with curious eyes, one or two men. All looked at her with confused glances. Yerty barrelled into a large man with bushy sideburns and grasped the man's arms. She whirled around and Corbin was standing there, puffing, a gentle smile on his ashen, sweating face.

"My dear child," Corbin said. "Come back and take your medicine."

"Stay away from me!"

Corbin smiled at the people who stared at him. "I am a physician, and my young patient here doesn't like the taste of her medicine." He turned to Yerty. "It's for your own good, child. You know that. Come now. Come take your medicine." Corbin approached Yerty and held out a pudgy hand.

"No, he's not a physician. Well, he is, he was, I mean, but he killed the other one, nailed him to a door. He's a monster!" People turned away, unwilling to become involved in what they clearly thought was an errant child's tantrum and lies. Yerty tugged at the hand of the man with the bushy sideburns, but he pulled away with a frown. "Please, sir. He's going to kill me."

Suddenly, and with a sinking heart, Yerty realized that this was exactly how many of her scams had played out, exactly this way. She'd assumed the role of frightened child many times in order to pilfer the pockets of trusting townsfolk, except that this time Corbin played Olaf's part.

Her lies and deceit would now come back to put her in the grave.

Corbin grabbed Yerty by the wrist and began to drag her away. She had to reveal something or be taken forever. She had to reveal the truth. "My name is Yerty!" she screamed. "It's my real name and this is not a trick. It's real! Please! I don't want your coins!" Pain shot up Yerty's arm; Corbin's fingernails were digging into her wrist and drawing blood. Yerty kicked and fought but the medic was too strong. He began to haul her back down the street to the quiet places.

"I'm telling the truth," Yerty pleaded.

Corbin snarled under his breath: "Time to take your medicine, child. It won't hurt a bit."

"Wait a moment," said the man with the sideburns. "Let the child be."

"She must take her medicine." Corbin did not stop.

"If she doesn't want it, then that's her business," the man said. "Hey, come back." The man with the sideburns approached the struggling child and the physician as several other people gathered around.

"I am a professional healer," Corbin said, "and this girl is under my care. Stand back, sir."

For a moment, Yerty thought the man with the sideburns was going to fold under the stern frown of the beast in the medic's coat. But he held his ground. "No. Unhand the child." The man put a hand on Corbin's arm.

Corbin let go of Yerty and without warning slashed at the man's throat with nothing but his fingers. Blood sprayed like mist in the afternoon heat and a stunned silence ended abruptly with screams as the man dropped like a sack of grain from the back of a cart. Yerty ran for her life as the group around the physician backed away in horror. Many of those still watching the parade turned at the shouts and curses. Yerty ran right through them and burst out onto the sunbaked main avenue. She found herself standing among a troupe of mummers dressed in gaudy costumes and wearing animal heads. An elephant, tiger, and bear stopped their capering and stared at Yerty with human eyes.

The crowd parted and Corbin, his pudgy face twisted in a feral snarl of frightening savagery, followed Yerty into the street. The beasts of paper mâché began to back away and run just like everyone else.

22

THE GAME

Cassie was glad to leave the elevator behind. Being suspended in the clammy darkness had been among the most terrifying experiences of her life. How had Julian made a habit of such a thing?

The evening shadows began to lengthen as Jacob led the way up a manicured path of fragrant white and purple flowers. Ivan edged ahead of Jacob, as eager as ever to deal retribution for the death of his son. The fat baker, John Cartwright, brought up the rear. Cassie walked next to Carl and judging from the jeweller's constant head turning, he was as nervous as Cassie.

The path led to a series of steps which, in turn, led to a plateau containing several low wooden buildings, each of a nondescript nature. Where the path ended and the cloister began stood a tall man in a black robe, his arms folded in opposite sleeves, motionless but expectant, as if he somehow knew of their coming. He watched the arrival of the five with a haughty disdain.

"I am Prior Blackwing," the man said. "Only the ordained may enter our community. Lay Brother Jacob, what is the meaning of this intrusion? Why are you here and not manning the elevator?"

Before Jacob could answer, Ivan blundered ahead. "I am Ivan Levin and I seek the murderer of my son!"

Prior Blackwing, oddly, ignored the outburst and focused on Cassie. "Women are not allowed on monastery grounds. This is strictly forbidden."

"We are also here to look for a boy," Cassie said. "Dylan is his name. He has striking green eyes. Have you seen him?"

"I have not. I say again, women may not walk on our property."

Jacob cleared his throat. "These men and this woman invoke martial law."

"Martial law does not apply to God," Blackwing said to Jacob as if the big man was a pupil who had forgotten the most basic of lessons, "which is something that you should know, lay brother."

Ivan exploded in rage. "Did you not hear what I said, man? My son was *murdered*, and I have reason to believe his killer hides among you!"

The tall superior looked down his nose at the tanner. "Why do you think your son's murderer resides within the Brotherhood?"

"This." Ivan held out the purple opal. "*This* was found on my boy. We have reason to believe it comes from up here. This woman"—he indicated Cassie—"was given an identical stone by a Monk of Ulfur. She is here to identify the man."

The superior arched an eyebrow, and his gaze burned a hole through Cassie. He said one word, and that word was etched from ice. "Who?" But before anyone could answer, Blackwing put out a hand. "Stop, do not say it. I already know. Lay Brother Julian. You seek Lay Brother Julian."

"Yes." Ivan nodded vigorously, his retribution finally at hand. "That is the name."

"He is gone," the superior sniffed. "He ran away last night."

Silence settled upon the group, the only sounds those of the whispering winds, now beginning to grow in intensity over the cliff face. Ivan's visage changed; his bloodshot eyes narrowed in suspicion. "No, you hide him. You protect your own."

"I assure you the man is gone," Blackwing said. "Julian is a thief and was exposed as such two days ago. Caught stealing what meagre possessions the brothers share. Before he could be punished, he absconded. We must now add murder to the list of the man's crimes against God, and child murder at that. I grieve for your loss, sir."

Ivan shrieked, "I care nothing for crimes against God! He has committed an atrocity against *me* and will be gutted for it. Tell me where he is!"

Blackwing was unmoved. "The shock of your loss has seen you lose control of your tongue, but I ask you to guard it all the same. This is God's place, and His will reigns here."

Several monks had by now gathered to witness the confrontation, their faces concealed within the shadows of their cowls. The superior's black robe sheened silver-grey as the moon began to make the top of the cliffs far above. Cassie was tired. It had taken a day's hard trek to make it here and a return to the city at this hour would be impossible. At some point, regardless of the results of the search, they would have to bed down in the community of monks. Prior Blackwing, however, did not seem about to extend an invitation.

"I will hunt him down." Ivan stormed off.

"Wait a moment," Blackwing said. "We have nothing to hide. Brother Rollant, come forth." One of the monks, a small, thin man with a sharp nose and deep-set eyes, stepped forwards and pulled back his brown hood.

"Yes, Prior Blackwing?"

"Brother Rollant, as a show of good faith, escort these men ... and *woman* around our community."

The small thin man raised an eyebrow. "Even the chapel and the library, your eminence?"

"Such as they are, Brother Rollant. Meagre though they may be. Yes."

Rollant stared blankly. "Of course, Father. I will take them."

Blackwing layered on the magnanimity. "I want no stone unturned. Our innocence must be demonstrated to our guests. Am I understood?"

"Yes, Holy Father."

The tall prior pointed to Jacob with a long finger, the nail of which appeared manicured to a sharp point. "Lay Brother Jacob, you are to return to the lower station."

"No," Cassie said, startling everyone, even herself. All eyes turned to her. "He is a chosen estimator, a juror, and must remain with the group until Julian is found or his absence is confirmed."

Prior Blackwing stared at her with obvious distaste but eventually nodded. "Trial under martial law, you say? Martial law is the rule of animals. You have until midnight to complete your search and then the rule of God reigns once more."

With that he turned and stalked away, black robes flapping about his long, lean body.

———

The wooden door creaked open. Abbot Howard, dressed in his finest pure white habit trimmed with silver, did not look up from the board and the arrayed pieces.

Prior Blackwing swiftly closed the door, the draught causing the flames of the three candles illuminating the board to dance on the edge of extinction, but they flickered, recovered, and seemed to burn with more vigour than before. The man in black crossed the floor silently and took his place on the other side of the table. The tall superior examined his game pieces, stroking at his cheek absentmindedly. It had been several weeks since his rosacea had magically disappeared, a condition that had afflicted him from his early teens, yet he stroked his cheeks by force of habit. He reached out and moved a black playing piece into alignment with several others.

Abbot Howard leaned forwards and studied the eleven-by-eleven stone board and the black and white pieces arrayed thereupon. Howard's side of the board was comprised of red squares upon which his white pieces waited. "You lay siege, Blackwing," the abbot said. "But you shall not break my defences."

"We face our own siege, Father Abbot."

"Oh?" The abbot ran an idle finger through several shining stones at the side of the board. These were not pieces designed for the game but rather precious gems: opals, rubies, even sparkling diamonds.

Blackwing watched as the abbot casually raised a diamond between forefinger and thumb and pressed it to his lips. "Men from the filth pits below have arrived seeking a murderer of children."

Intent on his next move, the abbot in white did not take his eyes from the board, nor the diamond from his lips. "Is that so? Then it has begun."

"Yes. More will follow."

"What is to be done, Superior?"

"What is the only thing to do when under siege?"

Abbot Howard reached out and took one of Blackwing's pieces with his white commander. "We break the siege. We break its back."

Blackwing nodded. "We must see to our defences, your eminence."

For the first time, Abbot Howard looked into the eyes of the other man. "Agreed. When I was sick, I thought I was going to die. But look at me now. By God's Grace I am still here and more robust than ever. I do not intend to die anytime soon. Come what may, I *will* live."

"Then you must kill."

The abbot returned the diamond to the table, but something continued to glint between his lips, something sharp reflecting the candlelight. "We kill in God's name."

"In God's name."

"Tonight, Superior?"

"These visitors cannot be allowed to leave this place with the truth of what we have become. Yes, they die tonight." After a pause, Blackwing added, "There is a woman among them."

"A woman?" Howard picked up a purple opal of beautiful mosaic pattern and both men gazed at it. "We must see them all off, especially the woman. You know the rules of the abbey."

Prior Blackwing moved another piece within striking distance of the abbot's king, and then rose from his chair. "I shall see to it."

"Wait, Superior. What of our game?"

Blackwing glanced at the stone board. "They are no threat to us. We shall resume our play when they are gone."

"No, you misunderstand." The abbot smiled. "The *other* game. The game you've been playing behind our backs all this time."

Blackwing hesitated. Finally, he said, "What game?" The tall cleric sat back down at the table, his face expressionless.

Howard leaned back in his chair, eyes locked on those of the man across the board. "You wish to be master of this community. You want to be the *abbot*. You have harboured this desire for some time."

Blackwing shook his head. "You are our leader, Father Howard. I have no ambition to usurp you."

Howard chuckled softly. "Liar. For months, you were making me ill and if it hadn't been for this"—he pulled out his sky-metal crucifix—"you would have succeeded."

Blackwing spoke with an innocent air. "I have no idea what you are talking about."

The abbot's crucifix glowed a soft turquoise, morphing into a subtle cyan. "As the resident physician, Blackwing, you are comfortable handling all manner of herbs, even the baleful ones. Is that not so?"

"That is so. But my use of the herbs was only ever meant to benefit you, your eminence."

The old abbot, though of quite youthful appearance these days—his hair now pure blond around his tonsure—clucked his tongue at the superior. "Come now. We have both ascended. This subterfuge is unnecessary. You were slowly poisoning me, but I forgive all your past misdeeds, as you shall forgive mine."

Blackwing stroked the faultless complexion of his cheeks. "There can be only one leader, Father Abbot. I live to serve."

"You're quite right, Blackwing. Remember that. One leader. We work together against a common foe."

"Yes, as you say." Blackwing stood, gave the kiss of life, and left the room.

The abbot leaned forwards and stared at the board. He put another priceless jewel to his lips and tasted it. Something glinted in his mouth, and it was not the gem.

"Earthly wealth," he muttered to himself. "Earthly wealth, indeed."

23
THE SCRUTATORS

Physician Corbin's breath snorted from his nose, sending puffs of dirt and sand up from the street. The man apparently possessed a set of lungs more powerful than those of a fighting bull, and like a bull in the arena, he took a moment to lower his head and paw at the ground, preparing to leap at Yerty and tear her to pieces right there on the avenue in front of a hundred witnesses. He did not seem to care about the public nature of his intended murder. His rage and desire for blood had ripped away any surface decorum or pretence at normalcy.

Corbin did not fear any retribution. He was beyond such things.

Several men had pulled knives and short blades, but only to protect themselves or their immediate loved ones. No one seemed willing to challenge the snarling medic more animal than man. No one was prepared to step between that creature and Yerty and risk their life for a street child.

Corbin lunged and Yerty screamed.

A metal star embedded itself in Corbin's forehead and he

stumbled and blinked. Howling, he pulled the object from his head.

"Leave the child be."

A woman spoke behind Yerty. Her skin was pale and her hair pure white. She wore a flowing white shirt and the leather belt at her waist carried several more metal stars. At her hip rested a long sword, which she now slid from its sheath. Beside her stood a stocky man with wild hair and a brown beard that had been braided into three forks. His legs were placed wide apart, and he carried a long-handled axe in his two hands.

"Leave the little one," the man growled.

Corbin hesitated, and then began to inhale dust and sand from the street, the particulate matter drawn to the man's mouth in a vacuum.

"Don't let him take a breath!" Yerty shouted.

The woman hurled another metal star at Corbin, striking him in the belly. The medic exhaled in shock and blew a gritty cloud harmlessly into the air. Corbin collapsed to his knees and grasped the star protruding from his stomach. He yanked it free in a spray of blood and gasped in pain. He threw it at the original owner, but the woman simply swayed aside.

Corbin leaped at Yerty. Before the creature could grasp the child, the woman's sword came down, and Corbin's hand separated from the arm and spun through the air in a bloody arc. He screamed in agony and turned on the woman. Wild-eyed, the medic flicked the blood of his wound at her, and she stepped back to avoid becoming blinded. A moment later, a stub of bone appeared at the fleshy stump of Corbin's arm, and within seconds the bone grew until it resembled a white blade.

"Merciful Christ alive," whispered the fork-bearded man.

Corbin laughed and went for Yerty with the bone dagger, but she was already scrambling behind the legs of her two saviours. Yerty prayed that the pair could take down the thing that Corbin had become. If not, she would be ripped apart and most likely eaten. Her blood ran cold at the thought.

The creature slashed and hacked at the man and woman, but they swung sword and axe, keeping it at bay. Yerty was torn between a sickening fascination to stay and watch the fight and run while she had the chance. She took the latter option.

Yerty ran.

The shouts of the combatants and terrified screams of the onlookers diminished behind her. The sound of running feet came close by, but it was only several others escaping the scene of madness.

Yerty's throat was dry, her tongue crinkled like parchment, but she couldn't afford to stop to find water. A man tried to grab her as she ran along a street. He was an old drunk by the looks of him, his manic grin revealing several missing teeth beneath a yellow-stained beard. Yerty easily sidestepped the man as he lunged at her. The drunk's face stuck in her mind—he had the same leering, hungry look that had overcome Corbin.

Was there a slow madness overtaking the city?

She rounded a corner and stopped to take a breath. She peeked back the way she had come. All clear. Yerty leaned against a sandstone wall and slid to the dusty street. She closed her eyes and took more gulping breaths. When she opened her eyes, the white-haired woman and the man with the trident beard were standing over her.

"Who are you?" Yerty said.

"I am Martha," the woman said. She had eyes of silver, almost mercury. "This is Gregor."

"Thank you for saving me. Is the medic dead?"

Martha nodded. "It required the separation of head from shoulders to stop the man. Come with us, child."

Yerty sighed in relief, but at the same time a sadness overcame her as she remembered what Corbin had been: a physician, a good one, and a friend to Miss Cass, and the Lord knew she had few of those. "No, no. I'm ... I'm expected somewhere."

"The archbishop will want to talk to you. This is not a request you may deny."

Yerty looked from one to the other. She was too exhausted to flee. "Alright, I'll come, but can I touch his horse?"

Martha and Gregor exchanged glances. "We'll see," Martha said.

———

Archbishop Courtenay watched as Edgar Thyme removed the sheet, revealing the body of Physician Corbin.

The bloated, ashen corpse had twisted and stiffened until it no longer lay flat on the table. A pushing motion of the hand could easily set the headless cadaver to rocking back and forth like a child's toy in a bizarre display of rigor mortis. But it was the hand that shocked, or more precisely the sickening protrusion of the bone blade that caused Courtenay to shake his head in dismay.

He turned from the corpse and stared at the girl, who was biting her fingernails as she observed the grotesque carcass on the table.

"Yerty, is it?" The child nodded silently. "I assume you know who I am, Yerty." She nodded again. "My scrutators"—the archbishop waved long fingers at Martha and Gregor standing silently nearby—"have told me quite the tale, quite the tale. Apparently, that creature on the table was intent on murdering you, and you alone. Why is that?"

"Because I know what it is, your holiness, sir."

"And what is it exactly?"

"It's Physician Corbin. He's gone mad."

The archbishop raised a fine black eyebrow. "Insanity is one thing, but this is quite another. This man grew a blade of bone from a severed stump. How is such a thing possible?"

Yerty paused and fingered her dirty tunic. "It's the metal. I think I understand it now."

The archbishop frowned. "What are you talking about, child?"

"It's in his pocket. I think. The metal thing."

The archbishop signalled for the coroner to come forwards. "Check his pocket."

"I have already done so, your excellency," Edgar Thyme said. "I found nothing."

"It must have fallen out," Yerty said. "If you find it, you mustn't touch it."

Courtenay found himself becoming irritable. The carcass on the table disturbed him, and he wanted answers. "Child, you'll need to explain. I do not understand."

Yerty took a deep breath. "My brother was taken. He is a child of the streets, as am I. Miss Cass was angry. She said nobody cared, that Dylan would not be missed, so no one bothered to look. There's something out there that wants to take children. And another boy died. Miss Cass thinks it could have something to do with the monks on the mountain and I think she is right. She's up there right now."

"Slow down. Who is Miss Cass?"

"She's ... she looks after us. I think she might be in trouble."

"And these monks?"

"Up the mountain, sir. On Mount Ulfur."

"Ah, you speak of the Brotherhood of Ulfur. I know of them. And this metal?"

"Several months ago, a meteor hit the mountain. Master Corbin went up there to help an injured man. He brought back a trinket with him, an amulet in the shape of a beetle, made from the very metal that fell to earth. It changes colour before your eyes. He was always playing with it, and I think it poisoned his mind and turned him into a beast. If I'm right, he's not going to be the only one."

The archbishop shook his head in wonder. "You say children are being abducted from the streets of Re'Shan, murdered, and the monks are responsible? That there may be more like"—he gestured to the bizarre corpse of Corbin—"this?"

"That is what I believe, your holyship."

"And furthermore, you believe the metal from ... this *meteor* is somehow corrupting anybody that encounters it?"

"I know it sounds mad, but I'm sure I'm right. Please, sir, you must save Miss Cass. She's in terrible danger."

"It will be done, rest assured, child. Leave it to me. Leave it to me." The archbishop observed Yerty fidgeting. She was clearly traumatized and had done well to survive an attempted assassination with grace. She was a solid character, but a child can only deal with so much. Courtenay clapped his hands together. "Thank you for granting me this interview, Yerty. I must consult with my scrutators. I gather that you like horses?" Yerty looked up at the archbishop with wide eyes and nodded. Courtenay clicked his fingers, and a page came forwards. "Take this girl outside and introduce her to the most magnificent animal in the Freelands. She may sit upon his back if she wishes." The page led Yerty away and the archbishop stared at the corpse on the table.

"The girl's tale is an unusual one, your excellency," Gregor said.

The archbishop did not take his eyes from the headless cadaver. "No doubt about that, yet the evidence is before us. I met with the Senate this morning. Senator Chace was distraught. His daughter is missing, taken in the night in a suspected abduction. These events cannot be unrelated." The archbishop clasped his hands behind his back and turned to address his scrutators. "The monks on Ulfur are an unauthorized sect, a cult. They do not operate under the auspices of the local diocese and have been a thorn in my side for quite some time. It now seems they have been struck down by some kind of collective madness."

Martha pointed to the table. "The physician wasn't a monk, your excellency."

"An unfortunate civilian casualty, the likes of which we must prevent from happening again. Gather the remaining scrutators and climb the mountain. Take the girl with you and glean any further information from her that may aid you. Make sure this sickness does not spill over and come down to overwhelm the city. Find this metal and destroy it."

"And the monks?" Gregor asked.

"The brief is quite plain. Kill all evil. Cleanse and purify. Simplicity itself."

Martha shifted her weight. "And if some of the monks remain untouched by this corrupting metal?"

Archbishop Courtenay looked into Martha's eyes of mercury. The woman was cold, unemotional: the perfect scrutator. "If there is any doubt, kill them all, for God knows who belong to Him."

24

JACOB'S WARNING

A chill wind whistled and moaned across the granite face of the looming cliffs, striking up a conversation with the mountain and tugging and pulling at tunic and hair. Cassie hugged herself against the cold wind and walked in Lay Brother Jacob's lee, the big man's body providing a wind-break of sorts.

Brother Rollant carried a torch that danced angrily in the biting wind, but he did not interfere with their search. He simply guided them around the compound and warned of potential unseen dangers in the darkness. They stopped at the large pit over which the Grand Chapel of the Brotherhood of Ulfur had once rested. A safety rope kept them from getting too close to the hungry maw of the black hole.

"Careful," Rollant said. "We've had an engineer up from the city and he says we are quite safe behind the rope, but you must not take one step past this protective barrier. Come, we have more to see."

When every monk had been identified by torchlight and every building in the compound had been inspected, from the storehouse and the goat sheds to the abbot's office, dormitories, and the chapel, Brother Rollant addressed the exhausted crew. Cassie had to take several steps closer to the thin monk to make out his words above the keening winds.

"I have been instructed," the skeletal Rollant said, "to offer you beds for the night. You will also be given food and water. Please, follow me." Brother Rollant led the group to the lay brothers' dormitory and, as the bells for compline struck, the compound emptied of clerics.

Ivan's frustrated need to murder someone radiated from him like hot embers. In the lay brothers' dormitory, he slumped down on a cot and pulled viciously at his boots. Cassie chose the bed as far from the sullen tanner as she could.

Carl put his hands on his hips and arched his back. As Rollant prepared to leave them, the jeweller addressed the gaunt monk. "Where is the source of the metal? The material that changes colour?"

Rollant looked at him coldly and pointed somewhere higher up the mountain. "It would be foolish to attempt the climb at this hour."

"May I inspect it in the morning?"

Rollant frowned. "This would be part of your search for Lay Brother Julian?"

Carl shrugged. "Perhaps." He looked at the others preparing to bed down for the night in the unadorned dormitory. "But you might also consider it ... business. I have a proposition for you and your masters." Ivan glared at Carl and the jeweller raised his hands in a pacifying gesture. "And of course, yes, it would be part of the search for the murderer, and the other missing child, Dylan."

"Very well. We will discuss your proposition in the morning." Brother Rollant nodded curtly and left.

Cassie lay back on a cot and put her forearm over her eyes. Good old Carl. Always ready to make a profit even in the most troubled of times and off the back of someone else's pain. She was bone-weary. She hadn't really expected to find Dylan up here, but she had hoped to find something, anything to indicate that the boy was still alive, or even that Julian was innocent. But the doe-eyed lay brother had been exposed as a thief and fled in the night. All signs pointed to Julian as not only a thief but also a child murderer. She had trusted him, fool that she was. She remembered the kiss on the rooftop and wondered how she could have been so wrong. Had she shared an intimate moment with Dylan's killer? No, she just could not believe it, despite the evidence. She reminded herself that this same evidence, the purple opal, had once pointed to *her* as the murderer of the tanner's son. Evidence could be read in many ways, so she wasn't prepared to condemn Julian just yet.

The skies rumbled and the winds howled at the windows and the seams between the wooden planking of the ill-constructed dormitory. An unhealthy draught played across her face. Cassie turned on her side to avoid it. Jacob was talking with the others, but their voices became a distant murmur. Cassie fought against the desire to sleep. She shouldn't sleep. Dylan was out there somewhere, cold and alone. Or dead. The thought sickened her. She had to stay calm, stay rational. Dylan had to be somewhere. The boy's disappearance had now extended beyond a week and Cassie, if she were honest with herself, had lost all hope of ever finding him. No, she wouldn't give up. She was missing something important, a clue to his whereabouts.

Someone tapped at her shoulder, and she opened her eyes, realizing that despite her best efforts she had drifted off. Lay Brother Jacob stood over her, his head brushing the ceiling. Cassie swung herself upright on the side of the bed and rubbed at her eyes. The big man sat on an empty bed opposite, the weight of his massive frame causing the bed to creak and strain.

"I will tell you this because the others will not listen to me," Jacob said.

"What is it? Tell me what?"

"Something is wrong. The lay brothers are absent."

"You mean Julian?"

"No. I mean *all* of them. There should be more than twenty men in here right now, for this room"—he swept his hand around—"is the lay brother dormitory, and each bed is usually occupied. The monks, the ordained monks that is, are present in the compound, but every *lay brother* is gone. I have seen no sign of any of them during the search this night."

Cassie looked around the mostly empty room. "Where would they be?"

The big man's face showed concern. "I had my own reasons for accompanying you to the community tonight. One of my crew vanished several days ago. This cannot be unconnected with the disappearance of the lay brothers, or that of Lay Brother Julian."

"You think Julian might be a ... victim of something? That he might be innocent?"

Jacob shrugged. "Tonight, upon our arrival at the upper station, I did not recognize the winch crew, but I know that they are fully fledged choir monks. Those men should not be operating the elevator. This is the duty of the lay brothers."

Cassie stared hard at the big man. "What are you saying?"

"I and my men at the lower station are the only lay brothers remaining on this mountain. Something is badly amiss. You and your people should get out of here. Now."

Carl and the others had by now pulled blankets about their chins, the conversation muted, dying, as sleep came for them. They weren't going anywhere, certainly not at her behest.

"Is the elevator still able to take us?" Cassie asked.

"It is closed for the evening, and we cannot return that way.

I would not risk it in any event." Jacob leaned in closer, keeping his voice low. "There is another way, a path known only to a few senior monks. I know of this path because it is my duty to get men and goods up and down by any means possible. Listen to me very carefully and I will tell you where—"

A boom of thunder, followed by a scratching at the window. Jacob fixed his eyes on the rattling glass.

"What was that?" Cassie whispered.

Snores came from the other end of the lay brother dormitory, the fat baker making enough noise to wake the dead. The scratching came again, but this time from above, something on the roof.

"I don't know," Jacob said. "A storm is building, but I heard something else. I will go outside to investigate."

"I'll come with you."

"No. Rouse your crew. You must prepare to leave, at once." The scratching came again, and Jacob lifted his bulk to his feet. "A moment."

Cassie held her hand out as the big man walked away. "Wait. The secret path. Where is it?" But Jacob had disappeared outside. Cassie approached the others and nudged the jeweller. "Carl, get up. All of you. We must leave."

Carl rolled over and muttered, "Fuck off, Cassie."

A single loud shriek from outside, high pitched and feral. This was followed by a deep guttural roar and then a chorus of animal sounds, a nonsensical cacophony of grunts, jabbering, and screams. Carl, Ivan, and John sat bolt upright in their beds, each man staring wide-eyed at Cassie, who stared back.

The window shattered as a monk came hurtling through it.

25

THE MAD MONKS

Carl cursed and John squealed. Ivan was on his feet, sword in hand.

The monk that had come flailing through the window stood, his face and hands lacerated, but the man merely grinned. Cassie stabbed him through the eye with her dagger and he dropped.

"What?" Carl gaped incredulously. "Cassie, what have you done?"

Cassie merely pointed with her bloodied dagger to the scene outside through the broken window: big Jacob bellowed in rage, striking out with closed fists at several dogs that snapped at him, trying to bring him to the ground. No, not dogs. Monks, perhaps half a dozen of them, teeth bared in feral grins and hands curved like talons.

Jacob roared, "A weapon!"

Cassie turned. "Carl, give me your sword."

The jeweller shook his head and clasped his weapon to him like it was the baby he'd never had. Cassie approached the baker and took the man's sword from where it lay beside his bed. The man was shaking in fear, the weapon of little use to him anyway. She sprinted outside, Ivan and Carl right behind her. Cassie swung the sword in vicious arcs, scattering monks and carving an opening to Jacob. The big man's arms and face were scratched and bleeding. He took the sword from Cassie and for a moment the monks stood off. Jacob walked backwards slowly, but the monks followed, grinning and muttering in a language Cassie could not recognize.

"The Devil has taken them all," Jacob said. He roared and lunged forwards, swinging the sword with all the power his massive arms and back could muster. The monks scrambled away and melted into the shadows. A full moon came out from behind scudding clouds and bathed the compound in a silver glow. The Monks of Ulfur were gone. Cassie exchanged horrified glances with Carl and Ivan. John crept out of the lay brother dormitory and shivered.

"What's happening?" the fat baker said.

Jacob scanned the compound. "Come with me."

Cassie followed the elevator keeper, her dagger held tightly in her hand. Several frightening noises came from shadowy places: a screech from behind the storehouse, the sound of grinding and snapping teeth from near the abbot's office. Every shadow seemed about to jump at them, fangs bared. They ran across the compound, heading for the path that would take them down the mountain to the entrance to the upper elevator. From the left and right, Cassie caught sight of fluttering and flapping monastic robes. The creatures appeared from pooling shadows and wooden structures, always behind or to the side of them as they ran. They were being hunted, hounded, shepherded. This was a trap, but Cassie realized it too late.

Suddenly, a dozen shapes loomed out of the ground ahead, blocking their path. Cassie turned and found more dark figures behind them. Surrounded. One monk came forwards and pulled back his cowl. The crucifix resting on his chest seemed to mimic the moon: a ghostly pulsing silver. The monk bared his teeth in a cruel smile. Cassie recognized him: Brother Rollant.

"Your bones will be sprinkled upon our gardens and to the earth your flesh shall return," Rollant said.

"You murdered Larson," Jacob said matter-of-factly. Rollant did not respond.

"And my son!" shouted Ivan, caught between terror and fear. "It was you!"

Rollant looked at the tanner with no discernible emotion. "Not I, personally."

"What kind of answer is that?" screamed Ivan.

"The only one you're going to get."

"Where is Dylan?" Cassie asked. Again, no emotion from Rollant. "And Lay Brother Julian? What have you done with him?"

This time the monk's face screwed up in ugly anger. When he spoke, his voice was shrill, full of rage. "He is no longer important. I have ascended. I am a true cleric, and the man's ineptness is no longer any concern of mine!"

Julian was clearly a sore point for Brother Rollant. Cassie probed a little harder. "Julian didn't run away. Where is he?" Perhaps if she found Julian, she'd find Dylan.

Rollant opened his mouth and then shut it. "No, no. None of this matters." He looked up to the moon and stars. "None of this matters! Earthly concerns no longer molest me. I have ascended. I am holy. I am holy. I am the moon and the stars. I am the distant black sun."

Jacob snarled, "You have forgotten your vows, Brother Rollant."

Rollant turned his gaze back to Jacob and he spat bile. "I have forgotten nothing! I am holy. You are a mere *lay brother*, a workhorse. Your strength exists only to serve our will. Do your duty, lay brother."

"And what duty is that, brother?"

"To die!" Rollant opened his mouth wider than should have been humanly possible, his jaws unhinged like those of a snake. His tongue protruded and slid down his chest, wrapping around the sky-metal crucifix on his chest.

Carl cursed and staggered backwards. John the Baker pissed himself, the sound of water leaking down a trembling leg to the hard wind-chilled ground. Cassie's stomach turned and her knees weakened, and she stepped back. Only Jacob and Ivan stood their ground.

"You'll pay for my son's death!" Ivan screamed, his voice cracking in fear despite the veracity of his words. Rollant's tongue flicked in the air like that of some obscenely grotesque toad, and he laughed, the horrid sound echoed by twenty more voices as the circling monks began to close in. Cassie glanced this way and that, looking for an opening, somewhere to run. There was nowhere to run.

"Three times three," growled Jacob, and every monk stopped and cocked an ear. "And your vows shall be three." The big man thumped the hilt of John's sword against his chest three times.

"Kill them!" screamed Rollant.

"Obedience," Jacob said. The monks did not move; they stood watching, waiting on his words, listening intently to the vows they themselves had uttered long ago. "The first of your vows is obedience to God."

Rollant clenched his fists. "Kill them! We have orders and I will see them carried out!"

"Stability." Jacob pointed the tip of John's sword at Rollant, no, *Jacob's* sword now, for he had claimed it at this moment—perhaps among the last moments of his life. The winds stopped. No one moved. Jacob pumped his chest three more times. In the deathly silence, he whispered, "Conversion of life. Death, death to the self brings life to God. Death to the self." Then, Lay Brother Jacob howled and let the killer that he had once been free.

Jacob fought with a savagery that caused the hairs on Cassie's arms to stand on end. Screaming in a berserk rage, he attacked, swinging and hacking with his sword. Several monks shrieked and fell, limbs sliced clean off, their lifeblood spurting onto the grass. The other monks, including the bizarrely tongued Rollant, backed away. Ivan and Carl, perhaps emboldened by the big man's bravery, lunged and stabbed with their own weapons. Cassie struck at a monk that grabbed at her, keeping the creature away with her dagger.

For a moment, the circle of monks weakened and broke. Jacob took the opportunity and ran for the mountain path, the others at his heels. The monks began to bark and shriek behind them, the high-pitched yips of feral hunting dogs in pursuit of their prey.

John the Baker was too slow and went down under a fang-toothed tide of flapping and swirling monastic raiment, his screams resounding across the mountainside as Cassie and the others hurtled down the path of gravel towards the elevators. John's screams turned to a rasping gurgle and then silence as the man's lungs were torn from his twitching torso.

Cassie had no time to feel guilt. They had to get out. She had to get back down to Re'Shan. These vile animals had taken Dylan, of this there was no doubt. She needed to get down to the city and get help from the City Guard, from the Senate, from anyone.

Suddenly, Jacob veered from the path. "This way," he hissed breathlessly. The big lay brother climbed a grassy bank and disappeared between two massive boulders on the ridge. Cassie, Carl, and Ivan scrambled after him, slipping and sliding on the moist grass. Cassie glanced back; no sign of their pursuers, not yet. Probably too busy feasting on the fat baker.

On the other side of the rise, Jacob was careening down an embankment towards a darkened cliff face. He must be leading them towards the secret path of which he had spoken. Yet there seemed to be no obvious way out. Still, it wouldn't be a secret path if it was obvious to everyone, would it, Cassie?

They came to a shallow pool of water near a cliff wall and Jacob waded in. Carl, Ivan, and Cassie exchanged glances, having no choice but to follow, for none wanted to meet the baker's fate.

Jacob, knee deep in water, turned sideways and disappeared into a hidden alcove in the cliff, the entrance practically invisible unless you were right on it. The jeweller and the tanner, each in the same sideways crab-like walk, followed. Cassie brought up the rear.

Jacob whispered a warning: "Steps." His voice came from somewhere above them. It was dark within the recess of the cliff. "There are five steps," Jacob repeated. "Up out of the water, come."

Cassie followed Ivan and Carl up several steps and they stood shivering on what must have been a small stone platform. "I can't see anything," Carl whispered. "We must wait until our eyes adjust to the darkness."

"We cannot wait," Jacob said. "The devils will be upon us. Many of the ordained are aware of this path, and they know that *I* know of it. If they do not find us at the upper elevator station, they will come here, and soon."

"We're going to break our legs in the dark," Ivan protested.

"There is a lighting station a few steps down," Jacob said. "I am trained to light the lamps in total darkness. About one hundred steps further down. Simply follow me and trust your instincts. We *cannot* wait here."

The big man's advice was good enough for Cassie and she pushed the person in front of her to get moving. It turned out to be Carl and he cursed her in the reverberating niche of the cliff wall.

"Silence," warned Jacob. Cassie heard the big man start walking, at first up several more stairs. They followed cautiously. Then, the stairs began to descend somewhere within the mountain itself.

True to his word, Jacob called a halt not far down. A scratching sound came muffled in the darkness. A moment later a flint sounded, and a spark appeared like a wayward firefly only to die out seconds later. Another strike of the flint and another spark. The third spark caught, and a candle wick began to glow, shedding a small patch of light, first over the metal frame that contained it, then on the rock walls glistening with damp, and finally to four frightened faces, well, three frightened faces and Jacob's dour one. The big lay brother continued to descend, the lamplight casting crazed shadows around the tunnel walls. Cassie realized that Jacob was walking in a stooped position as the tunnel roof did not allow for him to stand at full height.

Down they stumbled. Then, an animal shriek came from behind. Cassie had to evade Carl's sword before it punctured her gut, the man thrusting it out in fright. Cassie wanted to admonish the jeweller for almost killing her, but remained silent, listening for another sound. Something was in the tunnel with them, but it was impossible to tell if the scream had originated from above or below. Cassie prayed there were no murderous monks blocking the path ahead of them.

Jacob grunted and continued to descend. He, at least, seemed to believe the path ahead was clear. The thing must be behind them, then. Behind Cassie. She shivered and had to restrain herself from shoving Carl in the back and sending him sprawling on his face. There was little space to overtake the person in front. Cassie had never suffered from a fear of enclosed spaces, from claustrophobia, or *claustrum* in the Latin, but she damn well suffered from it now. To be torn apart in the small dark spaces beneath the crushing weight of Mount Ulfur: a bloody tomb, her flesh and bone sprayed and cracked in the airless, suffocating sepulchre of a mountain vein. She shivered and gathered herself. *Show some steel, girl. Show some steel.*

The sound of rumbling thunder came vibrating through the floors and wall, even here deep in the mountain. A storm of some ferocity was building. Still, Cassie would rather be outside in nature's volatile tantrum than trapped in here.

"Going to rain," whispered Ivan.

"I don't give a fuck," hissed Carl. "When are we getting out of here? How much further?"

Before Jacob could answer, another shriek came. This one closer.

"Not soon enough," Jacob said. "We must choose a place to stand and fight."

Carl protested that a tunnel was no place to turn around and make a brave last stand. He was right. At least not when Cassie was the one at the back end of the line. They soon came to an open space, a landing where the path diverged into two staircases carved from stone, one skirting left and the other right.

"Don't move. Not one step." Jacob took the candle from its metal frame and lit two other lamps set into recesses in the wall at either side of the opening. To Cassie's shock, she realized that they were standing at the lip of an open chasm. The landing upon which they huddled could have been no bigger than four by four feet. "Go left." Jacob indicated the curving staircase disappearing into the darkness. "Hug the wall and tread carefully, for the steps are slippery in places. Take the passage on the left where it branches and take the right at the following junction. Then a second left, but do not take any other path that branches from it. Follow the tunnel until you come out among the juniper trees. From there just keep going down until you intersect with the woodsman's track to Re'Shan. Can you remember?"

Cassie nodded. "First left, then right, then another left and stay on the path."

"Good. If you do not find the mountain track to Re'Shan, simply head down, always down." He attempted to hand the lamp to Cassie, but she didn't take it.

"What are you going to do?" Cassie asked.

"I will delay the pursuit."

Cassie looked around. "You can't fight here. There's no room to swing your prick let alone your sword."

Jacob grinned. "The same applies to them. They can only come at me one at a time." He gestured to the opening of the tunnel through which they had come. "I die today, but I will hold them as long as I can. Warn the city below. Tell them Lucifer is reborn on the mountain." Carl took the lamp from the big man and without a word he and Ivan began to descend. "Hurry," Jacob said to Cassie, "before you are left behind."

Cassie shook her head, wishing for something to say. She patted the big man on the arm and hurried to join the others before the light of the lamp disappeared, leaving her blind in the darkness.

———

Carl led the way, Ivan and Cassie close behind. Cassie reminded Carl of the appropriate branches to take in the maze of subterranean tunnels. After what seemed an age, the tunnel levelled out and came to a narrow crack in a cliff wall which opened out onto a forest of moonlight-tinged juniper trees, just as the big man had said it would. Small holes in the cliff face gave hand and foot holds for them to climb down to the forest floor about eight feet below. Carl blew out the candle and cast the lamp aside, sending it clanging onto some rocks nearby.

"God damn it, Carl," Ivan said angrily under his breath. "We have to be quiet, or those things will find us."

"We've left them behind, surely," Carl responded.

"We don't know that," Ivan said.

Rain had begun to fall in sparse but weighty drops, the pitter-patter on the rocks and grass and the heavier, damper thud of water on juniper needles and cones. The fresh scent of pine hung in the air, and something else: the tang of ozone from the rumbling, amber-charged storm. The sky lit up in a blinding flash, lightning streaking across the muddy clouds. The moon gave just enough light for them to pick their way among the rocks, shrubs, and trees.

Cassie estimated that they'd only descended about five hundred feet from the community of mad monks above. They wouldn't make it to Re'Shan before the sun rose. They'd be lucky to get to the city at all, especially if they could not find the woodsman's path.

Carl and Ivan careened through the forest, jumping over rocks and under low-hanging boughs. Cassie wanted to tell them to slow down, they'd blow themselves out within minutes. Panicking was only going to get them killed, one way or the other. Slow and steady, lads, because it was going to be a long night. Down they stumbled, tripped, fell, clambered up, and stumbled on.

Another flash of lightning. Cassie saw them: briefly illuminated figures up the mountainside about thirty feet on their flank, hunched and moving with great speed in a parallel line to their own. Carl and Ivan hadn't noticed them, but Cassie recognized the fluttering of monastic habits.

"I see them!" she shouted through the spattering rain and howling winds. The others turned frightened faces towards her and accelerated. Cassie put in a spurt of speed; this was no longer time for slow and steady. Jacob must have fallen, or these creatures had found another way down. It didn't matter.

They were all dead.

The sound of wet snapping juniper needles came to her in a lull in the storm: their pursuers close behind. They had to stand and fight, as Jacob had, but Cassie did not have the breath to shout for the others to stop and turn and knew that they would not do so in any case.

Ivan caught his foot under a tree root and fell. The man screamed; his ankle broken. Carl hurtled past him without so much as a backwards glance and Cassie did the same.

The devils take the hindmost.

Getting to his feet and ignoring the pain of his shattered ankle, Ivan the Tanner swung his sword and cleaved the head from one of the monks as the foul thing came leaping at him. Before the severed head tumbled to a halt in a pile of juniper cones, Ivan's arm had been ripped from its socket, both eyes punctured by taloned fingers, and his throat torn open. One monk reached in and wrenched Ivan's tongue from the gaping wound in his throat. They bit into him. Mouths coated in blood, three crazed monks cocked their heads, located the sounds of the other two fleeing prey, and resumed their pursuit.

Ivan lay dying, blinded, his throat filling with choking blood, a searing at the stump of his shoulder. Oddly, it was the broken ankle that really caused him pain. Despite his blindness, he somehow watched as his son, Jake, appeared through the blood and darkness and said, "It's alright, Dad." Smiling, his son placed a hand on Ivan's ankle and the pain disappeared.

Good boy. Jake had always been such a good boy.

———

Cassie couldn't run any further. Her knees threatened to fold, and her breath rasped in her throat. If she was going to die, she'd do it fighting. She stopped and turned, her chest heaving desperately. Carl had outpaced her. For a smoker and a drinker in his middle years, the man had revealed a surprising and very timely athletic talent. The bastard.

The rain had created a thousand rivulets pouring from darkened branches and the water hissed as it fell, making it difficult to either see or hear the monks hunting her. Cassie found herself in a small clearing lit by the cloud-streaked moon. She backed up against the bole of a spruce tree, her dagger out in front of her in one hand, the other wiping away the water spilling down her forehead and into her eyes: a hopeless last defence. A blind, deaf, stupid last stand.

Then the thing burst into the clearing, its head swivelling this way and that. It laid eyes on Cassie and came bounding at her.

"Keep away, you piece of shit!" Cassie screamed. She held her dagger out and the creature stopped and cocked its head. A moment later the thing pulled back its cowl. Cassie gasped. "Julian?"

Julian stared wide-eyed. "What are you doing here?"

"What am I doing here? What are *you* doing here?"

"I am hunted. From the look on your face, you find yourself in a similar situation. Have you seen them?"

Cassie lowered her blade. "If by *them* you mean those crazed fucking monks, yes. I've seen them."

Julian attempted to come closer, but Cassie raised her dagger once again. "Stay back."

"I'm not one of them, Cassie."

"How do I know that?"

Julian shrugged. "Well, right now, I'm not attempting to rip your throat out. That should be a good starting point."

"How can I trust you?"

Julian almost laughed through the rain streaming down his face. He exposed his teeth. "See any fangs? Am I slavering? No, I'm lucid, as lucid as could be expected under the circumstances. Come on, this is not the right place to talk. We must get out of here."

"But ... wait. I have so many questions. What's happening?"

Julian shook his head. "I can't explain because I don't truly understand it myself, but I can tell you one thing ..." He crouched low and moved away so that Cassie had to strain to hear his next words. "Dylan is alive."

26

SKULL FRACTURE

Carl ran until he thought his lungs would burst, but he didn't stop. John was dead. Ivan was dead. Hell, even Cassie must be dead by now. Carl had thought the Mistress of the Urchins would live forever. The bitch. He didn't know what had happened to the other militiamen at the lower elevator station. Dead as well, probably. Fuck, how did he get into this? What were these things hunting him down? Monks? They were all insane. This wasn't happening. It couldn't be happening.

Branches and twigs clawed at his face and the damp larch needles cracked dully underfoot. The rain got in his eyes, trying to blind him and send him sprawling to the damp earth. He wasn't going to fall like Ivan had, and he wasn't going to slow down like Cassie had. Fuck them both; he was going to make it. He'd made good speed, good distance. He had outdistanced his pursuers. He was going to be alright. He'd make the path down to the city soon and he'd be safe. He was faster than those things. He was faster.

His face was bleeding from the scratches he'd received in his frantic sprint through the brambles and trees on the mountainside, but they'd heal. A small price to pay for staying alive. He was exhausted. A pain clutched at his chest, and he slowed. Damn, it hurt. He couldn't get his breath, his armpits ached, and his jaw burned. Was he having a heart attack? No. He couldn't die like this, not after putting in so much effort to escape. That would be unfair.

The pain intensified and he had to slow further. Making sure that he was not pursued, Carl collapsed into a sodden ditch. He pulled a large fallen bough over himself and lay panting for several minutes, sweating from the exertion of his desperate flight as well as the pain in his chest. The rain pierced the branches above and drove relentlessly at his head. No matter how he tried, he could not get a satisfying lungful of air. His breath always seemed just shy of satisfying his body's need. Carl moaned as a new ache stabbed at him.

Water, he needed water. At least there was plenty of that. He pulled at a branch on the bough over his head, funnelling the rainwater into his mouth. He got a mouthful and swallowed. The pain subsided in his chest. That was better. Much better. His breath slowed and his heart resumed a more normal pattern.

Carl poked his head out of the ditch. No one about and no time to waste. He must be halfway down the mountain by now. Another three or four hours and he'd be in the city. He could do it. But he had to find the path. Why hadn't he already found it? Had he missed it in his haste? He decided to jog, not that he had a choice: his legs could no longer sustain a full-blooded sprint. He had not gone far before he found a well-worn path between the trees. This was it, the track. He'd found it. From here on, the journey would be unobstructed. If only the rain would ease, he'd be there in no time.

Lightning flashed and thunder crashed, sending a ringing around Carl's head. Nearby, a larch tree was smoking; its trunk split nearly in two as if God had brought a massive axe right down its centre. A close call but another sign that it was not his time to die. Carl trotted along the path as it wound downwards. He came upon a woodcutter's wagon with a broken wheel. For a moment he thought about climbing under it and closing his eyes. No, that would be foolish, they'd find him sooner or later. Turning away from the wagon, he found the path blocked by three motionless figures, cowls drawn over their heads. Carl went for his sword, but his scabbard was empty.

One of the monks was very tall and was flanked by the other two. The three men pulled their cowls back from their faces, revealing manic grins in the rain. Carl leaped to the other side of the wagon and slipped in the mud. The tall one closed the distance with obscenely long strides. He grasped the undercarriage of the wagon and in a show of inhuman strength flipped it, sending Carl sprawling into a puddle.

The monk spoke in a Germanic accent. "My name is Klaus, and I am a lay brother. Do you know what that means? To be a *lay brother*?" Carl got to his knees but did not answer. Klaus waved a hand at the other two monks. "Lawrence, Kristoff, and I, we are not ordained. Not holy. We may assist the clerics in their duties but not partake of these duties directly. Enlightenment is not yet ours." Klaus smiled. "But that doesn't matter, not now. We are all brothers, for we have all ascended and have found enlightenment in another form. Have you ascended, sir? Are you enlightened?" Carl could only stare with wide, horrified eyes. Klaus stepped closer and said, "I used to be just like you. Afraid. Afraid of this mountain and its dark, high places." He waved a long hand around the clearing and the path. "But you need not fear, all misery is gone."

Lawrence and Kristoff began to circle Carl. They leered at him. Carl could not control his bowels and soiled himself.

Klaus sniffed the air and laughed. "Do not fear." He

extended his hand and touched a sharpened fingernail to the underside of Carl's jaw. "Let me show you the path home."

Tears began to roll down Carl's face as Klaus made a small nick in his flesh.

"Stop." The commanding voice came from the trees, causing Klaus to whirl around.

Carl's breath caught in his throat. Could he be saved? A man in a robe of white, still white even amid all this darkness, rain, and mud, walked onto the mountain path. At his side was Brother Rollant, his tongue no longer obscenely lolling from his mouth.

Klaus looked puzzled. "Father Howard, what are you doing this far down the mountain?"

Carl breathed again. Could he be saved?

The abbot inhaled deeply and took a moment to admire the forest and the torrid skies. With a wave of his hand, the rain stopped falling, as if he had cast an invisible dome over them all. Father Howard said, "It has been some time since I had the strength to descend the mountain, Klaus, and I fully intend to enjoy the beauty of the storm. You're young and you take your health for granted. The young take many things for granted." The abbot turned to Carl. "The nearness of death gives one insight, does it not, friend?"

Carl realized the abbot was talking to him. "Wh ... what?" Carl wiped the remaining rainwater from his eyes.

"Do you not have a newfound wisdom?" Howard said. "Can you not see your life and all your mistakes more clearly?" Carl was confused. Was he saved? Father Howard addressed Klaus. "Have you found him? Is he dead?"

Klaus lowered his eyes and shook his head. "No, Father Abbot. But he has not passed us, of this I am sure. He is hiding somewhere in the woods, somewhere close by."

Carl tried to follow the conversation. Who were they talking about?

The abbot turned his attention back to Carl. He smiled, not unkindly, and knelt to bring his eyes level with those of the jeweller. "I think you may be somewhat confused by what you have seen this night." He held out his fist to Carl and opened it. A diamond sparkled within the abbot's palm. Carl stared at it. It was beautiful, a perfect cut. The abbot followed Carl's gaze. "An earthly treasure. I once desired the likes of this, as you do, but I realize now that this diamond represents both secular and sacred value. It is holiness in and of itself. But you know this, Carl Braithwaite. You're a man who has worked with precious stones for many years."

Carl's eyes widened. "How could you ... how do you know me?"

Father Howard winked. "I have been gifted with ... knowledge, you might say. You have a small trace within your blood."

"A small trace ... of what?" Carl stared once more at the precious stone in the abbot's hand.

Father Howard closed his hand into a fist. "Not the diamond. No, not that. You have something else within you, something far more unique. You have been touched by the *metal.*"

Was Carl saved? "I don't understand. Are you going to kill me? Please, I don't want to die."

The abbot casually placed the diamond to his lips. He smiled, pulling his lips back and baring his teeth. Carl gawked. Oh Lord, the teeth. The abbot's teeth were gone, replaced by jagged diamonds lining the upper and lower gums, embedded in the man's mouth and glinting like dagger blades. The abbot's smile was a bizarre, horrific grin of immense worldly value.

"The young look for all the wrong things, in all the wrong places," Father Howard said. "You have just a whisper within you, Carl Braithwaite, but it's not enough. You are not one of us." The abbot suddenly seized Carl's head in his hands and bit off the jeweller's nose.

Carl was not saved.

He shrieked and tried to jerk his head away, but the abbot was inhumanly strong. The cleric bit again, taking a chunk of bone from Carl's brow. Carl gurgled as blood streamed down his nose into his throat, choking him. The abbot snapped again, causing Carl's skull at the forehead to pop and splinter. Carl gave a garbled, choked squeal and only stopped struggling when his brain had been exposed to the cold night winds.

When the abbot had finished eating Carl's face, and a large section of his skull and brain, he let the featureless corpse collapse to the damp earth of the mountain path. He stood and wiped the sleeve of his robe across his bloodied mouth and jaws. The robe was no longer pristine white, but smeared with midnight red.

Abbot Howard stretched his neck, cracking the vertebrae this way and that. He turned to Klaus and said, "You must find him. Prior Blackwing believes that there will soon be a war between us and those below and I tend to agree with the man. Find Julian and kill him. Then return, for we must draw up our battle plans, do you understand?"

Klaus nodded and backed away. The tall German, and his companions Lawrence and Kristoff, melted away into the trees, on the hunt once more.

27
BIRTHDAY CAKE

The tall man in black just stood there looking down on Dylan silently from the shadows of his hood, not saying a word as the beeswax candlewick burned down. The man's scent was familiar to Dylan: oily and cloying, a hint of decayed bird bones lingering in the dank air. This was the man who had brought him here, taken him from Yerty and Miss Cass.

The man in black robes, if man he was, gestured for Dylan to join him outside the small cell. Dylan had no choice but to obey, for death would come swiftly on the cold wings of a crow were he to refuse. The man placed a hand on Dylan's shoulder and guided him down the hallway. The cells were empty. In the quiet moments, the children had exchanged names and Dylan made a point to remember all of them. Two of those names had recently disappeared. Dylan hoped that Georgina and Rico had somehow escaped the catacombs. The other possibility did not bear thinking about. Nine children, including Dylan, remained. But today, every cell stood empty.

Was Dylan the last one alive?

He simultaneously shivered and breathed a sigh of relief

when the crow man ushered him into a long room with a low ceiling. The children sat huddled together on a reed mat at one end of the room. At the other end, several brown-robed men sat around a low-hanging copper censer giving off curling, languid smoke the colour of an overcast sky. The men, monks by the looks of them, sat dull-eyed, heads lolling to one side or another, heavily drugged by whatever alchemy inhabited the censer. Other monks, faces hidden within hoods and hands clasped together, stood close to the children, watching them.

The crow man shoved Dylan forwards to join the frightened group of children. Dylan joined his companions and sat beside the girl called Carmelita, her large brown eyes wide with fear. Dylan gripped her hand in his and felt it tremble in waves as if she were a sick dog.

"I want my mama," Carmelita whispered.

"Silence!" the crow man shrieked. Each child jumped involuntarily. The man in black approached the censer and reached within his robe pocket. He sprinkled something on the censer, and it hissed, producing substantially more smoke and a strange acidic tang in the air.

Dylan recognized one of the men sitting drowsily at the table, his bald head haloed in drug smoke. *Martin*, his name was. Dylan thought back to the day before, or had it been the night before? Or two days ago? Within the catacombs in the mountain, time wandered lost like a confused child. But whenever it was, a voice had come to him in the darkness, whispering to him. The disembodied voice was familiar. But this was not the voice of a child, not one of the others nearby seeking company in the cruel darkness. It was a man's voice.

"I am Julian," the voice had said.

"I am Dylan," Dylan had replied.

"Dylan? Cassie has been looking for you. She will be greatly relieved to hear you are alive. Do you remember me? You tried to sell me mule shit."

"I remember you, sir. Miss Cass has talked about you."

"I don't have much time. How did you come to be here?"

Dylan related how wings had enfolded him and his head had spun above his feet, how the world had turned upside down and the mountain hung over him, then below him in a sharp wind. He spoke of the smell of a large seabird that had suffocated him.

"Blackwing drugged you," Julian said.

"He flew me up the side of Ulfur, sir, the crow man did."

Julian did not respond, and doubt laced his voice when he eventually spoke again. "You are confused by the man's drugs. Men do not fly. Listen to me, I awoke here not long ago, also a victim of the man's poisons."

Dylan whispered, "Where are you? I can't see you."

"Behind the wall, bend your head to the ground, follow the draught." Dylan did as he was bid and sure enough, a crack at the base of his cell gave vent to a cold channel of clammy air. "I am going to try to get you out," Julian said.

"All of us?"

"All ...? How many?"

"Nine of us, sir."

Another pause from outside. Julian hissed, "Damn it." Dylan understood the difficulty facing the lay brother. He could not possibly rescue them all, undiscovered. "I'll come back," Julian said. "Yes, yes, that's it. I'll get out and I'll come back for you, with help."

"Will you bring Miss Cass?"

"Yes, if I can. You'll have to sit tight, Dylan. Can you do that?"

"Yes, sir."

"Tell Martin I'm coming back to save him, do you hear? If

you see him, my friend Martin, you must tell him. Do you remember him? The … hush, Dylan. Someone is coming."

Dylan heard nothing, and then footsteps. Later, he thought he heard shouting from somewhere far away. When he whispered to the man on the other side of his cell, no response issued through the crack. Julian was gone. He hoped the doe-eyed lay brother made it out alive. Dylan wasn't sure just how much time remained to him, but now, at least, there was hope.

But that hope was fading fast. The crow man had them all gathered in the room with the smoke haze of drugs. There was nowhere to run.

"Happy birthday, children," the crow man rasped, nonsensically. "My name is Prior Blackwing. Welcome to your birthday party."

Dylan frowned and his stomach began to turn sour. *Birthday party?* Today wasn't his birthday and he was sure none of the others had one either. This man was insane, and very dangerous.

The children huddled closer together. The lay brothers, for Dylan recognized them as such by the black of their habit hoods, continued to sit dreamily at the table, each slack face blurred by the smoke. Dylan knew the smell, there were some in Re'Shan who would spend their evenings inhaling the opium, and they were among the easiest of marks to steal from, some even giving away all their money to the urchins, replete with beatific smiles on their faces. The lay brothers were victims of opium.

"Cake," Blackwing said. "Shall we eat cake?" He removed a sackcloth from an object on a smaller side table, revealing a small brown cake, the texture of cliffside shale. As unappealing as the cake looked, some of the children's faces lightened. Perhaps, there was nothing to fear after all.

Don't be fooled, Dylan thought. Don't eat the cake.

Blackwing cut the cake into small pieces with a glinting knife. "Eat, children," the crow man said. "Come, come."

The children were hungry; they'd barely eaten anything aside from stale bread for days. Blackwing must have known this for a sick smile spread across his dark face as the first of the children tiptoed towards the table. Dylan's head began to spin. The opium haze was everywhere by now. Perhaps it was this that relaxed many of the children, made them forget their fear. Dylan grabbed Carmelita's wrist as she made to stand and approach the table. The girl looked into his emerald-green eyes and Dylan shook his head.

"I'm hungry," she whined under her breath, pleading to go and afraid to at the same time.

"Don't go," Dylan whispered back. "Please don't go, Carmelita. Stay here."

Several children drifted across the room towards the cake, reaching out with hunger-weakened, trembling fingers. The lay brothers' eyelids flickered open at their approach, some of them taking out their crucifixes and kissing them. Strange colours winked through the smoke, drawing the eye. But the children soon ignored the lights as hunger brought their attention to bear on the cake.

"Eat." The same sickening smile stretched across Blackwing's face. "Eat."

Dylan's heart began to race. He realized that the crow man wasn't talking to the children. He was talking to *the lay brothers*.

And he wasn't referring to the cake.

Dylan tried to shout a warning, but his voice would not come. Carmelita had gone over to the table, somehow, though he couldn't remember letting go of her hand. Dylan reached out for her, grasping nothing but opium smoke. One of the lay brothers put a hand on Carmelita's shoulder. She ignored it and stuffed cake into her mouth. Another of the lay brothers smiled dreamily and patted his lap, into which a small boy, even younger and frailer than Dylan, stumbled and collapsed. The lay brother sat him upright like a child's puppet and gave the boy cake. The child ate it from the man's hand, and the man smiled.

Dylan stood and, his every step a quivering loss of balance, staggered to the table. The cake looked more appetizing than it had a moment before. Perhaps one piece.

Martin took Dylan's hand and Dylan wondered at the feel of it, soft and unthreatening. Martin was smiling dreamily, saliva issuing from one corner of his mouth. The Black lay brother clasped the back of Dylan's head and brought the child's head to his chest and cradled it softly.

Dylan whispered, "Julian is coming to free us."

Martin let go of Dylan and blinked, peering at the child as if seeing him for the first time. Martin swallowed hard and looked around. He shook his head and stood, steadied himself at the edge of the table, and then walked away, lurching this way and that to collapse in a corner. Blackwing frowned, anger blossoming on his face.

Several lay brothers remained at the table, smiling and fondling the hungry children on the head, or brushing a strand of hair behind an ear, small acts of decency and kindness. But it was not kindness. It was sickness. It was horror. Dylan screamed and all eyes turned to him; many lay brothers seemed to snap out of their stupor and stare at the children on their laps in confusion. Blackwing crossed the floor in two long strides and backhanded Dylan across the cheek.

When he awoke, Dylan was in his cell once more. He whispered into the darkness and was relieved when a child's voice came back to him. Dylan whispered urgent questions. The other voice answered. Two, it said. Two of the children had not returned to the cells after the *birthday party*. Carmelita was one of them.

Dylan squeezed his eyes shut, but tears seeped through anyway. He clenched his fists and hoped against all hope that Lay Brother Julian would return soon and bring fire to purge and burn. To bring vengeance to flay the skin from their backs. To bring sharp knives to gut all their bellies.

To bring righteous pain and death to the wicked.

28

TWO DAGGERS

"Dylan is alive?"

Julian did not respond to Cassie's question. The lay brother moved swiftly through the undergrowth, keeping low. Several times Cassie thought she had lost him in the darkness and the hissing rain, only for a ghostlike hand to reach out and pull her in a certain direction.

"Hurry up," Julian said. "We need to find a place to sit out the night, somewhere out of this rain."

Their shoes sank into the clutching, sucking mud. Before long, Julian jumped into a long ditch, just as a lightning strike crashed through the charged atmosphere, illuminating him in midair and giving him the appearance of a bat with outstretched wings of sacerdotal cloth. Cassie followed Julian down into the ditch and the two of them crawled under a natural roof of fallen bough and brambles. The rain penetrated the foliage above them but only in drips. They would be relatively protected from the storm here.

Julian spoke in hushed whispers, barely audible above the falling rain. "What are you doing up here?"

"Looking for Dylan. And for you."

"Me? You shouldn't have come alone. That was very foolish."

"I came with a group, but we've been separated. Listen, more children have been taken from the city, and the tanner's son was found murdered near the mountain path. Some believe that *you* murdered the boy."

Julian stared at Cassie. "Me? Why would I be suspected of such a horrible crime?"

"Because I ... I may have suggested you were responsible."

"What?"

"An opal was found with the boy, identical to the one you gave me." Cassie shrugged. "I suppose people like to jump to conclusions."

"Well, it wasn't me."

"I believe you. I've run into any number of potential candidates. What's happening up here?"

"Madness. They're all insane."

Cassie blew warm air into her numb hands. "Jacob told me that the lay brothers are gone. He said that he and his men are the last on the mountain."

Julian frowned. "Jacob and his men are in danger. They must get out."

"I think Jacob's dead. He stayed behind to make sure we'd have a chance to make it. He saved us."

Julian slammed his fist into his palm. "Curse those bastard fiends."

Cassie looked around frantically. "Hush. Stay quiet, Julian. Their senses are keen beyond ours. They might hear us. Where's Dylan? You said he's still alive."

"Yes. I ... I found him in a cell in the darkness."

"Are you sure it's him?"

Julian nodded. "I was able to speak to the boy."

"Is he alright? What did he say? Can we get to him?"

"Slow down. We can't go back up there. We need help. You said you came with others. Where are they?"

"Dead, I think. John and Ivan are dead. I don't know where Carl is. There were a few more men, but they stayed at the lower elevator station."

"Shit. They'll be slaughtered if they don't get out."

"Then we have to go back up and tell them."

"Damn it, Cassie, we can't. You saw those things. You were lucky to escape with your life, as was I. We go down to Re'Shan, call for aid, and then return when the odds are in our favour."

"How did you escape?"

Julian took a deep breath and leaned back against the side of the ditch. He put his hands to his face and rubbed at his eyes with the heels of his hands. "Onion and leek soup."

"What?"

"They drugged us. The evening meal of onion and leek soup contained sedatives. Blackwing is responsible, I'm sure of it."

"I met him. Unpleasant man, he and his toady, Rollant. And I do mean *toady*. Have you seen the man's tongue? What could alter a person like that?"

"I don't know, but I suspect ..." The lay brother trailed off and remained silent.

Cassie leaned forwards and almost shook Julian by his habit collar. "What? What do you suspect? Tell me."

"I can't be sure. I have ... indistinct memories. I'm not even sure how I managed to escape but I recall finding Martin and the other lay brothers imprisoned in the darkness. They were still stupefied, and I couldn't ... I couldn't get them out. I heard noises, voices, so I ran and hid."

"Was Dylan with them?"

"No, they're keeping the children in another place."

"How many?"

"Nine, or so Dylan told me."

Cassie gasped. "*Nine?* Why, why are they taking children? Why kill the tanner's boy and keep the others alive?"

"I don't know. Everything I remember is so ... confused. But the children are held somewhere in the underground places in the mountain. I came upon them by chance as I stumbled blindly through the deep passages. They are frightened but unharmed."

Cassie started softly crying. "We have to get them all out."

"I was discovered before I could ... I couldn't do anything. I'm sorry, Cassie."

Cassie sniffed and wiped away her tears. "How did you get out? How was it that no one found you?"

"They did find me." Julian held up his dagger. "I fought my way out."

"With one short blade? How is that possible?"

"They can be killed. They bleed and they die. What are you suggesting? That they *let me go*? That I am *one of them*?"

"No, I'm not suggesting that. But we must get the children out."

Julian's eyes glazed over. "It is the blood of innocents. Always we desire innocence."

Cassie frowned. "What did you say?"

Julian blinked. "It's something I overheard one of the foul creatures say. *Always we desire innocence.*"

"Is that why they want to abduct children? For their innocence? What, is it some kind of currency to them?"

"I don't know." Julian shook his head. "It doesn't matter. We must get to Re'Shan to call for aid. We can do nothing alone."

"Let's go, now. We must not delay."

"No. They are watching the mountain further down, waiting. They have the advantage at night. As you said, their senses are sharper than ours. But at daybreak, we have a chance."

"Can we wait until daybreak?"

"We have no choice."

The rain began to ease. Instead of a hissing downpour, it had turned into a thin pattering above their heads. Cassie leaned forwards and said, "Somebody must get word to the City Guard and the Senate. Another sunrise may be one too late for the children."

Julian turned his palms out in a gesture of helplessness. "I know little of what the monks have become, but I know that the night is their domain. They'll find us and kill us before morning if we attempt to move further down. I've been trying to get out all night, but they know I'm here and have blocked the way down."

Cassie looked around and hugged herself against the chill. "How much longer until sunrise?"

"Three hours, give or take."

"I'll go now. I can make it."

Julian reached out and gripped Cassie's forearm. "You have courage but running alone in the darkness will mean your death."

Cassie fought back more tears. "Yerty wants her brother back."

Julian squeezed her forearm. "Then we have to stay alive, because you and I are the only people who know what's going on."

"You fought them and lived. I can do it, too. Don't you want to free the children and your friends?"

"Damn it, Cassie. You know I do. Martin is still up there. But I was lucky to make it out. We need help, do you understand? We'll need an army to take this mountain. Our first objective is to stay alive until sunrise. Then, we make the run down to Re'Shan."

Cassie was about to argue when she heard the snapping of a

branch nearby. Somebody or something was close. Julian raised his dagger and balanced on the balls of his feet, head cocked, finger to his lip in a gesture of silence.

The rain had now stopped completely, only the dripping of water from needles to the damp earth. Cassie thought she heard whispering voices. The noise of the rain had hidden her and Julian, but no longer. The mad monks would hear everything, every word they spoke, every breath. The monks were close; the hair on the back of Cassie's neck stood on end. She gripped her own dagger tightly, her hand trembling.

The brambles above them disappeared and a leering face obscured the moon.

"I've found them!" Kristoff screamed. Julian sprang up and drove his dagger into the man's throat. Kristoff gurgled and fell backwards. Julian and Cassie jumped from the ditch and sprinted headlong through the bracken, under bough and branch, once more the hunted.

Shrieking laughter all around them. Cassie stuck at Julian's heels, following him in the hope he knew where he was going, in the hope that he would lead them both to safety. But hope was a damp, tired thing here on the side of Mount Ulfur. Hope would not see the dawn. Hope's legs had turned to jelly. Hope was about to have its throat torn out.

Klaus jumped unseen from a tree and knocked Julian off his feet. Cassie struck at the tall German with her boot and then her blade, missing her target but giving Julian a moment to gain his feet. Kristoff, blood still streaming from the gash in his throat, sprinted into Cassie's back and something in her spine cracked as she fell face first to the ground. Lawrence appeared through the trees and raised his sharpened fingernails, baring his teeth like a feral dog. Julian pulled Kristoff off Cassie, plunging his dagger once more into the man's neck and chest. Kristoff screamed and backed away, blood pouring from his wounds. Julian stood over Cassie, swinging his dagger. A sharp shock cut through Cassie's right arm as she struggled to get up. She ignored the pain and stood back-to-back with Julian: two mortal daggers against three sets of supernatural claws and fangs, against hell unleashed on the mountainside. Their weapons and courage would not be enough.

"Julian, Jules, my friend, calm down." Klaus raised his hands placatingly as he walked closer. "What's happening here?"

Julian pointed his dagger at Klaus. "You trying to kill us is what's happening."

"Only because you haven't ascended. But look." Klaus reached in his habit pocket and held out a crucifix made of sky-metal. "I have this for you. They told me to kill you, I admit it. But I don't want to. Join us, for you still have time."

Julian frowned. "Another crucifix? You and Vernon both. Why offer it to me?"

"Don't you understand?" Klaus looked exasperated. "This is what allows us to ascend, to attain enlightenment. We've worked it, Lawrence, Kristoff, and me. We've swum in it. We need no crucifix, for it's *in* us."

Julian backed away, shaking his head in confusion and staring at the crucifix as it shimmered in ever-changing colours. "What are you talking about?"

"Just shut up and put the crucifix on," Klaus pleaded. "The woman must die, but once you put it on, that won't matter."

"Fuck that!" shrieked Kristoff as he pawed at the gashes in his neck and chest, blood covering his trembling pale fingers. "Julian tried to kill me! End him!"

Klaus waved Kristoff away. "Jules doesn't understand. He didn't mean to hurt you. You will heal, Kris. Look, already the blood stops flowing." Klaus pointed to the affronted lay brother and sure enough the blood had congealed, the edges of the wounds in his neck sealing themselves shut.

Kristoff was having none of it. "But he tried to kill me. You can't deny it. He's not one of us. We have orders, Klaus. We follow them or *we* will be the ones torn asunder."

Klaus sighed. "Let me try one last time. Come, Jules. Join us."

Julian swept his dagger this way and that. "What are you going to do with Martin? Why do you hold the lay brothers and the children against their will?"

Klaus spread his hands wide and shrugged innocently. "Martin is safe and well, as are the children. No harm shall come to them."

"They're lying," Cassie said.

"Of course we're lying." Lawrence took a step towards Cassie. He stopped as she raised her dagger. Lawrence snarled, "Run, woman. This is none of your concern."

Cassie squared her feet. "You took Dylan. Come closer, fucker, and you'll see just what concern I hold in my heart for the boy."

Klaus slipped the crucifix of sky-metal into his habit pocket. "A shame. It's a gift, a gift that you spurn without truly understanding. Look at me, Jules. I fear nothing now. I'm free. I'm strong." Klaus looked around and his eyes came to rest on a thick branch on the ground. He picked it up and broke it in two effortlessly. Cassie shuddered. Power like that could allow Klaus to snap bones as cleanly as he had snapped the tree branch. "I no longer fear the night," Klaus said. "I no longer fear the mountain. It is Mother and God to us now." Klaus began to shake with emotion. "I'm not afraid anymore. You should have joined us, Jules, we're brothers. But you have turned your back on me, on us. You've turned your back on God."

"Stay back." Julian held out his dagger. Cassie swiped back

and forth with her own weapon, but Lawrence and Kristoff merely smiled and kept on coming. Lawrence grabbed at Cassie's dagger and missed. His teeth seemed to be sharpened points. He growled and cackled and lunged again, his fingers grasping Cassie's knife briefly. Blood sprayed as Cassie pulled the dagger away, nearly severing the lay brother's fingers, but Lawrence did not seem to care. He shrieked with laughter.

A wolf howled from somewhere nearby. Klaus jerked his head around, his face screwed up in fury, and now confusion. Lawrence and Kristoff backed away, licking at their sharpened teeth. The wolf call came again, followed by a sharp whistle, and then two men stepped out of the shadows at the edge of the clearing and into the moonlight.

One of the men, the bigger of the two, pointed a finger at Klaus. "It is *you* that has turned your back on God."

"Who are you?" Klaus hissed. "Are you enlightened?" Klaus sniffed the air. "No. No, you are yet stained by the unholy filth of the city."

The second man, the smaller pale one, turned to the first and said, "You see? You need a bath. Been saying it for weeks."

Both men drew weapons and advanced.

29
KILL THEM ALL

Klaus did not desire to kill Julian, but his former friend's refusal to put on the crucifix and join them enraged the tall German.

And now, to confound matters, two men had emerged from the trees and joined forces with Julian and the woman. But when Klaus saw how the two newcomers moved, his rage dissipated, replaced by anxiety. These men were not simply good shepherds coming to the aid of innocent sheep that had wandered from the flock. Not at all. Look how they handled their weapons, how they came in swinging fearlessly. The big one with the ginger beard wore a sleeveless leather vest under a wolfskin cloak, the wolf's head still attached. The muscles in his arms bulged and flexed as he swung his massive sword. The other one was lithe, dressed in a flowing shirt of white silk, his face thin and pale, his weapon a strange cutting tool that looked like a dog chain with serrated teeth along its metallic edge. It cracked viciously as it cut this way and that through the air.

These men were not here by chance. Word had already

reached the city below and now they were coming. This was merely the vanguard.

We need more time, Klaus thought. Prior Blackwing had promised they would have more time. Klaus had to run, to get word to the others above. No, no, he would not run. He, Kristoff, and Lawrence were ascended, enlightened, possessed of supernatural strength. They would slaughter Julian, the woman, and the newcomers, regardless of their fighting skills. No mortal could defeat the sky-metal Ordained.

Kristoff screamed as his arm was almost severed at the elbow by the slender warrior's serrated whip in a flashing strike that defied the eye's ability to follow it. Blood coated the long, snaking weapon as it hissed through the air, biting again and again. Kristoff shrieked in fury and pain and clutched at his useless limb, backing away.

The fear that Klaus had worked so hard to suppress returned in a heated wave that set his heart on fire.

———

"Are you afraid?"

Yerty looked up into the eyes of the woman sitting on the other side of the fire. Martha sat cross-legged, her back straight, hands upturned on her knees, adopting a meditative pose. The two of them sat between several spruce and larch trees, protected from the recent rain by a tarpaulin resting over low branches overhead.

"There are evil things in the shadows," Yerty said. "Yes, I am afraid."

"Evil that took your brother?" Martha asked. The woman's sword rested beside her and at either hip was a curved hunting knife in a sheath. Her belt contained metal stars with sharpened points. Yerty had never seen a woman, or a man for that matter, so well-armed.

Yerty nodded. "Yes. It took my brother." Her skin prickled at the sight of Martha's eyes glowing in the firelight, eyes seemingly formed from liquid silver, the pupils almost indiscernible under her eyelashes. Her hair was pure white, tied back, and falling behind her ears like a misted waterfall. *A ghost*, Yerty thought. *I sit at a fire with a ghost.* The overall impression of a wraith was accentuated by the gossamer thread of the woman's white silk shirt.

Martha threw a handful of twigs on the fire. "Do you believe?"

"Do I believe what, ma'am?"

"Call me Martha. Do you believe in God? The Lord gives life beyond death to his followers. If death cannot touch you, why should you fear any man?"

"It is not man that scares me. It was something else that took Dylan. Something born from the Underworld." The wind blew through the trees, chilling Yerty's neck and back. "I fear for my brother's soul."

"There is no more dry fuel for the fire." Martha reached within a knapsack and pulled out a green shawl. She gave it to Yerty to wrap around her shoulders.

Yerty took it. "Thank you, ma'am."

"You may call me Martha. I insist."

"Thank you, Martha."

"Sweet child. Do not fear for your brother. Pain is brief, suffering short. Heaven is eternal." Yerty lowered her head and nodded. Martha sighed. "My words are ill-chosen. Forgive me. I have no talent for consolation."

Yerty swallowed hard. "There's nothing to forgive. But I won't let Dylan go just yet." She brightened and said, "Miss Cass thinks he may still be alive. She came up here to look for him. She's brave, Miss Cass is, but I don't think she quite understood what she was getting into."

Yerty flinched at the dull cracking of damp twigs: something moving off in the darkness. Martha made no sign that she had heard the noise. A moment later a man entered the firelight, holding an armful of dry branches. Gregor eased the dry wood to the forest floor and sat down beside Martha.

With a wink at Yerty, he placed some more branches on the fire and in a gruff voice said, "The Ice Maiden never smiles." It took Yerty a few seconds to understand he was referring to Martha. "I hope you haven't caught your death of cold merely from her presence."

Martha did not, indeed, smile, nor did she frown, yet reproach laced her voice when she spoke. "Gregor, the child does not appreciate your attempt at humour."

"How would you know what she appreciates?" Gregor scoffed. "And who says I'm joking?"

"Where are the others?" Martha asked.

Gregor's brown beard had threads of grey. Frown lines creased his brow; smile lines webbed the corners of his eyes. He was not young, perhaps approaching his fiftieth year. "Anguilla and Ulf are scouting ahead. Forrester is trying to convince the woodcutter to stay with us, but the man is fearful and insists on returning to Re'Shan."

"What is he fearful of?"

Gregor looked at Yerty and his eyes seemed to burn with pale fire, a stark contrast to Martha's eyes of cool mercury. "The same thing this child is. Monsters in the dark."

Martha gave a slight shrug. "Let the woodcutter go. The man has brought us this far and must return to his family. Besides, he has described the path above adequately. We do not need him anymore."

"We do not know what we face," Gregor said. "It would be good to have another stout heart on our side."

"We have another stout heart." Martha nodded towards Yerty. "Perhaps the stoutest of us all."

Yerty lowered her head and spoke softly. "I am not brave. I'm shaking with fear."

"I see no such shaking," Martha said. "Gregor, do you see the girl tremble?"

Gregor ran his gaze of pale fire over Yerty. "No. This one is warrior born."

Yerty looked up, her eyes wide. "I am a child. I am told that I am sickly and frail. How can I be a warrior?"

Martha leaned forwards and whispered, "It's not the size of the warrior that counts. It's the size of the fight in the warrior."

Gregor grunted his approval. Yerty wondered if the two were making fun of her, but when she realized they spoke in earnest, something swelled within Yerty's chest. Could she truly be *warrior born*?

"Speaking of stout hearts," Martha said. "Take this." She removed one of her hunting knives and its sheath from her left hip and handed it to Yerty. "Do you know how to use a knife?"

Yerty slid the curving blade from its leather sheath and threw the weapon into the air. It spun three times until she caught it by the hilt. "Yes, I do. Miss Cass taught me."

Martha nodded appreciatively. "I like the sound of this Miss Cass. Child, listen to me. If Gregor and I fall, if the others fall, and you find yourself in danger, strike out with this weapon and do not stop until your enemy is dead"—Martha helped Yerty tie the sheath to her waist with a thin leather cord—"or you are."

"Get some sleep, both of you," Gregor said. "We continue up the mountain at first light."

A wolf howled in the distance, and then the harsh voices of

men echoed from the same direction. Gregor made a rumbling sound in his throat and both he and Martha got to their feet.

"That is Ulf's call," Martha said. "He and Anguilla have found something. Come, Yerty. No sleep for us, not yet. We are on the hunt." Martha buckled on her sword and moved off into the trees, Gregor at her side and carrying a long-handled axe.

Yerty scurried to keep up.

———

Kristoff's arm had been destroyed by the pale warrior's flexile, serrated chain. Clasping at the wound to staunch the flow of blood, he ducked and weaved in a desperate attempt to evade a fatal blow. Lawrence had by this time engaged the man in the wolfskin, sliding under and around hefty sword blows with supernatural agility. Lawrence managed to get in and slice at the big man's stomach with sharpened fingernails. The ginger-bearded warrior's leather cuirass, now torn, was the only thing that prevented his guts spilling out onto the forest floor. The Wolfman howled in feral battle rage, ignoring the blood seeping from his wound, and swept his massive sword in a horizontal arc. Lawrence easily evaded the blow once more.

Klaus slashed at Julian and Cassie with his sharpened fingernails, and they returned swift attacks with their daggers, neither side finding its mark. Klaus shrieked in frustration. This confrontation must end swiftly. There was no time to dance here with these fools, for Klaus had no doubt that more were coming, more warriors with death in their hearts. He must inform Abbot Howard and Prior Blackwing. They would know what to do.

As the lifeblood flowed from his arm, weakening him, Kristoff began to cackle. He lifted the hem of his habit with one hand and did a jig, tapping his sandalled heels together. The bizarre behaviour caused a temporary lull in the battle as all eyes turned quizzically in his direction. The blood stopped flowing from the gory wound at his elbow. Kristoff stopped dancing and stood motionless. The moon seemed to shine brighter, illuminating the sweat trickling from his forehead. Kristoff snorted and spat a globe of bile. It landed on Julian's leather sandal and hissed as it began to eat its way through the leather. Julian screamed in agony and pulled his sandal from his foot and cast it away, the smell of burning meat wafting on the night breeze. Kristoff snorted and spat acidic bile again and again, causing his enemies to scatter like chickens before a fox.

While this was going on, Lawrence seemed to light up in myriad sparks. When the light faded, he stood transformed. His eyelids had turned inside out of their own volition, revealing red flaps of flesh. The skin on his face and hands, and indeed his entire body, had hardened into a leathery, dimpled organic armour of a sickly green sheen. The pupils of his eyes narrowed into reptilian slits.

Klaus smiled at the shocked stares from the enemy. Now these fools would understand that the ordained could not be stopped.

Lawrence ignored the Wolfman and lunged at Cassie, but she struck him in the chest as he moved in, her dagger merely bouncing off his reptilian armour. Julian stepped in and brought his knee up into Lawrence's midriff, but again could deal no hurt to the man. Both Julian and Cassie struggled with Lawrence but could not bring him to the ground, their weapons now useless, his strength quickly overpowering theirs.

Suddenly, a shouting. Klaus whirled around. Three more figures entered the clearing: a man with a forked beard, a pale woman with long white hair, and, oddly, a female child. Klaus cursed out loud. The trident-bearded man screamed a battle cry as he came in swinging a long-handled axe. Kristoff spat at him, catching the man in the chest with his acidic bile, but the burly newcomer did not stop, nor call out in pain. He merely cut Kristoff's head clean off with a well-aimed swing of his axe.

Klaus nearly wet himself as his friend's headless corpse dropped to the forest floor. He backed away, preparing to run. The woman with long white hair leaped upon Lawrence, who had Cassie pinned to the ground, despite Julian's best efforts to pull him off. The newcomer brushed Julian aside and reached her hand over Lawrence's head and buried her fingers in his eyes. Lawrence screamed but did not relent. Blood dripped from Cassie's nose as Lawrence throttled the life from her. The pale woman removed a hairpin at the back of her head and inserted it neatly into Lawrence's eye socket, burying it deep into his brain.

Lawrence shrieked and jumped ten feet into the air, twisting as he did so. When he landed, he thrashed, screaming, about the forest floor, sending up a shower of damp pine needle and cone. The slender warrior with the metallic whip slashed at the prone Lawrence but could not penetrate the protective skin-armour. The Wolfman came in howling with his massive sword raised over his head and brought it down with a tremendous effort. This time, the organic armour gave and Lawrence, like Kristoff, lost his head.

Julian knelt beside Cassie. She was neither conscious nor breathing. Yerty rushed to her side, calling out her name. The hunters turned their eyes to Klaus. No one noticed the subtle translucent lights spilling dreamily upwards from the corpses of Kristoff and Lawrence. A moth floated through the clearing, its wings limned in the moonlight. It settled on Klaus's bony shoulder. The next moment a wind built up between the tree boles. But this was no natural wind. A cloud of insects, as numerous as locusts in the wheat fields, burst into the clearing:

moths, dragonflies, cicadas fluttering at mouths, eyes, and ears, threatening to suffocate, blind, and deafen.

Julian gagged on the dusted wings of moths and segmented bodies of cicadas. He couldn't see anything, couldn't breathe. He put his arm around Yerty's shoulder and together they leaned over to shield Cassie from the choking storm of insects. He felt Cassie's breath on his face and realized that she was still alive.

Then the cloud of insects dissipated like a puff of hashish smoke in a breeze. Klaus was gone.

Cassie coughed and opened her eyes. "Yerty?"

"Oh, Miss Cass." Yerty brushed Cassie's hair back from her forehead and then placed her check on that of her mistress. Cassie clasped the girl to her.

Julian sat back on his haunches and surveyed the clearing. The four warriors stood together talking. He tried to catch what they were saying as he retrieved his sandal, now with a sizeable hole in it thanks to Kristoff's acidic bile. He slipped it on tenderly, his foot still raw where Kristoff's spit had touched it.

The Wolfman held his sword up towards the slender warrior in the white shirt. "You see, Anguilla, that is why the sword is a superior weapon to your whip. You could not cut the creature's head from its shoulders, and yet I managed to do so."

"You also managed to take a blow, Ulf. Are you hurt?"

Ulf looked to his torn leather vest and the trickle of blood. "It is nothing. It will heal. What are you suggesting?"

Anguilla shrugged his lean shoulders. "Merely that your large weapon makes you slow."

Ulf bridled. "I struck the killing blow. I, not you."

The pale man gestured towards the woman with liquid mercury eyes. "Martha killed the man with her hairpin. You simply added the final flourish."

Ulf took an outraged breath. "Bullshit. Everyone saw it. You disabled an arm, but I took a head."

"It doesn't matter who did what," Martha said. "Stop measuring your pricks against one another. We must hunt down the tall one."

"And Forrester?" Gregor asked, looking to Anguilla and Ulf. "Where is he?"

Ulf slid his massive sword into its equally massive scabbard. "Last I saw him, he was escorting the woodcutter back down the path." The man rubbed at his ginger beard. "Do you think he is in danger?"

Martha pointed to Gregor's chest where the leather vest smouldered.

Gregor, noticing it for the first time, patted it down with a rough, calloused hand and said, "The Devil cavorts on this mountainside, but if he runs into Forrester, the Devil had better watch his arse."

———

Forrester watched the tall man in the monk's habit bound past him like some frantic, oversized hare and caught the whiff of Satan in the man's passing.

What had the girl said? The monks were cursed, crazed by some supernatural metal that turned mortal man into monster. Here, clearly, was one of the beasts in human form.

Forrester moved out from behind a wall of bracken and fern, crouched low, and followed the fiend, making sure to stay in the darkest shadows of the larch and spruce. Despite the obscene speed with which the creature loped through the forest, it could not evade or outpace him, for no man or monster knew the ways of the woods better than he. Forrester was God's chosen Woodsman, the greatest of the Lord's Cutters.

Forrester sniffed brimstone on the air and caught sight of robes flapping up ahead. He sprinted after the monk, choosing only soft bare earth, his sharp eyes picking out the most silent path as his feet found secure and noiseless passage through the trees.

Putting a hand to the hilt of his sword to silence it, Forrester approached the unaware monk from behind as he stood panting in a small clearing. He must surprise the foul creature, not allow it to transform, mutate, or present whatever powers the Devil had gifted it. The archbishop had been clear in his instructions: this growing evil must be stopped, sawn in two, and toppled like Lucifer's rotten tree, its roots pulled from God's earth.

And Forrester the Woodsman was just the man to do it.

30
ON BLACK WINGS

Klaus stopped, his breath rasping in his throat. Where was the entrance to the hidden paths in the mountain? He stood before an abandoned woodsman's hut a few yards from a cliff face and looked around. Klaus did not recognize either the hut or the small clearing it occupied. In his haste to escape the hunters, he had become disoriented in the woodlands.

Kristoff and Lawrence were dead. This was not possible. They were sky-metal Ordained. How could God have allowed this to happen? Why gift such wondrous powers, only to have death erase them forever? He sobbed as he remembered once more the taste of Kristoff's lips on his own, recalled Lawrence's firm, slick flesh pressed between them.

Klaus swallowed his tears and closed his eyes, sending out mental waves. He felt the responses of the spiders and huhu beetles and the cicadas in the spruce and larch, each insect giving off a distinctive echo in his mind, but it was not these he sought. He searched further until he found a single vibration of the appropriate size and shape. He called that one small creature to him, and then that one called more of its ilk. An amber mist appeared at the edges of the dilapidated woodcutter's hut, the lights within the mist pulsing and flickering like lightning behind storm clouds. Fireflies, hundreds of thousands of them, swirled into the clearing and around Klaus. The tall German gave them instructions, urging them to hurry.

Show me the way. Find the entrance to the hidden paths.

The skin at the nape of his neck crawled and Klaus glanced behind himself to make sure that none of the crazed warriors had managed to pick up his trail and come upon him before he could escape. Something came hurtling towards him and Klaus jerked his head away. Sparks buzzed in the air, but not those of the fireflies. Klaus collapsed backwards to the forest floor, his control of the fireflies dissipating, causing them to disperse in random patterns. Blood flowed from his mouth and nose, an injury that could have been fatal had he not sensed the attack and moved before the blade could land flush. Klaus rolled as a sword slashed a long divot in the damp earth where he had lain just a split second before.

Klaus had been gifted the supernatural speed of the ascended, but the hunter bearing down on him possessed an unearthly quickness of his own. Klaus had no time to assess the wound to his face, but he suspected that several teeth were missing, and his nose cut in two. This did not matter, for he would heal.

If he had time.

The warrior in black leather vest and leggings gave Klaus no time. He was short and squat, a flared cross of Saint George shaved into his head. No, not shaved, tattooed. It was the man's head that was shaved.

Klaus barely evaded another swing of the man's sword. Mentally, he reached out, seeking to connect once again with his insect allies, but the squat warrior seemed to understand and came in again roaring, swinging, pressing the attack so that

Klaus could not gather the mental concentration necessary to call for aid, all his resources focused on staying alive.

"I am Forrester," the man said, taking another swing. "And I am here to cut you down and purify your spirit."

The wet, warm stickiness of blood coated Klaus's neck and stomach, his habit torn at the abdomen, and he realized that the crazed warrior had somehow struck him at least once more. The man, despite his short stocky build, was inhumanly graceful and lethally quick.

His strength beginning to fail, Klaus made one last attempt to rally his insectile army. And then, against the light of the morning sun now breaking through the treetops in shards of blinding glory, a dark shape appeared, feathered wings spread wide as it descended at great speed behind the unsuspecting Forrester. The birdlike creature crashed into the squat warrior, sending him sprawling face first to the ground.

As Prior Blackwing stood over the unconscious body of Forrester, a child's shrill scream came from nearby. Blackwing turned and, his arms still outstretched, displayed the obscene structure of feather and ligament attached to his ribs and underarms. He shrieked in a high-pitched response to Yerty's terrified shout.

The others stood there with Yerty. Julian and Cassie, Gregor and Martha, Ulf and Anguilla, all of them rooted in shock at the unholy sight of the corvid in human form.

"That's the one what took my brother!" Yerty screamed, pointing at Blackwing.

The superior raised his head in defiance, his eyes narrow slits, his nose hooked and sharp, more beak than nose.

Forrester groaned and began to stir, spitting damp earth from his mouth. Blackwing raised a clawed hand to strike at Forrester before the Woodsman could rouse himself. Martha was faster and threw a metal star. Blackwing howled in pain and leaped back, unable to land the killing blow on the prone Forrester. Blackwing grabbed Klaus around the waist and leaped into the air. Another metal star tore through an obscene wing. The monstrous birdman gave a harsh caw of agony and anger but continued to rise, flapping and squawking in a grotesque mockery of a bird taking flight.

And then, Blackwing and Klaus were gone into the morning sun.

31
WE NUMBER EIGHT

Forrester had taken a bad gash to the back of his head from Blackwing's talons. The hunters had decided to rest in the decaying woodsman's hut while Martha tended to the wound.

"I'm alright," grumbled Forrester.

"We stay together," Martha said as she finished stitching the back of Forrester's head. "No more running around alone in the mountain woods. That goes for all of you." She took in Gregor, Anguilla, and Ulf in a glance.

Forrester huffed, "Caught me by surprise, that's all. I wasn't expecting a flying man."

"None of us know what to expect. That is precisely why we stay together." The mercury-eyed woman smoothed a pungent ointment over the completed stitches. "It's lucky you have no hair to interfere with my work."

"Did that devil spawn harm my tattoo?"

"No." Martha tapped Forrester's skull. "The cross of Saint George remains untouched, though I'm not sure the same can be said for your brain."

In the corner of the empty hut, Cassie sat with Yerty on a

carpet of mostly dry mint-smelling needles that had blown through the long-broken window. Cassie held the child's hand. She had not yet told Yerty that Dylan was alive, if he indeed still lived. Perhaps Julian had simply mistaken another child for Dylan. Cassie did not want to get Yerty's hopes up, but perhaps hope was all that they had, so she kissed Yerty's hand and whispered, "Dylan is alive. He's up there." She pointed in the direction of the community of monks. "Julian has spoken to him." At first Yerty looked at Cassie in confusion, then she frowned. Finally, the young girl cried. Cassie hugged her close.

"What are we dealing with?" Gregor asked gruffly to no one in particular.

All eyes turned to Julian, who sat half-dozing against one wall. The young lay brother opened his eyes and examined each hunter in turn before croaking in a dry, tired voice, "Why are you all looking at me? I'm not one of them."

Martha put away her sewing kit in a tan leather bag strapped across her shoulder. "It would appear not. Ulf and Anguilla"—she gestured towards the big man in the wolf's head cloak and the pale, lithe warrior standing watch in the doorway—"say that you and Cassie were attacked by those ... whatever they are ... demons in monks' clothing. This exonerates you as far as I'm concerned."

"But you *are* one of them." Gregor twirled his axe handle in a gnarled fist.

Julian turned sharply to the trident-bearded man. "No, I'm not. I think we have established exactly the opposite. I'm *not* one of them."

"But you *were*," Gregor growled. "A monk, I mean. You were up there when the possession took place."

"Possession?"

Gregor sighed in irritation. "The evil that inhabits the

monks. You know what has taken them. *You* know what we're up against."

Julian let out a long breath. "All I know is that the ordained clerics have gone mad. They hold the lay brothers against their wills."

"And the children," Cassie said.

"Yes." Julian nodded. "They have imprisoned several children, a boy called Dylan among them." Yerty had by now stopped crying. She hugged Cassie's upper arm and examined Julian with wide green eyes, entranced by the mention of her brother.

"Can you get us up there?" Forrester asked, rubbing gingerly at the stitches at the back of his head, only to have Martha slap his hand away.

"We don't need him," Gregor spat before Julian could reply. "I say we take the fastest route, the elevator, and attack them head on."

Cassie spoke up. "Jacob, the man who operates the elevator, is dead, a victim of the monks. I don't think we can operate it without him."

"The elevator would be a trap anyway," Julian added. "The monks won't let you just wander in through the front door. They'll have cut the ropes or such like. You won't make it to the top."

"Is there another way?" Martha asked.

Julian paused, and then nodded. "Yes. There are paths within the mountain itself. I took them to escape. And so did Cassie."

All eyes now turned to Cassie. "I ... Julian's right, I used them to escape, but I was disoriented, running for my life. I don't know where the entrance is."

Martha turned back to Julian. "You know the way. Lead us there."

Julian shook his head. "You cannot possibly hope to defeat the monks with only five of you."

"We number eight," Gregor said.

Julian frowned. "Surely, you cannot be suggesting that Cassie and Yerty accompany you? Or that I go for that matter?"

"And why not?" Martha asked, her eyes cool liquid metal.

Julian almost laughed. "Five or eight, it will make no difference. You're outnumbered. The girl and Cassie at least should be allowed to return to Re'Shan."

"They would be hunted down and assassinated before they made the city gates," Martha said. "They will be safer with us. Besides, Yerty is in training."

"In training?" Cassie said.

"Yes, I believe she will make an excellent scrutator."

"Scrutator? Is that what you people are? Judge, jury, and executioner?"

"Just the executioner part," Gregor growled, his axe still twirling in his fist.

"I won't allow it," Cassie said. "When this is over, she's coming home with me."

Martha put her hands on her hips. "To what? A life on the streets? With us, she will have regular meals, duty, and a sense of honour, a purpose to her life."

"No, no," Cassie said, waving Martha away. "She's a child. I have placed her in harm's way, this I know. There's always risk in the life of a thief, but what you suggest ... is madness. She is no warrior in training, no scrutator."

"Our life is one of hardships, true," Martha said, "but it is life in service of God. What more could a child—"

"No, no. She's not a ... a murderer."

Gregor laughed abrasively and Martha scowled. "Nor are we. Let the child decide. If she wishes to join us, I will see that it is done."

Yerty still clung to Cassie's arm, but there was something in the way she attended to the conversation that suggested she might be considering Martha's offer.

"I think you're missing the point," Julian said. "None of you will survive this."

"He's right," Cassie said. "This isn't the first time I've climbed this mountain with an armed group set upon a righteous course. The last endeavour didn't end well. The militiamen lie dead all over the mountain."

"We are not a poorly trained militia," Martha said.

Julian sighed heavily. "You're asking Cassie and Yerty to enter the most dangerous place in White Cloud, the very den of the Devil. At least allow the child to return."

"I agree with Julian," Cassie said. "This is no place for Yerty."

Yerty jumped into the conversation with a shake of her head. "No, Dylan is up there. He's alive. I'm going to rescue him. We all will."

Martha nodded in satisfaction. "You see? The child is a born scrutator."

Cassie wanted to argue, but the newly lit flame of hope burning in Yerty's emerald eyes quelled all resistance. Yerty had hope, at last she had hope, and Cassie simply could not bring herself to dampen the girl's newfound spirits.

"Besides," Martha said. "Yerty must come along as she appears to be the key to all of this."

Julian looked from Yerty to Martha. "What do you mean *the key*?"

Martha shrugged as if the answer were obvious. "She has identified the cancer that has allowed Satan dominion on this mountain."

Julian turned to Yerty and addressed the green-eyed girl. "What is she talking about?"

Yerty stood up and linked her fingers together, her head bowed. A moment later she looked up into Julian's eyes. "It's the metal, sir. It's the sky-metal from the meteor that drives them all mad. I worked it out. You see—"

"No." Julian got to his feet in turn. "It's something in Blackwing's potions. He's poisoned everyone, driven them mad. I mean, that's the only thing that makes sense." Yerty did not respond, and Julian scratched at the stubble of his tonsure thoughtfully. Cassie wondered if the lay brother would speak again, so long was the silence that filled the interior of the abandoned hut. Then, his eyes widened. "You could be right." Julian paced the hut. "That's why they bade me wear the new crucifix. Why the lay brothers were not similarly affected: their crosses were constructed of wood alone. That's what Klaus meant when he ..." Julian stopped pacing and silence descended once more as he looked around with an expression of distaste.

Gregor eyed Julian suspiciously. "Go on. When he said what?"

Julian frowned hard. "They worked with the metal every day, Klaus and the others, even swam in water infused with the metal. It's in their blood. That's what he said."

"And what exposure have *you* had to this so-called *sky-metal*?" Martha asked coldly.

Julian glanced at Martha, then at Gregor and the others. "I ... I ... none. I have never worn the metal. I refused it."

"Nor swum in the water that you speak of?"

"No." Julian swallowed hard.

Martha folded her arms and stared at Julian. "That is your first lie, lay brother." Gregor growled and took a step towards Julian, axe in hand.

"No, wait, wait." Julian held his hands up and walked backwards. "I fell in the water, once and only for a few seconds. I swear that was all. I was pushed in but got out immediately."

Martha waved Gregor away and stepped closer to Julian, examining his face carefully. After a time, she nodded and turned to the other scrutators. "I sense nothing untoward in the man."

"Keep an eye on him," Gregor growled. "Last thing we need is a surprise from within our group."

"I'm not like them," Julian protested. "I'm not. I'm clean. I swear."

"Then we are agreed," Martha said. "The sky-metal is the source of all this woe. It must be destroyed as must all those it has infected."

"Hang on," Julian said. "No, no. You don't understand. The others, Martin and the others, are being forced to wear the metal. The monks are trying to turn them, don't you see? You can't kill the lay brothers. They're innocent."

"Then we had better get up there quickly," Martha said, "before they turn, for *if* they turn, we must execute our duty."

Cassie shivered at the ghostly woman's choice of phrase: *execute our duty*. These people were committed to their course of action, no doubt, almost fanatical in their enthusiasm, but Cassie would rather be on their side than stand against them. She put an arm around Yerty's shoulder and pulled her closer.

"Inaction is the enemy," Gregor said with a grimace. "The civilians of Re'Shan below are the only true innocents in this matter and must be protected. We'll not sit idly by and watch doom enfold the city."

"Inaction is the enemy," Forrester repeated. The bald, squat man put his hands on his broad hips. "How many fiends inhabit the mountain, Julian?"

"At least a hundred," Julian said. "A frontal assault with so few numbers is tantamount to suicide. We must—"

"You let us worry about the numbers, boy," Gregor growled. He ran a thumb over the flat of his axe blade. "And what of these strange afflictions that the monks bring to bear? We have witnessed a man with the wings of a raven, another with skin that hardens like that of a crocodile. The tall one controls insects. Are we to understand that no two of the accursed creatures have the same abilities?"

"It appears so," Julian said. "This I cannot explain."

Martha turned to her comrades. "This does not bode well for us. We cannot formulate a battle plan when confronted by such peculiar attacks. We must be ready for anything."

Stroking his ginger beard, the massive Ulf pushed himself off the door frame. "Chop their fucking heads off. There's your battle plan."

"Your braggadocio impresses no one." Martha nodded towards Yerty and winked. "Not even the child." Yerty smiled and winked back. "Without a plan," Martha said, "all our strength counts for nothing. We need information. We must be armed with foreknowledge of what they are and what to expect."

Gregor jabbed a finger at Julian. "If it's information you want, there's your information. Tell us, boy. Where are the creatures now?"

"They inhabit the community on the mountain. That is our ... their home and has been for a hundred years."

"Can you get us up there?" Martha asked. "You say there is an alternate route?"

"Yes, the internal paths, as I said, but ... I was dazed when I found my way out through the tunnels."

Martha raised a gossamer eyebrow. "Can you do it? Can you take us there? If not, then you are of little use to us."

Julian's face froze and Cassie, too, understood the latent threat in the statement. Julian had better answer in the affirmative or find himself surplus to requirements.

"I think so." Julian swallowed. "But I urge you to reconsider. You don't have the numbers to succeed."

"We have no time for doubt," Martha said. "The children need us. You will lead us, Julian. You are the only one who can."

Julian threw his hands up. "This is insanity. We must return to Re'Shan to gather a stronger force."

"*We* are God's force," Forrester said. "*We* have made a promise to the Lord." Blood seeped through the stitches in his head, but the squat warrior paid it no heed. "You, surely, understand the concept of holy vows. We will destroy those corrupted by the metal, or we will not leave this mountain."

Julian looked from one warrior to another. "But ... but Martin and the other lay brothers are innocent. Martin has done nothing wrong. It is not his fault, do you understand?"

"We do not deal in fault," Martha said.

"But Martin is clean."

Martha turned away. "Let's hope he remains so."

———

"*Anguilla* is the Latin term for *eel*. Correct?"

Anguilla turned to Cassie as the group climbed a treeless embankment covered in scree, heading directly for a rock face lit up by the midmorning sun.

"Yes, that is so," he said.

Cassie walked beside the man, or more precisely, the man walked beside her and Yerty, assigned, apparently, to protect them in the event of another attack by the mad monks. Anguilla moved with a strange suppleness, and though the others lost their footing repeatedly on the small sliding stones, Cassie's lean bodyguard did not stumble.

"You have a pale complexion, much like Martha. She is your sister, yes? A twin, unless I am mistaken."

Anguilla raised a diaphanous eyebrow in surprise. "Also correct. She mentioned this?"

"No, but Yerty has a twin brother. I recognize the way that twins behave around each other."

The pale man nodded and then smiled at Yerty. "She told me of her brother. We will rescue him, girl, do not fear. The Eel gives his word."

Yerty gripped Cassie's hand tighter. Cassie fervently hoped they were not building the child's expectations too high, only to see them buried forever.

Cassie pointed to a necklace around Anguilla's neck. On a black leather strap hung a thousand small nails of white colour. But they were not nails. They were teeth from countless eels, razor-sharp points of calcified plates.

"Nice necklace," Cassie said. "I see *the eel* is your name and your emblem."

Anguilla nodded and removed his whip. It, like the necklace, contained razor-sharp teeth moulded to resemble those of an eel, though the flexile blade itself was fashioned from metal. "Ulf over there," he said, pointing to the ginger-bearded man up ahead, "thinks he is a wolf. In his language *ulf* is the word for *wolf*, you see? All fanged power and pride, but it is the eel that possesses the most powerful bite of all. These"—he touched the necklace—"once graced the powerful jaws of an extinct animal, but the teeth remain as sharp today as they did when the creature died in the times before time itself." Ulf turned around to look back at them, but he was out of earshot and soon lost interest.

Anguilla went on with a secretive smirk, "The large brute thinks he is the greatest warrior who ever lived. The Wolfman thinks his sword will cut the horns from Lucifer's head someday. But the sword is an ineffective weapon, for it is weighty and causes a man to move too slowly, especially one as ungainly as Ulf."

"I can hear you," Ulf called out from ahead.

"Quiet, you fool," Gregor hissed. "Look, the entrance. We enter the mountain's fouled womb." Up ahead appeared a crack in the cliff wall, a jagged black hole against the midday sun.

Gregor entered first, Martha behind him. Forrester went next. Julian turned to Cassie and the two exchanged glances. Ulf shoved Julian into the opening and the Wolfman disappeared within soon after. Anguilla bowed and with a theatrical flourish of his wrist bade Cassie and Yerty enter the passages within the mountain.

As the damp, echoing darkness of the mountain swallowed Cassie, she wondered if the scrutators were their protectors or something far more sinister.

———

Despite the danger, despite the mad monks running crazed through the internal corridors of Mount Ulfur, potentially jumping on them around the next bend in the passage and unleashing their bizarre and apparently idiosyncratic abilities, Julian wanted for nothing more than to lie down and sleep, even here in the damp, cold belly of the beast.

He hadn't slept since awakening from a drugged, night-mare-infested half slumber ... when? He couldn't remember how many hours or days had passed now. But they needed him, the hunters—the *scrutators* as they referred to themselves—they needed him, or so they said. Mount Ulfur was honey-combed with passages: a catacomb of low-roofed tunnels. It would be easy to get lost, but Julian had a general idea of the path to take. In fact, there was only one main passage. All you had to do was not turn down a tunnel narrower than the one you were currently following and always head upwards. Or downwards depending on where you wanted to go.

The only light came from a torch held in Gregor's meaty hand, and by this wavering flame Julian directed them ever upwards, towards their inevitable deaths, for it could only be death ahead of them. Blackwing was a human crow. He could *fly* and had vicious talons. How could they hope to overcome such monstrosities? A hundred more men, cursed by the sky-metal, awaited them. However, Kristoff and Lawrence were dead, evidence that the creatures could be killed. A flicker of hope in the darkness.

But against the entire Brotherhood, they had little chance. Probably a fitting end, Julian thought. A fitting end for all his wrongs. He felt sorry for Cassie and Yerty, however. They didn't deserve to die like this.

He did, but they didn't.

Wooden children's toys, crackling and curling in the flames. Flesh crackling and curling in the flames. Julian remembered the dream. Remembered the waking nightmare that it had been. No, not a dream at all.

He had wanted to tell Cassie but could not bring himself to do it. Damn it all.

A thought came to him. Perhaps *this* was redemption: to save Martin and Dylan or die trying. *This* was what he'd been preparing for all this time. The thought soothed him against the fear. Yes, if he was going to die, he'd do it for a worthy cause. He would perish on the side of good and all his sins, perhaps, would not weigh him down and drag him to the eternal abyss.

Atonement, after all, was truly worth something.

3²

TOOTH AND CLAW

Abbot Howard shielded his eyes against the midmorning sun and watched the black shape float gently down from the heavens like some angelic raven.

Monks scattered as the creature came in with its wings flapping and then stretching taut to gather the mountain updrafts. The thing's landing, however, was an ungainly event compared to its flight. Prior Blackwing and Lay Brother Klaus crashed to the ground, creating divots in the mountain grass and knocking the air from both men's lungs, though just what lungs Blackwing now possessed, Abbot Howard could not possibly guess. He was a freakish amalgam of man and bird. Still, God wished it so and it was so.

Monks crowded in to burble questions, but soon moved away when Abbot Howard swept forwards, the glow of monastic aristocracy surrounding him like a halo.

"Stand back," the abbot commanded. "Give them room to breathe."

Klaus got to his feet first, his face a long study in amazement, no doubt stemming from the fact that he had just been carried half the height of Mount Ulfur under the arm of Prior

270

Blackwing. His face was also a study in blood, bone, and gristle, a gruesome injury having practically cut the young German's face in two.

Blackwing got to his feet more slowly, breathing hard, the exertion of his flight as telling on his face as pain and shock were evident on that of Klaus.

"I don't think I'll ever get used to those." Howard pointed to the feathered appendages under the superior's arms.

As his wings faded and his face lost its hawkish aspect, Blackwing, now naked without his feathers or clothes, stood tall and said, "They are coming."

Abbot Howard sighed. "I had hoped for more time."

"Hope will aid us no longer. Have the tunnels been stopped up?"

Abbot Howard looked around at the nervous faces of the brothers. "Several men have not returned from this task. They have either encountered difficulties or are ..." He did not finish the thought for fear of alarming the gathered men, who were already fearful enough. "How many come for us?"

Blackwing shook his head. "I cannot be sure. Only a handful at this time, but Julian was among them, and the woman from the city below."

The abbot shrugged and put on a confident show for the brothers. "A handful? What have we to fear from such small numbers? We have ascended beyond mortal man and have already seen off the first wave."

Blackwing shook his head. "You do not understand, Father. This is no disorganized militia of fat middle-aged business-men." Blackwing held up an arm. A large bruise could be seen around a very clear tear in the flesh of his bicep. "They nearly took me down. These people seek to do us harm, and I believe they have the means to do so."

"What means?"

"They are fanatics and have little concern for their own welfare. Fear of death does not deter them."

Howard nodded. "Mmm. That makes them dangerous. Very well." The abbot looked around and shouted at those monks still standing idle. "Get to it! Prepare yourselves. The enemy of God comes looking to wipe you from His chronicles! Look within yourselves for whatever gifts God has planted there and urge them to bloom! We fight tooth and claw this day!"

The monks dispersed, squawking and chittering among themselves. Abbot Howard scurried away, and Prior Blackwing, after a moment's hesitation, followed him.

———

The room echoed to the clink of pieces moving on the board, but little else, for the two men seated at the table, the one in white and the other in black, studied the board in silence.

It was the one in black who finally ended the silence. "Your call to battle was stirring, Father Abbot"—Blackwing rubbed at the blemish-free skin on his cheeks—"but I fear we need a strategy."

"Strategy?" The abbot leaned back from the board. "This is not a game, Superior. The enemy comes seeking our doom."

"All the more reason to have a strategy, your eminence." Blackwing reached across the board and placed a black piece in position, completing a semicircle of white attackers and cornering Abbot Howard's king. "I win."

Howard swallowed his disappointment, took his king, bit its head off, and chewed on it. "What do you propose?"

"We seal ourselves within the mountain."

The abbot nearly choked on the head of his king. "That would allow us nowhere to run if ... the worst comes to the worst."

Blackwing folded his arms. "We know the depths of the mountain better than they do. Even if they find us—"

"If they find us, we'll be trapped. I don't like the idea. I say we stay above ground and fight in the open. Perhaps if we ascend high enough, then the frozen conditions on the mountaintop will deter any pursuit. Besides, what good will those wings of yours do you down there?"

Blackwing demurred. "The heights of the mountain will not stop them. If it is to come to a battle, and it will, then we must choose the battleground. Familiarity with the dark places is our weapon and we must use it to our advantage."

"My instincts rally against your suggestion."

"Then we must go our separate ways, Father. Those who agree with me will accompany me into the mountain."

Howard frowned. "I command this abbey, Blackwing. You've been planning a coup for some time now, and you see the forthcoming attack as the perfect opportunity to execute your power play. Admit it."

The superior waved the abbot away as if to indicate the suggestion was ludicrous. "Survival. We all seek survival. I will put it to the brothers. Those who wish to go down are free to accompany me. The others remain with you."

The abbot threw his headless king across the room with a clatter. "This schism you propose will only weaken us! We stay together. I insist." To make his point the abbot grinned without mirth, showing two lines of razor-sharp diamonds embedded in his gums.

Blackwing said nothing for a moment but simply stared.

Abbot Howard shifted in his chair. He was aware that Blackwing's transformation into a human corvid would bring talons and a beak as capable of rupturing flesh as easily as his own teeth. If the superior attempted to transform, Howard had every intention of leaping across the table to bite the man's throat out before his transmogrification was complete. He monitored Blackwing's thoughts, but if the man had any, he was shielding them from the abbot's mental probes.

Blackwing did not alter his appearance. "Very well," he said. The man in black stood and excused himself with a bow and the kiss of life.

As the door closed, Abbot Howard wondered from how many sides he had to defend himself. The losing position of his pieces on the game board gave him pause for thought. Blackwing was crafty. Very crafty indeed.

Howard hoped that he had the resources to win when it truly counted.

———

Brother Rollant hated Klaus. He had hated him upon his arrival more than a year ago and he loathed the man now.

Klaus was a lay brother. A *lay brother*. He had no right to hold his hands out to receive the gifts given by the Lord. Rollant, himself, had spent two years working his body to the bone and the flesh of his spirit to the nub for one reason and one reason only: to be a choir monk. To be ordained. To be enlightened. To ascend.

But now that prattling German was one of them, just like that, with a mere clicking of God's forefinger against His thumb and a rock from the sky. It wasn't fair. The bastard had at least another year of servile duty, another year of getting Rollant's boot shoved up his mewling arse before he could be considered an equal. And even more galling, Klaus now seemed to have Prior Blackwing's favour. The superior had dragged Klaus from the very clutches of their persecutors and flown him bodily up the mountain to safety. And now here they were, talking closely together, just the two of them.

Rollant made sure to keep out of sight as he watched them through the window of the refectory. The superior's hand was on Klaus's shoulder and his lips close to the German's ear, whispering, whispering, whispering something, the two of them limned by the light of candles within. It was cold and windy outside, but Rollant remained motionless except for his chattering teeth. Something was up, secrets exchanged between the two. Abbot Howard would want to know about this. He had warned Rollant to keep an eye out for just such signs of conspiracy. The community was fracturing, and that German bastard had something to do with it.

Rollant had to find out what Klaus and Blackwing were up to. It would not do to go to the abbot with unsubstantiated speculation. Time was running out. Better to tackle this head on. Rollant waited until Blackwing swept from the refectory and disappeared.

When Klaus left the monks' dining hall, Rollant followed, keeping to the shadows.

33

THE WHETSTONE AND THE BLADE

"You have a spider in your hair."

Cassie flicked at her short brown locks. "Is it gone?"

"Yes," Julian said.

The slick walls of the rock tunnel seemed luminous in the torchlight. At certain points the tunnel narrowed, and the roof became so low that they had to crawl through on hands and knees until the passage opened out again.

"These are not the paths that I took when fleeing the monks," Cassie whispered, getting to her feet after one such narrow crawl space. She helped Yerty to stand and dusted off the child's tunic. Cassie knew that Yerty hated dirt, but the girl remained stoic. She would swim through a sewer to save her brother.

"How would you know?" Julian whispered back. "One tunnel looks much like another."

"When we came down, not once did we have to crawl through any small apertures. Jacob certainly wouldn't have fit through any. This is a different path, I'm sure of it."

"Well, I don't pretend to know all the secrets of the mountain. This is the way that I came, at least. I think."

"You think?"

"Like I said, one way looks much like another."

Gregor stopped where the tunnel opened into a junction, left and right paths leading off, the left angling down, the right ascending. Behind him stood Forrester and Martha. Julian, Cassie, and Yerty formed the middle section of the party while Ulf and Anguilla followed up behind.

"I assume," Gregor growled, "that we take the right-hand path."

"If it's heading up," Julian said, "we follow it."

"Your method of orientation seems rather simple," Forrester said. "Are you saying we always go up?"

"That's what I'm saying," Julian replied. "If you want to reach the monks, you go up. Makes sense, yes?"

Forrester grunted. Neither he nor Gregor looked convinced.

"Normally, in situations like this," Forrester said, "the most obvious solution is not always the best. Paths tend to double back on themselves or even come to dead ends."

Julian scoffed. "And just how many times have you been in a situation like this? Do you and your allies make a habit of chasing feral quarry through the insides of mountains?"

"You'd be surprised, young fellow," Forrester said. "You'd be surprised."

"Who are you people?" Julian said. "Where did you spring from all of a sudden?"

"What does it matter?" Forrester said. "Without us, you and your lady friend would be dead."

"I'm not complaining," Julian said. "I am simply enquiring as to your origins."

"We represent God," Forrester said. "We are His scrutators. Archbishop Courtenay has the ear of the Pope in the Old World, and we—"

Martha cut the squat man off. "I don't think this is the time or place to be discussing this. We are here in the capacity of *scrutators*, as Forrester said. Let that be enough. Which path do we take?"

Julian shrugged. "Up. The right fork."

"Very well," Martha said. "We go up."

The crew continued to ascend through the belly of Mount Ulfur, the only sounds to accompany them those of their own breathing and footfalls bouncing off the circular tunnel walls. They soon came to an open space, the torchlight barely illuminating the chamber roof several feet above their heads.

Gregor paused in the chamber and the others came to a stop behind him. The trident-bearded warrior held his torch out towards one of the cave walls. "Do you see that?"

"I see nothing," Forrester said.

Julian stepped up beside Gregor and squinted. "Pull the torch away."

Gregor removed the torch from the wall and took several steps back. A shimmer began to appear in cracks in the wall, like the moonlight reflected from distant waves on a dark ocean.

"It's the metal," Julian whispered. "Traces of the sky-metal embedded in the undersides of the mountain."

"Stand back!" Forrester pulled Julian away. "If this is the accursed material that has corrupted the brothers above, then you must not go near it." Veins of shimmering colour now became clearly visible in the rock wall.

"It's beautiful," Yerty whispered, transfixed by the oddly pulsing rivulets of purple, pink, and sky-blue. Cassie dragged her away from the rock wall. This was the source of the evil on the mountain, the reason for the children's abductions, and Cassie didn't want Yerty anywhere near it.

"Beautiful things have the power to entrance," Martha said.

"But a thing's true nature often remains hidden. Do not be fooled by this. We must look away."

One by one, with great reluctance, the members of the party turned their backs on the translucent veins of sky-metal. They found a passage leading from the cave and followed it. At the next junction, a noise issued briefly like a cold whisper.

"What was that?" hissed Ulf. When no one responded to his question, the ginger-bearded warrior shook his head in concern. "This was a foolish idea. We cannot fight in these narrow spaces under the mountain. We're vulnerable to any number of traps. We should have stayed outside."

Anguilla patted Ulf on the shoulder. "Is your fear of the small places unnerving you?"

"I said nothing of fear," Ulf responded curtly. "A true warrior needs the blue skies overhead. We are not bats or insects. To blindly scuttle through the darkness is to allow our enemy the advantage."

"Steady, Wolfman." Anguilla smirked. "I'll not have your tears staining your beautiful red beard, or your reputation as a hard man."

"I'll stain my beard with your fucking blood in a minute."

"Quiet, the both of you," Martha snapped. "Listen." A slight tremor rolled through the floor along with the sounds of what seemed like harsh sand falling in an hourglass.

"We must light another torch soon," Gregor said. "We cannot stand idly around and let the next one burn through, or we will find ourselves truly blind. Do we go on or turn back?"

"We go on," Martha said.

Ulf shook his head. "I don't like it. This smells of death. We must go back. The fiends are intent on entombing us within a sepulchre. We must get outside before the mountain becomes our grave. We could try for the elevator."

"You heard Julian," Martha said. "There is no way up via that avenue."

"Here, perhaps." Julian pointed into the darkened tunnel leading slightly upwards. "As good a way as any, I suppose."

Ulf balked. "You seem an unsure guide and that is a dangerous thing. Without a clear route we simply wander aimlessly until the monks have sealed off all our escapes one by one. I say we go back down to the outside. Right now."

"Quiet," Martha said. "I hear something."

Silence settled on the group like bone dust on a crypt floor, only to be disturbed a moment later by soft, scuffling footfalls coming from the untried passage. Something approached them, something big enough to create a draught, shunting the very air at them as if it could not share the same passage with a creature so large. Gregor covered the torch as best he could, and darkness swallowed them. Then, the shuffling stopped somewhere up ahead; the subterranean breeze died off. The group listened and it seemed as if the other thing had stopped to do the same. Two forces in the darkness, listening.

Forrester broke the silence. "We have come for you, Devil Spawn. There is no place you can hide. Fear the wrath of the Righteous God."

A laugh, deep and echoing, came from just outside the torchlight. "I'm not hiding. And God's wrath rides with me, friend."

Forrester held his sword in two hands, pointing into the darkness. "Step into the light. Reveal yourself."

Into the torchlight stepped a man in a brown habit with a black hood, a large man, big enough that he had to bend over, and in this section of the tunnel not even Ulf, the huge Northern Wolfman, had to do that.

"Jacob!" Julian and Cassie shouted at the same time.

Jacob grinned in the torchlight. Julian pushed his way past

Gregor and Forrester to greet the big man. Julian gave the monastic kiss of life, but Jacob just pulled him into an enveloping hug, patting Julian on the back forcefully.

"Lay Brother Julian. It is good to see that you are alive," Jacob said. "And not insane."

"I am relieved to see you well, also. Wait—" Julian raised his hands to his eyes. Blood coated his fingers. "You're hurt."

"A scratch. Anyway, most of it is not mine. Who are these people?"

Julian turned and swept a bloodied hand around the party. "They ... they have come to help."

Jacob nodded. "I could do with a little help."

"Who are you?" Forrester asked.

Jacob bowed his massive head. "Lay Brother Jacob of the Ulfur Monks."

Forrester measured the massive man in the habit. "The elevator keeper? And what of the elevator and its crew?"

Jacob shook his head in the flickering torchlight, his face sober. "The crew is gone."

"Dead?"

"I do not know. They are simply gone."

Cassie spoke up. "And what of the other men I came with? The members of the militia?"

"I have found no traces of anyone at the lower elevator station. The elevator itself is inoperable. The platform and winches sabotaged."

"And we are simply to take your word for it?" Ulf said.

Jacob eyed up the big warrior. "I care not if you take my word. It is the truth, regardless of your credulity."

"What are you doing in these tunnels?" Martha asked.

"Some of the monks are in here attempting to block the tunnels to the upper reaches of the mountain. I have stopped them from doing so. For the most part, the passages above remain clear."

Martha appraised the massive lay brother as he stood motionless. "Good. We are here to remove the threat on this mountain." Jacob merely nodded at Martha's statement of intent. She went on, "You are not going to advise against this action? You won't tell us that the odds are not in our favour, that we face certain death?"

"Hah," Jacob laughed. "All of those things are true. But I won't advise against it. I know a one-way killing crew when I see one. Nothing I can say will turn you back."

"You're right. And you, Jacob? Will you join us in this endeavour?"

"You've got it around the wrong way, fair lady." Jacob raised his bloodied sword in the torchlight and grinned. "You're somewhat late to the festival. You'll be joining me."

———

Leaving the constricting passages behind him, Julian breathed fresh air and felt the late afternoon sun on his cheeks. The crew had made it out of the subterranean passages alive and Julian was pleased. He turned and assessed the quality of the men and women gathering on the small grass verge near the cliff face: the massive strength of Ulf and Gregor, the compact brawn and single-mindedness of Forrester, the calculating skills and precision of Martha, the otherworldly dexterity of Anguilla. Cassie, too, could handle a blade. They would kill many monks before they were done. But they would fall, in the end. The forces against the hunters were too numerous, yet they would drag scores with them to the next world. Of that, Julian had no doubt, especially with Jacob among them.

Ulf gasped for air like a man arisen from a watery grave. "Christ, it's good to be outside where a man can die properly."

"I have no intention of dying just yet, boy," Gregor huffed as he peered up the mountain. "It's those monks we'll send screaming to Hades."

"We do not choose when we die, old man," Ulf said.

"I'll choose when I go," Gregor replied flatly.

"That is not the philosophy of the Northern folk," Ulf answered.

Gregor scowled. "You can stick the philosophy of the Northern folk up your arse. I am Gregor the Watchman, Gregor the Vigilant, and I die when I choose, you ginger-faced cunt."

Ulf stalked towards Gregor, his face a mask of anger, but the older man was not cowed. He gripped his axe and jutted his thrice-braided chin out in challenge. Martha stepped between the two warriors, the shadow of a smile on her ghostly face. A tense moment later, Ulf laughed mirthlessly and moved away.

Jacob grinned and turned to Julian. "Interesting crew you have brought with you."

"Yes. You could say that."

Forrester came to stand in front of Julian and folded his stocky arms. "Where are they?"

Julian pointed at a ridgeline. "Just over there, a path will take us a further six hundred feet and we'll be at the compound."

"And the children?"

"Somewhere underground. I cannot exactly recall where."

Forrester grunted. "First, we clear the grange and the community above ground. If needs be, we will delve back into the mountain to find the lost children. For now, we eat, rest, or otherwise prepare ourselves. We leave in an hour."

Julian cast a puzzled glance at Jacob and then back at the squat warrior. He gestured to the darkening sky. "Night approaches. You will battle the mad monks without the aid of the sun? Is that wise?"

"We possess courage in great amounts," Forrester muttered, walking away. "Nobody said anything about wisdom."

———

Anguilla approached Ulf and winked at the big warrior as he sat sharpening his sword on a whetstone in the gathering shadows. The Eel gestured towards Jacob as he talked to Julian and said, "There is a man to match your size and more. The lay brother is enormous."

Ulf stood and straightened his broad shoulders as he gazed towards Jacob. Then, he shrugged. "What of it?"

"His cock must outsize yours, Wolfman."

Ulf frowned. "What do I care for the size of the man's cock? What the fuck is wrong with you?"

"I thought all you Northerners compared your genitals in your public baths. Sexual competition is the height of your culture, or so I am led to believe."

"You're insane, little Eel. Go bother someone else with your pathetic talk. We die before the sun rises, and I won't meet God with your inane prattle ringing in my ears."

Anguilla's lip curled at one side of his mouth in a display of mirth. "How can you be so sure? We are strong, and with you on our side, how could we possibly fall?"

Ulf grunted. "It is better to expect death and be pleasantly surprised than expect to live and receive a bastard of a shock. Do you understand me, Worm Dick?"

"*Worm Dick?*" Anguilla nodded in appreciation. "Imminent death brings out the best in you, Wolfman. Outstanding comeback."

Ulf sat down and returned to sharpening his massive sword,

slicing at the blade with the stone in vicious, angry strokes. "You all mock me because I was not born under the Christian God like you were. You think me a pagan, but I am as true as any of the others and I will prove it. You will see."

Anguilla fell silent, his face unreadable. The winds whistled across the cliff face but did not seem to touch the pale man's white hair. "No. You have that wrong, my Northern friend. I mock you because you are overly earnest and are very thin-skinned. But I do not question your faith. That I would never do."

Ulf looked up at Anguilla suspiciously, as if the pale man was leading him into a trap. "Then, we have a mutual respect?"

Anguilla bowed at the hip. "Respect."

"And do we have a cessation in hostilities?"

"Ah." The Eel smiled more broadly and shook his head. "That I cannot do, for I must stay sharp and you, Wolfman, are my whetstone."

Ulf pointed his sword at Anguilla. "Careful your blade does not break on the sharpening stone, little man."

Anguilla laughed and walked away to where Gregor was squatting over something on the ground. Martha and Forrester stood beside Gregor as he mixed a strange yellow powder and a green liquid in a small wooden mortar. From his knapsack he took several empty glass vials and laid them on the grass. When the powder and liquid had merged, Gregor carefully poured the mixture into the small vials and stoppered them.

"What are you doing?" Yerty asked as she came to observe.

"I'm making fireworks," Gregor said. "I will create a display the likes you have never seen, child."

Cassie frowned. "Are those dangerous?"

Gregor grinned and passed several of the vials to Martha, who put them in her bag. Gregor stored the remaining bottles in his knapsack. "Only in the wrong hands. And these"—he held up his gnarled hands, which he clenched into meaty fists —"are the right ones. God's chosen hands. With these hands, what could possibly go wrong?"

———

The door to the Second Chapel creaked open and Brother Rollant entered to find Klaus kneeling at the altar.

"What are you doing in here, Klaus? You are not ordained."

Klaus got to his feet and turned to face Rollant. Though the makeshift chapel was a pale shadow of the original one, the altar contained a jewel-encrusted candelabra, one that Rollant had not noticed before. The crisis facing the community had brought out the good tableware, apparently. Aside from the two of them, the chapel was empty.

"We are all ordained now," Klaus said. "God cares nothing for monastic rank."

"Shut up, you whining bastard." Rollant placed his bread knife up against Klaus's abdomen and whispered, "Don't bother summoning your insects to help you. They'll arrive only to lay eggs in your guts, which I will gladly bury in the garden along with the rest of you if you do not tell me what's going on."

Klaus's eyes widened at the knife at his stomach. "Going on? What ... Whatever do you mean?"

"I saw you talking to Prior Blackwing. You're involved in some kind of conspiracy. Don't deny it. What did Blackwing whisper in your feeble ear, Klaus? Go on, tell me or I'll spill your secrets, my way." To illustrate his point, Rollant pressed his bread knife harder against Klaus's abdomen. "Tell me."

To Rollant's surprise, Klaus gripped his wrist and twisted, causing the bread knife to fall to the floor. He endured another moment of surprise when Klaus threw him across the floor of the chapel, where he slid to an abrupt halt against the door.

Klaus bared his teeth and stalked towards the stunned monk. "Fuck you, Rollant. Who do you think you're talking to? The old Klaus is dead. I'm ascended, enlightened, whether you like it or not. The new Klaus is not afraid of you, or anything."

Someone attempted to open the door, but Rollant still lay against it, preventing anyone from entering. Recovering his wits, Rollant got to his feet and lashed out with his tongue, intending to leave his mark across the impertinent German's face, but Klaus merely grasped Rollant's elongated organ in his fist and jerked him forwards. Both men tumbled to the floor as a dozen monks flooded through the chapel doors, among them Father Howard and Prior Blackwing.

"Stop this!" Howard shouted. "There will be no fighting among ourselves. We have a common enemy on our doorstep and must bond together to face them, or we all fall."

Rollant and Klaus stood and brushed dust from their habits. Several monks looked sideways at each other, and Rollant was aware of the accusatory glance that Howard gave Blackwing, a glance that the tall superior ignored. The Brotherhood was pulling apart like stitching at a weak seam. Rollant instinctively blamed Klaus: the German was not ascended, not a true brother; proper rank and station must be maintained. Without adequate respect for one's status, the foundation of the Brotherhood of Ulfur could not support its own weight. Why could no one else see that?

Abbot Howard put his hands to his temple and took a staggering step. He fell and was helped to his feet. "They're here," Howard said. "I sense them. They have somehow made it through the tunnels. The enemy is here."

34
ONE-WAY KILLING CREW

Heads on stakes in the torchlight.

The features drooped slackly in death, and she had never been overly familiar with them in the firmness of life, but Cassie recognized them all the same: the missing members of the militia, guildsmen from the city below. Their heads had been impaled upon stakes at the base of the three hundred and thirty-three steps leading to the compound of the Brotherhood of Ulfur Monks. A horrific warning to stay away or suffer a similar fate.

Cassie pulled Yerty to her chest and clasped the child in such a way that she could not gaze on the wide-eyed fear and death on the faces of the beheaded militiamen. "This is no place for children," she whispered angrily. But she knew it was useless to argue with Martha and Gregor and the other scrutators. Cassie, Yerty, and Julian were now bound to them as the thick hide of a mule was bound to its own flanks.

In his thick calloused hand, Gregor held out a torch and examined the severed heads. Martha held a second torch in her more refined, yet equally lethal, fist. Forrester carried the third and final torch.

"They mean to weaken us with fear," Gregor growled. "It shall avail them little."

As they walked past the dead men's already desiccating skulls, Ulf patted one of them and said, "We shall avenge you, friend."

Cassie saw the concern on Jacob's face. No doubt he was wondering what had happened to his fellow lay brothers: the lower station elevator crew had disappeared along with the militia men, but their heads did not adorn any pikes, not at this point anyway.

Gregor had spoken of fear, and fear indeed threatened to suffocate Cassie, not fear for herself, but for Yerty. As far as Cassie was concerned, she had made the most of her own opportunities, had squeezed as much as she could from life. Yerty's own life was only beginning. She could not but help resent the hunters, these scrutators as they called themselves, for dragging the girl along. This resentment eased a little when Cassie recalled Yerty's insistence at joining them. Cassie realized that no one would have been able to keep Yerty away and this thought soothed her troubled mind somewhat. *Strong, brave girl*, Cassie thought. *I pray that you have a long life of mistakes and tears ahead of you.*

Each of the hunters held their own unique weapon at the ready, and even Yerty gripped a curved hunting knife in a white-knuckled fist, but the cloister of the Brotherhood of Ulfur was dark and empty.

"Let's not play these games," Gregor said into the early evening shadows. "Come out, reveal yourselves." No reply came, only the night winds whispering about the compound.

"We need more light," Martha said.

Martha, Gregor, and Forrester moved forwards and set their torches to a small wooden structure nearby. It would not catch because of the recent rain, so Gregor took a small glass container from his knapsack and hurled it at the structure. The hut now caught fire and blazed and smoked furiously. Julian put his hands to his head and turned away, upset at the destruction wrought upon the community, even if its inhabitants had descended into madness. Cassie understood that this place had been Julian's home for the last year and now was about to go up in flame. The man was obviously conflicted, despite everything that had happened to him.

"We're going to destroy it all!" Forrester shouted. "Come out and defend yourselves, your property!"

Flames flared and crackled into the chill night air, chasing shadows away. With the addition of a second structure, the blaze increased and lit up every nook and cranny in the cliff walls surrounding the compound. There was nowhere to hide.

Cassie marvelled at the audacity of the scrutators. Outnumbered twenty to one, if Julian had assessed the numbers of infected monks correctly, and without an apparent strategy, they had just wandered into the lair of the beast and challenged it to an open battle. Either they had greatly overestimated their own skills, or the scrutators had yet to reveal their true capabilities.

The group edged deeper into the compound. Forrester spat on the stones of the central courtyard in a challenge. "Come out and fight, demons! Come face God's wrath!" Gregor moved off to the edge of the courtyard and set fire to the abbot's office.

Anguilla turned to Cassie and said, "Close your eyes and block your ears when I signal." Before Cassie could ask just what the signal was, the Eel walked away. Cassie passed on the warning to Yerty and Julian. The big lay brother, Jacob, seemed to have melted into the shadows.

"Where's Jacob?" Cassie whispered.

Julian shrugged. "He was here a moment ago." Gregor,

Martha, and Forrester set fire to the lay brother dormitory. Julian looked on the verge of tears. The undersides of the clouds far above seemed to glow with reds and oranges. The compound was now a conflagration.

Cassie, Julian, and Yerty joined the others as they began to cross the central courtyard towards the dark maw of the pit where the Grand Chapel had once stood. It was the only place that the savage heat could not reach them.

Gregor scowled at Julian. "Where are they? You said they would be here."

"I ... I don't know."

"This way!" Through a gap in the smoke, Jacob emerged. He had to shout over the crackling flames, but everybody heard him clearly. "The monks are this way!"

————

Vespers. Abbot Howard loved vespers. *Vesperas* as it was once known by the Romans, *aefensang* by the ancient race that fought them. *Evensong.* A beautiful cleansing of the day and preparation for the night vigil, and Abbot Howard had come to live for the night.

For the night was when he truly felt alive.

Since his health had returned to him, thank the Merciful Lord, he had begun to prowl the mountain at night like a panther, his vigour and strength unlike anything he had known even in the hot flushing springs of his youth. Yes, he was powerful in mind, body, and spirit. He would never grow old again. *He would never die.*

The door to the Second Chapel opened and Brother Rollant stood there wringing his hands. "They come," he said.

Howard sighed and admired the monks, heads bowed in

prayer around the candlelit altar. The enemy could at least have waited until vespers was over. The abbot clapped his hands. "It is time, brothers. It is time!" Each monk lifted his head and began to snarl.

Rollant glanced around the chapel. "So few of us? Where is Blackwing? Where are the others?"

Howard grimaced. "In this, our hour of trial, he has fled. He shall burn in the fires of the damned for his lack of faith. Many of the brothers have followed him, and they, too, shall be judged."

Lay Brother Rollant whispered, "The intruders have set fire to the compound. Everything is ablaze."

Howard patted the gaunt man on the shoulder as he walked out of the Second Chapel. "Do not fear. We shall rise from the ashes as we always have. We will be here forever."

As the abbot walked away into the night, something nuzzled at Rollant's hand. He looked down into the eyes of a goat, a vacant expression in its eyes as it chewed, oblivious to the approaching danger. Rollant screwed up his brows. "I remember you. Elsie, isn't it? What kind of idiot names his goats?" Without another word, Rollant grasped the animal by its stubbed horns and violently twisted, breaking Elsie's neck.

––––––––

"The scrutators form a wall," Martha said to Cassie. "Keep the girl and yourself behind that wall. Do you understand me?"

They stood at the top of a winding path leading down to a goat enclosure and the Second Chapel. Cassie watched as monks came hurtling from the chapel, ascending the path with astonishing speed, loping, slavering, their posture and their guttural shrieks more animal than man. Feral shadows in the deepening gloom.

"Do you understand?" Martha said again.

Cassie nodded. "Yes. I understand."

"We have seconds now," Martha said. She winked at Yerty. "Do not fear, all will be well."

Cassie grabbed Yerty and together they stood back as Martha, Gregor, and Forrester formed a line. The Wolfman and the Eel positioned themselves at either end, extending the line. Behind them stood Jacob and Julian. If the monks got through this second line of defence, it would be up to Cassie to protect Yerty.

Cassie gaped. Dozens of them, each monk capable of rending a body limb from limb. She had hoped the hunters might have a chance, but here, now, seeing the monsters clambering with inhuman speed towards them up the grassy mountain path, she realized that they could not defeat the murderous onslaught of tooth and claw.

Gregor shouted into the wind, something as equally guttural as the screams of the monks, his axe held high over his head. Anguilla turned to Cassie and calmly pointed to his eyes and ears. Remembering the warning, Cassie pulled Yerty towards her.

"Close your eyes, Yerty," Cassie said, "and don't open them until I say so."

Cassie felt the child nod against her chest, her own eyes squeezed shut. Cassie clamped her hands over Yerty's ears, and the girl, in turn, reached up and covered Cassie's ears.

The creatures had closed the distance to mere yards when Gregor threw a glass vial that shattered in their midst and sent out a light brighter than a sudden sun at midnight. Monks screamed and shielded their eyes. Martha threw a glass globe of her own. When it shattered, an incomprehensible whooshing sound created a sucking vacuum in eardrum, mouth, and nose. Like a sea disappearing from the beach before a tidal wave, nothing happened for a moment, no one breathed or could breathe, and then the air came rushing back in a compressed roar, blasting the senses. The monks collapsed to the earth, blood streaming from their ears and noses, and the one-way killing crew went about its business. Within moments, a dozen monks had their heads separated from their shoulders by Ulf's sword and Gregor's axe or their brains pierced ear to ear with Martha's hairpin. Anguilla swung his whip and joined the slaughter. Forrester lopped heads from necks as if out chopping wood on a bright spring morning.

Cassie's ears rang in nauseating echoes. She held Yerty's head in her hands. "Are you alright?" Cassie's voice was muffled by the clanging in her ears. Yerty nodded. Julian was on his hands and knees, retching. Big Jacob shook his head as if merely clearing a moment's fogginess and he, too, joined the destruction of his once-brethren.

As their senses returned, those monks with heads still attached scrambled to their feet, their numbers savagely culled. Droplets of colour like a slow summer rain seeped upwards from the corpses of the dead monks, small shimmers of pale purples and pinks, mint greens and ruby red sparkles, though none had the time to stand and admire the beauty of the event.

Several monks fled in terror at the sight of their brothers' mutilation, but many remained to fight, enraged at what they perceived as unjustified murder. These monks were ready to die, for men and righteous monks they still believed themselves to be.

Ulf howled in canine joy as he swung heartily, dark blood splatter coating his lighter ginger beard. Martha ducked and weaved, her martial grace mirrored by her twin brother, Anguilla; the two pale warrior-siblings formed a matching choreography of sword and sharp-toothed whip. Gregor and Forrester relied on pure brutality. Paying no heed to their own safety, the two scrutators hacked and hewed with sword and axe, dismembering anything in their path. Jacob brought his sword down on the skull of a man he had once exchanged words with on the elevator platform, cleaving the monk's head open.

One of the monks evaded a swing from Ulf's sword and latched onto his upper arm with its teeth. Ulf howled in feral rage and grabbed the thing's face in his left hand and squeezed. The monk's jaw and face disintegrated, and the creature dropped to the ground. Retrieving his sword, Ulf beheaded the monk with one blow. Cassie slashed at a monster that had managed to penetrate the defensive line of sword, axe, and whip. The thing seemed to be going for Yerty, its eyes fixed hungrily on the girl. A second came rushing towards them. The hunters were losing the battle against sheer numbers. Julian moved towards one of the monks trying to get at Yerty, easing under a slashing sweep of claw and stabbing it in the heart and cutting its throat in successive smooth flowing movements. The monk dropped silently to the damp grass. The second monk swung around in alarm. Julian's hand flicked out like a snake and the monk's eyeball popped. Reflexively, the creature put both hands to its eye, but before it could shriek in pain, Julian's dagger had buried itself in the thing's heart and neck. The creature collapsed, dead.

Cassie and Yerty exchanged astonished glances. Julian was no simple cleric-in-waiting. He was another killer in lay brother's clothing, much like Jacob.

Someone screamed from behind Cassie. "There will be no females on the mountain!"

Cassie whirled in time to see Abbot Howard leaping from a boulder. Yerty swung her dagger as he came down on her. Howard rolled to his feet and touched the blossoming blood-stain on his white robe at the midriff.

"Now, child," the abbot said sternly, wagging a remonstrative finger at Yerty. "*That* was insolent." The abbot snarled, baring his diamond-encrusted gums. Yerty shrieked in fear from where she lay on the ground.

"Julian!" Cassie screamed.

"Father Howard, step back." The abbot looked up to see Julian standing there, dagger poised. "I saved your life, Father. Do you remember?"

The abbot cocked his head. "Yes, I remember. I am eternally thankful for my life, my boy. But I'll be damned if I let you take it back now."

"I ask you to step away from the child and the woman."

The abbot's face glazed over dreamily. "I would be dead if not for you. It's true." His eyes snapped back to focus. "Take this as a reward." Abbot Howard threw a concealed handful of jewels at Julian and the precious stones tore and sliced at the skin on his face. Julian staggered and Howard went for Yerty.

Yerty threw her dagger at the monk, but it landed hilt first and bounced off.

"Stop that!" shrieked Howard, stopping in his tracks. "Willful child!" Madness seemed to overtake the abbot and he snapped at the air with his deadly teeth.

Julian, still blinded, struck out but the abbot laughed and moved in low, preparing to eviscerate him and the girl. Jacob grabbed the collar of Howard's white robe and pulled him away. The abbot turned and snapped at Jacob, but the big man let go of the collar and moved out of reach. Jacob's right arm was bloodied, and he carried no sword.

Two monks leaped upon Jacob from behind, tearing at the flesh of his back. The abbot rushed in, and Jacob staggered under the weight of the three feral monks. Cassie screamed and stabbed wildly at Jacob's attackers, but another monk joined the assault on Jacob and the big man disappeared under a writing mass of brown habits, like maggots squirming in a festering wound. Cassie hit the jugular of one of the brown-robed furies and the thing squealed and rolled away. Jacob hurled another off himself. Cassie's heart skipped a beat when she saw the horrific bite marks that had torn Jacob's habit apart at the chest and stomach. Julian had recovered his senses and stabbed one of the mad monks in the skull. Jacob roared as he got back to his feet. He held Father Howard at bay with one large hand around the abbot's throat, the feral cleric still slavering and snapping at Jacob's face. Jacob headbutted the abbot and nearly knocked himself out. Shaking his head, the big lay brother looked around. Spying his sword, he picked it up while keeping Howard at arm's length. When Jacob stood again, Howard's feet were dangling in the air. Jacob neatly inserted his sword in the belly of the abbot and sliced this way and that, gutting him. Howard shrieked as his innards spilt steaming to the cool damp mountain grass. A few moments later, he stopped kicking and Jacob dropped the carcass of the abbot of the Ulfur Monks to the ground, beheading him for good measure.

The sounds of battle began to diminish. Despite his wounds, Jacob entered the fray once more. The last of the monks fell. It was over.

Martha sheathed her sword and gave two small bows: one to Julian and one to Jacob. "You two fight well for monks."

"They weren't always monks," Cassie said.

"What were they?" Martha asked.

"I don't think either of them are telling."

Martha turned back to find Julian on his hands and knees. "What are you doing?"

Julian was feeling for diamonds and rubies in the darkness, the ones flung at his face by the abbot. He stuffed them in his habit pocket. "Investing in my future."

"What does a monk want with earthly wealth?" Martha said.

Julian looked up sharply, his bloodied face grim. He gestured to the dead abbot. "Recent events have led me to reconsider my career choices."

35
A FINAL TASTE OF GIN

Julian stepped around several casks and barrels limned silver in the moonlight and approached the large tub and grinding wheel set against one wall. The acrid smell of unripe juniper berries hung in the air. Julian had never set foot within Brother Vernon's gin mill in the entire time he had been on the mountain. He'd tasted plenty of the gin, but never seen where it had come from. A scuffling noise from a separate room at the back of the mill drew his attention. He approached a doorway and pushed back a cloth partition. The windowless room emanated tangible darkness, like oozing black blood.

Julian stood in the doorway and listened. "Is there anyone in here?" He raised his dagger and took a step forwards.

"Julian, my boy, is that you?"

Julian recognized the voice. "Yes, Brother Vernon. It's me."

A candle flickered to life on a long wooden table, and then another. "Come. Come, sit. Drink with me." The old monk smiled and gestured to several pewter mugs on the table. He took one of the cups from the table and offered it to Julian. Vernon's expression changed from a hearty welcome to one of concern. "What happened to your face, my young friend?"

Julian touched a finger to his stinging, jewel-shredded cheeks. "Earthly wealth," he said, ruefully. Julian inspected the corners of the room for fear that a crazed monk might be lurking in the shadows. Vernon, himself, did not seem threatening and so Julian sat down opposite the old monk but kept his dagger grasped in one hand under the table.

"Drink, drink, my boy." Vernon offered a cup already filled to the brim with pungent clear liquid. "God is good."

Julian did not take the cup. "Do you understand what is happening here, Brother Vernon? You are sitting at this table drinking gin while the world falls down about you."

The old man paused with his pewter mug to his lips. He blinked several times and placed the cup back on the table. "It's ... it's not ... things have been bad of late, I know, but with God's grace, we shall see it through."

Julian shook his head. "Not this time. Blood and death. That is all that is left on the mountain."

Vernon whispered, "Is it so bad out there?"

"Blood and death. Innocence lost." The old man winced at that. "Where is Martin? Where are the children and the other lay brothers?"

"You do not remember?"

"The last time we spoke I was ... befuddled with Blackwing's drugs. I need you to tell me where they are. We must find them."

The old man looked about. "We?"

"I did not come alone. This, you must know."

Vernon nodded and his hands trembled as he once again picked up his mug and sipped. "Yes. They have come to wreak their revenge in the guise of retribution."

Julian sighed. "I'm not here to discuss the right or wrong of it. Where are the children? They do not deserve to be held captive."

Vernon nodded again. "Yes, yes, I agree. They are innocent."

A noise at Julian's back. Martha brushed aside the cloth partition and stepped into the room.

Vernon sat back, his eyes widening as Gregor and Forrester followed the female scrutator. The old monk swept a hand around the room. "Welcome to the tasting room. Taste with me, drink with me, friends. Peace, I wish you no harm."

Martha examined the room at a glance and turned her attention to Brother Vernon. She approached the man, her hands raised peaceably. She touched a finger to her chest and said, "Your crucifix. Do you wear it?"

"Always," Brother Vernon said.

Julian shook his head sadly. The old monk had just signed his own death warrant. "Show it to me," Martha said. Vernon pulled out the sky-metal crucifix from under his habit. Martha pursed her lips, stepped back, and nodded. "Thank you, old one."

"Drink." Vernon offered a cup of gin to Martha. When she did not take it, he held it to Gregor and Forrester. Neither man's expression altered from their grimness. "We are all friends here," Vernon said. "We haven't all f ... fallen. There are good people up here, still."

"Aye," Martha said. "Good people." She took the hairpin from the back of her head. Julian met the woman's mercury eyes, and for a moment, he considered pleading with her on Vernon's behalf.

But he knew the Ice Maiden had settled on her decision.

Gregor and Forrester turned their backs and left the room. Martha stared at Julian, and he understood the period of grace she was giving him. *Leave if you cannot watch.* Julian patted Vernon on the shoulder and stood.

The old monk reached out. "Wait, Julian. A drink, for all the goodness we once held in our hearts." Julian paused, nodded, and took the cup. The gin was bitter. It had always been bitter. "The children," Vernon said absentmindedly. "Yes, I know where they are." Martha frowned and then put her hairpin back in the secret sheath at the back of her head. Vernon got to his feet, hitched his habit, and walked, stooped, from the tasting room into the gin mill proper, where Cassie stood with Yerty and Anguilla.

"What's happening?" Cassie asked. "Who is this?"

"I am Brother Vernon." The old monk gave the kiss of life.

"I've heard of you. You are the gin maker."

"One and the same. I have something to show you all. But first, a drink?"

Ulf poked his head inside the gin mill, his right upper arm heavily bandaged. "Did someone say *drink*?"

Vernon nodded enthusiastically. "Yes, yes, here." As Ulf entered the room, Vernon passed a cup to the man.

Ulf swallowed the gin in one hearty mouthful. His face screwed up and he gasped. "It's good. Good stuff. I think Jacob needs a drink."

At the mention of the name, Brother Vernon started. "Jacob? Lay Brother Jacob? Where is he?" Ulf nodded outside and Brother Vernon hurried out into the moonlight. Jacob sat against the exterior of the gin mill, his face ashen. The bloodied and sweat-soaked bandages around his torso were visible through his shredded habit. He had his head back and his eyes closed.

At the sight of the badly wounded lay brother, Vernon put a hand to his mouth and exclaimed, "Lay Brother Jacob. What happened to you?"

Jacob did not open his eyes when he spoke. "I have lapsed back into my old ways, brother. I have killed again, but for a worthy cause, if I may excuse myself in such a way. For a worthy cause."

Vernon placed a cup into Jacob's trembling fingers and shuffled back inside. "What transpired out there?"

Martha folded her arms. "Your abbot and his friends took several bites out of the big man."

"Oh, my Lord."

"And your brethren tried to murder us all."

"Oh no. That is ... that is terrible."

Martha nodded. "Indeed, gin maker. Terrible. What did you wish to show us? I suggest you make it quick."

"Here." Vernon pointed to a rectangle of moonlight on the gin mill floor. "Step back, if you would."

Martha, Forrester, and Gregor took a few paces back from the spot indicated by Brother Vernon. The old monk bent over and grasped a small ring. Pulling on it, he revealed a trapdoor that opened to a patch of pure darkness below. "You may come out," Vernon said. "It's safe. These are friends. You may come out."

The first small, dirty, and frightened face to emerge from the darkness was Dylan's.

Yerty squealed and embraced her brother as several more children came blinking out into the moonlight. Cassie simply stood, unmoving. Then she, too, embraced Dylan and tears came in shuddering waves from all three of them.

———

"Children are resilient," Martha said. "Look at them."

The children sat in a circle in the corner of the gin mill, eating heartily of the last stores of bread exhumed from the bread ovens. Anguilla and Ulf stood guard over them, smiling as the little ones shoved food into their mouths and talked merrily, as if the trauma of their recent lives had never happened. Yerty sat beside her brother Dylan, listening attentively to a story the children were passing between themselves.

Gregor watched as Cassie applied a salve to Julian's face. The elder scrutator spoke gruffly. "There are more monks? Is that what you are saying?"

"Yes," Julian said. "As far as I can tell, the dead make up less than half of the total number of monks on the mountain."

"Then where are the rest of them?"

Julian hesitated. "I believe they are ..."

Gregor twirled his axe. "Well?"

"They have retreated to the Grand Chapel."

Cassie stopped applying the cream to Julian's face and stared at him. "But you said the chapel fell."

"It did. But I remember when I awoke within the mountain, after Blackwing drugged us, I remember thinking the place was familiar. I believe the Grand Chapel still remains intact, more or less. Brother Vernon has confirmed my suspicions." The old gin maker of whom they spoke currently remained under the floor of the gin mill, where the children had been kept, until his fate was decided.

Gregor huffed. "Then we must go down to find the monks and clean the mountain of evil once and forever."

"Ulf won't be happy," Martha said.

"Fuck Ulf," Gregor said. "We go where God tells us."

"What are we to do with the gin maker?" Forrester asked, pointing to the gin mill floor. "We cannot let the man walk free. He must be cleansed."

Julian frowned. "If by *cleansed*, you mean murdered, I cannot agree. He helped the children. He got them out. He saved them where I could not. The man's a hero."

Cassie handed the salve kit back to Martha and said, "Julian is right. The old man seems harmless."

"Pah!" Gregor spat and spittle caught in his thrice-forked

beard. "What of the other innocents? The lay brothers. He didn't help them. Nor did he reveal the children immediately. He was hiding them beneath the floor until he had no other choice but to tell us of them."

"He hasn't hurt anyone," Julian said. "He's not like the others."

Martha shook her head. "I'm sorry, Julian. He wears the metal about his neck. It is only a matter of time before evil corrupts him."

"Then take the crucifix away from him."

"It's in his blood by now. The fact that he has not turned already is a testament to the old man's healthy heart, his right-eousness. Let him die now, while he still retains this goodness."

"He can hear every word we're saying," Julian whispered, gesturing to the floor.

Martha shrugged. "That does not matter. He cannot be allowed to threaten anyone in the days to come. If we do not finish him today, then the future deaths of innocents stain our hands. We take no chances."

A choking sensation tightened Julian's throat. "This is wrong."

"You need not fear for the man's immortal soul," Martha said. "Quite the contrary, if he meets God today, then he shall be taken to His side. If we wait, it may be Lucifer who claims him as he has claimed the others." Martha nodded to the other end of the room. "Cassie, take the children outside. I will send the old one home."

"Hasn't there been death enough today?" Cassie said.

Martha stared at the other woman, the cool mercury eyes of the one in sharp contrast to the pained brown eyes of the other. "We do not do this for the joy of it. The monks took the chil-dren, have murdered at least one. Vernon is complicit in this.

None can argue otherwise. No more children shall be taken. Are we agreed?"

Cassie could not hold the gaze of the other woman and turned away. Martha nodded towards Ulf and Anguilla and the two men gently began to usher the children outside.

"To do it in such a cold way. It's cruel," Cassie said.

Martha opened the trapdoor to the cellar. "It must be done."

"Damn it!" Julian said. "Then I'll do it. If it must be done, let me do it."

Martha bowed her head and stepped away from the opening. "When it is over, bury him deep in the cellar, along with the metal. Don't touch it with your exposed skin. Do you understand, Julian?"

Julian nodded sullenly and took a candle and a mug of gin. As he descended the steps of the ladder Cassie walked outside to sit with the children and listen as they babbled together. These children would never be truly innocent again, not after what they had experienced, but for now they maintained something of childlike wonder, and Cassie sat close and tried to absorb as much of it as she could, tried to remember what it was to be a child, tried to smile along with them.

She hoped Julian would be kind. Something about the lay brother told her that he would. He would send old Vernon home with kindness.

And with a final taste of bitter gin.

36
ATONEMENT

The Second Chapel burned brightly with a hundred candles. The children were lying on makeshift beds around the outer edges of the nave, many of them asleep. Jacob lay prone before the altar, his hands clasped on his chest like some kind of statue of a martyr in repose.

"Stay with us," Cassie said.

Julian shook his head from where he sat on the wooden floor. "I can't. I must go. Martin is down there. I have to get him out along with the other lay brothers."

"What if the monsters come when you're gone?"

"There should be no danger here," Julian said. "The monks that remain have fled within the mountain. We can't take the children down there. Someone has to watch them."

"Very well. Do you think Jacob will live?"

Julian glanced over at the resting form. "He's a strong man. He'll make it. If we're not back by morning, you must get the little ones back to their families in Re'Shan. If Jacob can't walk ... leave him."

"No, no. I can't do that."

"You have to get the children home. Jacob will understand."

"I'll come with you," Cassie said. "Down below."

Julian looked at her in surprise. "No. You are reunited with Dylan. I believe that he and Yerty constitute your family now. I would not separate you again, not so soon. You stay here tonight. There should be little danger as I believe the scrutators have cleared the mountain, at least its surface. Besides, it's my turn now."

"Your turn for what?"

Julian lowered his head. "I became a monk to ease the burden I have carried. To find some kind of redemption."

"What burden? Redemption for what? Am I finally going to get that confession?"

Julian looked up. "I was a soldier, once."

Cassie showed no surprise. "In the service of King Lyle of Otago, that much I know."

"Yes. In the name of my king, I was asked to put down a rebellion, though this *rebellion* was nothing more than a group of peasant farmers protesting the unjust rule of their masters. It just so happened the land barons had the ear and favour of the king. We were instructed to make an example of them to deter any future trouble."

Martha stood leaning against the chapel door, eyeing Julian. It was time to go. The scrutators were now ready to delve deep and burn the scourge from the belly of Mount Ulfur. To lance the wound and squeeze the pus from the sore.

Cassie shifted uneasily, dreading the answer to her next question. "What did you do, Julian? How did you put the rebellion down?"

"The farmers had families." Julian glanced at the sleeping children. "In my duty to my king, I became something that makes the monsters we hunt seem almost civilized. I cannot ... I cannot utter my misdeeds in words. I fear that I would foul this holy place and turn you against me, if you are not already so."

Cassie could not find the appropriate response and so remained tight-lipped.

Julian's face reddened. "I fled after it was over. I could not reconcile my actions with my own sense of honour." Julian clenched his fists. "They tried to find me, and still hunt me, I believe, for desertion of duty." He stood up. "I go to do some good against the shame that forever haunts me, though I know it will never be enough."

"We all have our sins," Jacob whispered from where he lay. "But you are a true brother. Perhaps the last good man on the mountain."

"Thank you, Jacob. I ..."

"You don't need to tell anyone what you did in the past. That's between you and God. Kill the evil that lurks below and free the lay brothers. Adjust the scales before you die, for that is all any of us can do."

Cassie knew that Jacob spoke as much for himself as he did for Julian, that both men had chosen this life on the mountain to escape what they had once been. With a sickness in her stomach, she watched Julian walk away. She considered running after him, to tell him that she forgave him for whatever it was that he had done.

But she didn't.

———

Five men and one woman stood at the edge of the gaping pit; the smouldering embers and wispy flames from the dying fires around the monastery cast no light into the abyss. Nor did the moon, now riding high in the black star-sprinkled skies, reach below with her silver light.

Julian had nearly died down there in the initial collapse of the Grand Chapel all those months ago, but somehow, he had survived. The Grand Chapel had survived, too.

"Christ's shit," Ulf said. "We can't be going back into the dark places." The big Northerner was pacing and glancing nervously down into the darkness.

"That's where they are," Gregor said, "so that's where we're going. Anybody not man enough"—here he glanced at Martha and cleared his throat—"or *woman* enough, can go back to the chapel to childmind. But I'm ready to do some more of God's good work."

Forrester grunted in agreement and ran his hand over his head, lingering at the place on his skull where the tattoo of the flaring Saint George's cross stained his skin. "Aye, our task is not done. But how do we get in? We don't have enough rope from the looks of it."

"Julian?" Martha raised her diaphanous eyebrows. "How would they be getting in and out? Not all of them can fly, I assume."

"No," Julian agreed. "Not all of them can fly, but I believe, with hindsight, that certain members of the Brotherhood have been going down to the Grand Chapel for quite some time. There has to be something nearby that allows access." Julian began to search the areas around the pit. The others dispersed and did the same.

"What's this?" Anguilla said after a few moments. The crew joined him, and there, at the midpoint between the pit opening and the cliff face, was an iron rung embedded into the side of a boulder the height of a man. Using the rock as an anchor, it would be possible to lower themselves safely into the pit.

"Looks like we'll be needing a longer rope," Forrester said.

———

Julian was the first one to descend into the darkness. The rope-sling that held him was a makeshift effort: Forrester's own rope simply tied to a fire-damaged rope found in the compound above. It could hardly be safe, Julian thought. The scrutators all had knowing smiles on their faces as they lowered him down, especially Gregor, the bastard. He seemed to be enjoying all this death and destruction.

Julian sighed and tried to control the fear. Here he was once again, suspended in the darkness within Mount Ulfur, just like his first day as a lay brother coming up on the elevator, and in the moment when the Grand Chapel had fallen after his rescue of the old and frail abbot. The Grand Chapel had taken Julian along with it on its ride down to Hades and put him in a month-long coma. But he had lived through that and now he was back for more. He hadn't had enough, clearly. What kind of idiot would come back for more of this? Never again. Live or die, never again. He would become a pig farmer somewhere on a muddy plain that stretched to the horizon. The flat places, yes. No more mountains for him, no more caverns. No more abyssal spaces.

Never again. Lord, just let him live through this.

Julian's feet touched something, and he shouted up that he had made solid ground. His voice echoed loudly; every mad monk in the mountain must have heard him, but no response came from up above. Where were the scrutators? Had they left him here to die? Julian shouted again and this time he heard Martha's answering call. How far down, she wanted to know. How stable. Untie the sling and sit tight and a torch will be lowered to you. True to her word, a burning torch came down on the rope like a slow version of the alien fireball that had changed his life on that fateful day, changed all their lives. The torch had been tied so that its flaming head would not set fire to the rope. Julian grasped the torch, pulled it from the knot, and tugged on the rope. The rope disappeared above, and Julian held the torch out. He stood on a platform much like that of the lower elevator station. There seemed to be something carved into the rock several feet away. Taking tentative steps towards it, fearful of falling through the wooden platform beneath his feet, Julian approached the rock and gasped: narrow stairs carved into the very rock walls, winding downwards. The stairs could fit one, perhaps two abreast, but there was no handrail. The monks must possess excellent night vision and the sure footing of a mountain goat, although not even that was a guarantee of safety, as Julian well knew. He wondered if—

A hand grasped his shoulder and Julian jumped.

"Calm yourself, lay brother." Martha smiled.

"Please announce yourself next time. You're very quiet."

"I think we should all be quiet." Martha examined the stairs. "Whose work is this?"

"The monks, I suppose."

"They built a staircase into the rock face within the mountain, and you knew nothing of its construction?"

Julian began to sweat, despite the cool conditions within the mountain. "We lay brothers are very busy at our day-to-day tasks. I can only assume that this was done under cover of night, when the lay brothers were abed."

"Perhaps," Martha said. "Or perhaps it's been here for many years."

"To what purpose?" Julian asked.

Martha shrugged and turned as her brother alighted on the platform. Anguilla stepped out of the rope-sling and tugged at the rope.

"How are we getting back up?" Julian said.

"Who says we're getting back up?" Anguilla said with a wink.

"My brother is joking," Martha said. "He is an excellent

climber and will find a way for us. I have seen him scale the tallest trees in Dysael to taste the sweetest of fruits that grow there. Or was that feat merely to impress a maiden?"

The Eel gave a theatrical bow. "The maidens do love sweet fruit." Panicked shouting and cursing came from above. Anguilla gave an exaggerated sigh and rolled his eyes. "That would be Ulf. He lacks gainliness. Not for him high-flowering sweets, or maidens for that matter."

"Settle, brother. He may hear you."

"There *is* something of an echo in here, isn't there?" Anguilla said. "Shall I repeat myself? I said that Ulf is an uncommonly ugly ragamuffin from the North who could not bed a woman if his life depended on it."

"I heard that," Ulf said, landing on the platform. "You'd better—" A creaking sound stopped him midsentence.

Anguilla tut-tutted. "You're too fat, Wolfman. I keep telling you to lose some weight. Come, before you fall through and disappear into the depths and take us with you. Over here."

Ulf released the rope from around his large buttocks and tiptoed fearfully towards the others, who now stood on a shelf of basalt rock at the top of the stairs. "Christ, I hate it in here," he said. "A man should—"

"Yes, yes," Anguilla interjected. "A man should die in the open spaces with the wind in his beard and the sky as his coffin lid. We've heard it all before. Shut up about it."

"You shut up, you pale little runt."

"Both of you shut up," Martha said. "Your bickering must stop. I won't die with your idle prattle in my ears."

"That's what *I* said," Ulf complained. "But he—"

"Enough." Martha cut the air with her hand. "Enough. We are complete." Gregor and Forrester crossed the platform to join them, both men simply having clambered down the rope, hand over hand. Forrester lit a torch from the one burning in Julian's hand.

Martha patted Julian's cheek and pointed at the lethal stairway. "As a Monk of Ulfur, *you* will lead the way."

It was very unsettling how she referred to him as a Monk of Ulfur. Something in the way Martha said it. Something not entirely friendly.

37
A FINAL DESCENT

In the darkness, Prior Blackwing traced his fingers along the damp stone walls, examining each cell as he passed by. Too many were empty. Too many had chosen to stay above with Abbot Howard. Blackwing knew that the abbot would be furious when he discovered his absence, along with that of a good portion of the Brotherhood. That was of little concern to the superior. If the abbot was still alive and chose to seek some kind of retribution, Blackwing would deal with him when the occasion arose.

They were most likely dead, in any case: those who had chosen to stay in the community above. Probably dead at the hands of the hunters.

Blackwing sighed. The abbot had been right about one thing: the Brotherhood was fracturing. The schism comprised three factions: those who had followed Blackwing, those who had stayed with Abbott Howard, and the others, the ones who had chosen to flee. They, too, would be hunted down, either high up on the mountain or down in the city below if they were foolish enough to try to integrate back into the world of secular affairs. No, the only safe place was within the shelter of the all-protecting Mother, Mount Ulfur herself.

The scraping and scratching sounds made by Blackwing's sharpened fingernails stopped as he came to a cell occupied by a solitary monk, his head bowed.

"Brother Simon," the tall superior said. "Are you ready?"

Brother Simon looked up from the cold cell floor lit by a single candle, his pudgy face sheened in a clammy sweat. "I have not ascended, Father. I ... I have failed." The monk clasped his hands to his face in shame. Blackwing examined the soft hands, their lack of strength, their lack of sharpened claws. He sighed again. This did not bode well; he needed every man in fighting shape. It was time for war, not prayer.

Blackwing entered the cell, removed the hands, and gently lifted Brother Simon's cherubic face. Simon smiled weakly, but the smile collapsed as the superior began to choke him. The monk struggled as his face turned red, then purple. He clawed at the hands around his throat in a futile attempt to break Blackwing's supernatural grip. Brother Simon's eyelids began to flutter as he lost consciousness. Blackwing released his grip and slapped the man, who coughed and began to breathe in great heaving sobs.

"Anything?" Blackwing said. Tears streamed from Brother Simon's eyes. He did not possess the breath to reply. Prior Blackwing began to choke the man again, only to revive him at the last moment. Blackwing repeated the cycle twice more. When Simon collapsed back onto the floor gasping and begging for mercy, the tall superior shook his head in disappointment. "Nothing," he said. "Still, you need not feel ashamed. Your talent will come to you in moments of great stress, and then it shall set you free and you will ascend to God's perfect weapon. I apologize, Brother Simon, that I could not facilitate its birth. Now, prepare yourself to fight as best you can."

As he turned away from Brother Simon, Blackwing felt the presence of his latent wings below his skin, and he ran his tongue over his teeth, teeth ready to erupt into wicked fangs at his bidding. The superior had hoped that more of his men would ascend, for they would have need to fight the enemy at their door. True, some of the monks had found their inner powers as gifted by the sky-metal, but too few. There were too few of them in killing shape. But Blackwing trusted God and Mother Ulfur to protect them when it came to the final battle. The hunters would find Blackwing, at least, ready to fight with sharpened beak and claw.

———

Martin leafed through the pages of the book. It had not taken him long to pick out and identify certain symbols. The pages were just beginning to give up their secrets, the knowledge within blossoming like the desert lilies. Librarian Cohen had told him that he was a naturally gifted reader. Martin's father would be proud, indeed. Father had wanted for nothing more than to see Martin get an education, become inducted into the holy monks. Proud, he would be proud.

No. It was all wrong. The blackness outside the windows of the library was a constant, no dawn, no dusk. They were underground, in the sunken Grand Chapel. The shock of waking up to find where he was had been compounded by the rapid introduction to the library. The books had been promised to them after their formal induction into the Brotherhood, but that was still a year away. Why had they been allowed the *lectio divina* so soon?

And Julian? A thief and a murderer who had betrayed the Brotherhood of Ulfur? Martin did not believe it. It was all wrong. He wanted to see the sky again, but every time he asked,

Librarian Cohen and Prior Blackwing had told him the same thing.

Soon. This is all part of your initiation into the Brotherhood. Patience. Soon, soon you will be ordained.

Ordained? It was all so unexpected, so rushed.

And then, there were the strange dreams. Children, he was a child again, or was it ...? Something about children. Fuzzy images of strange things. His stomach turned and he shook the dreams from his head.

Several lay brothers sat around the table, at other tables, books open in front of them, but they did not appear enthused by the activity of reading. Many of them simply stared listlessly around the library, as clearly lost and confused as Martin was. A flapping caught Martin's eye. Prior Blackwing had soundlessly entered the library and approached a middle-aged monk bent over a book at a small circular table.

"Are they ready, Brother Cohen?"

Librarian Cohen stood, bowed, and removed small circular spectacles. "I ... I'm not sure, Father Blackwing. I've been monitoring their progress, but ..." The librarian worried away at the spectacles in his hand.

"Let us see." Blackwing swept past the flustered librarian towards the lay brothers.

"Father Blackwing," Martin said. "Why are we—"

The superior cut Martin off with a raised palm. "If men came here seeking your deaths, how would you respond?"

"We would defend ourselves," said one of the lay brothers beside Martin.

Prior Blackwing folded his arms. "Show me." Each of the lay brothers took their pulsing, sky-metal crucifixes from beneath their habits. "Good, good. How go your reading lessons? Is Brother Cohen a competent instructor?" Several men nodded and the superior smiled. "Enough of books. The time is come for more primal actions. Are you with us?"

"What is happening?" Martin asked. "I don't understand."

"War, my young friend. Between our kind and theirs. We have need of your talents."

"*Our kind?*" Martin looked to his lay brethren. "What do you mean ... *kind?*"

"It's too soon," Brother Cohen said as he came up behind Blackwing. "It's too soon."

Prior Blackwing gave the librarian a withering glare. "They are ready. They must be. The enemy is upon us."

Librarian Cohen gasped, and Blackwing turned to see what had caused the surprise. A book was floating in the air before Martin, its pages turning slowly of their own volition, at first slowly and then faster and faster.

"What is this?" Martin said in amazement. With every page that turned, Martin understood each word written thereupon, his mind expanding and swelling with the rapid influx of information. Martin stopped breathing. Was Blackwing doing this? No, not from the way the man gawked. It was Martin. *He* was doing this, himself. Lifting the book with his mere thoughts, absorbing its contents. His heart hammered in his chest and a thrill shuddered through him unlike anything he had experienced before.

Blackwing stared. "You are ascended. You are a true brother now. Ordained, as of this moment. As are you all." Blackwing nodded in satisfaction. "Yes, we are ready. The hunters come here to kill us, but it is they who will find that Mount Ulfur is indeed their tomb."

38
VERTIGO

Some of the candles died and the Second Chapel darkened.

Cassie did not choose to relight the candles. Let the children sleep. Let them forget about the terror of their abductions at the hands of the mad monks.

Dylan whimpered and kicked his legs as he slept. Yerty held her twin brother's hand. Several other children began to toss and turn on their blankets.

"Relight the candles," Jacob murmured from where he lay. "They are frightened of the dark."

Of course, how could she be so foolish? The children now feared the dark: the light was a comfort, not a hindrance to their sleep. Cassie got to her feet and took a burning candle. She walked around the chapel and touched the candle flame to those wicks which had been extinguished, and she moved them to a place more protected from the draught. For good measure she lit several more candles and placed them in various nooks.

"You should also sleep," Cassie said to Lay Brother Jacob as she sat down beside him.

"I hurt too much," he said with a sharp intake of breath.

"You must leave me here at first light and get the children out. Get them home."

"I can't leave you here."

"I belong here. Despite what has happened, this place is still my home."

Cassie did not reply. The big man had saved her life, and she did not want to abandon him to his pain, for his wounds were indeed grievous. Abbot Howard had taken several meaty chunks out of Jacob's torso. A man of lesser spirit would be dead already, but Jacob's spirit was as colossal as his corporeal frame.

Dylan continued to whimper and Yerty spoke softly to him. Soon, the young boy sank back into a disturbed slumber. Yerty looked at Cassie with concerned eyes. "What's wrong with him, miss?"

Cassie could not find the right words to explain. She did not know what Dylan had seen, what he had undergone, but it could not have been pleasant. "He ... he has seen some bad things. He'll ..."

"Your brother's soul has been tainted by the evil done to him," Jacob said, his eyes still closed as he lay on the chapel floor. "He will never be the same again. He will be older in his head, more prone to anger and dark moods. You must be prepared for this."

Yerty nodded, seemingly satisfied at the explanation. "But he'll be alright? Parts of him?"

"He'll be alright," Jacob said. "Parts of him."

Cassie silently thanked the big man for putting it in a way that a child could understand. "Why did the monks take them?" Cassie whispered to Jacob. "Why the children?"

"The monks seek to alleviate the discomfort of their wickedness."

"By hurting innocent children? How does that make sense?"

The big man grunted quietly in pain and said, "The soul of an innocent is a salve to the infected wounds of their own souls. For a while, this innocence eases their suffering, but before long they destroy the little body that contains the pure soul, abandon it, and thus seek more. At least, that is what I conjecture."

"They're ... eating innocence? Feeding off the souls of children? It's sickness. It's madness."

"Yes. That it is."

"I hear something," Yerty whispered.

Cassie turned to the child in alarm. "What is it? What do you hear?"

"There's someone outside."

Jacob sat up with a grimace of pain. "Help me stand."

Cassie tried to protest, to tell the big man to stay down or his stitches would burst, but he did not listen. The door to the Second Chapel opened with a creak and Brother Rollant peered inside. He entered, licking his thin, cracked lips with his toad-tongue. Behind him came several monks. They padded into the chapel quietly, yet the children, sensing the presence of something malevolent, awoke as one and began screaming. Cassie shouted for the children to get to the back of the chapel, and there they huddled as Rollant, a slow smile spreading across his thin, vicious face, calmly strolled across the nave towards them.

Jacob's face was ashen, and his sword hung limply in his hand. The keeper of the elevator was in no condition to fight. Cassie grimaced. Damn it, the scrutators were supposed to have cleared the mountainside. She gripped her dagger and stood beside the big man, who was swaying unsteadily.

The more the children cried and shrieked in fear, the wider Rollant's smile became. His grotesquely protruding tongue lolled from his mouth, swishing this way and that, tasting the air.

"Well, well, what is this?" Rollant said thickly, his words fighting for space with his bloated tongue. "What do we find in our chapel, the holiest of all our holdings? Children, a lay brother, and a woman. This is a sacred place"—Rollant gestured around the chapel with his obscene, dripping organ—"and your mere presence here makes it unclean. None of you have the right to be here. I, on the other hand, was ordained in this place. Do you hear me? *Ordained.* You have no right. You must all be punished."

"Stand down," Jacob said. "Go back to the pits of hell, fool. You are no more ordained than my last shit was."

The skeletal monk snarled. "You've forgotten your place, lay brother."

"Fuck you, Rollant. My place is with my hands around your scrawny neck."

"*Brother* Rollant!" the thin man shrieked. "*Brother* Rollant! *Brother! Brother!* I'll purify this place with your blood!"

Jacob looked at the floor. He stood in a spreading pool of his own ichor. "Too late. Come closer, unholy little cunt, and I'll gut you like I gutted your demon abbot."

Rollant's eyes bulged, his tongue flicking about in a fit of rage. "Kill him! Kill the woman and succour the children!" The monks moved in but were hesitant. Despite his savage wounds, his loss of blood, Jacob was still a man to be reckoned with and the monks knew it. "Kill him!" Rollant shrieked again without showing the courage to approach the big man himself. "He murdered your brothers, murdered your abbot! Take vengeance!"

"You all!" Jacob roared at the monks and pointed at Rollant. "How is it that this man orders you about? He was a lay brother until recently. What makes him your master now when you were ordained first?"

For a moment, the monks stopped and darted glances at each other.

Rollant squealed, "Don't listen to him! Father Abbot passed on his authority to me! We follow his orders, even in death. Kill all the outsiders, those not ordained!"

Jacob's sword slipped from his grasp and clanged to the hard wooden floor. The monks jumped nervously at the harsh sound, but smiled a moment later when Jacob knelt to retrieve his weapon. The big man's hands and wrists were soaked in blood, his grip on his life weakening every moment. Cassie's heart sank. Jacob had torn his stitches and was rapidly bleeding to death.

Smelling weakness, the monks lunged.

Cassie went for Rollant as the monks went for Jacob. If she could take him down quickly, it might end the fight before it began. The idiotic gape on Rollant's face indicated that he had no idea what she was planning. She even managed to bury her blade into the toad man's chest. The fucker, however, had no heart, or at least it wasn't where it should be, and he did not die. With a pained shriek, Rollant swatted Cassie away with his distended tongue. It hurt like a bludgeon to the side of the head and Cassie's vision swam as she fought for consciousness.

Jacob impaled the first monk on his sword and simultaneously kicked another in the balls. Then he slipped on blood, his own and that of the impaled monk, and went down, his sword still buried in the body of the first monk. Two more of the enemy leaped onto Jacob but the big man was not yet defenceless. He buried his fingers into the eye sockets of one of the creatures and ripped the monk's skull apart. Cartilage, bone, and brain exploded. The surviving monks used their crucifixes as blunt blades and began to stab and tear at Jacob.

Rollant tried to kick Cassie, but she evaded his foot easily. The toad man decided that his bloated tongue was a more effective tool and so attempted to strike her across the face once more, but Cassie was on the move, ducking and weaving.

Jacob's strength had almost dissipated, the majority of his blood now spilt onto the chapel floor, his body gashed, and his flesh torn everywhere. With a last show of immense power as he lay dying, Jacob hugged two monks to his bloodied chest and squeezed. Spines cracked and eyes popped. Jacob felt their final, noiseless exhalations caressing his cheeks. It was a warm, comforting thing. Jacob sat up and with his last reserves of strength removed his sword from a corpse and beheaded the two prone monks to make sure they would not be reborn. But Jacob's strength was gone and a final thrust from the surviving monk's crucifix pierced the big man's valiant heart.

Jacob fell back to the chapel floor, dead.

The monk creature stood breathing hard, looking to Brother Rollant for guidance. It was clear that neither of them had expected Jacob to put up such a fight in his condition. They had been caught out, had been overconfident, and had lost much. But the big man was dead; only the woman and children remained.

Cassie leaped on the monk and stabbed him in the groin. If they had no hearts, she was damn sure they still had cock and balls. The monk took a step back and then staggered. He put his hands to his groin and felt around. Cassie knifed him in the throat. The monk vomited blood and fell forwards onto his face, unmoving.

Yerty had crept up behind Rollant and buried her knife in his arse, and the gaunt monk screeched. Once again, he had been caught out. Cassie shouted at Yerty to get away, but Rollant grabbed her by the tail of her tunic as she attempted to escape. Dylan rushed forwards to help his sister, but Cassie held him back. Children screamed. Rollant shrieked, threatening to kill Yerty as he held her by the hair, his fingernails poised across her throat.

Cassie held her dagger in one hand, the other hand open. "Wait a moment, Brother Rollant. Stay calm. Stay calm. We can talk this out."

"Come one step closer, and I'll tear her throat out," Rollant snarled.

"Alright, alright. Just let her go and—"

The chapel door creaked open, and everybody turned. Klaus stood there, alone, the blackness of night behind him, candlelight sheening his long face. Cassie cursed and her heart sank. She'd fought so hard. Jacob had fought so hard. She could not defeat Rollant and Klaus both.

"Lay Brother Klaus," Rollant said. "I never thought I'd be so glad ... help me. Tell this witch to put down her blade, or I shall kill the child."

Klaus walked down the nave slowly, his eyes taking in the corpses on the chapel floor slick with blood. Cassie pointed her blade at him. "Don't come near me, or I swear I'll kill you. Don't touch the children."

"The woman is insane." Rollant clutched Yerty tight to his chest like a shield. "She murdered poor Brother Shaw, stabbed him in his private parts just now. She's an animal. Kill her."

Klaus looked from Rollant to Cassie and back again. "Elsie is dead," he said.

Rollant frowned. "Who is Elsie? What are you waiting for? Kill the woman."

"My goat. Elsie."

"We are under assault! They've come to destroy us! We must defend ourselves. Kill the woman!"

"Her neck ... broken." Klaus seemed to be talking to himself. "Who would hurt Elsie?" His dreamlike gaze turned to Rollant. "Did you do it? Did you murder her? Murder my Elsie?"

Rollant's face went slack in disbelief. Then it blossomed into anger. "You stupid German bastard! Who cares about a goat at a time like this!"

Klaus scratched at his temple. "I remember now. You threatened to cut her throat. Do not deny it."

Rollant stared as if he couldn't comprehend what he was hearing. "Yes, I killed it! What does that matter? We're beyond all of that now, stupid mewling fuck! Don't you understand? They've come to kill us!"

Klaus's eyes narrowed grimly. "*They* are unnecessary."

Rollant's face skewed in fury and confusion. "What did you say?"

A cockroach appeared at Rollant's shoulder and scuttled up his neck. The gaunt monk shrieked as it began to burrow into his ear. He lost his grasp on Yerty, and she scampered away. Rollant slapped at his ear and missed the insect. He grasped the cockroach in his bizarre tongue and spat it away. Klaus smashed him in the face with a fist. As Rollant went down, Klaus kicked him in the ribs, shattering many. Rollant coughed blood, but Klaus did not stop. He straddled Rollant where he lay and began pounding the man's face with his bare fists. Rollant attempted to hit back with his tongue, but Klaus merely tore the organ from his mouth as Rollant gave a strangled gurgling moan. Cassie contemplated striking at Klaus with her blade while the tall German was occupied in caving in the smaller monk's face. She hesitated, half wanting Klaus to finish the job on Rollant. She grabbed Yerty and ushered the children into a corner of the chapel and stood in front of them, legs spread in a stable stance should the German come for them after killing Rollant.

For kill Rollant he did, and a little more. Rollant's skull had cracked and splintered like an eggshell dropped from a great height, the yolk of his brain now smearing the chapel floor along with the blood of many men, both good and evil.

Klaus stood and stared at Cassie, his fists bloodied pulps. Cassie swallowed hard and levelled her dagger at Klaus. The German merely blinked and turned away. He walked from the chapel without a backwards glance. Cassie clasped Yerty and Dylan and cried in relief, shock, and sadness. Cassie cried for the children, those present and those gone, and she cried hard for Jacob.

———

Klaus stood in the winds at the precipice of a sheer cliff and looked down at Re'Shan twinkling far below at the edge of the dark desert. He recalled with a strange fondness the vertigo that had once overwhelmed him. How strange that he should miss that, of all things, about his former life. He approached the lip of the precipice and stood on the very edge with his arms outstretched. He had no fear. The vertigo was long gone, his anxiety gone, everything that made him human, gone. An eagle called from somewhere below, far down the vertical cliff. He admired the city and the dark golden desert one last time. Such a beautiful view.

Klaus took a step forwards and embraced his humanity once more.

39
THE SUNKEN CHAPEL

The narrow basalt steps hugged the internal rock walls of Mount Ulfur, twisting downwards.

Julian led the way, Gregor and Martha right behind him. Forrester, Ulf, and Anguilla formed the rear guard. All around them a tar-like darkness stole the torchlight, leaving them with precious little vision. Julian's foot lost its purchase on a misshapen step, and he slipped on the edge of the dark hungry abyss waiting below. Martha reached out and grabbed his habit collar. His balance now under his control, Julian took a deep breath and steadied himself.

"Thank you," Julian said.

"You are welcome," Martha replied. "I would hate to see you die so soon."

Julian's skin crawled as he wondered just what would be an acceptable time to die.

Gregor sprinkled something from his satchel over Julian's torch and it flared briefly, nearly setting Julian's overgrown tonsure on fire. Julian's curses died in his throat at the sight ahead. By the light of the quickened torch, he saw the sunken

Grand Chapel, nestled between two massive crags at the end of a rope bridge leading across a chasm. Then the torchlight faded.

Gregor made to add more of the material to the torch, but Martha whispered, "Save the powder. We shall need it. Soon now."

Julian approached the beginning of the rope bridge. Surely the supporting ropes had been cut or the catwalk planks weakened. If the monks had retreated to the inside of the mountain, they would not allow passage to their sanctuary to remain intact. But then, how would they get out? Even the mad monks had to eat. Especially them.

"Go on, Julian," Martha said. "You go first."

"Oh, and if I don't fall to my death, you'll follow along safely?"

Martha shrugged. "Something like that." Even here in the darkness, the Ice Maiden's mercury eyes sheened translucent silver.

"I guess I'm expendable."

"Only God is not expendable. Wouldn't you agree, brother?"

Julian didn't bother to reply that he no longer considered himself a Monk of Ulfur, or a lay brother. Or in the least a holy man. No, now he just wanted to get Martin and the other innocents out alive. He sighed and approached the bridge.

"We'll be right behind you," Martha said.

Julian bit back a caustic reply and stepped gingerly out onto the rope bridge. It seemed stable enough, comprised of wooden planking within two guide ropes at waist height. Solidly constructed and not sabotaged by the feel of it. Martha followed only a few paces behind.

Something whizzed by Julian's face in the darkness. It might have been an insect. When the next object bounced off his skull and caused his knees to buckle, he shouted, "Hurry, they're throwing stones!"

It wasn't just stones. Bats screeched and swooped at them, perhaps controlled by one of the mad monks, or simply in a murderous mood all of their own. Julian ducked and stepped onwards as fast as he could. The rope bridge set to rocking and he couldn't maintain a solid foothold. He fell to his knees at exactly the same moment something much larger than a bat grasped at his shoulders. Tear marks in his habit around the collar proved ample evidence that he had just avoided death.

"Blackwing!" Julian shouted. "He's here!" Sword, axe, and whip sliced blindly through the air and now the bridge began to tilt dangerously. "Stop!" Julian shouted. "You're tipping us over!"

Gregor fell. Martha screamed his name and reached out for him but missed. A shrieking call echoed in the darkness and then disappeared. The group clung onto the swinging footbridge.

The walkway steadied and Gregor's frowning face appeared at the edge of the wooden treads. Martha and Forrester hauled him back up. The pelting rain of rock and stone continued and Ulf roared his rage and swung with his massive sword.

"Run," Martha called. "Run for the end of the bridge!"

Madness. If any section of the bridge had been purposely weakened, they were all hurtling towards a trap. Julian could not believe his luck when he made a set of stone steps at the other side of the chasm. Here, the rock throwers could apparently not target them, for the hail of sharp stones ceased. Martha, Gregor, and Forrester came barrelling into Julian, knocking him over. Ulf and Anguilla followed, elbowing each other to get off the bridge first.

Julian caught his breath and looked around. He had dropped his torch in the mad dash across the bridge, but torches surrounding the main entrance to the Grand Chapel provided sufficient light. The gentle flames seemed to be beckoning them to enter the spiritual home of the Monks of Ulfur.

"I lost my satchel," Gregor said. "On the bridge when I slipped."

"That is not good, Watchman," Martha said.

Gregor clenched his jaw. "I know it's not good, Ice Maiden."

Forrester rubbed his hand over the tattoo of Saint George's cross on his scalp and walked away, shaking his head. Ulf and Anguilla exchanged dour glances.

"You have doomed us all," Martha said matter-of-factly. The woman's approaching death seemed not to concern her in the slightest.

Julian looked from Martha to Gregor and back again. "What was in the satchel?"

"Our last weapons that are not steel," Martha said.

"You mean that bag of tricks you used up above? Those odd flashes and bangs?"

"That is what I mean."

"We're going to be torn apart as soon as we walk inside the chapel, aren't we?"

"That is a possibility, Julian. Would you like to turn back?"

"Is that an option?"

Martha's face showed little expression. "No."

Julian approached the entrance of the Grand Chapel and took one of the torches from its sconce. Handing it to Martha, he said, "In that case, you go first this time."

———

The glass panel doors to the first-floor prayer chapel were closed. Martha eased them back on their rollers and they opened smoothly. Either the quality of the original build was so sound that the doors, and indeed the entire building, had survived the fall basically intact all those months ago, or the Monks of Ulfur had repaired the entire edifice without alerting Julian and the other lay brothers. Both suggestions seemed impossible, yet the structure remained solid and stable here in the dark belly of the beast known as Mount Ulfur. Julian had desired to enter the Grand Chapel on his first day on the mountain. Now, he wanted to run the other way.

Something clattered across the dimly lit prayer chapel floor. Martha took a deep breath and stepped into the large room, the torch held at the length of her extended arm. The others followed.

The grey columns and mosaic floor of birds in flight glinted in the torchlight. The central nave was empty, but there was a figure at the altar, no, not a single figure, several, moving all over the semicircular apse at the back of the chapel.

"Give yourselves over to the Lord!" Forrester shouted.

A voice from a dark recess responded, "Oh, we have, friend. That we have. Come join us." Several gold cups, rubies, opals, and other precious items came clattering across the nave to rest at the scrutators' feet. No one moved to retrieve them. Julian swallowed and stared in wonder at the objects of immense value, but he remained motionless. This was clearly a trap.

"Join us," the voice said again, and this time six crucifixes whirled through the gloomy space to land with a clinking among the gold cups and gemstones, one for each of them. These objects changed colour before one's eyes: formed of the sky-metal.

"Lucifer's cross," Gregor spat. Several hisses came from the shapes in the shadows. "What makes you think we would forego our immortal souls for such bullshit? We shall not be damned to the Underworld as you are. Fools."

The hissing became louder. More monks seemed to materialize from behind columns to the side of the nave. Julian's pockets were weighted with diamonds thrown at him by Father Howard. He'd never been so wealthy in his life. But all of this availed him nothing now, not here in the depths of the abyss. He reached into his pocket and took a handful of the priceless stones.

"Earthly wealth," he whispered as he cast them to join the sky-metal crucifixes and opals, rubies, and gold goblets on the nave floor of the prayer chapel.

With a whooshing sound, the torch in Martha's hand went out. The sound of feet scuttling on marble, confusion, Gregor shouting to get another torch. When Anguilla returned inside with another flaming torch from the entrance, the prayer chapel was empty.

Forrester rubbed at his scalp. "What was that all about?"

"They're trying to buy us off," Gregor said. "Not enough riches in this world."

Martha took the torch from her brother's hand. "What now, Julian?"

"Up to the sleeping cells, second floor."

————

The long corridor was pitch black and silent. Martha edged her way forwards, the torch in her hand illuminating the dank stone floor in a ghostly orange flicker. The first few cells were empty; only a rat scurried away in startlement from the invasive light.

A dark shape lay curled up on a thin straw mattress in a cell halfway down the corridor. Forrester edged his way into the cell, sword poised.

"Wait," Julian hissed. He entered the cell and knelt beside the still figure on the mattress. Julian turned the man over and placed two fingers on the neck of the unresponsive figure. "It's Lay Brother Waldron. He's alive."

The stocky Forrester lowered his blade, only to raise it again. "Is he infected?"

Julian patted at the sleeping man's habit. "No. There's no sign of the sky-metal at his breast. He's clean."

Gregor entered the cell and spoke in a low voice. "Clean? We don't know that."

"He's clean, but heavily sedated. Prior Blackwing's potions, no doubt."

"I don't like this," Gregor said.

"Check the other cells," Martha said. Anguilla and Ulf moved off down the corridor.

Gregor jutted his chin at the sleeping lay brother. "I say we kill them all."

"You would slay a sleeping man?" Julian said. "An innocent man?"

Gregor growled. "I don't know any innocent men. Do you?" The Watchman turned to Forrester with a brutish frown. "Forrester, are you with me?"

The squat warrior sighed and slowly nodded. "Aye. We can't take the risk."

Julian held his hands out. "No, no. I told you. The lay brothers are innocent. They haven't yet become tainted." Julian looked to Martha. "Please."

Martha's face showed indecision for the first time. She glanced at Gregor. "Wait."

"If we hesitate," Gregor said, "we will pay the price. You know this."

"We wait," Martha insisted.

Anguilla returned to the cell. "There are more down here."

Julian got to his feet and followed the Eel. He stopped at the entrance to another cell and gasped. There, in the flickering glow cast by the torch, slept Martin.

Julian called his friend's name and cradled Martin's head in his lap. "Martin, wake up. Wake up."

And Martin opened his eyes. "Julian?"

———

Six lay brothers. They had found six lay brothers sleeping in various cells. Each was roused from his stupor and given food and water. The hunting party had now effectively doubled in size. The lay brothers, however, remained without weapons to defend themselves.

"Where are the others?" Julian said to Martin. "There's only six of you. Where are the other lay brothers?"

Martin rubbed at his eyes. "I don't know. They separated us. I can't ... I can't remember. They gave us drugs, vile things, and I pretended to fall unconscious."

Julian patted his friend on the shoulder. "Don't worry, Martin. We're going to be alright. We've got you now. We can get out."

"Not until we purify the mountain," Martha said flatly. "We do not leave this place until our work is done."

"What ... what is she talking about?" Martin breathed huskily.

Julian sighed. "Never mind." Julian sat back on his haunches and ran his hand through his unkempt tonsure. "We stay together. Let them carry out their task ... and then ... well, I don't know. We have to get out of here first. But I've found you now. Everything will be well."

Martin grasped Julian by the arm. "No. It's all gone wrong. Blackwing is insane. He wants to kill you, Julian. And he'll kill us and the children, too, when he finds that we have joined you."

"I know. I know. But it's alright. The children are safe. They're with Jacob and Cassie. And now you're safe, too. It's all going to work out. I promise. Come on." Julian helped Martin to his feet. The other lay brothers followed more slowly, stretching backs and rubbing at knees.

"Damn it, boy," Gregor growled to Julian. "Where are the rest of them? The accursed ones?"

Julian pointed up. "The library is above our heads. One floor up. And above that ..."

"Above that?"

"The rooms of black and red marble."

"Let's move," Gregor said.

Julian held up a hand. "We can't ask Martin and the others to accompany us. Let them rest here."

"No. We stay together."

"They're in no condition to fight. They barely know what is happening to them."

"Tough titty, boy," Gregor said. "They are either with us or against us. I really don't care. But if they're not with us ..."

Julian silently cursed the fork-bearded hunter.

———

The library of the Monks of Ulfur was famed throughout the Freelands. Scholars would come on learning pilgrimages from all over the land, at least until the library had disappeared into a gaping hole in the mountain. News of its loss had mortally wounded more than one young historian or scribe hoping to harvest the secrets of one of the greatest knowledge granaries in White Cloud.

But the library had, in fact, survived. It remained extant, though none in the outside world knew it. The double doors were ajar. Julian remembered catching a glimpse of the library the day the Grand Chapel had fallen. Then, everything had been chaos, but now, as they entered the library, Julian could not help but admire its order. Everything was as it should be. Every book in its appropriate place. Reading candles were placed in sconces on the walls giving plenty of light. Julian sniffed and smelled the intoxicating perfume of vellum and parchment, of ink and leather and beeswax.

Judging by the stern expressions on the faces of Martha, Gregor, and the others as they cautiously entered the library with their weapons at the ready, the scrutators were not avid readers.

Martha nodded to her twin and Anguilla disappeared behind a large bookstack on the right, Ulf at his heels. The Ice Maiden glanced at Gregor and he and Forrester moved off to the left. Julian gestured for Martin and the other lay brothers to wait by the door, where they huddled together tightly, casting nervous glances around the room. Julian and Martha cautiously walked the central area of the library with its circular and rectangle reading desks.

A book lay open on one such table and Julian craned his neck to look at it.

"Reading will get you killed," Martha said.

"I sense no mad monks within the library," Julian whispered in response. "If I could have but a moment to just touch the book, turn its pages."

"I wasn't referring to the monks," Martha said. "Reading, in general, will shorten your life, fill your head with absurdities."

"You can't read?"

"I read very well. Thus, I know the poison which lies within the pages of these tomes, put there by the poisonous minds of men."

"Well, I shan't argue with you. I would simply suggest that there is much to learn from these books."

Martha did not turn to Julian when she spoke. "There's nothing a book can teach me. Not one written by a man at any rate."

Anguilla appeared up ahead to their right and shook his head. Gregor poked his bearded face out from behind a shelf to their left. "All clear," he said.

"The library is empty," Martha said. "Where are they?"

Julian pointed to the ceiling. "One level remains. I can think of no other place that they could be."

"Are you ready to die, Julian?"

Julian's breath caught in his throat. "No. No, I'm not."

Martha turned on her heels, heading for the door and the stairwell to the topmost level of the Grand Chapel, scattering the lay brothers as she powered through the library door.

Julian had to hurry to catch up with her as she reached the stairwell and began to ascend into the darkness.

40
ENDGAME

At the top of the stairwell, a cool draught against Julian's cheek suggested that they were now in a large open space. The light from Martha's torch did not illuminate either wall or ceiling. The entire upper level of the Grand Chapel was gone, perhaps destroyed by fire, but the floor remained as a large open platform. Red marble reflected the torchlight at their feet as they moved forwards, cautiously avoiding the edge of the platform and its precipitous drop into blackness.

A flame flared to life somewhere ahead of them, and there stood Blackwing thirty yards away, a pool of black marble around him.

Prior Blackwing's voice echoed in the cavernous space, a malicious smile in his voice. "I believe that your eyes are not quite as accustomed to the darkness as ours. Let me assist you."

The superior's torch came to rest against an object that resembled a sack of grain, yet the sack moved. A monk shrieked as his habit, now consumed in flame, came hurtling across the black marble floor and onto the red section upon which Julian and his comrades stood.

The scrutators scattered. Julian leaped to avoid the burning monk, but the man changed direction and came right at him. Ulf grabbed Julian by the habit collar and hauled him out of the way. Julian crashed into Martin and the two men fell. They scrambled to their feet before the flaming monk was upon them.

Ulf roared and swung his sword but missed. Anguilla cracked his whip and Julian felt the draught of the blow pluck at his ear. The burning monk's leg separated at the ankle, and he fell screaming, clutching at his severed leg.

"Why isn't it dead yet?" Gregor roared.

"It is corrupted," Martha said. "Impervious to fire. Move!"

Anguilla's whip cracked again, and this time the monk lay still. By the light of the flaming corpse, Julian could now see several more monks creeping towards them across the black marble. The scrutators fanned out in a line on the red side, weapons at the ready. Julian realized with horror that he had dropped his dagger in his attempt to escape the burning monk. Where was it? He spied it several yards away and moved to retrieve it, but the dagger began to slide away from him. Julian gasped in shock, but before he could call a warning, the dagger slapped hard into Martin's outstretched hand. Martin stabbed Martha in the back with the dagger.

Julian screamed as the Ice Maiden fell. Martin raised the dagger again, but Julian had him by the wrist, shouting for him to stop. The lay brothers attacked the scrutators from behind as the ordained monks attacked them from the front. The lay brothers had turned, gone over to Blackwing. It was a trap. Julian screamed again. "No, Martin!"

But it was too late.

"Stop, Martin. We're friends." Martin tried to headbutt Julian in the face, but Julian turned his head, and the blow glanced off Julian's cheek.

"We're friends, Martin!"

Blood poured from Martha's back, staining her white shirt in a growing patch of dark red, but she was moving, trying to gain her feet. The lay brothers leaped upon her, kicking and punching, and Martha collapsed under their combined weight.

Gregor fought against a monk that crackled with yellow sparks. The burly warrior swung his axe and missed. As his weapon touched the sparkling aura around the monk, a shock passed through the axe into Gregor's arm, and he howled in pain.

Ulf and Anguilla struck out at their enemies, both men preoccupied with staying alive and unable to assist Martha. Julian tried to wrest the dagger from Martin's grip but whatever had possessed Martin gave him immense strength.

Forrester fought two monks. He swung his sword, and it passed through the body of one of them, leaving the man untouched. The squat warrior screwed his face up in bewilderment. He swung a second time and his weapon again passed harmlessly through the body of his enemy as if the man's flesh was comprised of nothing but smoke.

One of the lay brothers picked up Martha's sword and urged his comrades to get off the woman and make way for the killing stroke.

Julian tried one last time. "We're friends, Martin."

But Martin did not respond. Julian snapped Martin's fingers backwards and tore the dagger from him. He stabbed Martin through the eye. Martin shrieked but didn't fall. With two precise strokes Julian shredded his friend's throat. Martin dropped and Julian jumped on the man with Martha's sword. He struck out with his dagger and the lay brother crumpled. The other lay brothers backed away, looking at Julian in fear.

As Julian reached down to help Martha to her feet, something hit him from behind. The light from the still-burning corpse of the monk seemed to spin around him, and Julian almost lost consciousness. Pain shot across his shoulders and the back of his neck. He rolled and narrowly avoided Blackwing's second swooping attack. Julian got to his feet and tried to take in everything. Hunters and monks everywhere, locked in combat, Martha on her feet, sword back in her hand, swinging and killing the remaining lay brothers, men with whom Julian had once shared his life. He looked away as the Ice Maiden beheaded them all.

Gregor swung his axe, clearing a space like a farmer with a scythe reaping grain. The hunter's triple-braided chin jutted menacingly as he sliced this way and that. Forrester continued to hack away at one of the two monks near him, but again his blade passed harmlessly through the monk's habit and flesh. Suddenly, a metal star embedded itself in the throat of the monk hanging back and the combatant nearest Forrester disappeared.

"A phantom," Forrester murmured. Silently thanking Martha for the revelation, the squat hunter closed in on the choking, gurgling monk who had apparently produced the apparition of the other. Blood spurted from the man's throat and a great deal more spurted onto the marble floor after Forrester sliced his head off.

The light from the burning corpse diminished and darkness crept towards them from the outer reaches of the marbled platform. Martha threw another metal star at Blackwing as he flapped overhead but missed. The woman was now bleeding profusely from the gash in her back.

"Are you alright?" Julian asked, coming to Martha's side.

Martha's voice rasped in her throat. She coughed and bloody spittle laced her chin. "A lung is pierced. We need light, Julian, or Blackwing will tear us to pieces in the darkness."

Ulf went down under several monks, but Anguilla, whip in

hand, expertly flicked the serrated chain through the clammy air. Somehow, he managed to carve the monks into bleeding chunks without touching the big ginger-bearded warrior. Ulf muttered his thanks as he got back on his feet. The Wolfman and the Eel stood back-to-back as several more monks jumped at them from the encroaching darkness.

Gregor swung his axe and disembowelled a monk. Forrester approached another who was rubbing his palms together, attempting to call to action whatever power the Devil had gifted him. The man's eyes grew wide as the tattooed warrior approached, and he frantically increased the pace of his rubbing. Forrester cleaved the man in two, from skull to sternum, before he could accomplish whatever he was attempting.

Martha took a few unsteady steps forwards. The marble floor was coated with the blood of the monks and several of the scrutators. Martha stood straight and cocked her head. She turned as Blackwing swooped down but made no attempt to evade him as the horrid birdman clutched her in his talons. Julian threw his dagger at Blackwing's receding form but missed. As his dagger disappeared over the edge of the marble platform and began its slow descent into the abyss, Martha's sword clattered to the floor.

Anguilla screamed his sister's name, but Martha was gone.

Many monks and lay brothers were stretched out dead on the red and black marble. Several cadavers began to twitch and flex as the sky-metal in the dead men's blood diffused through cell and vein, organ and flesh, drifting upwards in twinkling droplets of colour, beginning the long journey back to the stars.

A monk, eyes wide in fear and wonder, stood in the middle of the melee, among the mutilated corpses of his brethren and the slow upwards ascent of the sky-metal. Julian knew the man by sight and recalled his name: Brother Quinn. The monk's astonished face was awash with colour, the entire chasm now illuminated in the same soft glowing light, a slow upwards cascade of glinting yellows and bright golds, purples, oranges, and greens of every shade climbing ever higher and casting light against the chasm walls. Brother Quinn raised his trembling hands and a moment later the air left Julian's mouth and a growing pressure built in his ears. The monk was sucking all oxygen from the battlefield. Ulf clutched at his chest and dropped to one knee. The other hunters suffered similarly, each struggling to hold those monks still living at bay. But the enemy, too, began to stagger. Brother Quinn was about to destroy them all, friend and foe alike.

A flapping and screeching echoed from high above. Bathed in the brightly coloured sky-metal rising into the dank air, two figures tore at each other. Martha clung to Blackwing, stabbing at the man's head, neck, and chest with her hunting knife. One of the superior's wings was shredded and the creature was losing elevation. As Martha plunged her blade into Blackwing's flesh, so, too, did Blackwing strike at Martha with sharpened beak. The two figures were dripping blood, their own and that of the enemy.

Blackwing struggled desperately to fly higher, attempting to rip Martha from his body as if she were a deadly leech attached to his skin. For a short moment Blackwing climbed through the air despite the violent embrace of the Ice Maiden.

And then Martha landed the killing blow. The superior's foul heart burst, punctured by the woman warrior's blade. In his death throes Blackwing's distended limbs wrapped around Martha and the two figures plummeted. With a sickening cracking of bone and rupturing of flesh, Martha and Blackwing, his body now reverted to its human form, crashed to the marble platform behind Brother Quinn and the man's head snapped around, his vacuum spell briefly faltering.

Gasping in air, Julian took full advantage of the lapse in the monk's concentration and threw himself forwards, rolling towards Martha's sword and grasping it. Coming out of his roll, he carved a chunk out of the side of Quinn's neck. The monk stumbled and clutched at the gushing wound. Julian hacked again, lopping Quinn's head from his shoulders.

The surviving monks fled and jumped from the roof. Julian saw ropes leading away from the marble platform towards ledges and caves in the chasm walls, ratlines providing a last-minute escape. Gregor slashed at the nearest rope while Forrester went for another. Screams of falling monks pierced the brightly lit cavern, but many more made it to safety and disappeared.

Anguilla knelt at his sister's side, his fingers feeling for a pulse at her bloodied neck.

"Martha is dead," he said. The Eel's face showed no emotion.

Gregor stared. Forrester shook his head sadly and turned away, running his hand over the tattoo of Saint George's cross on his scalp and the stitches that Martha, herself, had put there. Ulf began to cry.

"Not Martha," Gregor whispered. "Not Martha."

Anguilla brushed Martha's matted hair back from her bloodied face. One of her eyes had been plucked from her head. Anguilla closed the other eye and rested his forehead against hers. He whispered something and then kissed his sister's cheek.

Martha's broken body lay stretched out on a rectangular reading table in the library. Gregor and Forrester sat in silence at the table, their heads bent low. Julian sat alone at a circular table nearby. The book that lay open in front of him no longer spoke of mysteries, its allure faded to nothing but ink on paper. It had all been for nothing. He had failed Martin. He had been forced to kill his friend to save Martha's life, and he had failed in doing that also. Two more deaths to add to the long list that blackened his soul.

Ulf stood by Anguilla as the smaller man stared from a window out into the black, cavernous spaces. The Wolfman reached out and laid a sympathetic hand on the Eel's shoulder. Gregor raised his head slowly and spoke in a husky voice.

"Our work is not done. We must hunt down the remaining monks before they kill again, before those who have not done so discover their abilities. We must kill them now before they become something stronger." No one responded to Gregor's muted exaltation. "Anguilla? I know that this is difficult, but ..."

The Eel turned and nodded. "I understand. Martha would wish for no delay in our duties. For her, we kill them all."

"Wait, wait." Julian closed the book and got to his feet. "They're not all corrupt. Many of the lay brothers are absent. I realize now that Blackwing was not able to turn them all. Don't you see? That's why there were so few. There are innocents, still, on the mountain, and within it."

Gregor's face turned red as he slowly stood. His eyes of pale fire rested on the cold, still form of Martha. "She trusted you." His voice trembled in barely contained fury. "I warned her, but she trusted you. And your friend stabbed her in the back. I'll have no more talk of innocence, no more. We trust no one, we take no chances. We kill them all for God knows who are His." The old hunter's face set in a grim mask. "I'll go further. As far as I'm concerned, you're one of them. I should do you right now." Gregor bared his teeth and hefted his axe from hand to hand. He took steps towards Julian.

Anguilla placed a hand on the gnarled hunter's forearm. "I understand your pain, but she was *my* sister and would not wish this. Leave the lad alone. Control, remember? The first thing we control is ourselves, or what are we but murderers?"

Gregor's eyes bulged; his jaw muscles worked incessantly. Ulf came to stand behind Anguilla and glared at Gregor. Julian flicked his eyes to the door, ready to run if need be.

"Don't make the same mistake your sister did," Gregor growled low.

The Eel shook his head. "Stand down, Gregor."

The Watchman's rigid stance eased somewhat, and he finally nodded. "Alright. But guard your back."

Anguilla frowned. "Are you threatening me?"

"Not you." Gregor nodded towards Julian. "Him."

A noise came from somewhere outside. "The monks have returned," Julian said.

"Good." Gregor twirled his long axe handle. "Saves us the trouble of hunting them down."

The library door rolled back and several military men in black and grey surcoats cautiously entered the library, swords poised. Upon seeing the scrutators, the lead soldier sheathed his weapon and said, "My name is Captain Walker of the City Guard. I believe you know this woman." He gestured over his shoulder as Cassie walked into the library.

41
RATLINES

"What happened down here?" Cassie asked. "Julian, are you alright?"

The doe-eyed monk appeared to be sleeping with his eyes open. He was sitting with his back against a bookshelf in an isolated part of the library, his head thrown back and staring at the ceiling. Voices murmured from nearby, those of the City Guard and the scrutators.

Cassie tried again. She reached out and patted Julian's knee. "Julian? What happened down here?"

Julian blinked, came out of a trance. "Martin is dead. The other lay brothers ... many of them dead. I don't know where the survivors are. They're going to kill them all, innocent or not. Martha is dead."

Cassie sat back and sighed. "I'm sorry to hear about Martin and ..." She supposed she was sorry to hear about Martha as well but couldn't for the moment decide if that was the appropriate reaction.

Shouting and the sound of quick footsteps. Cassie jumped to her feet and went for her dagger. Gregor was roaring. "Bloody fools! What have we risked our lives for? What did

Martha die for? To have you carry the disease out of here in your blood?"

One of the City Guardsmen had been knocked to the ground by a punch from Gregor. Near the soldier's outstretched hand lay a crucifix of sky-metal. Gregor hurriedly applied a leather glove to his right hand, picked up the glowing sky-metal, now translucent amber, and threw the object from the library window into the dark chasm.

"The sky-metal in all its forms must never leave this mountain," Gregor said, turning from the window. "Never touch it with exposed skin." He pointed at the dazed soldier. "Put that man under watch for the next year." The soldiers in black and grey stared at each other.

"You heard the scrutator," Captain Walker said. "This man will not be left unattended for a year." Two men hauled their colleague to his feet and sat him on a chair in a corner, where he worked his mouth and prodded at his jaw.

Captain Walker looked about the library. "This place must be sealed off forever. The entire edifice."

"Bring more explosives," Gregor said, "and I will see it done."

"All the bodies on the rooftop"—Forrester pointed upwards —"throw them into the chasm, along with the metal. Remember, don't touch it, and if you must, never with exposed skin."

Gregor gestured at the battered soldier still rubbing his jaw. "That stupid prick may as well throw himself off the edge as well."

Captain Walker nodded at two soldiers, and they began the climb to the rooftop.

Cassie turned back to Julian. The man's face was pained. His friend's corpse was to be thrown away like offal into a sewer.

"Bastards," Julian whispered.

"The children are safe," Cassie said, sitting down beside

Julian. "They're safe, Yerty, Dylan, too. The City Guard are escorting them to Re'Shan as we speak."

Julian brightened at that. "Good. Something good has come from"—his eyes glanced at Martha's corpse and the men talking around it—"from all this. Where is Jacob?" Cassie opened her mouth but could not form the words. She cast her eyes at the floor. Julian's face darkened again. "More death."

"But the children are going to be alright," Cassie said.

"Yes. The children are safe. I'm happy to hear that, Cassie." Julian rubbed at his face with his hands. He looked ill. "How did Jacob die?"

"He fought bravely until the very end. He saved my life and the children's. He died a hero and a good man."

"I can only hope for a death of equal merit."

Cassie spoke with a hint of anger in her voice. "Stop talking about death. You're alive. You have fought well and on the side of good."

"Have I? Good? Is that what side I'm on?"

"You battled evil men. No, not men anymore. Foul things, monsters. Surely, you have no doubts as to which side you fought for, or still fight for."

"I have nothing left but doubts."

Cassie sighed heavily. "It's over now, isn't it?"

"No. Not while a single one of the monks yet lives, and I still don't know where the other lay brothers are."

"I think," Cassie said, "you need to get off this mountain. Make a new start somewhere. I can—" She stopped and stared.

Julian frowned. "What's wrong?" He followed Cassie's gaze. Blue sparks danced around Julian's hands. He held his hands up and unfurled his fingers. The bright blue lights flickered in and out of existence, slowly revolving around his fingers like tiny rings of star dust in orbit around a planet. Julian balled his hands up and the lights winked out. In horror, he whispered, "Fuck. Gregor was right. It's in me. It's in me."

"My god. What ...?" Cassie put her hands over her mouth. "What are you going to do?"

Julian's eyes darted towards the scrutators deep in discussion, and then back to Cassie. A moment passed between them in which neither spoke. Julian gave a long exhalation and pushed himself off the library floor. He edged his way behind a bookstack towards the door. Before he disappeared into the shadows, his fearful eyes met Cassie's once more.

Go, Cassie mouthed. *Go*.

Julian nodded and was gone.

A few seconds later he stood at the lip of the marble platform on top of the Grand Chapel, his eyes searching the darkness. He found what he was looking for and, making sure Captain Walker's men were occupied in the task of pushing corpses over the edge, climbed quietly onto the last surviving rope and clambered hand over hand across the ratline.

And Julian, once more, found himself suspended above the black abyss.

ACKNOWLEDGEMENTS

A heartfelt thanks to Ronnie Smart for his feedback and encouragement in the writing of this novel. His wisdom and enthusiasm have made all the difference. I write to music and this time around found great inspiration in the works of Greg Dulli and his varying projects. Also, a huge thanks to A. M. Rycroft and the team at Epic Publishing for having faith in my work because this book wouldn't be here without them.

ABOUT THE AUTHOR

Cameron Scott Kirk has published many short stories, won a Best of Fiction award, and is the author of the novel *The Mad Trinkets*, which has been adapted to audiobook featuring the amazing voice artist Alister Austin. He has been known to slay dragons, fight off invading aliens, and match the hardiest dwarf in a drinking competition. When he's not doing that, he's writing about it. Cameron lives with his wife, Penny, and daughter, Cody, an aspiring storybook author and illustrator in her own right.

EXCERPT FROM PATH OF THE WOLF
BY TONY-PAUL DE VISSAGE

Chapter 1

Aux-le-Piémont, France,
April, in this Year of our Lord, 1499

It was early in the spring when Isabeau de Montaigne first met the man who would become her lover.

France was at war with Italy; that very day, the country had suffered another defeat in its continuing conflict begun by their king, Louis, the twelfth of that name. It was also the day when, after an absence of three months, Isabeau's husband returned to Aux-le-Piémont.

Skirts clearing her ankles, so they wouldn't brush the damp grass making up the untended meadow calling itself their front courtyard, she met François on the path joining their cottage to the highroad. If the sluggishness of her movements was any indication, she was unenthused in welcoming him home.

The first time he went away, when she woke to find him throwing a change of clothing into his knapsack along with his

357

sketchbooks and charcoals, she thought he was abandoning her. He swore otherwise, that he'd come back "when I've found what I'm seeking."

It had happened so many times since, she didn't worry if she awoke and her husband was gone, didn't wait in quiet distress for the sight of his silhouette on the highroad. Sometimes, she hoped he wouldn't come back.

Being an abandoned wife would've been sheer heaven.

Recently, he'd been approached by *le église de Rue Jean-Baptiste Amélioré* about painting a mural depicting their sainted namesake. François accepted and set off on a quest to find the man who'd be his subject.

This time, he'd been gone so overlong she wondered if perhaps *le bon Dieu* had finally granted her unspoken wish. Then she thought, *Why should he? He never has before.*

Now, as if to underscore that belief, François was back, and this time, he wasn't alone.

There was a dog with him, restrained at the end of a length of rope; a big lumbering brute, loping clumsily behind him. Its gait was odd, as if its forelegs were shorter than the hind ones.

Merde, Isabeau thought resentfully. *Something else for me to tend after he loses interest.*

Like the bird he bought from a Spanish sailor off a ship supposedly having sailed to the newly discovered land to the west. Or those exotic flowers that wilted and died as soon as the first cold wind blew off the mountains. Of course, he used the bird in several paintings, but after that, it sat in its cage, ignored. Isabeau was the one cleaning its droppings, taking it out and letting it fly around the cottage and sit on her shoulder, until one day it flew away never to return.

She hoped it had made its way over the mountains into the warmer climes of Italy.

Now, her husband stood before her again, sweaty and

travel-worn, the dust of the highroad surrounding him like a cloud, begrimed into the sleeves of his linen shirt and the shoulders of his doublet.

Briefly, she was tempted to stalk back to the house, refusing him the welcome he expected he deserved, but, as usual, duty overcame anger. What would be the use of turning away? When she looked back, François would still be there and so would that dog or whatever it was.

He stopped. So did she.

The creature dropped to its haunches.

Without preamble or greeting, she said, "Did you find what you sought?"

Not that she really cared.

"Yes," he answered. "I did. I found my St. Jean."

"Where is he?" She looked past him down the track, expecting to see some beautiful boy on horseback, hurrying to catch up. It was usually the handsome son of a noble family whom he'd entranced with promises of immortality on canvas.

She saw no one. The path was empty.

"Here." He held up the rope.

Her gaze traveled its length to where it wrapped around the animal's neck, only to have her attention caught and held by the oddest eyes she'd ever seen. They were the color of molten copper, flecked with glints of bronze-patina-green, under heavy brows meeting in a single line, looking out of place in what she could see of the mud-bedaubed face.

Isabeau thought, *These are not the eyes of a beast.*

Frowning, she studied the creature's face. An odd countenance, no snout, no muzzle with a wet bulbous nose, though fur-covered and whiskery, as uncomfortably disturbing as its eyes.

She glanced at the creature's body, at the long coarse hair growing in a tangled mane around its neck and down its back, spreading over dirty shoulders. A matted pelt encircled its hips, part of its texture and color like the skin of another creature, the rest its own flesh, and the legs... hairy but relatively bare, as were the feet... but so filthy.

With a start, she was certain she was looking not at an animal, but a man, a dirt-caked man, squatting at her husband's side, his fingers digging into the grass. A man, watching her with curious but intelligent eyes.

Oh, surely not.

As if sensing her unease, he growled, a rough, low grating, deep in the throat. Isabeau took a step backward.

"Steady," François said, but whether to her or the creature she wasn't certain. "Don't be afraid. It's only that he doesn't know you. Hold out your hand."

When she didn't move, he repeated, "Hold out your hand. Let him get to know your scent."

As if he's a dog. She wanted to tell him she wasn't afraid, then thought, *Why bother?*

Her fear, or lack of it, didn't matter to François. Defiantly, as if she were dealing with one of her Uncle Étienne's hunting dogs, she offered her hand to the beast.

He sniffed at it, running his nose along her fingertips and against her palm, snuffling loudly. He barely touched her, a mere brush of flesh against flesh, but it made her skin chill slightly, though she managed to hide its shiver.

With a whimper, he thrust his head against her hand. Automatically, Isabeau's fingers stroked the filthy hair, creeping around the side of his head to one ear, over its slightly pointed tip, scratching behind it as she'd often done to her uncle's dogs. He grunted with pleasure, leaning against her palm.

His tongue shot out, brushing her wrist. She forced herself not to recoil, made her fingers continue their scratching movement.

"He likes you. Good." François looked satisfied, as if *he* had something to do with the beast's acceptance of her.

She pulled her hand away. The creature stared at her. Reproachfully, she thought. He'd liked having his ear scratched.

Her hand felt greasy. She forced herself not to scrub her palm against her skirt. She hoped he didn't carry fleas or other vermin.

"I'm hungry." François' belly growled, underscoring his words. "For the past mile, all I could think of was a bowl of Mathilde's good lamb stew. Is supper ready?"

As if the cook had nothing more to do than prepare a meal to sit and spoil waiting for his return.

"It should be soon." Isabeau put reproach into her next words. "We didn't expect you."

"No reason you should."

No apology for appearing with no warning. It wasn't in François' nature to think of others or show regret at their inconvenience.

"Tend to my pet." He tossed the rope to Isabeau. She nearly missed it, scrabbling to keep it in her hands.

"What shall I do with him?" She was resentful. As she'd suspected, she was to assume care of the thing.

"Put him in the room inside my studio." His answer was offhanded, as if every day he appeared leading a creature that might or might not be a man masquerading as a beast. "There's some chain there. Replace the rope and fasten him to one of the window-bars so he won't run away. He may be restless, being in a new place."

He took a key from his purse and lobbed it to her. François always kept the key to his studio with him. As if he didn't trust Isabeau not to snoop during his absence.

Isabeau caught the key more easily than she caught the rope.

He continued to the cottage.

———

For the release date and other details about *Path of the Wolf*, visit the Epic Publishing website (www.epic-publishing.com/books). To keep up to date on all of Epic Publishing's newest releases, follow our blog (www.epic-publishing.com/blog).

www.ingramcontent.com/pod-product-compliance
Lightning Source LLC
Chambersburg PA
CBHW010647100726
47901CB00009B/2467